KT-451-260

EAST FINCHLEY
LIBRARY

~~~ ~~~~ 201~

Please return/renew this item by the
last date shown to avoid a charge.
Books may also be renewed by phone
and Internet. May not be renewed if
required by another reader.

www.libraries.barnet.gov.uk

BARNET
LONDON BOROUGH

'Two unusual people with a very real love story. A uniquely beautiful read'
Image Magazine

'Beautifully written and deeply strange . . . Allan writes about neglect and
transgression very well . . . Wonderfully taut' Leaf Arbuthnot, *Sunday Times*

30131 05710794 5

LONDON BOROUGH OF BARNET

'This is a very singular book indeed, one punctuated by dark, strikingly densely imagined fairytales, which share disturbing parallels with Andrew's own life. Blurred boundaries are, in part, what this unsettling, intricately constructed and teasingly elliptical tale of misfits, outcasts and outsiders is about . . . The award-winning sci-fi writer's talents are evident' Stephanie Cross, *Daily Mail*

'Haunting and beautifully written, the plot unfolds as a story within a story' *Candis Magazine*

'Sometimes, all you can really do is applaud . . . So achingly clever and well constructed it's a bit like a magic trick. A dazzling little puzzle box of a novel, one that interleaves multiple voices, moods and genres. Intricate, measured and subtly creepy, this is the sort of book that invites you to find your own path, and decide for yourself just what the story is' Nic Clarke, *SFX*

'There's something wonderful about taking a step into an uncertain world. Especially when you're in the hands of someone as capable as Nina Allan . . . There's more than a touch of Angela Carter to it . . . It's really rather magical . . . It's the two characters at *The Dollmaker*'s centre that makes it such a compelling read. Allan offers the narrative skill we've come to expect, accompanied by a real tenderness and heart' Jonathan Hatfull, *SciFi Now*

'An unusual love story full of magic' *Good Housekeeping*

'A compulsively unsettling story and hypnotic prose make this a must read' *Literature Works*

'*The Dollmaker* is the sort of novel that speaks to the power of fiction and the possibilities it contains: I couldn't shake the thought that my imagination was playing an active role in shaping the narrative. I won't read a better book this year. Every character is beautifully drawn and every moment feels both authentic and magical; this novel is an enchanted castle of stories upon stories, a dizzying labyrinth. I wanted to go on reading it, and living in its world, forever' Blair, Goodreads

'Her literary sensibility fuses the fantastic and the mundane to great effect' *Guardian*

'This is a most unusual novel, both weird and wonderful. I loved it. Neil Armstrong' *Mail on Sunday*

'From her literary toy box, Allan conjures the scary, the surreal and the ordinary in a work of dazzling originality' Rose Shepard, *Saga*

Nina Allan is a novelist and short story writer. Her previous fiction has won several prizes, including the British Science Fiction Award for Best Novel, the Novella Award and the Grand Prix de L'Imaginaire for Best Translated Work. She lives and works in Rothesay, on the Isle of Bute. *The Dollmaker* is her third novel.

Also by Nina Allan

THE DOLLMAKER

Nina Allan

riverrun

First published in Great Britain in 2019
This paperback edition published in 2020 by

riverrun

An imprint of

Quercus Editions Limited
Carmelite House
50 Victoria Embankment
London EC4Y 0DZ

An Hachette UK company

Copyright © 2020 Nina Allan
Illustrations © 2020 Helen Crawford-White

The moral right of Nina Allan to be
identified as the author of this work has been
asserted in accordance with the Copyright,
Designs and Patents Act, 1988.

All rights reserved. No part of this publication
may be reproduced or transmitted in any form
or by any means, electronic or mechanical,
including photocopy, recording, or any
information storage and retrieval system,
without permission in writing from the publisher.

A CIP catalogue record for this book is available
from the British Library

Paperback 978 1 78747 256 3
Ebook 978 1 78747 253 2

This book is a work of fiction. Names, characters,
businesses, organizations, places and events are
either the product of the author's imagination
or used fictitiously. Any resemblance to
actual persons, living or dead, events or
locales is entirely coincidental.

10 9 8 7 6 5 4 3 2 1

Typeset in Monotype Fournier by CC Book Production
Printed and bound in Great Britain by Clays Ltd, Elcograf S.p.A.

Papers used by Quercus Editions Ltd are from well-managed forests and other responsible sources.

To Lindsey Hughes (1949–2007)
With love and thanks

Der Zwerg

Im trüben Licht verschwinden schon die Berge,
Es schwebt das Schiff auf glatten Meereswogen,
Worauf die Königin mit ihrem Zwerge.

Sie schaut empor zum hochgewölbten Bogen,
Hinauf zur lichtdurchwirkten blauen Ferne;
Die mit der Milch des Himmels blau durchzogen.

'Nie, nie habt ihr mir gelogen noch, ihr Sterne,'
So ruft sie aus, 'bald werd' ich nun entschwinden,
Ihr sagt es mir, doch sterb' ich wahrlich gerne.'

Da tritt der Zwerg zur Königin, mag binden
Um ihren Hals die Schnur von roter Seide,
Und weint, als wollt' er schnell vor Gram erblinden.

Er spricht: 'Du selbst bist schuld an diesem Leide
Weil um den König du mich hast verlassen,
Jetzt weckt dein Sterben einzig mir noch Freude.

'Zwar werd' ich ewiglich mich selber haßen,
Der dir mit dieser Hand den Tod gegeben,
Doch mußt zum frühen Grab du nun erblassen.'

Sie legt die Hand aufs Herz voll jungem Leben,
Und aus dem Aug' die schweren Tränen rinnen,
Das sie zum Himmel betend will erheben.

'Mögst du nicht Schmerz durch meinen Tod gewinnen!'
Sie sagt's; da küßt der Zwerg die bleichen Wangen,
D'rauf alsobald vergehen ihr die Sinnen.

Der Zwerg schaut an die Frau, von Tod befangen,
Er senkt sie tief ins Meer mit eig'nen Händen,
Ihm brennt nach ihr das Herz so voll Verlangen,
An keiner Küste wird er je mehr landen.

Matthäus von Collin

The Dwarf

The mountains fade into the greyish light
As the queen and her dwarf set sail
Their ship swaying upon the polished ocean waves

She gazes up into the dome of the sky
Into the shimmering blue distance
Shot through with milky threads of cloud

'You stars have never lied to me,'
She cries. 'You tell me I am soon
To die, yet I cannot deny I'm glad to go.'

And then the dwarf falls upon the queen
Weeping, blinded by agony
He binds a red silk cord about her throat

'This hell is of your own making,' he says.
'You left me for the king. The only thing
That can bring me joy now is your death.

'I'll loathe myself forever for your murder
But I can't help myself. I'll send you, pale ghost
To an early grave.'

She clasps her breast, so full of young life
As bitter tears rain down her face
She lifts her eyes to heaven, praying

'I don't want my death to cause you pain,'
She says. The dwarf kisses her pale cheeks
As in that same moment she slips away

The dwarf gazes upon the woman, fixed in death
He commits her body to the waves
And yet the longing in his heart will not be still
He is doomed to roam the seas for evermore

Matthäus von Collin (translation by Nina Allan)

VI: Death, Funeral and Burial of Dolls

Sometimes these are quite isolated from each other and from sickness, and some-times all follow in due course. Of all the returns available under this rubric, 90 children mentioned burial, their average age being nine; 80 mentioned funerals, 73 imagined their dolls dead, 30 dug up dolls after burial to see if they had gone to Heaven, or simply to get them back. Of these 11 dug them up the same day. Only 9 speak of them as dying naturally of definite diseases. 15 put them under sofa, in drawers, attics or gave them away, calling this death; 30 express positive belief in future life of dolls, 8 mentioned future life for them without revealing their own convictions, 3 buried dolls with pets and left them, 3 bad or dirty dolls went to the bad place, 14 to Heaven; 17 children were especially fond of funerals. 12 dolls came to death by accidental bumps or fractures, 1 burst, 1 died of a melted face, 2 were drowned (1 a paper doll), 1 died because her crying apparatus was broken, 1 doll murdered another, was tried and hung. Dolls of which children tire often die. 30 children had never imagined dolls dead. This parents often forbid. 1 boy killed his sister's doll with a toy cannon, 3 resurrected dolls and got new names, 5 out of 7 preachers at dolls' funerals were boys, 1 was the doctor; 3 doll undertakers are described. 22 cases report grief that seems to be very real and deep; in 23 cases this seemed feigned. The mourning is sometimes real black and sometimes pretended. 19 put flowers on dolls' graves, 1 'all that week'; 28 expressly say that dolls have no souls, are not alive, and have no future life. In 21 cases there was death but no burial; in 10, funerals but no burials; in 8, funerals but no death.

(From 'A Study of Dolls' by A. Caswell, Ellis and
G. Stanley Hall, *Journal of Genetic Psychology* Vol 4,
Granville Stanley Hall, Carl Allanmore Murchison
Journal Press 1897)

A Knyght ther was, and that a worthy man
That fro the tyme that he first bigan
To riden out, he loved chivalrie,
Trouthe and honour, fredom and curteisie.

(Geoffrey Chaucer, Prologue,
The Canterbury Tales)

MY FATHER DIDN'T WANT me to have her but in the end he gave in. My mother managed to persuade him he was over-reacting. One evening, long after I was supposed to be in bed, I sat in the dark at the top of the stairs and listened to them arguing about her.

'I won't have it in the house,' said my father. 'You don't want to encourage him, do you? That's exactly how these things start.'

'Don't be ridiculous,' my mother countered. 'He's only seven. He'll have forgotten all about it in a week.'

I understood that my father was angry, but I didn't know why. I had never heard my mother call my father ridiculous before, and the idea that I was the source of conflict between my parents was unnerving but strangely thrilling. Not that I dwelled on the matter for long. What mattered to me was not the argument, but who would win it.

HER NAME WAS MARINA Blue and I loved her on sight. In a world that was confusing and occasionally frightening, she gave my heart a focus. In a shop full of bisque-headed mannequins, it was she who brought the others to life.

In reality she was nothing special. Dolls like Marina Blue roll off the production lines in their thousands and are of little value to the collector. Yet there was something, even so, that set her apart from such generalities. She drew the eye, as all things born of sentient creativity are bound to draw the eye. She had presence. More than that, she had dignity. I knew from the moment I saw her that she would change my life.

THE TOWN I GREW up in was small, not much more than a village. There were three pubs and a small hotel, one main shopping street and the old cinema, which had recently been converted into an indoor antiques market. There were two parks. One was at the top of the town close to the Rivermead housing estate and had infamously been the site of an abduction. The other, whose official, unsuitable title was the Heathfield Pleasure Gardens, was frequented by drug users and petty criminals through the hours of darkness and turned instantly to quagmire whenever it rained. I was not allowed to play in either of the parks. I was not allowed to go into town at all unless my mother was with me.

The school I attended was called Martens. I used to believe it had acquired its name from the dozens of house martins that nested beneath the eaves, though when I was older I discovered it was named after its founder, a Pieter Martens who came to Britain from Copenhagen to study at Oxford. At the time I was there, the school still had outside toilets and that species of enormous, green-painted radiator that dated from before the war. There were around fifty pupils. My ordeal did not properly begin until I graduated to St Merriat's, the upper school, but there were intimations of trouble, even so. My classmates were growing quickly. In spite of their apple cheeks and choirboys' voices, they had started to mutate into men. I was a moon-faced, pot-bellied, grub-shaped boy with wet-looking hair and glasses. Still less than four feet tall, I was too weak to kick a football, too small to scramble a fence. Boys who had happily included me in their games just the summer before began to take note of these differences, and draw away.

The school day ended at three. My mother collected me at the gate and afterwards we would go shopping. Not the serious, fort-nightly shopping that required a car but small, pleasurable errands such as buying sewing thread or fruit cake or the *Radio Times*. My favourite shop was Prendergast's, the stationer's, where my mother bought her writing paper and envelopes, and which doubled as a toy shop. I was allowed to browse the shelves while she completed her purchases. I soon learned that if I mentioned any particular toy often enough, I would usually be given it eventually. On the day I first saw Marina Blue sitting in Prendergast's window, there were still a full three months to go before my eighth birthday. I immediately became convinced that someone would buy the doll before then, that I would never see her again. It never entered my head that there was more than one Marina Blue, that in all probability there was an entire warehouse stacked with them. Her eyes were a deep sapphire, her glossy, waist-length hair the perfect shade of chestnut brown. Her head, hands and feet were made of unglazed bisque porcelain, her body of cotton twill stuffed with kapok. She wore baggy, bell-bot-tomed trousers and a red hooded top. Her square-heeled, lace-up ankle boots were sewn from real leather. I felt weak and slightly nauseous at the sight of her, as if I were about to faint.

'Come along Andrew, don't dawdle. We need to get to the bakery before it closes.' My mother grabbed me by the hand and tried to pull me away from the window, but I resisted her. For perhaps the first time in my life I was torn between my usual habit of compliance and the dark and delicate thrust of my own desires.

'I want to go inside,' I wheedled. 'I want to see the little girl in red.'

'That's a doll,' said my mother. She glanced quickly towards the window display and then away again. 'Dolls are for girls.'

I felt close to tears. 'It's nearly my birthday,' I said. 'That's what I want.'

'You'll change your mind long before that. You know what you're like.'

In fact this was untrue and both of us knew it. I had always been a child who loved certainty. I gazed at my mother in despair, then allowed myself to be led away in the direction of the bakery. In the weeks that followed, I made sure to mention Marina Blue every day, speaking with the studied nonchalance I had previously employed in pursuit of other treasures I had coveted: the miniature kaleidoscope, the magnetic dragonflies, the pewter monkey. In its early stages, my gambit met with a seeming indifference that was easily the equal of my own. Then, with less than a fortnight to go before the day itself, I overheard my mother and father having their argument. This was the endgame and I knew it. When I finally sneaked off to bed that night it was in the expectation and fevered hope that the victory was mine.

SHE CAME IN A cardboard box, nestled in yellow crêpe.

'It could be valuable one day,' my father said. 'You know what

4

they say about antiques of the future.' He rubbed his hands together as if he were cold.

'I hope this is still what you want,' my mother added.

I felt as if something was expected of me – a particular turn of phrase in expression of gratitude – but I was too marvellously overwhelmed to say anything at all. I briefly fingered Marina Blue's red jacket then put the lid back on her box. I took exaggerated pleasure in the other gifts I had been given: a mint-green anorak, a pack of playing cards on the theme of capital cities, a carton of sugar mice. I blew out the candles on my birthday cake and afterwards the three of us played charades. It wasn't until later, alone in my bedroom, that I felt able to hold her. She felt heavy in my arms and wonderfully real. Her hair smelled of pinewood. When I laid her on her back, her eyes slid closed.

I placed her box gently on the chair beside my bed. Even with the lid on, I found I could remember her in every detail.

A GREAT DEAL HAS been written on dolls. There are volumes on the history of dolls, the provenance of dolls, the value of dolls, heavy catalogues filled with lavish illustrations, images that quicken the blood and stimulate desire. I have read that the doll is a surrogate: for friendship or for family, for love. Most children grow out of dolls eventually, but not the collector. The true collector, like the poet or the idiot, remains prey to the intensified sensibilities of childhood until the day they die.

In the introduction to her memoir, *A Brief History of Wonderland*, Doris Schaefer, the renowned doll collector and curator of the

Museum of Childhood in Bad Homburg describes the moment when she first saw an Ernst Siegler 'Gabi' doll at an auction in Frankfurt. Schaefer was thirty years old at the time, a partner at law with a flourishing practice, but her encounter with the doll was an epiphany. She gave up the law the following year and devoted her life to the creation of the museum.

I AM FOUR FEET nine inches tall. Most of the puppy fat fell away in time, but because of my restricted height I still appeared round. In addition to that I wore heavy National Health spectacles, which seemed to accentuate both my shortness of stature and my pudgy physique. For my sixteenth birthday my parents gave me a pair of glasses with tinted rectangular lenses and narrow black frames. The new glasses streamlined my moon face, at least a little, but did not stop me resembling a diminutive schoolmaster, which is what everyone assumed I would become.

Most of my classmates called me the Dwarf, though there were other names, too. I knew from an early age there was no point in my even trying to belong, that aspiring to be like them would, in some mysterious way, increase their contempt. Rather I regarded my schoolfellows as members of another tribe, whose customs were mysterious and filled with savagery.

My intelligence I took for granted. I enjoyed all my school subjects, but my true interests already lay elsewhere. The school library had little to offer me, but the public library in Welton was surprisingly well stocked. There was also *Ponchinella*, a monthly magazine filled with articles on all aspects of dolls and doll collecting. I saved my pocket money so I could buy it the day it came out. I read each new issue from cover to cover and then read it again.

Even my father came gradually to accept that my passion for dolls was not something I was about to grow out of. In the end he stopped worrying about me. I think he was able to come to terms with my obsession by convincing himself that my hobby would eventually pay off. A lifetime in business had taught him that anything can become valuable, given time and the right circumstances, be it piggy banks or Victorian underwear or used beer bottles. One memorable Christmas he presented me with *Merrick's Price Guide to World Dolls*, an indispensable textbook that had thus far been well beyond my means.

'We'll have you working for Christie's at this rate,' he said. He smiled at me, and it was a good smile, open and friendly and relaxed. I don't think I was ever the son he had imagined for himself, but we always found plenty to talk about and, in any case, I liked my father. I didn't see any reason to trouble his mind by explaining that the goal of the true collector is not the accumulation of riches, but the consummation of passion.

I remember how my father adored his cars, both the steel-blue Volvo he drove for work and the vintage Jaguar that lived in the garage and was taken out only at weekends. The Jaguar was racing green with chrome trim and soft, chestnut leather upholstery. My father cleaned the Jaguar once a fortnight without fail. I was sometimes allowed to buff the upholstery, using a chamois leather moistened with a yellow polish called Heller's Wax that came in a tin. I loved the smell of the Heller's, resinous and woody as ambergris. I think my father hoped that by letting me help him with the Jaguar he might be able to spark my interest in cars in general, but although I listened carefully in an effort to please him, I invariably forgot most of what he told me more or less as soon as we went back inside.

I never learned to drive, and after my father died I stopped pretending I ever would. By the time of his death, both the Jaguar and the Volvo had been sold. He ran an Audi saloon instead, a car he always despised, though I never knew why.

I have always found it interesting, the way people and their vehicles can become inseparable in the mind. My dear friend Clarence drives a white Ford van with a cracked rear windscreen and a large dent in the passenger door. She flexes her muscles as she gets into the driver's seat, like a soldier climbing into a tank. Often when I think of Clarence, I think of that action, the way the van has become identified for me with her strength, her chaotic yet indefatigable way of being.

INFORMATION (biographical/bibliographical/photographic) on the life and work of EWA CHAPLIN AND/OR friendship, correspondence. Female, single, mid-40s. Main interests: dolls of Germany and Eastern Europe. Please reply to: Bramber Winters, PO Box 656 Bodmin UK.

2 .

ON THE BACK PAGE of *Ponchinella* there was a Personals column. I always read it, as I read everything else in the magazine, and in many ways Bramber's advertisement was no different from the thousands of others I had seen there over the years. What first drew me to Bramber Winters was the beauty I found in her name. I vaguely recalled that Bramber was the name of a place, and when I looked in Coastage's English Almanac I found I was correct: Bramber was a small village in East Sussex whose chief visitor attractions were a ruined castle and a pipe museum. When I asked Bramber if she had ever been to the village she said she had never heard of it.

Later in our correspondence I sent her a postcard of Bramber Castle I happened to find on a stall at Camden market. The photograph was in black and white. It showed a grassy mound, surmounted by a number of toppled stones. A near illegible copperplate script covered most of the reverse. The Horsham postmark was dated July 1972. The recipient was a Mrs Hilda O'Gorman, of East Mersea, Essex. I wondered what Hilda O'Gorman was doing now, if she was still alive. As always when I handle old letters, I felt a frisson of energy, a tiny secret acknowledgement from out of the past. I could almost convince myself that both sender and recipient knew of my plans for their postcard, and approved.

When it came to Bramber's request for information about Ewa Chaplin, I was on less certain ground. I had heard of Ewa Chaplin, of course I had. An artist of high renown and vanishingly small output, Chaplin was a Polish émigrée who had arrived in London at the outbreak of World War Two. Some accounts insisted she was penniless, others maintained she came with the ubiquitous hoard of gold coins sewn into the lining of her shabby overcoat. All agreed she had turned to seamstressing and later to dollmaking as a way of making ends meet. Her dolls are unique, prized by museums around the world, sought after by private collectors, who pursue them with a zeal that can seem excessive even by the standards of the doll fraternity. I had never felt particularly drawn to them myself. I found there to be something cold in Chaplin's creations, an edge of the uncanny I did not care for. Not that I said so to Bramber. I told her I was making enquiries, that I had a lot of contacts among European dealers and that I might even be able to get her an interview with Artur Zukerman, who had photographed dolls all over the world, including – famously – the American Chaplins. The first of these statements at least was true. As for the rest, I told myself those were bridges that could be crossed if and when I came to them.

When I asked Bramber what it was, in particular, that drew her to Chaplin's work, she said she first became interested when she happened to see a play based on one of Chaplin's stories. *It was when I was at school*, Bramber wrote. *My best friend Helen was in it. Ewa Chaplin wasn't afraid to make dolls that weren't comforting*, she added. *She seemed to know that dolls are people, just like us.*

I had never read Chaplin's stories. As I understood it, Chaplin first began writing when she was a student in Krakow, though her work had not been published until after her death. I did know that Chaplin had supposedly based many of her dolls on the characters in her stories, but I never felt particularly curious about them, probably because I found the dolls themselves so unattractive. I could see what they meant to Bramber, though, and the candour of her words touched me deeply. I had never found anyone whose feeling for dolls appeared to accord so closely with my own. The experience was thrilling to me and almost shocking. I think that was the moment I first intuited the depth and intimacy of our connection.

I HAD BEEN WRITING to Bramber for more than a year before I understood that we were destined to be together. The next time I wrote, I included my phone number. When Bramber wrote back, she said there was no payphone at West Edge House, and that she didn't have a mobile. I wasn't sure I believed her – who doesn't own a mobile these days? – but on reflection I decided she was simply one of those people who dislike using the telephone. This small insight into her personality only endeared her to me further. Certainly I didn't perceive it as a problem. Soon she would come to trust me as I trusted her. And in the meantime there were our letters, which I looked forward to as harbingers of a new reality, a reality in which we would confess our togetherness, becoming more fully ourselves in a way that is only possible in the presence of that rarest of human sympathies: mutual love.

The idea that I might go and see her did not occur to me at first.

I had not been invited, after all, and I was hardly the sort of person who could present themselves at someone's door in the sure and certain knowledge of being welcomed inside. My life thus far had taught me enough about rejection not to actively court it. But once the initial seed had been planted – a television documentary about the decline of the tourism industry in the West Country – I found myself unable to uproot it. I would go west, I decided. And even if my bravery was not rewarded, at least I would have the satisfaction of knowing where I stood.

For some weeks, months even, the idea of the thing and then the planning of it – consulting route maps, perusing railway timetables and gazetteer entries for the places of interest I hoped to visit along the way – was enough to sustain me. But as April became May and drew closer to June I knew I must act, or find myself ensnared in a cycle of regret. After browsing for information online, I discovered the existence of the West Country Rover ticket, a travel card with a three-month validity that would enable me to access any part of the Devon, Cornwall and Somerset public transport networks, switching freely between bus, coach and train as my itinerary demanded. The woman behind the counter of the travel agent's where I purchased my rover card had pink hair and blue eyes. Both made a startling if not altogether unpleasing contrast with the leopard-print fake fur boa draped across her plump shoulders.

'Going on holiday, are we?' she said. 'Fancy a spot of sunshine on the English Riviera?'

'The sun isn't really my friend, I'm afraid. I prefer a nice breeze.'

She smiled at me brightly, as if my answer had told her everything about me she would ever need to know. She pressed a button to release my ticket from the machine and tore it off along its perforated edge. She selected a plastic wallet from the drawer underneath the counter and slipped the ticket inside.

'Best keep it safe,' she said. 'Better safe than sorry.'

West Edge House
Tarquin's End
Bodmin
Cornwall

Dear Andrew,

Thank you for your letter. I was so excited when it arrived. I've always wondered whether anyone actually reads the personal ads in magazines and now I know they do. I would be delighted to correspond with you, if you would like to. There's no one here I can talk to – not about dolls, anyway. I'm sure you understand!

I have thirty-six dolls in all: twenty German, ten English and six French. The first doll I ever had was a 'Marianne' by Claude Muriel. She was given to me by a friend of my mother's when I was ten.

So you live in London! I haven't been in the city in twenty years. I think about going sometimes – I would love to visit the museums – but then it seems so far, and my job here makes it difficult for me to get away.

Tarquin's End is a small village, not much more than a hamlet, really. Some of the people at West Edge House – Diz and Jackie, for instance – have been here for years.

I want to thank you for the postcards you sent. I love the Paul Chantal doll. She reminds me of a student from Lyon who used to give French conversation classes at my secondary school. Isn't it strange, the way dolls always seem to bring back the past? I suppose it's because they never age.

The post came early today. Our deliveries sometimes don't arrive until after lunch. Dr Leslie says they leave us till last because we're least likely to complain, but I once heard Diz saying to Jackie that really it's because the postman is afraid to come up here. Diz's real name is Derek Ryman. Sylvia Passmore – Sylvia is the housekeeper here – told me he used to be a doctor. Diz spends most of his time with Jackie, though you couldn't imagine two people less alike.

The postman brought a parcel this morning, but Jackie wouldn't open the door to him. She stood stock still in the passageway between the stationery cupboard and the entrance to the visitors' lounge, staring through the glass partition at the letters that were already on the doormat. She was wearing her yellow ribbed tights, the ones that make her legs look like corncobs. When the postman rang the bell again, Sylvia Passmore came out of the office, moved Jackie aside and went to open the door.

'Don't let him in,' Jackie said. 'He'll kill us all.'

'Parcel for Maurice Leslie,' said the postman. 'Can you sign?' Sylvia signed the paper on the postman's clipboard with a red biro and then he gave her the parcel. Sylvia closed the door and came back inside.

Jackie stuck both hands behind her back, flattening herself against the wall. 'Don't put that near me,' she said. 'You don't know what's in there.'

Sylvia made a tutting sound and marched off down the

corridor. When I touched Jackie's arm I found she was trembling, although when I saw her an hour or so later, sitting in the garden with Diz, she seemed perfectly all right again. It's hard to tell why she gets herself in such a state over such ordinary things, how much she remembers afterwards. There are days when she chats away to the postman as if she's known him for years.

Both Jackie's parents are dead now. Every couple of weeks she has a visitor, a tall, straight-backed woman with glasses. Sylvia Passmore told me this woman is Jackie's daughter. A couple of Sundays ago the woman turned up here and asked if she could take Jackie for a drive in the country. Jackie wouldn't get into the car at first, but then Diz said he'd like to go too and so things turned out all right.

I wanted to send you a postcard of Bodmin, but Jackie refused to give me one, even though she has a whole stash of postcards – hundreds of them – hidden under her bed. I'm very fond of Jackie but I have to admit she can be unreasonable sometimes. I was born in a village called Heath, which is not far from Bodmin, but I grew up in Truro. We moved there just after my first birthday because it was easier for my father to find work there.

My father was a car mechanic. My mother liked to say he was a mechanical engineer but he never did any exams, he was just good at mending things. I don't only mean cars. The first thing I remember him mending was an alarm clock, the battered old Westclox from beside my parents' bed. I was six at the time. He sat me between his knees and let me watch what he was doing.

'I'm not sure what's wrong with her, Ba. Let's get her on the table and then we'll see.'

He took the clock to pieces and when he put it back together again it started ticking immediately. He couldn't charge as much as the qualified garage mechanics because he didn't have the certificates, but customers came to him anyway. They could tell he had an instinct.

Our house was on Harlequin Road. My mother liked to say their bedroom had a view of Truro Cathedral, even though all you could see was the tip of the spire. I liked my own room better because it overlooked the builders' merchants at the back. They were called Groat & Sons and they started work early. I used to make a gap in the curtains and watch the men in their blue overalls loading bricks and wood and scaffolding on to lorries. Dad sometimes did odd jobs there, mending broken machines.

My first real memories date from my fifth birthday, when I was given a glass snow dome with a model of Hampton Court Palace inside. Although the snow dome was mine, I wasn't allowed to keep it in my bedroom until I was eight. My mother was afraid I might break it.

My mother and father used to drive over most weekends and take tea with Dr Leslie. In the end they stopped coming – they were bored, probably – and I told Jennifer Rockleaze they were dead, just like Jackie's parents. Jennie was new here then. Later, after we became friends, I told her the truth.

Looking forward to your next letter!

Yours always,
Bramber

18

3 ·

I HAD NEVER HAD SEX with a woman. There was a girl I liked at school, a plump and gentle redhead named Angela Madden. I loved the soft rotundity of her forearms and cheeks, the whispery, luminous timbre of her voice. She had a way of lowering her eyelashes so that only a sliver of bright blue iris remained visible. Her hair was smooth and shiny, like Marina Blue's. Unlike the others in my year group, Angela did not seem unnerved by me and we ended up spending most of our break times together, devising complicated games with marbles and coloured chalk. One day I went into school to find her gone. No one said anything and a couple of days later I discovered she had moved with her family to Oxford.

The other girls in my class skirted me warily, as if even the most cursory contact would be to risk immediate and summary rejection by their peers. The boys still called me names, although as we all grew older they seemed to derive less enjoyment from that particular pastime. I felt relieved, though no less alone. By the time we were all doing 'O' Levels, some of the more bookish individuals in my year would at least deign to speak to me, but I couldn't honestly have called them friends. By the time Wilson Crosse came into my life at the age of fifteen I think I had resigned myself to my solo existence.

I even believed I preferred things that way, perhaps because it was the only kind of life I had ever known.

I met Wil in Welton public library. I visited the library at least once a week, not just to borrow books but because I liked the ambience: the waxed parquet flooring, the Victorian tiling in the lavatories, the inimitable odour and texture of well worn library books. Wil quite literally bumped into me in the antiques section, catching my shoulder as he strode past and making me drop the book I'd been reading.

'I'm terribly sorry,' he said. He had very fair hair, cropped short. He was taller than me, of course, but he didn't seem to tower above me like most other men.

He bent to retrieve my book, closed it then turned it over to look at the cover.

'Fanshaw's,' he said. 'Invaluable.' He tapped the book's spine with his index finger, as if stressing the point. The jacket photograph showed a Lucien Basquiat 'Julienne' doll with hand-stitched lace-trimmed bloomers and auburn hair. 'I'm no expert in dolls myself,' he added. 'I'm more a mechanicals man.'

'You mean automata,' I said. It sounded as if I meant to correct him. I could feel myself blushing.

'That's right,' he said. 'Only I prefer to call them mechanicals in honour of Shakespeare. You remember, the rude mechanicals? Some of mine are very rude indeed.'

He raised an eyebrow and grinned, making creases around his pale eyes. He handed me back my book, brushing the tips of his fingers against my palm. 'I have a full set of Fanshaw's at home,' he added. 'You could come and have a look at them, if you like.'

For the first few weeks he barely touched me, restricting himself to the kind of harmless intimacies that might easily be explained away as avuncular affection: stroking a finger the length of my wrist bone, an arm slipped around my shoulders from behind. He liked to take off my glasses and pinch my cheek. I was unused to such caresses – my father would ruffle my hair sometimes and my mother always kissed me goodnight but that was all – and the attention Wil bestowed on me made me feel flattered, privileged even, as if I had finally been allowed a glimpse of the kind of life most people seemed to take for granted.

The first time Wil had sex with me was on the couch in the smaller of his two downstairs reception rooms, the room he habitually referred to as the snug. It happened so quickly I barely had time to register what was going on. He held on to me tightly, ramming his narrow penis inside me with a force and an urgency I had never for a moment suspected he possessed. The pain was substantial, but not so great as my distress and bewilderment at Wil's transformation into an entity I barely knew.

'Go upstairs and wash,' he said when he had finished, and so I did. I could hear him moving about in the kitchen, putting plates on a tray and running water into the kettle. By the time I came back downstairs he was the same as always. On subsequent occasions he took me up to his bedroom, and afterwards there was always a fresh pair of underpants waiting for me, identical with the brand I normally wore. What he did with the old ones I never found out.

I dreaded these episodes, but at the same time I became used to them. They were no longer frightening so much as unpleasant, like being forced to eat a food you cannot stomach. I reassured myself with the knowledge that out of all the time we spent together, the interludes in Wil's bedroom were mercifully brief.

Wil never spoke of what happened between us. We talked instead of the other things we had in common: antiques and automata and, of course, dolls.

I adored his house, a substantial Victorian villa at the top end of Rhodesia Street. Behind the house lay half an acre of garden Wil had left to go wild. He loved insects and plants and trees, and declared himself against most forms of gardening, which he described as ecological vandalism. By contrast the inside of the house was a temple to order and cleanliness, a fact that seemed remarkable not just in view of the garden but also because of the profusion of fragile objects on display. There were books, of course, many hundreds of them, but that was just the beginning. Wil's rooms were crammed with beautiful things: snuff boxes, lacquerwork, netsuke, Japanese fans. His passion though was for automata, of which he possessed several dozen and all in working order. The 'rude mechanicals' – the erotic esoterica that formed the centrepiece of his collection – were able to perform the most remarkable feats, and were marvels of the clockmaker's art. Wil's favourite was an eighteenth-century French piece, in which a Roman centurion coupled first with a lady, then with a soldier and finally with a tow-headed boy.

'It's so rare it's not even catalogued,' Wil confided. 'Objects like this were banned at one time. You could go to prison simply for looking at them.'

I didn't care much for the mechanicals. I found the relentless circularity of their motions pointless and faintly sinister. Wil did not own many dolls, though there was one I coveted desperately, a

Schindler 'Amy' with her own silk-lined rosewood travelling case. Wil used to joke about bequeathing her to me in his will, but in the event he gave her to me as a present when I went away to college.

We wrote letters at first, and in the Christmas vacation of my first year we took tea together in a café in Pangbourne but I never visited him in his home again and by the following autumn we had fallen out of touch entirely. Wil had seemed older but then so did I. I found I could no longer tolerate his touch.

MY PARENTS NEVER KNEW about Wil – on those occasions when I went to his house I always told them I was visiting a school friend. Had they dwelled on the matter more closely they might have questioned me further, for I had no school friends. As it was, I think they were so relieved at the idea that I *might* have that they were reluctant to spoil the illusion by delving deeper into it. I did tell Clarence – one night when her husband Lucan was away and we were both rather drunk. I was surprised by how clearly they came back, those memories. Clarence insisted I had been Wil's victim. She actually called him a vampire, which struck me as funny – Wil was so pale, after all. She was right, I suppose, but I had never seen our relationship in those terms, or at least not until then. I did know that Wil was terrified of us being found out, but no more than I was. Whether there were others like me before or afterwards I have no idea. It would be naive of me, I suppose, to assume I was the first.

Was I simply a doll to him, one of his rude mechanicals? Clarence seemed to think so. For a while she tried to persuade me that I should report Wil – shop him to the cops, was how she put it – but

I wouldn't hear of it. The thought of having to confront him across a court room – to see him again anywhere – was something I could not countenance. I found it simpler and more effective to think of Wil and our time together as little as possible. I told Clarence I'd rather we didn't talk about him any more and in the end she agreed. Clarence is stubborn but she knows when she's beaten. I think part of the reason we work so well together is that we respect each other's privacy. Clarence was the only person in the world who knew about my relationship with Bramber. She seemed pleased at first – she said it was good for me to have friends – but when I told her about my planned trip to the West Country her attitude changed completely.

'You have told her you're coming?' she said.

'Not yet,' I said. 'I want it to be a surprise.'

'Not everyone likes surprises. You can't just turn up on her doorstep. You barely know the woman.'

I prevaricated, saying I wasn't about to make some grand announcement, not when I was just passing through. I didn't want to put Bramber to any trouble. Clarence changed the subject, and I did my best to pretend the conversation had never happened, although I have to admit I was hurt, not by what she said but because I had believed she would understand.

I had recently asked Bramber if I might come and visit her – testing the water, you might say – and she had replied by return of post, insisting it would be impossible because West Edge House didn't cater for guests. I didn't believe her, the same way I hadn't believed her about the telephone. I wondered if she was just shy, or if there was something more sinister behind it. You hear about places, don't you? Nursing homes and private clinics that are supposed to offer seclusion and care and a respite from the world but that are closer to being prisons. The thought of Bramber being locked away in a place like that, afraid to say anything unless it made matters worse – the idea made me feel ill. I said nothing to Clarence about my fears. Her earlier reaction had left me in no doubt that she disapproved of my feelings for Bramber, that she would be happier if we broke up. I did briefly wonder if she might be jealous, but dismissed the idea as ridiculous. Clarence has Lucan, after all, and Clarence has Jane.

THE DAY OF MY departure finally came. I arrived at the bus station early. People were already queuing for the Reading coach. The two women immediately in front of me were wearing identical camel-coloured car coats.

'Did you remember to pack the sandwiches?' said one to the other.

'You know I did. You saw me putting them in.'

I found myself picturing the flat they shared, a warren of dim purple rooms filled with china ornaments and the scent of lavender. The rest of the queue comprised a middle-aged man in a business suit and a teenage girl with a pasty complexion who looked as if she'd been crying. I too had packed sandwiches for the journey, together with Ewa Chaplin's famous stories. The book had not been easy to come by. When I asked for assistance at my local bookshop, the bookseller scrolled silently down his computer screen for ten minutes then informed me that the volume I was after was an American publication. 'A new translation,' he added. 'It'll take six weeks for us to get hold of it. At least.' Whether that last was meant as an apology or as a disincentive I couldn't be sure. I told him I was in no hurry, that I was happy to pay a deposit if that was what was required.

In the event the book arrived in slightly under a month, an attractive paperback whose cover illustration happened to feature – a coincidence, I'm sure – a reproduction of Corot's subtle and nostalgic painting, *Girl with a Doll*.

What was I to make of these stories? The title of the collection was *Nine Modern Fairy Tales*, yet a cursory glance through its pages gave me no clues. I skimmed the introduction and the short essay on the translator, Erwin Blacher, who had apparently once shared a breakfast table with Ewa Chaplin during a symposium on European folklore, but the truth was, I was still far less interested in Chaplin herself than in what she meant to Bramber. As the coach headed out of London I found myself unable to concentrate on the book and in the end I returned it to my travel bag.

I HAD ORIGINALLY PLANNED to pass through Reading without stopping, but a week before the start of my journey I changed my mind. I had not been in the town since my schooldays and I was curious to see how it had changed. As a boy, I had thought of Reading very much as the big city, a dour and vaguely frightening place that, even though it lay less than half an hour away by car, I seldom visited and only ever in the company of my parents. My clearest recollections of the town were tied up with the old-fashioned gentleman's outfitters where my father bought his suits, and a Polish delicatessen that sold chewy dark sourdough bread and chocolate-covered pretzels. Staring through the window at the tangle of roundabouts and industrial estates that rolled in tidal waves against the town's ruddy Victorian defences it occurred to me that the Reading of my boyhood was almost certainly gone, obliterated in the tide of development like so many other places. I had been foolish to think of coming here. Too late now.

I had booked into one of the faceless corporate hotels opposite the station, a decision that now seemed as inappropriate as stopping off in the town to begin with and mitigated only by the knowledge that it would be for just the one night. My room was on the second floor – two dozen identical doorways leading off a grubby magnolia corridor floored with brown corduroy. I deposited my holdall on the fold-out luggage rack then headed outside.

The town, as I had feared, seemed completely alien, and if someone had told me that it was not, after all, the place I had once known but some peculiar counterfeit I would not have been surprised. I spent what seemed like hours roaming the streets around the centre in a fruitless search for the Polish delicatessen, before admitting defeat and stumbling into an Italian restaurant on one of the side roads off Friar Street. I felt dispirited and footsore but the restaurant's warmth and soft lighting had a revivifying effect and when the food arrived I began to feel better. I took my time over the wine and even ordered myself a brandy to round off the meal. It felt late to me, though when I returned to my room at the hotel I discovered it was not yet nine o'clock. I made coffee in the white plastic kettle and switched on the TV. The news came on and then a film, a noisy drama set at the time of the Vietnam War that I kept watching more to pass the time than from genuine interest. The film finished and I went to bed. I switched off the light, but the persistent traffic sounds outside, coupled with my own circling thoughts, made it impossible for me to sleep. I decided I would read instead, the first of Ewa Chaplin's *Nine Modern Fairy Tales*. The story was strange – something about a young theatre actress who decides to murder her husband – but it held my interest. I was even beguiled, a little.

I closed the book and put out the light again. This time I slept soundly in spite of the street noise. It was as if the hotel and the town outside belonged to two different worlds.

THE DUCHESS

by Ewa Chaplin

translated from the Polish by Erwin Blacher 2008

'Y ou're Nelly Toye,' said the dwarf. 'I saw your *Duchess of Malfi.*'

Nelly's thoughts were so far away she hadn't noticed the beggar in his soiled overcoat, had almost stumbled over him in fact. He was huddled against a ventilation grating – for warmth, she supposed. The heat of Süssmayr's ovens rose steadily from the bakery's basement sixteen hours a day. Süssmayr's Pâtisserie, who had continued producing their magical confections even in the depths of wartime, had defined the ambience of this part of town for as long as Nelly could remember, yet the familiar, sweet aromas of baking dough and butter icing and caramelised sugar seemed unpalatable suddenly, almost noxious. Her stomach rolled.

How can he bear the torture? she thought. He's like the beggar at the feast. She glanced down at the man on the pavement and then quickly away again. For a second she almost believed it was Adrian she was looking at, her beloved older brother Adrian, who had perished in the mud of Paschendaele. She shook her head, feeling the warmth of a blush staining her cheeks. How could she have imagined such a thing? The man in the street wasn't a dwarf either, she could see that now, he was an injured soldier. Both his legs had been amputated above the knee, the wooden trolley he used to propel himself about the city serving also as a repository for his worldly goods. Like so many who had returned from the war with their minds as well as their bodies blasted to wreckage, he was clearly destitute. Nelly's husband Mason had frequently expressed the opinion that this new influx of beggars and social deviants should be cleared from the city. One couldn't feed them all, he maintained angrily. The state should do something. Didn't he pay his taxes, after all?

This man with her brother's eyes, though. What was that he had said about seeing the play? That could not be true, surely – yet he had spoken her name. All at once this seemed to Nelly like a bad omen, like in the scene at the beginning of *Anna Karenina*, where Anna sees the little peasant, hammering away at a stanchion at the side of the railway line. Seconds later a station guard falls on to the track and is killed. Anna sees the dwarfish peasant again at the end of the book, just moments before she throws herself under the train.

Nelly pulled her fur stole more closely about her shoulders then fumbled in her pocket for a coin. She dropped the coin into the tin plate at the beggar's missing feet. She remembered how in Tolstoy's novel Vronsky gives the stationmaster money for the dead guard's family. Nelly's friend Cecily argued that his gesture meant nothing, that it was a ploy to gain the approval of the woman he was about to seduce. To Nelly now it seemed more like the kind of bargain people in operas strike with the devil: an attempt to buy off a fate that will ultimately lead to the destruction of all they hold dear.

As she hurried off down the street, almost tripping on the cobblestones in her eagerness to be away, Nelly found she could still feel the soldier's eyes burning into her back. Later that morning, when Konrad Binewski first showed her the painting of the duchess, she tried to tell herself that the incident with the beggar had nothing to do with it, that it had nothing to do with anything. In all likelihood this was true. Yet it is equally true that if Nelly had not encountered the soldier, she would not have been thinking about him, and so would not have made a point of altering her route to walk past Süssmayr's three days later. This is where our story truly begins.

No doubt there will be others among you who insist that without this first meeting, there would have been no second meeting. I'm not of the mind to argue, either way. Theatre people are terrible about omens though, have you noticed? Those plays whose titles they won't repeat, those phrases they don't dare to utter before a performance? You could say that Nelly Toye was the victim not of omens so much as the tradition she embodied.

Konrad Binewski was getting old. Nelly had known Konni all her life. He had been a friend of her father's since they were first at university together in the 1860s, which made him seventy years old at least. Frightening, if you thought about it, which Nelly tried not to. She kept her eyes on him as he moved about the shop, the way he staggered, ever so slightly, each time he put down his right foot. Arthritis of the knee, he had told her, and as Nelly reassured herself, no one ever died of arthritis.

Losing Konni would be like losing her father all over again. The shop itself, with its sun-flecked interior, was like a portal into the past: her father and Konni drinking Schnapps together in the back room after hours, the boisterous political discussions that occasionally degenerated into a full-blown shouting match. Konni's wife, Lizaveta, yelling down the stairs that supper was ready, God damn it, *ready*, so would the both of them just shut up and come upstairs?

Liza had been a playwright, and often unwell. Nelly believed it had been the combination of these two aspects, their shaded glamour, that first kindled her own enthusiasm for the stage. The idea that Liza might truly be mad – mad as Ophelia, mad as Lucia – seized her youthful imagination with a romantic zeal. When Liza was well, she attended theatre premieres with the actors she wrote for, penned excoriating anarchist diatribes in the radical press. When Liza was sick, she became a deadening, attic-dwelling presence, whom no one but her husband was permitted to see.

Nelly was fifteen when Liza committed suicide – an overdose of morphine, it was whispered, though Nelly and Adrian were told simply that she died in her sleep. It was only then that Nelly began to grasp how much, in reality, Liza had suffered, how she had been crippled by the depression that finally killed her as surely as the typhus that killed her schoolfriend Käthe in the first year of the war.

Nelly's father and Konni had become close as brothers again after Liza killed herself. Konni and Liza had had no children, and now that Adrian and her father were dead too it was just Nelly and Konni, leftovers from a life that was gone for good.

Cecily believed that Nelly's marriage to Mason had been a reaction to her father's death, coming so soon after Adrian's, an attempt to insure herself against future losses.

'You do realise what your fiancé thinks about people like Adrian?' Cecily had said to her just a week before the wedding. 'He believes all homosexuals should be sterilised. How can you even think of marrying someone like that?'

They had a huge row and then made up again, though Nelly found it impossible to forget some of the things that had been said on either side. For a while at least she stopped visiting Cecily quite as often as she had been used to, retreating instead to Konni's shop, the place she felt most secure and where she knew that whatever happened she would not be judged. Nelly was in the habit of dropping in on Konni at least once a week, whether she had business to conduct with him or not, though on the day she first saw the soldier she had been on her way to his shop for a genuine reason: an evening bag of hers, a black, beaded creation given to her as a gift by Mason soon after they met, had snagged and broken its delicate chain-link handle on a protruding doorknob. Konni had promised to mend it for her, and Nelly was anxious to have the bag back, preferably before Mason noticed it was gone.

'Here's the fellow,' Konni said. He laid the bag gently on the counter, its glittering jet tassels clattering like ebony nails on the polished woodblock. 'Good as new.' The handle was indeed as good as new, so flawlessly mended it was impossible to tell it had ever been damaged. 'A pretty thing, certainly. Turkish, I believe.'

Nelly nodded, smiling at Konni's hesitancy, the familiar self-deprecation that belied a knowledge as extensive as that of many encyclopaedias. As a student, Konni had been something of a firebrand, railing against the evils of capitalism and bent on leading a life of monastic seclusion, devoting himself to poetry and philosophy like his hero, Hölderlin. Then he met Liza and everything changed. Liza needed time to write, so Konni took over the family antiques business, just as his father had secretly hoped he would.

'I've been happy,' Konni always insisted, and Nelly felt certain that for the most part he had been, as much as anyone had the right to hope for, anyway. Did he still sometimes dream of the other life he had once imagined for himself: the garret room, the brilliant friends, the slim volumes of poetry published to glowing accolades? Nelly had never asked him. She didn't see the point. Hölderlin went mad and wasted away, in any case – everyone knew that.

'How are you, Konni?' she asked him, once she had finished admiring the mended bag.

'Mustn't grumble,' he replied at once, though he sounded distracted. He cocked his head, as if he were listening for something, glanced quickly towards the door, though there was no one there. 'Listen,' he said. 'I found something interesting. Would you like to see it?'

'What do you mean, interesting?' Nelly laughed lightly. She had that feeling again, as if events had been set in motion behind her back.

'You'll see. A dealer brought it in, one of my regulars. He said – well, none of that matters. Just have a look.'

He dipped down behind the counter and retrieved the object, which turned out to be a small oil painting on a round canvas some twelve inches in diameter. The painting was of a woman in an ermine stole, seated in a baize-green armchair against a darkened background. Beside the armchair stood a dwarf, broad-chested and stumpy-legged, his luxuriant chestnut hair contrasting vividly with the sober, coarse-looking fabric of the cloak he wore.

The dwarf's cloak was fastened with a pin, in the form of a dagger.

The woman in the ermine stole was Nelly Toye's identical twin.

Nelly drew in her breath. She had never seen a ghost – she had never believed in them – yet this was like seeing her own ghost in reverse, an

34

image of herself from before she was born, her pale face gleaming mysteriously from beneath the varnish. The sensation was unsettling, like coming face to face with her own reflection in a muddy puddle.

'Remarkable, isn't it?' Konni said. 'You understand why I wanted you to see it?'

'Do you – know who painted this?' Nelly said. Her only thought was that the picture must be the work of a contemporary artist, something done on commission. For an overenthusiastic admirer, perhaps – God knew the theatre attracted some peculiar types. The painting looked old but age could be faked, she felt sure. She even remembered Konni confirming as much, that even the world's greatest museum experts were likely to be fooled by a forgery at least once in their careers.

That the painting showed Nelly in a role she did not recognise and had never played was disconcerting, but not so strange, after all, not now she'd had a moment to think about it. Didn't people say the power of the imagination was infinite? The dwarf was a coincidence. His presence meant nothing.

Konni was shaking his head. 'Not a clue. The artist's signature is here, look – Nikolaus Schilling – but the name means nothing to me. I could probably find out more, if I did some digging. The painting is old, but not as old as it looks, you can tell by the varnish.'

'I don't understand,' Nelly said. The facts were leaping away from her again. Konni gave her a look. He appeared to be as confused as she now felt.

'The subject isn't actually you, if that's what you were thinking. That would be impossible. This woman was painted three decades before you were born at the very least. If I had to lay money on it, I would say this work is a modern interpretation of an historical subject matter, either a copy of an earlier painting, or a straight pastiche. A very good pastiche, mind you. Herr Schilling was certainly talented, whoever he was.'

'Really?'

'Really. The painting is clearly inspired by Velazquez, not just the subject matter but the colours, too – the red of the woman's dress is unmistakable. But the influence is so ostentatious it's almost as if the artist is inviting us to share a joke at his own expense. I rather like it.'

'I'll take it,' Nelly said. That was one of the advantages of being married to Mason – she could see a thing, and make it hers, no questions asked. So far, this was a privilege she had barely exercised. The house she now shared with her husband on Golovinsky Street was filled with furniture and objets d'art acquired by Mason during the first forty years of his existence, a time that had proved as inaccessible to Nelly as the locked room in *Bluebeard's Castle*.

'They're his first wife's things, probably,' Cecily had scoffed. Nelly had little interest in finding out. This painting, though – this would be hers. She even knew where she would hang it – in the small upstairs sitting room where she took her coffee when Mason was absent, where she went over her lines. It would look perfect there, on the wall just behind the sofa and above the old sideboard that had been the one piece of furniture she had brought to the marriage. The sideboard had been her mother's, though the only person who knew that was Cecily.

Did she like the painting? She had no idea. She only knew she had to have it with her.

'Don't feel you have to, Nelly.' Konni looked embarrassed. 'It'll sell in a heartbeat.'

'No, I want it. Really.'

Konni named a price, an amount that would have seemed exorbitant to her in the old days but that was now – not so much. She had the feeling the painting was worth more though, that if Konni hadn't had his overheads to think about he would have given her the picture for nothing. The war had made such generosity impossible, at least for most people. She added twenty per cent to the bill, because she could and because she knew Konni needed the money.

Konni looked troubled. 'I wish I'd never seen it,' he said.

Nelly frowned. What a strange thing to say. Konni had seemed so animated about the painting earlier.

'But I'm delighted to have it. I'm going to surprise Mason. He'll find it amusing, I know he will.'

Their eyes met, just for a moment, and then they each looked away. The idea that Mason Gehrlich might find amusement in a work of art was a joke in itself, and both of them knew it.

'Goodness,' Cecily said. 'What a marvellous find.'

She held the painting at arm's length then leaned it upright against a stack of books and began scrabbling around in the top drawer of her writing desk. After a moment or two she drew out a watchmaker's loupe on a metal chain. She bent down to peer at the artist's signature.

'Do you think she looks like me?' Nelly said.

'You know she does, or you wouldn't have bought the thing. You've never gone in much for acquiring art, have you, Mason or no Mason?'

The remark might have stung more, had Nelly not understood that it was Mason Cecily was aiming her darts at, not her, though it was true she had no idea what her taste in art was, none at all. She knew how to choose clothes, a rug maybe. Anything more ambitious felt risky, as if she were liable to make a fool of herself at any moment. In any case, knowing about paintings had always been Adrian's department.

She thought, as she had often thought, that it was all right for Cecily, who still had both her parents, this commodious, book-lined apartment at the museum. How could she fully grasp what it meant to her, the house on Golovinsky Street, the red velvet cushions on the daybed in her sitting room, the polished parquet flooring? Her lovers before Mason had been other actors, a stage manager, once – disastrously – the brother of her understudy in the part of Iphigenie. Mason Gehrlich had been another proposition entirely: powerful, self-confident to a degree that made him seem dangerous and attractive in equal measure. And rich, of course. Rich in spite of his divorce, his almost-grown children, his recreational gambling habit.

Nelly had stopped believing in love, or so she told herself, when Adrian died. In exchange for love she had Mason, and the bulwark he provided against the world. He didn't give a damn about her acting career, but so what? If she knew nothing about finance, Mason knew even less about the theatre, and Nelly felt secretly glad that once the first, frenetic months of their courtship were over, he barely even took note of where she was playing.

'Do you recognise the artist?' Nelly said to Cecily.

'Nikolaus Schilling? I've heard the name, but that's about all. Why he isn't better known I have no idea.'

'Is he any good, do you think?'

'Absolutely. He's so indebted to Velazquez it's almost brilliant. A lesser artist would have tried to impose his own, inferior ideas. This Schilling fellow flaunts his indebtedness, like a red rag to a bull.'

'That's what Konni said.'

'Well, Konni was right.' She continued examining the painting's surface through the loupe. 'I can't tell you who these people are. Not yet, anyway, you'll have to leave it with me. A painting like this would most likely have been a commission. Just look at them,' she said. 'There'll be a story, I'm sure. He was probably her lover. Court dwarfs often ended up in bed with the queen. You won't find much about that in the history books, but it's a fact, nonetheless.'

Nelly laughed nervously. The subject made her uncomfortable, though she could not have said why. 'You're not serious,' she said.

'I most certainly am. You know what aristocratic families are like – hardly a healthy gene pool. A good number of queen consorts found themselves married off to men who were impotent, or homosexual, or who had longstanding mistresses already. These women were expected to remain sane, and produce heirs, and yet if they were caught out taking a lover they could end up facing banishment or even execution. A court dwarf wouldn't count as a lover though – he barely even counted as a person. Certainly he had no rights. Court dwarfs were seen as possessions, part of the household inventory. What a lady chose to do with her possession, in private, was no one's business but her own. Not that these liaisons were always a secret. There's a famous account in one lady-in-waiting's diary of the *ménage à trois* that existed between her mistress, the court dwarf, and king himself. The king was incapacitated as the result of a war wound, but he still liked to watch. He used to pay the lady-in-waiting to let him conceal himself in a window alcove, so he could spy on his wife having sex with the dwarf. The diary reports that after the dwarf had finished pleasuring the queen, he would help himself to a plate of stew in the palace kitchens then sneak up the chimney stairs to the king's apartments and give him a right royal seeing-to.'

'That can't be true, surely?' Nelly's heart pounded. She felt the space between her legs ache then contract. What on Earth was wrong with her? She gazed upon the painting, upon the glowing chestnut hair of the dwarf as he stared out at her from the frame.

Who are you? Nelly thought. Don't I know you from somewhere?

Which was impossible, of course, but again, his eyes . . .

'Why shouldn't it be true?' Cecily countered. 'Can you begin to imagine how boring it was, being queen? Boring and dangerous. Apart from anything else, you'd need someone to talk to.'

Yes, you would. But that would be like . . .

What?

Nelly sighed.

Your own perfect, secret existence. A kingdom of two.

'I'm so tired,' Nelly said. '*The Duchess of Malfi* must be getting to me. I've not been sleeping.'

'Are you sure that's all it is?'

Nelly nodded. 'I wish we could go away for a week, to Salzburg, just the two of us.'

'And bring an end to those marvellous notices you've been getting?'

'You're always telling me you never read the papers.'

'Usually I don't. I'll let you know about the painting.'

'Are you sure you can spare the time?'

'Even if I couldn't I would. I'm addicted to mysteries. I know all the Sherlock Holmes stories by heart, remember? Leave it to me.'

After saying goodbye to Cecily, Nelly went to the theatre by way of Süssmayr's Pâtisserie. She expected the soldier to be gone – homeless people never seemed to stay in any one place for long – but he was there, after all, pressed up against the grating with his tin plate in front of him just as before. He looked dirty and cold. He glanced up as Nelly approached.

'Good day,' he said. In the world of a week ago, he would not have dared to greet her in such a fashion – as if he knew her, as if the two of them were acquainted. Now everything was changed. How this had happened she did not know. She felt her cheeks burning.

'Did you mean it,' she said, 'when you said you'd seen *The Duchess of Malfi*?'

The soldier nodded. 'I've seen it twice. You were magnificent, both times.' He stared at her levelly, daring her, she supposed, to contradict him. Beneath the smuts and grime of the street his face was fine, handsome even, she could see that, but what good were such thoughts, what was the point of them? Whatever he had been before, he was ruined now. It came to her that it might have been better if he had died out there in the mud, instead of being found and sewn together and dumped out here on the street like so much garbage.

'I know the doorman,' he was saying. 'I used to work at The Majestic. Before the war, I mean. We were friends, sort of. He lets me shelter inside the theatre sometimes, if the boss isn't in. There's a place you can go, a little cubby hole under the circle. It used to be the lighting man's room, my friend says, only it isn't used now. You can see right on to the stage. It's like,' he paused, inhaled, 'being offered a fleeting glimpse of another world.'

'That's from *Anthea*.' Nelly found herself smiling, in spite of herself.

'I've seen them all.'

Nelly straightened up. 'Wait here,' she said, cursing herself inwardly for her tactlessness. What else was he supposed to do? She dived into

Süssmayr's, where she purchased a fragrant, still-warm Zwiebelbrötchen and a slice of apple tart, wrapped in the ochre-coloured, rose-stencilled paper that was a hallmark of Süssmayr's. She laid them carefully on the boards of the wooden cart beside the tin plate. She saw the way his eyes fixed on the food, the way he continued to hold it at arm's length, mentally. He would not touch it until she was gone, Nelly realised. He still had his dignity, at least for a while.

'Is there anything else?' she said, suddenly terrified of what he might ask of her.

'Cigarettes,' he said. 'I never used to but my comrades all smoked so I took it up. Awful habit but I miss it.'

She nodded and hurried away without turning back. The following morning, when she returned with the cigarettes, she asked him why his former employers at The Majestic had not seen fit to offer him aid. The soldier laughed, and for the first time she noted an edge of bitterness in his voice.

'My old boss would have helped me for sure, but he's gone. Left for the United States. Said it wasn't a good time for people like him to be in this city. People like him – whatever that means. Herr Bakst was a gentleman. The new manager doesn't give a damn. Told me to clear off and if he caught me begging anywhere near their hallowed portals he'd call the police.'

The soldier's name was Harald Leiermann. Before the war, he had studied civil engineering part-time at the university, working night shifts as a hotel porter to make ends meet. He had wanted to build bridges, he told her, magnificent bridges, which would grace their rivers and alpine valleys as intricate silver bangles might grace the ankles and wrists of a beautiful woman.

'I expect you think that's ridiculous,' he said. 'People like me, we don't get to build bridges. Even without this.' He made an angry gesture at his missing legs. 'My father was a railwayman, a guard. My mother takes in sewing. There were six of us at home.' He took a cigarette from the cardboard carton and lit up with one of the matches she had also brought him. 'They think I'm dead, my mother and sisters, and I'll let them keep on thinking so. I can't go home – they can't afford to feed me. With my father gone they barely get by.'

The next time she saw him he had washed and shaved. His friend the doorman, he explained, had let him use the theatre cloakroom after hours. Nelly brought him goulash from the street kiosk on Parmenterallee, more cigarettes. She stayed and talked with him for half an hour, breathing in the smell of the cigarettes and thinking how much she liked his voice, not just the sound but the way he spoke. He had grown more forthright since the last time, more confident. Mason would have said mind your step, he's after something, his type always are.

This man has lost everything, Nelly thought. Why should he not be after something? She remembered some words Adrian had said, about how robbing the poor even of their desires is the first step in robbing them of their humanity.

She felt sorrow for all Harry had suffered, great waves of it that threatened to choke her, yet it was more than that, she knew already. Had it begun when she asked him his name, when she bought him the pastry, when she dropped the coin into his plate? Or had it been earlier than that, much earlier, when she told herself she had stopped believing in love after Adrian died?

Not that it mattered. Things were as they were. Love, as Cecily had once said, was a disease. Once contracted, it is more or less impossible to shake off.

A month after their first meeting, Nelly signed the lease on a ground floor studio in the theatre district. A modest apartment – two rooms, with a stove and washing facilities – but it was dry and pleasantly furnished. It was a place to be.

'I can't accept this,' Harry said. 'Not when I don't have any means of paying you back. I don't want your pity.'

'You think this is pity?' she stormed, stung to the heart. She told him she didn't care in the least about money, though he could repay the loan in his own good time, if it mattered so much to him. What she wanted was for him to return to his studies at the university. 'You can achieve everything you ever wanted to,' she insisted. 'More – because we are together and that makes us stronger.'

She spoke the words earnestly, even though she and Harry had not so much as kissed yet. How could they, out in the open, with no place to be? Once Harry had relented and moved into the apartment, Nelly stayed away for three days. She told herself she was giving him time to settle in, to grow accustomed to his new situation. In reality she was terrified of the turn her life was about to take. Everything she had done for Harry so far could, if the need arose, be explained away as charity. One more step and she was done for. Had this really been what she intended, when she began?

Would she feel the same about this stranger, now that the impossible was suddenly a reality? Would Harry's injury – his disability – repel her? Could he still be a man?

When on the fourth day she arrived at the apartment it was to find Harry seated at the scrubbed-down table, a saucer of cigarette ash at his elbow and sketching furiously in a ring-bound exercise pad. His crutches were propped close to hand against the back of his chair.

His expression, as he turned to face her, lay somewhere between stoical indifference and incredulous joy.

'I thought you'd changed your mind,' he said, simply.

Her stole slid to the floor, slipping from about her shoulders in a liquid glide.

'I was,' Nelly began, but never completed the sentence or even the thought. She was overcome by the strength of her emotions, the sense, simultaneously, that she had known him all her life, that here *was* her life, beginning at last. Very soon they made love, the fur stole pooled beneath their bodies like a shed skin.

How did this not happen sooner? Nelly thought, in wonderment. She could not have imagined his body to be more beautiful.

The following week she purchased for him one of the new wheeled chairs, an 'invalid carriage' that would allow him free movement about the studio, to direct himself along the street, to sit undisturbed in the park where he liked to study.

A moving castle of silver tubing and polished leather, the chair provided the very latest in assisted mobility.

'Invalid carriage,' said Harry doubtfully, when he first laid eyes on it.

'This is not an invalid carriage,' Nelly assured him. 'This is a miracle of engineering. This is freedom.'

Later, when it was dark, Nelly wheeled the battered wooden cart out into the street. She left it by the side of the road a couple of streets away from the apartment. By mid-morning of the following day it had disappeared. She hoped someone had found a use for it, if only for firewood.

'Your Nikolaus Schilling was something of a renegade,' Cecily said. She had cut her hair. It sat close to her head, like a skull cap. Nelly's first reaction had been shock. The more she thought about it, the more she found such a reaction ridiculous. Why should the socially permitted length of a person's hair be determined by their gender? Besides, the new style suited Cecily – it suited her well. Nelly decided she liked it. 'He was drawn to transgressive subjects,' Cecily was saying. 'Siamese twins and royal eunuchs, demons consorting with children, that kind of thing. He was elected to join the Academy on account of his technical skill, then thrown out again three years later when a scandal erupted over a painting of his called *The Magdalene*. It showed Christ cavorting naked with prostitutes, apparently. Schilling made a lot of enemies, mainly because he really was a good painter. The older Academicians loathed him. They became determined to ruin his reputation and for the most part they succeeded.'

'How come he isn't more famous now, though? If he was so good, I mean.'

'A large number of his most important paintings were destroyed in a fire. There were rumours that it was arson, but that was never proved. Anyway, Schilling went abroad after that, disappeared from view. He has his fans, of course, and those paintings that did survive tend to get snapped up quickly when they come on the market. The painting you bought is actually quite valuable.'

'You were able to track it down, then?'

'It wasn't that difficult, once I got started. The woman was a minor aristocrat, Duchess Sophie of Marienbad, born in 1603. Her husband the duke was well thought of, if something of a recluse – he lost his older brother in the Thirty Years War and never got over it. He was older than Sophie, but not disastrously so and their marriage seemed amicable, or at least it did at first. But as time wore on and there were no children, rumours began to circulate that the duke was underperforming in the bedroom department, that the marriage hadn't been consummated even. At some point, Sophie became friendly with the duke's chief treasurer, Nyall Lysander.'

'Lysander was the dwarf?'

Cecily nodded. 'Though he was never what you would call a court dwarf in the traditional sense. He was a brilliant man, by all accounts, and fun to be with. Unlike many in his position he held considerable power, not to mention being a favourite of the duke. Sophie clearly needed more excitement in her life and what started as a friendship quickly evolved into a passionate love affair. For a long time they were able to hide the true nature of their relationship because no one believed that a duchess would be willing to risk everything – her marriage, her position in society, her fortune – all for the sake of what many would have considered a circus freak. They were found out in the end, though. Sophie became pregnant, and hatched a hare-brained scheme to murder the duke and make it seem like an accident. Things didn't end well.'

'What happened?'

'Lysander was hanged, and Sophie was made the subject of what might be termed a cruel and unusual punishment: her left eye was put out, with a fire iron. The duke's advisers persuaded him it would make the

47

duchess less attractive to future rivals, though they clearly saw Sophie as a political force to be reckoned with and wanted her diminished. Nikolaus Schilling made up the double portrait of Sophie and Lysander from contemporary sources as a satirical commentary on a society affair that was causing ructions at the time. It was exactly the kind of sensational subject matter Schilling had been criticised for in the past. The painting didn't do him any favours with the Academy, but I'm sure he didn't have a problem finding a buyer for it, and you wouldn't either. I can make some enquiries, if you like.'

'I don't want to sell it,' Nelly said quietly. The story had shaken her. She was trying not to imagine what it had been like for Sophie, knowing her lover was to be executed, being subjected to a senseless and wanton disfigurement too gruesome to contemplate. What had become of her, finally? Cecily would be able to tell her, no doubt, but maybe it was better not to know.

History swept on remorselessly, dragging everyone in its wake. Schilling's painting was all that remained.

'You're very quiet, all of a sudden,' Cecily said. 'Did I say something wrong?'

'I think I'm in love,' Nelly said. The words rose from her spontaneously, unbidden, though if she had planned to tell anyone at all it would of course have been Cecily.

'You're not serious?'

Nelly stared at her hands. She was sitting where she always sat when she visited Cecily: in the armchair under the window, her feet drawn up beneath the plaid rug that she always drew over her knees, regardless of the weather. She had always felt safe in Cecily's rooms, yet she had stopped feeling entirely safe anywhere now, she realised, even here.

'He's an engineer,' she said softly. 'I met him – he saw me in *The Duchess of Malfi* and things started from there.'

It was a reasonable enough story and more than half true. The round reality of the thing – Harry's injury, the apartment she was paying for – seemed too complicated all of a sudden.

Nelly hadn't slept properly in days. A week even. Two.

'What are you going to do?' Cecily said. 'Are you planning to tell Mason?'

Was there an edge of triumph in Cecily's voice, a hint of I-told-you-so? Nelly thought not, though she didn't believe that she would blame her if there was. Cecily was only human, after all.

'I can't. Not yet, anyway. I don't know what he might do.'

'You're frightened of him.'

'Of course not.' She laughed. 'I need time to think, that's all.'

'This – man. Does he know about Mason?'

'He knows I'm married.' Which again was true, though she and Harry had not spoken of Mason directly, all this time. It was almost as if they believed that to say his name was to utter a curse, that not speaking it would hold him at bay, like an evil spirit.

'Are you happy, Nell? At least tell me you're happy.'

Happier than I've ever been, she thought. *Happier than I believed was possible. Sick with terror.* Nelly had come to believe that every performance she had starred in until then had been a species of fraud – acting from above the waist, as her old mentor, Katerina Spitz, had been fond of putting it. Her love for Harry had illuminated the poetry of Ibsen, of Shakespeare, in new and terrifying ways. Had she believed, before Harry, in the calamity of love, its vicious aftermath? She did not think so.

She thought she had been so clever, marrying Mason. Instead, she had been a fool. She had forced herself into a trap of her own devising.

'I wish I'd listened to you, that's all,' she said at last.

'Don't be ridiculous. None of us can see the future. And I'm the last person you should be taking advice from when it comes to romance.' They both smiled. Cecily had been involved in an agonised correspondence with a married artist for the best part of a decade, with no discernible resolution, forwards or backwards. Nelly had always privately thought Cecily preferred things that way – all the drama, without the practical inconveniences of a life together. But as the last few weeks had proved, what did she know?

'I will sort things out,' Nelly said. 'Thanks for finding out about my picture.'

She left soon afterwards. She had intended to go home before heading off to the theatre but she had left it too late. She lay on the couch in her dressing room instead, the lights off to avoid interruptions and the conversation with Cecily coursing through her brain like a repeating sine wave.

Tell Mason, Cecily had said. Or: are you going to tell Mason?

Telling Mason would be like ripping away the backcloths from a theatre set: the dusty darkness beyond, the bare hanging wires. She could lose everything, and worse. She had seen how vindictive Mason could be when it came to his business rivals. She hated to think what steps he might take to jeopardise her future if he discovered her treachery.

How would they manage then, she and Harry? It did not bear thinking about.

'If only he were dead,' she said to Harry a month or so later. The feeling had been growing in her, as the evenings lengthened and the darkness deepened, as the first freezing flurries of snow made it more difficult for her to flit about the city on a whim, that the only solution to the problem of Mason lay in Mason's demise. So far at least it had been an abstract idea, a wish rather than a plan, although it was not difficult, Nelly soon discovered, to find justification for such a wish in the real world. The way Mason bullied his driver, Johan, for example, the way he eyed the buttocks of Minna the housemaid as she knelt to lay the fire. The way he railed with increasing vehemence against the so-called degenerates who clogged the doss-houses, the filthy foreigners and starving farm-workers begging in the streets.

One evening he came home tight-lipped with anger after being forced to sack a man he had previously earmarked for promotion.

'Turns out he's a faggot,' Mason said. 'I can't have animals like that in my office. There should be a law against these people.'

There is, Nelly thought. There are many.

More and more, if he was in a foul enough mood, Mason had begun fulminating against the decline of moral standards amongst her theatre colleagues, insisting Nelly should steer clear of them socially, that he didn't want her inviting them back to the house when he wasn't there.

Parasitic riff-raff, he called them. Nelly had been married to Mason for two years. He still told her he loved her, frequently, still liked to treat her to expensive dinners, surprise her with overnight stays at luxury hotels.

She still allowed him to have sex with her, because what else could she do? His body seemed crude, excessively heavy, a blunt instrument. His lovemaking still excited and repulsed her in equal measure.

How long, how long, how long? How much longer could she stand it?

Harry looked at her sharply. 'He doesn't need to be dead. Just leave him. Fetch your things and walk out. We can get by.'

Harry had returned to his studies. He was now able to manipulate the wheelchair with confidence, able to access lectures, to move about the city independently and with a new light in his eyes. He was thinking about the future and seeing a life for them both in it. He had made a friend at the university, Jonas Arp. He chatted about Jonas constantly, wanted Nelly to meet him. The idea of stepping outside their accustomed parameters – the idea of being seen – made Nelly deeply anxious, even though being seen was what she did for a living.

She kept making excuses.

'You're ashamed of me,' Harry said.

'Never,' Nelly replied.

'It's him, then. Mason.' His name at last.

Nelly nodded. 'If someone should see us. And tell him.'

'So what? He can't keep you prisoner. I don't give a damn what he does.'

You would, though, Nelly thought. You have no idea how dangerous he is. Men like Mason will eat the world, if you let them. I've seen it happen.

She thought of the duchess, Sophie, in Schilling's painting. She had seen it happen, too. Before they took her eye.

'Just let me think,' she said to Harry. 'I'll find a way out of this, I promise.'

The critics had noted a new maturity in her *Duchess of Malfi*. *It is as if Toye truly lives the part*, one wrote, remarking on the duchess's famous speech in Act 1 V.

Rarely has a work of classic drama seemed to speak so acutely and so bitterly to contemporary concerns, observed another, drawing attention to the play's embedded power structures, Webster's commentary upon the disadvantaged position of women within a patriarchal society.

A goddess of war, ran the headline of a third.

When Nelly was on stage, all things seemed possible. Above all, she could say what she felt. There was talk of her going to Berlin to star in a film, a spy thriller in which she would play a double agent codenamed the Scorpion, who dispatched her victims with a stiletto.

'A stiletto?' Nelly smiled. 'Why not a gun?' She was having lunch with the movie's casting agent, in a restaurant close to the theatre.

'Because a gun always makes a noise, and because Rita – that's your character – is an expert swordswoman. She slides the stiletto in between the ribs and punctures the heart. The victim is dead before he knows it, and there's virtually no blood. We want the film to have a period feel, and the stiletto is part of that. The scriptwriter was directly inspired by seventeenth-century revenge dramas. Like *The Duchess of Malfi*.'

'It sounds exciting,' Nelly said. She had dreamed of being in movies ever since she and Adrian had queued around the block to see Tatiana Tcherepnin in Lubitsch's *Demons* during one of Adrian's furloughs. This was the break she had been waiting for, that she had secretly expected, but now that it was here all she could think about was the obstacles it presented. She dreaded to imagine what Mason would say – he loathed Berlin – and she could not consider relocating there anyway, not without Harry.

She agreed with the casting agent that she would travel to the German capital the following month to take a screen test. That would not commit her to anything, and in the meantime she could work out a plan.

'You've sometimes had swords and muskets here in the shop, haven't you, Konni?' she said. 'Have you ever heard of a thing called a stiletto?'

'A stiletto? You mean the weapon?' He did not ask her why she would be interested in such a thing, though she could see the question in his eyes as clearly as if he had spoken it aloud. She smiled, thinking that this was exactly what her character would do in the film: smile, and tell no one. Konni had known her since she was born. He would believe what she chose to reveal, and let that be enough.

'I'm doing research for a film I'm going to be in. Might be in, anyway,' she said. 'Nothing is definite yet. But I want to make a good impression when I go for the screen test.'

She told him about the spy thriller, and about the assassin, Rita, who routinely used the stiletto as her weapon of choice. 'The casting agent told me you could kill someone with one of those things without spilling so much as a drop of blood. Do you know if that's true? It sounds unlikely to me.'

Konni was nodding his head vigorously. 'No, no, it's perfectly true. For an experienced swordsperson, anyway. The trick is to pierce the heart in a single thrust. Stops beating then, you see, stops pumping. Hence no blood. The cause of death would become obvious as soon as you examined the body of course, but the killer could be miles away by then, and leaving very little evidence behind them. Clever, if you like that sort of thing. The stiletto has been a staple of Italian melodrama for centuries. Interesting that someone has chosen to use it in a modern context.'

'Have you ever seen one, Konni?'

'Of course I have. They come up on the market quite often, though armoury has never been a specialism of mine.'

'I know this might sound like a strange request,' Nelly said, 'but do you think you could get hold of one for me? I want to think myself into the part – to try and imagine what it might be like, to use a weapon like that, to kill someone. At the moment I have no idea how it feels even to hold a sword in my hand.'

'You're not planning to murder anyone, are you?'

They both laughed and laughed, then Konni made Turkish coffee, serving it in Liza's favourite gold-rimmed coffee cans. Nelly sipped her drink, wondering if Konni would remember this conversation later, when news came to him of the sudden and violent end of Mason Gehrlich, killed by an unknown assassin with a sword through the heart.

Mason had enemies, yes – men like Mason always did – but such a death, coming out of the blue, like something from the pages of Shakespeare, or Christopher Marlowe, or John Webster?

Yes, Konni would remember, but he would say nothing. Of that, Nelly felt certain. He had known her all her life. He was like a second father to her.

What a lovely thing it is, she thought. What a sweet little sword.

The blade was triangular, tapering to a needle-fine tip. Like a bee sting, Nelly mused. A sleeping man would barely feel it. He would simply go on sleeping – for all eternity.

If there was one thing she knew about Mason, it was that he slept like the dead.

'It's sixteenth century,' Konni explained. 'Forged on an anvil. The craftsmanship is exceptional. Go on, feel it. You won't cut yourself. One of the characteristics of the stiletto is that it has no sharp edges.'

He passed her the weapon, and she folded her fingers carefully about the handle. She experienced a sudden, tender warmth at the core of her, a sense of empowerment that was different from sex, different from money, different from everything.

It was similar to the power she felt within her when she was onstage, only earthier and more grounded, a deeper shade of red.

'Is this a dagger that I see before me?' she murmured softly.

'Suits you,' Konni said. 'I hope they find you a splendid costume to go with it.'

Nelly laughed aloud. She believed in the spy movie, suddenly – she believed in herself as the star of it. The Duchess, she would insist they named her, not the Scorpion. The Scorpion sounded too predictable. This was her part, after all, surely she should have a say in what she was called?

There were things she would have to do first though, and time was moving fast.

'I'd like to buy this, Konni,' she said. She pressed the dagger's point against the pad of her thumb, not hard enough to break the skin, just hard enough to prove that it could be done. 'I'd like to take it with me, to Berlin.'

If this were a play, the audience would guess everything in an instant. They would know the Duchess was lying to the old man, that she meant to use the dagger to kill her husband. They would be meant to guess, though, that would be the whole point. The old man would be the dupe, the innocent party, the only man in the theatre who didn't know the truth.

'You're not in trouble are you, Nelly?' Konni said. He peered at her over his glasses.

'Of course not. I'm nervous because of the screen test, that's all. I've never done anything like this before and it's a big chance for me. I want to make the most of it. You do understand?'

Konni was silent, and as the seconds ticked by Nelly thought about how the years they had known one another – the years of Liza's illness, the day the telegram came about Adrian, her father's funeral – had really all been leading up to this moment, the two of them in this room. Truth or dare.

'Well, Nelly,' Konni said at last, 'I won't sell you the dagger, but I will give it to you as a present. For good luck. It can be our secret.'

She had known from the start that she could not kill him at home. If Mason's body were to be found even within a mile of Golovinsky Street, Nelly would be the first to be suspected. Like Nyall Lysander, she would hang. The thought of such a fate – not so much her death, but the utter loss of dominion over her life – made the hairs at the nape of her neck freeze like thorns.

As for what would happen to Harry – the idea that he might end his days begging on the street was too dreadful to contemplate. The evening after acquiring the stiletto she went round to Harry's apartment and presented him with fifty thousand crowns in cash, together with the diamond earrings Mason had given her on their first wedding anniversary.

'In case anything happens to me,' she explained. 'There's enough here for you to keep on the apartment until you've finished your studies. The earrings would fetch another twenty thousand. Only be careful where you trade them – they could be traced.' She felt in her bag for her notepad, scribbled down the address of Konni's shop then tore off the sheet and folded it inside the case with the earrings. 'Konni will look after you. Tell him I sent you. He's a good man.'

'What's all this about, Nelly? Are you planning to walk out on me?'

Harry's face, the quiet hurt in his eyes, the shrouded desperation that had marked his expression when first they met.

'Don't be ridiculous,' Nelly said. It was terrifying, how much they needed each other. A world without Harry would not be incomplete so much as rotten in its foundations. 'This is just a precaution. What if I were ill, or had an accident? I'd go out of my mind with worry if I thought you couldn't manage. I should have thought of this earlier – I can't imagine why I didn't. It's only for a short time,' she added. 'Just until we're free.'

His expression darkened again. 'Whenever that might be,' he said.

'Not long now.' She knelt by his chair, began stroking his thighs. 'I have a plan. Trust me.'

'The only plan we need is you walking out of that house and not looking back.'

'I don't see why we should have to live like—' Beggars, she had been about to say. 'I don't see why we should have to struggle. I want what's mine, that's all. Please try and understand.'

Harry sighed, then Nelly kissed him and the whole subject of Mason and when they might be rid of him slipped sideways and fell away. Just before she began to undress, it occurred to Nelly that it wasn't about the house any more, or the things inside it, but about the Duchess.

The final act was approaching, the end of the play. Nelly found herself transfixed by the drama, as if she were in the audience and not onstage. How will it end? she kept wondering. She tried to think herself back to the early days of her affair with Mason, when she was still able to convince herself that the rush of excitement she felt upon seeing him might one day be transformed into love.

Once sexual attraction wore off, what you were left with was an ordinary person – like the princess and the frog, only in reverse. Whether that person turned out to be your lifelong companion or your sworn enemy seemed mostly down to chance.

I hate him, Nelly thought. She could not remember feeling hate before, not really, and the violence of the emotion surprised her. The only person who seemed to understand it was the Duchess.

There was a woman, Rosa. Nelly knew her vaguely through the theatre – she occasionally took parts as flower-sellers or harlots, violated servant girls – but really she had been a friend of Adrian's. Rosa had a small child, and earned her living serving in bars, though Adrian had hinted that she had once worked as a prostitute in real life. It took Nelly a while to track Rosa down, but eventually Wishart, who ran the box office, told her he'd spotted her working the bar at the Ponchinello, in the banking district.

It's like fate, Nelly thought. The banking district. Given world enough and time, Mason would probably have begun an affair with Rosa all by himself. Not that she could afford to leave it to chance. She felt embarrassed, having to ask Rosa to do what she needed her to do, if only because it meant Rosa would know that Nelly had heard and believed the rumours about her. She comforted herself with the idea of the money she would be paying her, enough for Rosa and her son to live on for many months. Years, if she was careful. And Mason was good looking. At least there was that.

'I want a divorce,' Nelly explained. 'This seems like the easiest way of getting one.'

'Let me get this straight,' Rosa said. She was making a good show of not recognising Nelly. A just punishment for her presumption, Nelly conceded, and one that carried the additional benefit of making their temporary association a great deal less risky. 'You're offering to pay me to have sex with your husband?'

Nelly nodded, then swallowed. Her mouth felt awfully dry all of a sudden. 'It need only be the once.'

'You've got a real nerve, you know that?' Rosa said. She was a striking woman, with lustrous blue-black hair and lavender eyes. She was also too thin, the reddened skin of her hands hinting at a life that Nelly had managed entirely to avoid. Nelly lowered her eyes. Shame stained her cheeks and burned her stomach, like acid. The Duchess would not feel ashamed, Nelly knew. She would see this woman as a tool, to be used as she saw fit and then discarded.

'I'm sorry to ask, but I'm desperate. You're the only person I can think of who can help me. I can't go on like this much longer – I can't bear it.' She let the tears rise up, huge, crystalline tears, the kind that had won her all those rave reviews in the role of Violetta.

'You're good, I'll give you that.' Rosa glanced back over her shoulder. The woman covering for her at the bar was looking daggers. 'When do I get the money?'

Nelly let out her breath in a rush. 'I'll give you half now.' She felt in her bag for the envelope. 'You'll get the rest by messenger the morning after.'

Rosa slipped the packet of money inside her dress. 'You're very trusting, aren't you?'

'I trust you.'

'Because of your brother?'

Nelly looked at the floor.

'Adrian was the best man I ever knew,' Rosa said. 'I'm doing this for him. Because he'd want me to help you.'

They stared at one another. Nelly tried to smile her gratitude, but found she could not. She had never before felt more distant from another human being. What she was doing to Rosa was wrong, so wrong that she had opened a gulf between them that could never be filled. Yet kings and emperors performed such actions every day. A queen or a duchess would not ask, she would demand on pain of death.

Nelly straightened her back. 'He'll be going away on business at the end of the month,' she said. 'It has to be soon.'

A hotel that was not too far from Mason's office, yet unlike the sort of place he might normally patronise. Not disreputable exactly, but down at heel. Nelly chose the Black Angel, a tall, narrow, suitably shabby pension, boxed in on both sides by cheap apartment buildings and overlooking the railway tracks. She explained to Rosa that she should behave exactly as she would under normal circumstances. 'You won't see the detective, but he will see you. When you leave, go by the back door – there's a yard, with a side-passage leading back out on to the street. Go straight home. Someone will call on you later, with the money.'

'What if he wakes up? Your husband, I mean.'

'He won't wake up. He sleeps like the dead, especially with a few drinks inside him. Just remember to leave the door on the latch. You'll never have to see him again.'

Nelly had concocted a story in which Mason had been having an affair for many months, that the woman was the wife of one of Mason's business associates, someone who – in spite of her betrayal – Nelly was fond of and did not want to see embarrassed. Far easier to hire a detective to catch Mason in flagrante with someone else, then threaten to unmask his mistress unless he complied absolutely with Nelly's demands.

'I want the house,' she said to Rosa, by way of explanation. 'Mason won't care about the money, he just hates losing. If I were to simply ask him for a divorce, he'd fight me through the courts and I'd end up with nothing. I need to gain the advantage.'

'How much of what you're telling me is actually true?' Rosa said. 'I'm only asking because I know your brother wouldn't thank me if I didn't look out for you.'

She crossed and uncrossed her hands in their black gloves, and Nelly thought about how this moment might play out onstage. *Act 3, Scene 2: Aronofsky Park. The DUCHESS and ROSA are sitting side by side on a wooden bench. The Duchess is wearing an expensive-looking grey overcoat and her mink stole. Rosa is wearing a red woollen dress coat with a velvet collar – stylish but insubstantial.* The coats would pass more social comment than two pages of dialogue. The audience would feel sympathy for Rosa, but this was not her story, hers was just a bit part. Once her scene with Mason was over she would disappear from the stage.

'Don't worry about me,' Nelly said. 'I know what I'm doing.'

'You might think you do, but you should be careful. You know what people say about the best laid plans?'

'Will you do it? I need to know.'

'I can't afford not to. But then you knew that when you asked me. You can still change your mind, though.'

'I won't change my mind.'

'Very well, then. It's your funeral.'

Funeral, Nelly thought. Funeral. She could not get the word out of her mind. She had put on long gloves, like Rosa's, the black lace cloaking her arms like the strands of a mourning veil. She would buy new gloves for Mason's funeral, she decided. Once the police had released his body for burial, no expense would be spared.

She imagined herself, pacing the empty rooms of the house on Golovinsky Street: the lamps dimmed, the curtains drawn, the tragic widow, glimpsed for a moment at an upstairs window then seen no more.

'She's not accepting visitors at the moment,' Minna would say when people called. 'I think she's still in shock.'

Nelly paused in front of the painting, the Duchess Sophie and her lover, Nyall Lysander. Would they have gone back on their plan, had they known what was to come? Nelly doubted it. Some things are meant to be. If Schilling's painting was about anything, it was about fate: the duchess, caught at the height of her power, the dwarf, saying this is what it means to be human. This is what it means to love, the way fire tears through trees. To know the awful future and still not falter. To grasp the universe and swallow it whole. To laugh in their faces when they come to take you to the scaffold.

ACT FIVE, Scene four: Angel Street, night. The DUCHESS stands stage left, facing away from the audience and watching the scene as it unfolds on stage. She wears a dark hooded cloak. The stiletto glints in her gloved hand. Enter MASON and ROSA from stage right. Rosa's coat is part the way open, and we see she is wearing a beautiful expensive-looking pearl choker. Mason is visibly inebriated but still coherent. They come to a standstill in front of the Black Angel hotel.

MASON: Is this what you are to me, then – my dark angel?

ROSA: You have called me your pearl, your rose.

MASON: If a pearl to ransom a goddess, a rose to intoxicate the senses unto madness [he grips her shoulders, turns her head roughly, forces his mouth on to hers] then all is as it should be, though 'tis your blackness that endures as an inducement.

ROSA: You believe me a deceiver, then, sir?

MASON: In no wise. You mistake my meaning. [He kisses her again, more gently.] A man who is weary and much travelled wears out all passion, eventually. How overfed blooms do cloy and sicken, how the jewels at the dowager's throat do lose their sparkle. But as for you, my angel . . .

ROSA: What of me?

MASON: You will be the death of me yet. [He grabs her hand, forces it against his crotch.] Even as I throb and strain, I would yet understand thy purpose.

ROSA: Purpose, sir?

MASON: How came we so perfectly together, madam?

ROSA: I know not your meaning, sir.

MASON: My meaning? I would have thought it transparent, and most especially to a being such as yourself, who needs must know all. As a man of business I have never worshipped at the altar of Felicity – Felicity be damned. Any man who trusts to luck will live to see himself swindled eventually, or called fool to his face. And yet – in my hour of doubt and

64

darkness here you are. In the matter of my marriage, here is your wisdom. You tell me my wife is true, even as you mark my helpless body for your conquest. You assure me of your faith, even as I glimpse the coin in your pocket from a common soldier. My faithful guardsman whispers your past acquaintance with my wife. Is this luck then, or vile rumour? You will call me a cad for asking, but I would call myself Tom Numbskull were I not to ask.

ROSA: Not your wife, sir, your wife's brother, a sweet youth, who is lately fallen honourably on the field of battle. He was my help, my faith, my confidant and I mourn him still. I know not your wife, sir, though I, as the world at large, have seen her pass by on the street and admired her in her finery.

MASON: Say I believe you. My sense yet insists that to be admired is not yet to be admirable, especially in matters of beauty, in which logic so mincingly surrenders to the heart, making mincemeat of us all. My wife is gone from me, though the scent of her still lingers. I will know the truth, and knowledge will seal my action, and there will be no mercy. She believes she outsmarts me. Lo, Duchess! You will feel my blade even as the air of treachery buffets your cheeks, you and your low charlatan. For now, for this blue night, I shall steep myself in roses. Come inside!

MASON grips ROSA by the arm, and together they mount the steps to the pension. As the front door closes behind them, the DUCHESS emerges from the shadows to face the audience.

DUCHESS: Oh ye who speak of treachery, take heed. I, feel your blade, sir? In those days of our first acquaintance I yearned to feel it, right enough, and rudely thrust. Yet withal such yearnings fade when love is absent, the surest blade grows blunt from being ill-used. You used me, sir, even as your vile assassins robbed me of my brother, even as the coin in your treasury puts fat on the bones of the captains who plot the next war. Why should I yet be robbed of my dowry, sent penniless as a beggar into the street? You know not your wife, sir. A woman is not a prize to be won, my lord. Thrust your blade, aye, and twist it deep, your cracked carapace borne aloft on the stew of roses. You will feel my wrath before morning. Your wife bids you adieu.

Nelly was shivering inside her cloak, an old thing of Minna's she had borrowed from the basement closet, hoping she could return it before it was missed. She longed for her stole, not just for the warmth of the fur but for the comfort of the identity it bestowed upon her. She had grown used to being admired, she realised. The sensation of being invisible was discomfiting.

Beggars lay huddled in doorways. Alongside the entrance to the covered market, a group of vagrants had a fire going. Nelly sat for a while on the fringes of the crowd, listening as an old man with a pockmarked face and a ruined nose recounted the story of his escape from the Siberian salt mines. She wanted desperately to be in Berlin, sipping a glass of champagne in a cabaret bar with a whole new life in prospect.

I am Nelly Toye, she thought, as if she needed reminding. She had told Harry about the screen test, that she would be away for a week and then depending on the outcome she would secure an apartment for them both, together with a guarantee from the university that Harry would be able to continue his studies in Berlin.

'This will solve everything, don't you see?' she had assured him excitedly. 'If I land this part it will mean money – real money. We won't need to struggle any more.'

She had promised to tell Mason she was leaving him as soon as she returned. She trembled inwardly at the thought of it, the outburst of rage and accusations and threats such a confession would provoke.

Luckily, it would not be necessary. By morning Mason would be dead, and Nelly would be on a train bound for Berlin. The police officer who brought the news of her husband's murder to the house on Golovinsky Street would be obliged to send a telegram instead.

This city had had its hour. It was time to leave.

Finally, she rose. Her hands in their threadbare gloves felt numb with cold. She crossed her arms, hugging herself for warmth as she made her way back through the maze of side streets to the small cobbled courtyard opposite the Black Angel. The air was midnight blue, and sharp with frost. She leaned upon the balustrade, and waited. Around a half an hour later, the front door of the pension eased open and Rosa emerged into the light from the carriage lamp over the doorway. She was wearing her red coat. Nelly recalled how three hours earlier Mason had seized Rosa's arms, forcing her up against the wall as he fumbled with his belt. *Christ, I'm horny*, he had muttered. Nelly had heard him quite distinctly. She had been horrified, convinced Mason was about to force himself on Rosa right there on the street, that they would never get inside the hotel at all. Rosa had pushed him away, laughing, said something about a nightcap. Eventually they had gone inside.

Rosa now looked perfectly composed, her coat buttoned up, her hair loose about her shoulders but not unduly dishevelled. As if nothing had happened, Nelly thought. In a little over two hours the dawn would be breaking, and this business would be over, once and for all.

She waited until Rosa was gone, then stepped forward from her hiding place and hurried up the steps to the hotel. The door opened soundlessly. A single lamp burned dimly in the hallway. Mason was in Room 16 – she had agreed this vital detail with Rosa beforehand. Nelly was surprised by how calm she felt, but then that was often how it was when she learned a new part: she would be nervous for weeks about forgetting her lines, then once she was actually on stage her fear disappeared.

Like opening a door and stepping through.

The building was old, and like all cheap hotels smelled faintly of dead chrysanthemums. The floorboards creaked as she climbed the stairs, but the guests, behind their locked doors, either did not hear or did not care to investigate. Room 16 overlooked the back – the yard and, beyond that, the railway sidings. The door stood ajar. When Nelly bent her ear to the crack she heard the low, unmistakable sound of Mason, snoring.

Put out the light, and put out the light, Nelly's lips formed the words. *Othello*. She wondered how it might feel, to die in your sleep. Was there a frantic, painful instant of passing over, or would you simply go on dreaming, never to awake? She felt in her cloak for the stiletto, the handle sliding into her palm softly as the light from the streetlamp spilling into the room. Mason lay on his side with his face in the pillow, the quilt askew. His bare shoulders gleamed like marble, a toppled god. There was something magnificent in his robustness, his certainty even in sleep that the world was his.

The Duchess drew forth her weapon, the lamplight flowing like mercury the length of the blade. She could hear her own breathing, rasping in time with her husband's snores.

'For thine is the kingdom', she whispered. She bent over his body, breathing in his scent, the raw, rich, life of him. The idea that such a life could be stilled at her behest, the earthy reek of his armpits, his groin might be turned in the space of a second to the stink of corruption seemed suddenly in this private darkness to be the worst kind of sorcery.

In the morning she would be a murderess. Harry need never know the truth of what had happened, but he would sense she had changed.

Nelly lay down on the bed, pulling up the quilt to cover her legs and resting her forehead in the small of Mason's back as she had done in the old days. Mason did not stir – he slept like the dead. Nelly imagined how if she were to wake him and confess everything – her affair with Harry, her deception with Rosa – he would make light of the whole business, assure her they need never think of it again, that this world of lowlifes and cripples and boarding houses was nothing to do with them and never had been.

He would buy her something beautiful and expensive, laugh about how she was always letting her imagination run away with her.

'You theatre types,' he would say, shaking his head. 'Honestly.'

The next day, or the day after, he would renew his suggestion that they emigrate to America, where his brother still ran the family business.

'We would have a good life there. Better than here. Europe is going to the dogs, everyone who's anyone can see it.'

She drew the point of the stiletto gently across his shoulder blades and then laid it aside. She was damned if she would let her hatred of this man, her husband, steal her future. Murder was too good for him.

Go back where you came from, Mason, she thought. Just – go.

She stood up from the bed. On the floor at her feet lay Mason's clothes, crumpled together carelessly like a discarded costume. From the top pocket of his jacket she drew his handkerchief and the onyx fountain pen he always carried with him, a gift from his father.

She spread the handkerchief on the dressing table, pinning it down with a half-empty wine bottle so she could write on it, taking care not to blot the ink.

I know you were here, she scrawled, in block capitals. She thought about signing her name, then decided not to. If her identity wasn't obvious it soon would be. The play was over.

The sky was powdery grey with the promise of dawn. As she came down the back steps and into the yard, Nelly heard the first train leaving the station, the familiar screech of brakes as it slowed down to cross the viaduct, in the silence that followed the chiming of hammer on metal down by the tracks.

A railway worker cursed. A burst of laughter.

You nearly had my thumb off.

Fuck you, granddad.

The Duchess pulled the cloak more tightly about her shoulders as she hurried along. She would buy Minna a new coat, she decided. Something warmer, and better quality. It would make a fine parting gift. For the first time in many weeks, she felt entirely free.

Dear Andrew,

I was given my first doll as a present, completely by chance.

In spite of his affinity with machines, my father never went anywhere by car if he could help it. He would drive to the outlying villages for work, but in his free time he preferred to walk, or else he took the bus. Our car always smelled of my mother, of her skin and hair and the soap she used, which was lemon-scented, and came in a cardboard box patterned with yellow flowers. My mother used to go driving most afternoons. She would wait until she knew I was home from school, then she would take the car keys from the china pot on the hall table and often wouldn't get back until six or seven in the evening. When my father came in from work he would cook supper for us both, then I would do my homework and he would watch *Nationwide*, and whatever came on afterwards. When my mother arrived home she would sometimes make herself an egg on toast but that was all.

Every now and then she would take me with her. She never told me where we were going. Sometimes we just drove out into the countryside around Truro and then came home again. Once we went to a small seaside town on the northern coast called St Clare. My mother parked the car then led me towards a café on the narrow high street. There was a woman waiting for us, standing outside on the pavement. She had polished red lips, and dense dark hair with a silver streak running through the middle of it, like Cruella de Ville.

'I don't like going in on my own,' she said to my mother. 'People give you funny looks.'

My mother didn't introduce me, but in the course of the conversation I discovered that the woman's name was Ingrid. A waitress brought tea and scones, and my mother talked to Ingrid about a concert she had heard on the radio. After about an hour we left and drove home again.

Our visit to Catherine Sharpe began in the same way, except that Catherine Sharpe lived in Truro. On the outskirts anyway, north-west of the city centre and almost in the country. Her house was large, set back from the road at the end of a gravel drive. She used to be my mother's singing teacher, though I did not understand that until a long time afterwards. She wore her white hair pinned high on her head in a style that reminded me of a picture of Marie Antoinette I had seen on the cover of a book in the school library.

My mother leaned forward to kiss her. Then she did an incredible thing.

'This is my daughter, Bramber,' she said. 'She likes making up stories.'

I blushed. I could sense my mother's hand, hovering beside my arm, curled into a shape that would have fitted my elbow exactly.

'She looks just like you, Lisa,' said Catherine Sharpe. 'It's strange to think that you have a child.'

My mother laughed. After that she didn't speak of me again. She seated herself on one of the large, chintz-covered sofas that took up most of Catherine Sharpe's living room and began talking about a record she had just sent off for, from London. Both women seemed to have forgotten I was there.

I moved around the margins of the room, examining the dark paintings in their ornate frames and the tiny gold carriage clock on the mantelpiece. Eventually I found my way out into the hall. There were four doors opening off from it, each revealing a narrow slice of the room beyond. The largest of the rooms had three tall windows overlooking the driveway and contained a grand piano. In the bathroom I hovered in front of the mirror, watching myself reflected against the dark blue tiles. In the room next to the bathroom stood a single brass bedstead and a glass-fronted bookcase crammed with sheet music. On top of the bookcase sat a doll. I gazed at her steadily and she gazed back. I couldn't get over the feeling that she seemed to know me.

She wore a plain brown dress and long, leather lace-up boots. Her hair was reddish and curly, and felt real. I grabbed her around the waist and lifted her down. I didn't notice that Catherine Sharpe had come into the room behind me. When I heard her call my name I almost dropped the doll, from fright. I felt certain Catherine Sharpe had been spying on me, following me around from room to room. Later I realised she must simply have caught sight of me on her way to the bathroom.

'Do you like her?' she said. I stared at her silently, not knowing

73

if it was safer to admit that I did or pretend I didn't care. 'Take her home with you if you like, she'll just be cluttering up the room otherwise.'

'I can't,' I said at last. My heart was thumping. I tried to think of a reason, of something I could say that wouldn't sound rude. I could already imagine my mother's silence in the car as she drove us home, her anger at the foolish way I'd behaved in front of her friend.

'Don't be silly, of course you can,' said Catherine Sharpe. 'It isn't valuable.'

She gave a funny little laugh, as if the whole incident had amused her greatly. She took me by the hand and marched me back to the living room. My mother was still on the sofa, leafing through a magazine.

'I've given your daughter that doll.' Catherine Sharpe waved a hand in my general direction and I realised she'd forgotten my name. 'You don't mind, do you? It's just some old thing that used to belong to my sister. I'd forgotten I had it.'

My mother turned slowly towards me. The magazine fell from her lap and slid to the floor. 'She's too old for dolls,' she said. 'Bramber has never enjoyed playing with toys.'

Neither of the women spoke to me directly, and after a moment's silence Catherine Sharpe asked my mother if she would like more tea. I understood that I would be allowed to keep the doll, so long as I stayed perfectly quiet and didn't do anything else to make my mother feel embarrassed. I sat down on a stool close to the window and held the doll in my lap. It seemed to me that both of us were waiting, on tenterhooks, holding our breath. Eventually, my mother got up from the sofa and kissed Catherine Sharpe on the cheek. Shortly afterwards we left. My mother drove most of the way back into Truro in silence. The lights of the oncoming cars kept turning her face yellow, stacking it with shadows.

Then, when we were almost home, she raised her eyes to look at me in the rearview mirror.

'I never imagined you wanting a doll,' she said. 'You never asked for one.'

'She was a nice lady,' I said. 'I was just being polite.'

My mother frowned, then turned her attention back to the road. When we reached the house I went straight to my room. Half an hour later my father called me down for supper. He dished up – it was omelette and chips – then started telling us about the JCB Groats had called him in to repair that afternoon.

'They're different from cars,' he said. 'A machine like that, it's more like a dinosaur, really.'

I laughed, but my mother was silent. She seemed miles away. When we'd finished eating she stacked the plates together and took them through to the kitchen. A moment later I heard the taps running and the sound of piano music on the kitchen radio.

Two of my dolls are wax dolls, a Gerhardt Rilling and a Leopold Toft. The Toft has a broken finger, which I know makes her less valuable but I would never part with her anyway, so it doesn't matter. I buy all my dolls online these days. I've never been to an actual auction, even though I know there are auctions in Truro that I could easily get to if I wanted. A couple of years ago I asked Dr Leslie if I could go into Bodmin on the bus, but he said he didn't think it would be a good idea.

75

'You know you're not good in crowds, Bramber. If there's anything you need you can always ask Sylvia.'

When Jennifer Rockleaze asked if I could go to Bodmin carnival with her and Paul, the same thing happened. Dr Leslie said it was nice of them to offer but he wasn't happy about me being out after dark.

Jennifer Rockleaze is my closest friend here. She comes up to my room sometimes, puts the kettle on and tells me about the computer business she and Paul are going to set up once they've finished helping Dr Leslie with his research.

Jennie said it didn't matter what Dr Leslie said, that if I wanted to go to the carnival I should just go. When I told her I'd changed my mind she looked disappointed.

'But we need you, Ba,' she said. 'To stop us getting caught up with the freak show.'

I know she doesn't mean it about her and Paul being freaks but it still upsets me when she says things like that and I suppose it must have shown on my face because she burst out laughing.

'Honestly, Ba,' she said. 'You do know that's what we would probably have been doing a hundred years ago, don't you? Turning somersaults and dancing for pennies.' She flung her arms around my waist. 'Nice work if you can get it. I wonder how well they pay.'

I once heard the postman referring to Paul and Jennie as dwarfs. I hate the word dwarf. It sounds stunted and ugly. Paul has achondroplasia. His arms and legs are shorter than normal, but he has a broad, strong chest and beautiful eyes, brown as velvet. He makes all his own clothes. He says he could buy children's clothes, like a lot of other little people, but he doesn't really like what they have in the shops. Jennie's arms and legs are perfect but she's tiny, a little under four feet two. When she drinks tea she holds the cup with both hands, as if it were a bowl. She makes everything around her look ugly – oversized and cartoonish. Perhaps that's what ordinary people are most afraid of when they see people like Jennie and Paul: losing their place in the scheme of things.

I once asked Jennie why she and Paul even stayed here, seeing as they can leave whenever they like.

'It's a laugh, and we live rent-free,' she said. 'We're saving up to get a place of our own.'

Jennie likes my dolls, she's even learned all their names. If I were to tell anyone about you it would be Jennie. You are exactly the kind of secret she would love to know.

It's been blazing hot here all week, almost thirty degrees. The downstairs rooms are stifling but Jackie being Jackie, she won't let anyone open a window in case the butterflies get in.

It was lovely to hear from you, Andrew. I hope you are well.

Yours always,
Bramber

4 ·

I FELT GLAD TO BE leaving Reading. The coach kept to the main roads at first, skirting Newbury and Andover and Salisbury, then just after Warminster we turned off on to a B road signposted for Wade. I had a room booked in Wade, which *Coastage's English Almanac* described as one of the most attractive villages in East Somerset. I planned on staying there three nights.

The coach pulled into a lay-by opposite the post office. There was nobody waiting to board, and as soon as I had alighted the coach released its brakes with a shudder and then ground off towards the next stop on its itinerary, which I believe was Frome. Once it was gone, the silence seemed to close in with a rush, as if it had been lying in wait. I crossed the road to the Bluebell Inn, trying to rid myself of the feeling that I was being watched.

There was a woman in the saloon bar, loading empty glasses on to a tray.

'I was planning to close for the afternoon,' she said. 'Seeing as we're so quiet.'

She was wearing a sleeveless cotton print dress, revealing plump white forearms sprinkled with freckles. Her voice had a soft lilt to it that I presumed must be the local accent. Red curls clustered about her forehead and temples. She reminded me — immediately and irrevocably — of Angela Madden.

'I'm not here for the beer,' I said, and smiled. 'Not yet, anyway.'

She stared back at me with confusion. Then she spotted my holdall and clarity dawned.

'Oh, you're Mr Garvie,' she said. 'You called about the room.' The realisation seemed to fill her with dizzy relief. She set the tray of glasses aside on the bar and came towards me, smoothing her hands across the skirt of her dress. Her movements were unhurried and graceful, so much like Angela's. I wanted desperately to ask the woman her name, but decided that in view of our earlier misunderstanding that would probably be a mistake.

She showed me out of the bar and into a narrow, windowless hallway and then up a flight of stairs. At the top there was a small square landing, three doors leading off.

'Front or back, it's up to you,' she said. 'We've no other guests at the moment.'

I went for the door on the left, if for no other reason than to avoid pushing past her in the confined space. I wondered where she slept herself, and supposed there must be a private set of rooms to the rear of the bar.

'I'm just downstairs if you need anything,' she said. 'Food starts at six.' She handed me a set of keys then disappeared.

The room I had chosen turned out to be at the front, overlooking the street. On the opposite side of the road I could see the post office and a newsagent's. A little further along there was what looked like a greengrocery, with crates of fruit and vegetables set up outside. Three women stood together outside the post office but otherwise

79

the street was empty. The village seemed not so much sleepy as dead. *Coastage's* described Wade as a bustling, vibrant community with a weekly farmers' market. I knew the book was some years out of date, but even so it was difficult to understand how a place could change so dramatically in so short a time.

My room was pleasantly cool, but the hours spent cooped up inside the coach had left me with a longing to be outside. The pub was so quiet that even though I'd been speaking to the landlady less than ten minutes earlier I could not escape the feeling of being alone in an empty house. The sensation unnerved me, for some reason. I used the bathroom across the hall then went back downstairs.

Outside, the women in front of the post office had dispersed. The sun stood high in a sky bereft of clouds. I realised then that I was hungry – I had not eaten since leaving Reading. I walked along the street to the greengrocer's, selected two apples from the display outside then went into the shop, where alongside the fruit and vegetables I discovered a small stock of basic grocery items. I chose a carton of Ritz crackers and took them up to the counter with the apples.

'Beautiful day,' said the man behind the counter. He slipped my purchases into a bag.

'It's a beautiful part of the world,' I said. I passed him a five-pound note.

'Certainly suits me.' He was a big man, with tanned muscular forearms and iron-grey shoulder-length hair. He had a London accent, and I couldn't help wondering what had brought him to Wade. In spite of what I had said to him, I was already beginning to dislike the place. It seemed isolated and insular, a long way from anywhere. I felt I had been lured here under false pretences. What I proposed to do with myself for three days I had no idea.

At its far end, what passed for the high street narrowed and divided. I took the right-hand fork, passing alongside a terrace of red-brick cottages and fully expecting the village to come to an end. Instead, I found that one street led to another and then to a third. I saw more of the red-brick terraces, but there were also more substantial properties, double-fronted whitewashed cottages, detached Victorian villas behind tall green hedges. The deeper I penetrated into it the more of Wade there seemed to be, the village expanding ahead of me like an endless, self-replicating mirage.

I walked for more than an hour. I polished off the two apples and then started eating the crackers straight from the box. Their saltiness made me thirsty and I cursed myself for not buying a bottle of water to go with them. I looked around, hoping to spy another corner store or pub but there were just more houses. The interlinking streets were curiously similar and I even began to wonder if I'd been walking in circles. At the junction of two identical terraces I came upon an off licence, a tiny branch of Thresher's, but it was closed. A little further on there was a hairdresser's called Betty's. There were pictures in the windows, black-and-white photographs of models showing off hairstyles from the 1950s. From somewhere in the depths of the building came the monotonous drone of a hairdryer.

I saw people from time to time, but none of them spoke to me. As I passed the access lane between two tall houses, a gate suddenly flew open and a woman came dashing out. She wore a full-skirted white linen dress with a shiny pink belt at the waist. She was young and strikingly pretty. Her high heels rattled on the cobblestones.

'Gordon!' she cried, and again, 'Gordon!' though there was no one else in sight. The weather was too hot for running, yet she ran nonetheless, passing close in front of me as if I were invisible. I continued along the street. After a minute or two I came upon an elderly gentleman, bending over a stem of ragwort that had managed to worm its way upwards through a crack in the pavement. He looked me straight in the eye but didn't speak.

At that point, my sense of adventure evaporated completely. I felt sweaty and exhausted, desperate to get back to my room at the Bluebell, to dump my shoes on the floor and lie down on the bed. I began to retrace my steps and after about ten minutes I found myself back outside the hairdresser's. Approaching from the opposite direction I noticed things I hadn't seen the first time: the gated entrance to a children's playground and, opposite the off licence, exactly that kind of junk shop I could never resist, its crowded windows and darkened interior acting as a powerful magnet to draw me inside.

The shop was called Magpie's. There was a row of mismatched wooden chairs outside, like rejects from a dentist's waiting room. I found it mysterious that I had somehow failed to see them when I passed by before. The dusty window framed all the usual items of bric-à-brac: fringed lampshades and china teapots, chipped willow pattern plates and a brass Art Deco lamp stand in the form of a cobra. A fake, probably. There was no one behind the counter. A door at the rear of the shop offered a glimpse of pale-blue walls and red terracotta tiles. A radio played Mozart. I heard the chink of a spoon against the rim of a cup.

I wandered contentedly among the white elephants, my feelings of disquiet dispersing amidst the familiar and comforting odour of second-hand books. I was not intending to buy anything as I did not want to add to my luggage but one glimpse of the doll – she'd been dumped in a tea chest, together with what must have been a hundred assorted napkin rings and three mismatched sets of pearl-handled cutlery – and my resolve was thwarted instantly. She had been dressed in a bright green baby's romper suit – well-worn and bobbly and quite hideous – but I recognised her at once as a Bedingfield, a 1909 'Laura Louise'. Her long chestnut hair had been twisted into dreadlocks and one of her eyes was missing but when I lifted her I heard it rattling inside her head. Otherwise she seemed undamaged. I was just starting to unbutton the romper suit so I could examine her more carefully when I heard someone come through the door at the rear of the shop.

'I've not seen that in ages. I thought it had been sold.'

A woman's voice. I turned to face her, and in a brief moment of utter confusion I thought it was the pub landlady I was seeing, the woman from the Bluebell who looked like Angela. Then I realised this woman was older, and thinner. The resemblance was remarkable, all the same.

'My husband picked that up at some auction,' she was saying. 'Part of a job lot, it was. Shame about the eye.'

'The eye can be mended,' I said, before I could stop myself. Even an amateur would understand that a damaged piece is a piece that can be bought more cheaply, especially when the seller has no idea of its real value. I knew these things – I had been reading books on auction-craft since the age of twelve – but in the case of 'Laura Louise' the knowledge was useless to me. Any dealer with even a modicum of experience can smell desire. If this woman was any good at her job, she would know I had already decided to buy the doll, even at a price that would make other, less impetuous collectors walk away from it in disgust.

'Is that right?' the woman said. 'It's like anything, I suppose – easy if you know how.'

'I wouldn't say it was easy,' I said, in a pathetic attempt to regain some ground. I would have to unstitch her head from her body to get at the eye. It was unlikely that I would be able to save her hair – it was too badly matted – and without her original clothes she would never be worth much anyway. I couldn't leave her, though, could I? It was out of the question.

'How much is she?' I asked.

'Ten pounds?' the woman said. She laid her head on one side, a blackbird eyeing a worm. I went away with the doll wrapped in a double sheet of newspaper, thinking that ten pounds was probably the most anyone had paid for anything in Magpie's, ever.

BY THE TIME I arrived back at the Bluebell, the evening was coming on and the heat had subsided. The landlady had just come outside to put out the food board. She asked me if I'd had a pleasant afternoon and I said yes.

'Food's just started serving if you'd like a bit of supper?' Her hair had been loosely plaited, then fastened to the back of her head with a tortoiseshell comb.

'I'll be down in ten minutes,' I said. 'I just want to wash my hands.' I also wanted to phone Clarence. I couldn't get a phone signal from my room, an inconvenience that seemed altogether typical of a place like Wade. Luckily there was a payphone, tucked away in a small vestibule between the bar and the public toilets. Clarence answered almost immediately.

'Are you having a good time?' she said.

'I think so,' I said, then told her about the Bedingfield.

'You're supposed to be on holiday, not snooping around for finds.'

I could hear Jane in the background, practising the piano. There was a focus, an intensity to her playing that was unusual in a child of ten, disconcerting even, but then Jane communicates much more easily through music than she does through speech. For those who don't know her, Jane can come across as backward in her intellectual development, though she is anything but.

'You know me,' I said to Clarence. 'I'm a workaholic. Did Lucan get back from Rome?'

'He missed his flight.' Clarence sighed. 'There aren't any seats until tomorrow afternoon.'

Lucan once telephoned me out of the blue and asked me to go for a drink with him. We met in a bar close to Mansion House tube, which was near where he worked. It was summer, one of those sweltering London evenings where it seems as if the light will never quite fade from the sky. Lucan became rapidly drunk – the heat, probably. He told me he was jealous of Jane.

'I suppose that's natural. She does need a lot of attention,' I said. I felt uncomfortable, being there alone with him. I found myself staring at the long, silvery hairs on the backs of his hands, the circles of sweat staining the underarms of his hand-made Italian shirt.

'It's not that so much. Or at least I don't think so. It's just that she seems so sure of herself. So sure of who she is, I mean. It's as if no one else exists, apart from her.' He mopped sweat from his forehead. 'Ignore me. I don't know what I'm saying.'

Jane resembled Lucan in every way, except that Lucan was beautiful and Jane was not. Her face was flat and pale, and when she played the piano a deep furrow of concentration appeared between her eyes. I sometimes wondered if it was the plainness of Jane's features that made people suppose she had learning difficulties.

Clarence didn't invite people round much in the evenings because Jane tended to be nervous around strangers. Lucan spent a lot of time abroad. I suppose he had affairs. Clarence never talked about it and I didn't ask. I felt guilty, I suppose, not just because Lucan had confided in me but because I had agreed to meet up with him without Clarence knowing. Some secrets feel harmful, even when from the outside there's nothing to them.

'Jane's sounding wonderful,' I said.

'She's had a good day today. She's been working on her Beethoven.' Clarence sighed again. She sounded tired, as she invariably did during the school holidays. I began asking her about the exhibition of studio ceramics she was helping to organise at a new gallery space in Camberwell but the pips went before she could answer.

'I'm about to be cut off,' I said. 'I've run out of coins. I'll ring again when I get to Exeter.' I put the phone down before she had the chance to ask if she could call me back. Clarence and I talked most days when Lucan was away but I had found our conversation that evening to be an unwelcome distraction. I went through to the saloon and seated myself at a table beside the open window. I caught the high, sweet smell of straw bales and beneath that the coarser, darker odour of manure. London seemed light years away and I was glad.

Several of the other tables were already occupied, mostly by couples. Three men – obviously regulars – were stood at the bar. One of them seemed familiar and after a moment I recognised him as the shopkeeper who had sold me the apples and crackers earlier in the afternoon. The man beside him was ribbing the landlady, trying to persuade her to let him have a pint on tick.

'Go on, Marian, be a sport.' He had brawny sunburned forearms and a florid complexion.

'Sport's one thing, fool's another,' she said. She turned pointedly away towards the shopkeeper. 'Pint is it, Geoff?'

Her name was Marian, then, not Angela. I felt obscurely relieved. I went up to the bar to look at the specials board. When Marian had finished dealing with the shopkeeper I ordered the chicken curry and a half of lager.

'I hear you met my sister,' Marian said, scribbling my food order on the back of a napkin. 'Lisa said you were interested in antiques. Dolls or something, she said.'

'That's right.' So they were sisters, which at least explained the likeness between them, though how Marian could already know of my visit to the junk shop was more of a puzzle. Some sort of village bush telegraph? The idea was slightly less unnerving than the thought that the sister – Lisa – had considered my presence interesting enough to move her to pick up the telephone the moment I left. 'I enjoy old things, that's all.'

'We've plenty of old things around here, that's for sure.' She stole a glance at the red-faced man who had managed to inveigle his way on to someone else's table. 'Thanks,' she added, as I handed her a ten-pound note. 'Take a seat and I'll bring it over.'

One of the locals wolf-whistled. I pretended not to notice, the strategy I have always adopted when confronted by ignorance. I fumbled my wallet back into my pocket and returned to my table. I had hoped to exchange a few pleasantries with the shopkeeper but he had gone to sit with someone else, a woman in a red dress. His wife, probably.

The curry, when it came, was bland but satisfying, a typical pub curry. I sipped at my beer, listening to the ebb and flow of conversation around me and wishing I had thought to bring something to read. I felt as conspicuous here in the saloon bar as I had done wandering the streets of Wade, and I thought about how much like families small communities are: not hostile necessarily but insular, in the way that all small groups of people who know each other too well are insular. A gang of office workers in the busiest city can be as closed to outsiders as the most isolated rural outpost – I knew that from my days at Clark Cannings.

The only way to become accepted in a place like Wade would be to marry in. Or else to make oneself amenable and curb one's opinions. Hardly an attractive prospect, either way.

I finished my food and returned to my room, cursing myself once again for having stranded myself in the village for another two nights. I felt unbearably restless, almost ready to head out into the streets once again. I told myself that would be foolish – there was nowhere for me to head to, after all – and decided to cheer myself up by writing a letter to Bramber instead. Bramber had once told me she enjoyed the way I described things, and although I had never considered myself anything of a prose stylist the idea that I was giving her pleasure spurred me on. I told her about the junk shop, Magpie's, recalling its interior and contents in some detail. I explained how I had discovered the Bedingfield – the tea chest stuffed with old cutlery, the green romper suit – and then gave an outline explanation of how I would repair her.

I made no mention of where I was. I was allowing Bramber to believe, I suppose, that I was off on one of my jaunts to the furthest reaches of London, the autonomous suburbs and end-of-tube-lines where the postcodes started to blur and the tidy hedges and tar-macked driveways of middle England began to set in. Such trips had remained a part of my life even after Ursula's vanishment. Bramber was accustomed to me telling her about them, even if I had never told her about Ursula.

I wondered if she would notice the Warminster post-mark. The thought of her noticing made my stomach flutter. We would be conspirators then, two people sharing a secret without having to name it. I sealed the letter inside its envelope and got ready for bed. It was past eleven by then, and the pub was deathly quiet again. I supposed there was a limit to the time you would want to spend in the company of neighbours you were bound to run into again the following day, and the day after that.

I turned out the light, imagining Bramber lying asleep two hundred miles to the west of me. Did she dream? I wondered. Did she ever dream of me?

I think it was in that moment that I truly understood the purpose of my journey: not simply to see Bramber and to speak with her, but to save her. I intended to take her away from West Edge House, and bring her home with me to London.

BY THE AFTERNOON OF the following day I had nothing to do. I thought I might pay a second visit to Magpie's, but in spite of wandering around the streets for the better part of an hour I was unable to find the shop again and in the end I gave up. I returned to the high street, then followed the lane that ran behind the pub until I came to open fields. I walked until I was completely out of sight of the village then lay down in the grass. The sun was high – hotter than the day before, even – and the constant whirring of crickets was almost hypnotic. The earth smelled dusty and yellow. A five-spot ladybird hurried in and out between the grass stems. *I'm nowhere*, I remember thinking. Then I fell asleep.

I awoke several hours later to find my right arm reddened from sunburn and my head spinning from the heat. I staggered back to the Bluebell, feeling nauseous and hoping that the pub landlady – Marian – would not be around to catch me in such a dishevelled state. Upstairs in my room I filled the hand basin with cold water and did my best to cool my burning head and arms. I applied some skin lotion and put on a clean shirt. Then I went in search of Marian. I told her I'd been recalled to London on a personal matter and would be leaving sooner than I had expected. The next day, in fact.

'I'll pay for the extra night, of course,' I added quickly.

'Not to worry,' she said. She smiled, as if in closet understanding of my situation. 'We're never that busy anyway, not as a guest house. It's the pub that pays the bills.' Each time she moved I caught the scent of her, the tart aroma of aniseed or some other herb, exacerbated by the heat. She still reminded me of Angela, though not so forcibly, and I wondered why the likeness had so unsettled me.

As I turned to go back upstairs she spoke again. 'You're not really a dwarf at all, are you? You're a nice-looking man, only small.'

'I suppose it depends on what you think dwarf means,' I replied. 'I don't often think about it.'

'I'm sorry if I was rude,' she said. 'I knew I shouldn't have said anything. Did you know you've got beautiful hands?'

'Do you think so?' I said. 'Thank you.' I looked down at her own hands, plump and daintily freckled, the gold wedding band on her ring finger. I wondered how long she had been married, and whether her husband was an incomer like the greengrocer or a local like the man with the red face who had tried to cadge a free pint. My own hands had remained smooth and ringless, almost unchanged from when I was a child. I wondered what it might be like to touch this woman – Marian – as I had never been given the chance to touch Angela Madden.

There are more than two hundred varieties of dwarfism. I know, because I looked up 'dwarf' in an encyclopaedia when I was eight. If I were to be classified as anything, it would be as a proportionate dwarf, what used to be called a midget. Still was, frequently and with gusto, when I was at school. The mutation is completely random, and brings neither the foreshortened limbs nor the associated spinal abnormalities that are common among achondroplasics. If I were a couple of inches taller I wouldn't even qualify as a dwarf, I would just be a shortarse, the way the kids at Martens noisily insisted. I've never actively sought out other small people – as a child I'm not sure I even knew there was such a thing – but when I encounter them, however rarely, in books or films I experience a flicker of – what? – fellow-feeling, especially more recently.

We cannot change the world but we can be in it. We can exist, at least. There – I said 'we'. I think that's a first.

I CAUGHT THE BUS from outside the post office at ten o'clock the following morning. It took the left-hand fork at the end of the high street, following a road that ran uphill through a modern housing estate, a part of town that, throughout my various explorations, I had still not come across.

As we reached the outskirts of the village and turned on to the broader, more evenly surfaced A-road that led to the dual carriageway I felt in my holdall for Chaplin's *Nine Modern Fairytales*. I found I was eager to while away the journey time with another story.

Amber Furness

by Ewa Chaplin

translated from the Polish by Erwin Blacher 2008

The brooch was shaped like a beetle, a golden cockchafer with fringed antennae and a long, tapering carapace. The beetle's wing cases were slightly parted, revealing the lacy silver folds of the wings beneath. Their roughened, filigree edges caught at the light.

The brooch would be beyond her means, Amber knew – the shops in this part of the city were mostly of the kind that discouraged casual browsing. Still, the piece compelled her, not only because it was beautiful but because she believed she recognised it as the work of Danka Olssen, a recently elected member of the Guild of Goldsmiths who took her inspiration from the natural world. Amber had written on Olssen as part of her higher study portfolio at the College of Art.

She pushed open the part-glazed door and stepped inside.

The shop was poky and dark, and smelled faintly of tobacco. A strange sound filled the air, a constant, restless murmur that after a moment's confusion Amber recognised as the diligent, measured ticking of many clocks. The shop was full of them: mantel clocks and carriage clocks, silver half-hunter watches on looping chains. There were grandfather clocks and grandmother clocks, their polished walnut cases inlaid with fine marquetry, and in a glassed-off alcove to the right of the door there were more than a dozen skeleton clocks, their delicate workings protected beneath crystal domes.

Every clock in the room showed a different time and it was the clocks that predominated. Amber had expected to see more jewellery, more precious artefacts, but there were none, just the tray of brooches and rings that had drawn her inside.

Behind the counter sat the shopkeeper, a man with a large, well-modelled head and shoulder-length grey hair. He wore a dark suit, with a paisley-patterned waistcoat beneath the jacket. The stool he sat on was high, like a bar stool, and as Amber stared at him she realised with a jolt that his feet, in their polished brogues, were way off the ground.

He's a dwarf, she thought. Well, so what?

'Can I help you at all?' he said. His voice was deep, chestnut-coloured, pleasant to listen to, and his wire-rimmed, owlish glasses reminded Amber of her old mathematics teacher in high school. The most extraordinary thing about him was his hands. There was a finesse about them, a dextrous delicacy that Amber found it hard to quantify. The hands of an artist, surely, or a musician.

'You have a brooch in the window,' she said. Her voice caught in her throat. She swallowed. 'I'd like to have a look at it, please.' She could feel herself blushing. She wondered if she should explain to him that there was no question of her buying the brooch, that all she wanted was to see it close to. She imagined his reaction: puzzlement, irritation, contempt even? But he was already leaning into the window casement, perched on a set of wooden steps that had previously been concealed behind the door. He lifted the tray of jewellery items carefully towards him.

'Let's see.' His fingertips were square, the nails beautifully cut and filed. They could have been a doll's hands, they were so perfect, or a storefront mannequin's. He placed the tray on the counter, his hands folding themselves together afterwards like the wings of a bird.

'This is the one you meant, isn't it?' he said, pointing to the golden beetle without the least hesitation. Amber would remember this later and find it strange.

'Yes,' she said. 'I thought it might be—'

'By Danka Olssen, yes. A beautiful example.' He unpinned the brooch from its velvet backing and levered it free. He laid it in his palm, contemplating it with what seemed a childlike pleasure. He's like King Midas, Amber thought, though she could not have said exactly where the idea arose from.

'Did you buy it at auction?' she asked.

'A probate sale,' said the dwarf. His eyes behind the wire spectacles were rainwater grey.

'I love Danka Olssen's work,' Amber said. 'I studied her in college.'

'Are you a collector?'

'Oh, no.' She laughed. 'I can't afford to be.' She blushed harder, embarrassed at how much of herself she had inadvertently revealed. Not just her poverty, but her studentship, which must surely point towards a lack of worldly experience. As she reached out to touch the brooch, her fingers brushed inadvertently against his wrist.

'You are an artist yourself, then?' he said. If he had noticed the contact, he gave no sign of it. He gazed at Amber steadily with his rainwater eyes.

'I'm hoping to be,' she said. Now he'll look at my hands, she thought. It's what everyone does, eventually. He didn't though, and Amber felt a momentary rush of gratitude, of kinship even. She supposed the dwarf knew everything there was to know about being stared at. 'I love your clocks,' she said. 'They're mesmerising.'

'I have always been in love with the idea of time.' He fell silent for a moment, gazing around the room. 'It's interesting, how it fascinates, is it not? The simple arrangement of numbers around a dial? Some people think it is their symmetry that makes timepieces so appealing but I have always believed it is because they are alive.'

'Alive?'

'I mean they have a function beyond being decorative. They do something. Having a clock in the room is almost like having company.'

'I think I see what you mean,' Amber said. She thought of the first clock she had owned, a tiny gold-plated wristwatch given to her by her parents on her eighth birthday. On those nights when the pain in her joints was bad enough to keep her awake, she would lay the watch on the pillow close to her ear. Its ticking had comforted her, as had its luminous green hands, sweeping their way incessantly around the darkened dial. A secret compass that showed her the way down into sleep.

'There is something else, too,' said the shopkeeper. 'A clock is the only instrument specifically constructed for measuring a quantity that is intangible.'

Amber laughed again. 'What about radiation?' she said. 'What about Geiger counters?'

'The atoms of radioactive substances can be quantified. They're simply not visible to the human eye. Not without an electron microscope, at any rate.'

'I've never thought about time that way,' Amber said. 'It makes me feel nervous.'

'That's because a world without clocks would not be a safe world. You would be surprised how quickly everything we have come to count on would fall apart.'

'Do you make clocks as well as sell them?'

'No,' he said. 'I have never possessed the requisite creative talent, unfortunately. I'm good at mending them, though. I have been told I have the hands for it, but I believe it has more to do with instinct than with mere dexterity.'

He looked down at his beautiful hands, as if the idea of their suitability for his chosen profession was still a surprise to him. 'Is it arthritis?' he said suddenly. He gazed at her steadily and without embarrassment, never lowering his eyes from her face.

'It began when I was five,' Amber said. 'It doesn't hurt any more, though. The doctors say I'm in remission.'

The fingers of her left hand were all but lifeless. She could use them to hold things down but that was all. The fingernails of her index and middle fingers were thickened and misshapen, like those of a very old man, the finger joints swollen and reddened in spite of the fact that the disease was not currently active. The fingers of her right hand were strong and agile, though the hand itself was twisted and slightly splayed. It looked as if someone had struck it with a hammer.

'When I was a child, the pain in my joints used to keep me awake at night,' she said. 'There were exercises I was supposed to do but they hurt so much and seemed so pointless I used to make things instead. The pain was still as bad but at least I had something to show for it.'

He took her left hand in his, raising it gently towards him with his delicate fingers. Amber had a momentary vision of their two hands together, the perfect formation of his artful joints, her clumsy deformity. The touch of his hand had sympathy in it, and a practised deftness, the touch of the hand of a man who mended clocks.

'I would like to see some of your work,' he said. He wrapped the gold beetle in a twist of cotton wadding, then packed it neatly away inside a small cardboard box. He placed the carton on the counter in front of her.

'Do you like music?' he said. 'There is a concert in the Old Town next week that I would like very much to attend. Do you think you might do me the honour of accompanying me?'

A bribe, Amber realised at once. My society, my *attention*, for the brooch. She had read of such things in fairy tales, but never in life, or at least never as they might be applicable to herself. Such unequal bargains never ended well, not in the stories anyway. But was this really so unequal? The man was clearly intelligent, and cultivated, and with a wealth of knowledge. He was also a dwarf, but again she thought, so what?

The dwarf and the freak, she thought. Was there any wonder he felt himself drawn to her? But then she liked him, she had to admit, at least a little. An evening in his company would not hurt either of them.

She reached for the box. 'I would love to,' she said.

'My name is Anders,' he said. 'Anders Tessmond.' He told her he had bought the lease on the shop and the flat above just the year before.

'What was the shop before you moved here, do you know?' Amber asked.

'Can't you guess?' said Anders Tessmond.

'A tobacconist's?'

Tessmond nodded, and they both smiled.

He was wearing a loosely tailored dark-grey smoking jacket, an exquisite diamond tie-pin in the shape of a rose. Amber couldn't help noticing how well the jacket fitted him. As if it had been made for him personally, she thought, as she supposed it must have been.

The first half of the concert featured a flute and piano duet. The flute player was tall, with long, heavy limbs, her white skin made to seem even whiter by her black velvet dress. The pianist had a bent, bony body, hunched over the keys, limbs akimbo like the legs of a gigantic insect. A cockroach perhaps, or a giant grasshopper. His fingers moved at a speed that seemed unnaturally fast.

The music itself left Amber unmoved. She shifted in her seat and glanced around. Anders Tessmond, she saw, had his eyes closed. His lips were slightly pursed, as if he were sleeping. They were beautifully shaped, Amber noticed, with the colour and texture of crushed pink silk.

'I don't care much for music,' Amber said in the interval. 'I know nothing about it. I'm afraid I must be disappointing company.'

They stood together at the crowded bar. The people around them chattered excitedly and she had to lean forward and slightly downward to hear what Tessmond was saying.

'Music should be an experience you respond to naturally. Knowledge is no substitute for love.'

'I'm sure you're right,' she said. She looked down at him, pressing the stem of her champagne glass tightly between her fingers. Anders Tessmond knew about this music, she could tell. He would be able to explain it in exhaustive detail if only she asked. Yet he seemed unbothered by her ignorance, at ease with it even. She did not know if this made her feel better, or worse.

For the second half of the programme, the flute player was replaced by a huge, bear-like man in a tuxedo. He had closely shaved red hair, just like his photograph in the programme, which identified him as Olaf Scherer, from Copenhagen. He took the stage commandingly, like a giant in a fairy tale, then proceeded to sing a series of unintelligible songs in a booming baritone that made her head ache.

The programme provided a list of the songs, together with translations of their titles. One of the songs was called 'The Dwarf'. Amber stole a glance at Anders Tessmond, wondering if he knew. Then she realised that he was bound to, that this was why he had brought her here.

'It's about a dwarf who murders a queen,' he told her, when the concert was over.

'Why does he kill her?'

'He is in love with her. He's been in love with her for years, and believes she loves him, too. But then the queen announces that she is to marry a young knight of the realm. The dwarf goes mad with grief. He cannot bear the sight of her. He kills the queen and then himself. That's the end.'

'But surely,' Amber said, 'he should have realised?'

Anders Tessmond smiled. 'What should he have realised, exactly? No one was closer to the queen than he was, no one knew her better. He had been her dearest companion since she was a child. She used to tell him everything. He had always believed her confidence meant love.' He raised his glass to his rose-coloured lips. 'Court dwarfs were very popular in Europe at one time. They appear in many famous paintings. Some even had their own servants. Others were fed in the kitchen, alongside the dogs.'

'That's horrible.'

'Well, it's odd, certainly. I have always considered it strange, not to say perverse, that the extent of a person's humanity might somehow be determined by their height.'

He continued to smile. Once again, Amber found herself staring at his hands, those smooth and perfect fingers that might easily have belonged to a pianist, or to a stage magician. Her eyes kept being drawn to the watch he wore, white gold, she thought, or maybe platinum, a Herzog. Its dial was transparent, the purest crystal – she could see the cogs and springs of its mechanism whirring behind. Like the workings of my brain, Amber thought, or some infernal machine. She could not imagine what had brought the word infernal so readily to mind, yet it continued to flicker there, nonetheless, like a captive fly.

'Why do all the clocks in your shop show different times?' she asked suddenly. She was anxious to stop talking about the music. It came to her once again, that Anders Tessmond had known beforehand that the song about the dwarf would be on the programme, that he had wanted her to hear it.

'Time is an illusion,' Tessmond said. 'It is a device invented by humans, to keep themselves sane.' He stared pointedly at the watch on his wrist. 'Have you never considered the lies these things tell? That is not their fault of course, it is we who put them up to it. But when you think about it clearly, the only clocks that show us what we choose to call the right time are those on a perfect par with the Royal Meridian. Move even an inch to the right or to the left, and your watch is a liar.'

'But time would still pass, even if there were no clocks.'

'Of course it would, in a sense, but it is only human beings who persist in their delusion of time's linearity. So far as the universe is concerned, all moments in time are equal and exist simultaneously. Which means that in terms of its own private universe, no clock can be wrong. If people understood this better, they would worry less about time's passing.'

'I'm not sure if I find that reassuring or not,' Amber said.

'All I am saying is that time is less rigid than most people think.' He raised his hand to touch her cheek, his perfect fingers brushing the corner of her mouth. 'The queen was foolish,' he said. 'No one could have loved her better than the dwarf.'

'Why do you say that?' Amber said. She found herself unable to move away.

'Because he saw her for what she was,' said Tessmond. 'He knew her from the inside out.'

They stood in the foyer, close together, the tide of their fellow spectators flowing around them as they moved towards the exit. 'Would you come home with me?' Tessmond said. 'Just to sleep,' he added hastily. 'There's a spare room, upstairs. I find it difficult to be alone after listening to music.'

Amber did not see how she could refuse, not easily anyway, not without damaging their budding friendship. Besides, she was curious. Curious about Tessmond, curious about his apartment above the shop. 'How can I?' she said. She laughed a soft, low laugh. 'I don't have my night things.' As if the mention of night things did not immediately call to mind the soft glow of naked bodies, his and hers, an image she felt sure he was seeing even as she denied him its reality.

'I have everything you need,' he said. 'There's no need to worry.'

Some steps you take because you don't know the trajectory of the road ahead, she told herself, and some you take because you do, and still you want to dare yourself. She asked herself which of these extremities lay before her now, and couldn't decide.

For her birthday, he gave her a pendant of polished amber.

'You must get this all the time,' he said, 'but I couldn't resist.'

The pendant was triangular in shape, an inch across at the base and bound in silver. There was a fly trapped in the amber, not the usual kind of gnat or housefly but a prehistoric monster, its spiky, jointed legs forever thrashing in the tide of the orange sea that had risen to drown it, the limbs of an impossible swimmer, aeons dead and yet still present, irrefutably there.

'My aunt gave me an amber ring for my twenty-first but it's too small for me,' Amber said. 'I could have had it altered, I suppose.' The ring was exquisite, a polished oval of tawny amber in a Georgian setting. Amber knew it must have cost her aunt a great deal of money, yet with her hands the way they were, the gift had seemed tactless, a mockery even. She had never even tried to put it on.

Tessmond lifted her hair aside and fastened the catch. His touch on her skin was so light she barely felt it.

'You look like a queen,' he said.

'You always choose such wonderful things.'

'The maker is still young, but he'll be famous yet. His work will end up in museums. Won't you come out with me now and show it off?'

'It's getting late,' Amber said, although it was not yet ten. She felt as she often felt when she was with him: uncertain of whether she wished to stay or get away.

'What time would you like it to be?' Tessmond said. He slipped the watch from his wrist, the platinum Herzog he had been wearing at the concert, with the skeleton dial. 'Try it on,' he said. He caught hold of her wrist, and Amber felt the surge of tension she always experienced when anyone touched or paid attention to her hands. She looked down at her fingers where they lay in his, and trembled. He settled the bracelet into place about her wrist.

'You see,' he said. 'It's not as late as you think.'

The Herzog's hands were pointing to seven fifteen.

Amber laughed. What harm could there be in going with him to Dyers' Mews, in enjoying a celebratory cocktail in the wine bar he liked there? When Tessmond opened the door to the street she saw it was still light outside, the radiant, silver twilight that characterised so many September evenings in the city. The birches adjoining the small park across the road linked arms against the sky, their fingers bunched and twisted just like her own.

'So do you live with him, or what?' Jaen asked.

Amber shifted in her seat. 'He has a spare room,' she said, although actually it was more than that. From a darkened inner hallway behind the shop, steps led up to Tessmond's private apartment. The living room at the front, overlooking the street, was hung with velvet drapes and lined with bookshelves. The room seemed to contain as many clocks as the shop downstairs. The bathroom and kitchen overlooked the yard, as did Tessmond's bedroom, though Amber could not have said what that room was like, because the door was always closed.

In the hallway next to the kitchen was another door. Amber had initially mistaken it for a linen closet, although in fact it granted access to the upper floor. The staircase was narrow and very steep, which led Amber to imagine that the space above would be equally cramped. She had regretted accepting Tessmond's invitation to spend the night there almost immediately.

'I hope you'll be comfortable,' Tessmond had said. Amber opened her mouth to tell him she had changed her mind, she had decided she would walk home, after all. Why she hadn't done so she couldn't remember – the expression in his eyes, so full of hope, the very narrowness of the staircase, which made it impossible to turn around without brushing against him. She climbed gingerly upwards, the uneven, uncarpeted treads creaking alarmingly beneath her feet. She emerged into a room that should have been impossible. Beamed and smelling faintly of sandalwood, the curved ceiling and polished floorboards putting her in mind of the cavernous space beneath an upturned boat.

A wooden bedstead and a bedside cabinet, an intricate Oriental carpet, a tall chest of drawers. A recessed doorway led to a well appointed en-suite bathroom.

Amber thought of her dingy flat, with its grumbling, inefficient radiators, the dripping tap her landlord had promised to fix six months ago but had never got round to.

'How is this here?' she breathed.

'I had it converted after I moved in,' Tessmond said. 'The builders were surprised by how much space there was. So was I.'

The thought flew through her mind, that he was lying, that the room had never existed before that night.

She felt like laughing aloud. Did she believe that Anders Tessmond was some sort of wizard?

There were many at court who credited the dwarf with magical powers.

'It's incredible,' Amber said. 'Are you sure you don't mind my staying here?'

Tessmond smiled, and inclined his head in the ghost of a bow. 'There's no point in it standing empty,' he said. 'A spare room needs a guest.'

At the time she met Jaen, who was apprenticed to the city philosophers and who worked at the Remarque Library to pay their rent, Amber had been living in Anders Tessmond's attic for most of a year.

'What's the deal?' Jaen asked, echoing Amber's own thoughts almost exactly. 'Are you – do you have sex with him?'

'Of course not.' She shook her head vehemently. 'He's a friend, that's all. A kind of – guardian.' Tessmond had never pestered her for favours or for greater intimacy. She came and went as she pleased, though when she had asked Tessmond for a key he had said there was no need, that she would never find the door locked against her and this, so far at least, had proved to be the case. She had given up the lease on her studio flat, telling herself it was goodbye and good riddance, though the very ease of her life with Tessmond continued to bother her.

'Guardian?' Jaen said. 'You mean like an angel? A eunuch? I bet he doesn't see it that way. You should be careful.'

'Careful of what?'

Jaen shrugged. 'I don't know. That he doesn't get the wrong idea, I suppose.'

'I can always leave. If things don't work out, I mean.' If things get complicated, she meant. Difficult. She had not told Tessmond about Jaen. When she went to see them, she told Tessmond she was going to the library, which was half the truth at least, it didn't feel like lying. There was no need for Tessmond to know about Jaen's quarters, deep in the cellar complex of the great Remarque building, which was where most of the scholars and prentice philosophers kept their lodgings.

Amber had never expected to fall in love. The presence of Jaen in her life still shocked her on a daily basis.

Jaen had been curious about her hands – they had asked questions, examined her joints – and for the first time ever, Amber was able to talk about her disfigurement with complete unconcern. She felt uncomfortable asking similar questions about Jaen's transition, however. Amber knew that full membership of the philosopher's guild was open only to women, though Jaen was open about their personal antipathy towards the old law and had aligned themself with a sept that was pledged to repeal it. 'Isn't that risky, I mean for a prentice?' Amber had asked. She hesitated to say more, for fear of trespassing against Jaen's privacy, but Jaen knew her too well.

'Because I'm ascended, you mean? You think they might demand I do penance on account of my penis?' Jaen laughed. 'We are allowed to talk about this, you know.'

'I'm sorry,' Amber said. She gently punched Jaen's ribs. 'Did you always know? I mean—'

'I didn't transition because I wanted to become a philosopher, if that's what you mean. Being a philosopher and being who I am are one and the same.' Jaen wrapped both arms around her waist, slid down their hands to rest between her legs. Amber gasped, the air cutting across the plane of her upper lip like a blade of ripe grass. She loved Jaen's body, the upright, muscular strength of it, the tightness of the flesh beneath the skin. Sometimes, upstairs in her room at Anders Tessmond's, Amber would bring herself to orgasm, remembering the ecstasy of lovemaking she had experienced with Jaen earlier in the day, Tessmond moving slowly about in the rooms directly below. The knowledge that he was there and maybe listening made her climax, when it came, all the more powerful.

'I think you should tell him,' Jaen said, later.

'About you?'

'About us.'

'I will, I promise. I need to pick the right moment, that's all. He's been so good to me.'

When Amber mentioned to Tessmond that the studio on Renfrew Street she'd had her eye on had been snapped up by someone else, Tessmond said he would investigate. Three hours later he returned to the shop with the contract, and the keys in his hand. Amber insisted on paying the rent herself. The studio was just one room above a butcher's shop, and now that she was no longer paying the lease on her old apartment she could easily afford it.

'What did you do?' Amber asked him nervously. 'The people at the rental agency told me there was no way their client would change his mind. He'd already paid his deposit.'

'He *would* have paid it, perhaps,' Tessmond said. 'But I have an idea that when he went to the agency yesterday to sign the lease, he discovered that somebody else had beaten him to it. He'll find another studio, I'm sure.'

Tessmond winked, then smiled. He had a lovely smile, open and warm. Amber found herself wondering, as she often did, how old he was.

'You turned back time,' she said, dreamily. She didn't believe it, of course. The photographer who'd paid the six-month deposit must have gone back on the deal after all, for some reason. But it was a nice idea, a sweet and harmless game they played together, just the two of them.

Truly, she loved Jaen. She knew her life here above the clock shop would have to end. There was something dishonest about it, dangerous even – Jaen was right about that. But still, it was difficult. More difficult than Jaen could properly understand.

'Is it him you love, or his power?' Jaen asked.

'His power?'

'You're afraid to let go, because you feel safe with him. He keeps the world at bay. Why don't you just fuck him and be done with it, if that's what you want?'

For the first time in their relationship, Amber imagined she heard an edge of contempt in Jaen's voice, a twitch of irritation. Her insides ran cold.

'Of course I don't. And I'll tell him. I'll tell him soon. I just need to find another flat first. You do understand?'

Jaen nodded. Philosopher prentices were not permitted to take an official companion until their five-year anniversary. Cohabitation was precluded until that time, although the guild's attitude to sexual relationships had become a great deal more relaxed in recent times.

Amber had recently secured a part-time post as factotum in the city archives. She had not told Tessmond about the job. One hint that she was short of money and Amber knew he would try and insist she accepted a stipend – it would not be the first time he had broached the subject. Instead, she let him believe she was spending more time at the studio.

The night following her argument with Jaen, she awoke with a start, convinced there was someone in the room with her. Her heart thumped in terror, but as her eyes gradually adjusted to the darkness she saw there was no one, that the room was just as always. Light from the streetlamp below filtered through the half-open shutters, unspooling in milky rivulets in the folds and creases in the discarded clothing on her bedside chair. She got up to use the toilet. The normalness of the action steadied her nerves a little, though she could not rid herself of the conviction that she was being watched.

What if he has always been watching? Amber thought. What if there are hidden cameras, secret apertures? She remembered the many times the idea of Tessmond's proximity had been a turn-on for her. For the second time in twelve hours she felt chilled to the bone.

She wrapped herself in her robe – an antique silk kimono that Tessmond had given her some months before, though what the occasion had been she could no longer remember – and tiptoed in her bare feet down the narrow staircase. Her heart leaped up with each creak, raucous as gunshots in the silence. Was Tessmond a heavy sleeper or an insomniac? Amber belatedly realised she had no idea.

The lower landing lay in darkness. The scent of tobacco was always strongest at night, for some reason – perhaps the stillness drew it out of the woodwork, like a living sap. She saw that the door to Tessmond's bedroom stood partly open, a sight that startled her as it had always been closed before. There was no light on, just a wedge of darker grey between the plane of the door and the angle of the frame, a neat, taut segment, like a hole into nowhere. Amber felt herself drawn towards it, as if the blackness were magnetic, and her upright, frozen body were made of iron. Just as she had imagined a presence looming over her in her bed upstairs, now she felt traumatised by the idea that she was, in fact, alone, that the house was empty and ruined, that the person of Anders Tessmond was and always had been a figment of her imagination.

'Anders,' she called softly. Her voice emerged as a creaky whisper, the hesitant, toneless mumbling of a senile old woman. She felt that she had stumbled, by mistake, into an alien world. It was impossible to believe that Jaen lay asleep less than two miles from where she now stood, their chin tucked into their elbow in that way they had, their lips curled sweetly around a phrase in the ancient language as they moved through some dream. Amber remembered how as a child it had been possible to feel safe from demons simply by leaping into bed and pulling up the covers. She made for the stairs and hurried back to her room, caring less about the sounds she made than about fleeing from the murky hallway and whatever it hid.

She sprang into bed, giggling now with the thrill of it, the horror. She no longer knew if she had really been frightened, or if her terror had simply been a manifestation of her guilt.

I can't leave, she thought. We belong together. She banished the thought, pushing it from her like a physical entity. Little by little her breathing steadied, and at last she slept.

'You look pale,' said Tessmond at breakfast the following morning.

'I was awake in the night,' she said. 'I don't know why.'

'Let me take you out for the day. The fresh air will do you good.'

He turned the shop sign over to 'closed' and they walked down through the city towards the harbour. A ship had recently docked. Uniformed sailors strolled about on the quayside, laughing good-naturedly amongst themselves, as if they had not been on dry land for many months. The sun sparkled in the rigging. Amber stood and watched as two able seamen manoeuvred the captain down the gangway and on to shore, a huge, burly man in a wheelchair, his naval cap jammed down tight upon his ginger curls. The lower part of his right leg was missing, the trouser folded in half and sewn together like a pocket.

'My brother dreamed of going to sea,' Tessmond said. 'My father said he'd see him hang first. He became a bank clerk instead.'

'You never told me you had a brother,' Amber said. She felt

muzzy-headed and slightly unwell. The air of the harbourside smelled fishy, rancid, the way it sometimes did before a storm.

'He died,' Tessmond said. 'He killed himself.'

Amber drew in her breath, coughing at the fish stench. 'I'm so sorry.'

'He brought the calamity down upon himself. The man he worked for was also a magister, of the rune sept. Rick swore him his allegiance and then broke his word. There could be only one end.'

'But if he changed his mind about his devotion?'

'You cannot change your mind, not without doing penance. The man had offered him his ring. You understand what that signifies, surely?'

They stood silently at the rail. Amber continued watching as the seamen began unloading cargo: crates of snapping gorgons, leather sea chests bounded with iron, vast sealed containers on trestle wheels, stamped with black-and-yellow biohazard stickers. Scenes like this conjured images of older times, the great age of sail, when the seas had been considered boundless and when the act of crossing the ocean had been to dice with monsters. A world that was gone now, mostly, to be recaptured only in dreams, or by reading the diaries and memoirs of long-dead explorers.

She turned to look at Tessmond, who was gazing up into the rigging where some small animal – a marmoset or a lemur, it was too high up to tell – capered and leaped with practised agility from rope to rope. Tessmond seemed both there and not there, his mind far away. Contemplating the tide of history perhaps, as she herself had been doing. His handsome head, his deep-set eyes, the ruby tie-pin on his lapel – these things set him apart, she realised, as much as his shortness of stature set him apart, if not more so.

He is not of this world, she thought. That is what draws me to him.

The promise that there might be an answer. To all of it, to the pain of living. Jaen was right – it is his power I am in thrall to. He has made me weak with it.

'How did he die?' Amber asked at last. 'Your brother?'

'He injected himself with cyanide. It was instantaneous.'

Amber folded her arms across her chest, clutching her sides. The waters of the harbour lapped at the concrete, viscous and black, like bitumen, she thought, or some other foul liquid. Then she realised there was nothing wrong with the water, it was simply darkness falling, the night curling itself around the ebbing twilight like a black feather boa.

That cannot be so, Amber told herself. We've only just eaten breakfast.

She turned to Tessmond in consternation. His face was barely visible in the dark.

'We will be permitted to board soon,' he said softly. 'I have reserved a cabin on the aft deck. The motion is less noticeable there, or so I've been told.'

She took a step backwards. 'What do you mean?' she said. Her lips felt numb. 'What have you done?'

He turned then to look at her. His eyes glinted in the firelight from one of the braziers. 'Our voyage will take nine months,' he said. 'Our daughter will be born three days after we make landfall. You will be anxious during the final weeks – who would give birth during a sea voyage? – but all will be well. The quayside hotel in Juno will have been alerted. They will set aside rooms for us. There is a doctor in the town. Everything will be provided, just as it should be.'

Amber looked down at herself, the flat, pure line of her belly, the modest curve of her breasts.

'I'm not—'

'It is time.'

She reached out with one hand, grasping at the harbour railings to steady herself. Around them, tides of bystanders ebbed and flowed. She could not help noticing that some were carrying luggage – suitcases, bulging haversacks, tooled leather travelling cases. She heard raucous laughter, a child's shrill cry, smelled the savoury aromas of frying onions and chargrilled lobster from the smoking braziers.

'There is something I need to tell you,' Amber said. Her teeth chattered together as she spoke, though it was a warm night, sultry even. 'I should have said something sooner, I realise that, but—'

'He waited six months,' Tessmond said. His voice was level and perfectly steady but it was impossible to mistake the fury in it, the low growl of contempt. 'He searched for you everywhere. He even came to the shop eventually, though you had forbidden it. He gave up in the end. What choice did he have? Give up, or go insane. He's a trained philosopher, after all – he considered the nature of insanity, and rejected it. He understood how dull it would be, how stultifying, to trade his freedom for the bars of an asylum. And what good would it do? You would still be gone.'

'Don't say he,' Amber whispered. She felt faint with disgust. 'Jaen is—'

'An emasculated cobbler's lad with ideas above his station. Good grades at school and a clever turn of phrase will never make of him what he aspires to. You are a queen, Ambergris. You demean yourself, playing in the dirt. But then you are young.'

'None of these things are true. I am no queen.' You're getting me confused with the song, she thought. What happens in the end? The queen dies and the dwarf is an outcast. He must be insane.

'Then allow me to inform you that you do not know yourself. But you will.'

He made a grab for her wrist, but she pulled back, evading him and backing away into the crowd. She caught her heel and almost fell, but a person in the crush behind her shoved her upright again. She elbowed someone in the ribs. They cursed loudly but moved aside. Amber dived through the gap in the press of bodies and found herself at the entrance to a narrow alleyway between two warehouses. She prayed it would not lead to a dead end. It was all too easy to imagine becoming trapped in a wired compound or in the backyard of an inn, sticky with refuse from overflowing dustbins, unable to retrace her steps for fear that Tessmond would still be waiting for her back on the harbourside. She had to take the chance though, she had no choice. Gasping with relief, she emerged on to an open road, somewhere north of the docklands, she thought. In truth she did not know exactly where she was and nor did she care. What mattered was that she had gained the advantage, she could get away. Tessmond stood no chance of catching her now – his bent, foreshortened legs, combined with the disproportionate weight of his torso made it impossible for him to run for more than thirty seconds without becoming breathless. Even an hour ago, the idea that she might have exploited his disability in this way would have horrified her but now she rejoiced in it, she felt exalted.

She dashed up the road, the hard night air sawing at her throat, the grogginess she had been feeling earlier forgotten. She ran with long strides, relishing her swiftness, slowing down only when she reached a brightly lit intersection, a small parade of shops that signalled to her that she was entering one of the outlying residential districts beyond the northern cordon. She still did not recognise her exact whereabouts but the lights and storefronts, the sight of people walking about were enough to reassure her she was bound to come to a tram stop eventually.

From there she could make her way – where? She could not return to the shop, not even to collect her belongings, it was too much of a risk.

She would go to Jaen. She would not be allowed in the prentice quarters, not after sundown, but Jaen would be permitted to speak with her, to take tea with her in the canteen even. They would talk, decide what to do, then Amber would go to a hotel for the night. She would be safe there, and everything would look different in the morning. She had a camp bed at the studio, she could easily stay there until she found something more permanent . . .

She stood at the kerbside, waiting to cross. On the opposite side of the road, a woman wandered the length of the mall and back again, passing from storefront to storefront, killing time. Her red hair blazed in the light from the streetlamps, the colour and density so like Amber's own hair that she could not help but feel comforted, experiencing that strange frisson of kinship that is always ignited in the presence of the familial or the familiar. It was not just the vibrant redness of the woman's hair that made her feel this way – something in the erectness of her posture, the briskness of her movements gave Amber the sense that she did indeed know her, that here was someone she could turn to, at least to ask for directions to the nearest tram stop.

As she reached the other side of the street, a heavyset man clutching several carrier bags printed with the name of a citywide liquor store cannoned into her, jabbing her painfully in the side with his elbow. He turned abruptly to stare at her. His skin looked blotchy and moist, with yellowish, ugly bruising beneath one eye.

'Watch where you're going, can't you,' he barked. 'Are you blind?'

She caught a whiff of his breath – cheap lager and pickled onions. 'Sorry,' Amber said, but he was already gone. She made her way to where the woman was standing, before the window of a small boutique selling leather goods and gift items. As Amber edged closer, trying to find the right words to frame her question, the woman performed a strange but familiar gesture, raising her right arm towards the window and thrusting it forwards into the light from the display.

She's trying to look at her watch, Amber thought, only she can't because it's caught in her coat sleeve.

The woman tugged off her glove and Amber saw that her fingers were deformed, twisted like a bunch of damp kindling. The watch on her wrist was gold, white dial and domed glass, the identical twin of the Aylward Tessmond had given to Amber on her name day the year before.

The woman shifted slightly before the window, allowing Amber to catch a glimpse of her reflection. The skin of her forehead was taut and shiny, like molten plastic. Both her eyebrows had been burned away and one of her eyes was missing, or permanently closed. Her bottom lip appeared to have burst, entirely erasing the line of definition between her mouth and the lower portion of her face.

Amber gasped aloud. The woman glanced at her sharply and recoiled.

'You should have got away,' the woman mumbled. Her speech was slurred and barely audible, mangled by the mutilations to her mouth. 'You should have listened.' Her single eye looked wet, bogged down, and after a moment Amber realised she was crying.

'I'm sorry,' Amber said. 'Sorry to bother you.' The words fell from her lips, hard as bullets. There seemed no sense to them. She stood paralysed in front of the window, her likeness merging with the woman's until she was unable to tell where the woman started and she left off.

What has he done? Amber thought. What has he done to me? She closed her eyes, inhaled. When she opened them again the woman was gone. Her own perfect reflection stared back at her from the window glass, overlaid with the ghosts of hand-stitched leather satchels and silver cigarette lighters. She turned back towards the street. A bus was just pulling up outside the liquor store, illuminated from within and stately as a battleship. Its brakes groaned as it came to a standstill. Amber hurried towards it and got on. She asked for Dolmen Street, which was the stop closest to the Remarque Library. The driver nodded and released her ticket from the machine as she fumbled for change.

The bus waited a few moments, then released its brakes and moved off into the traffic.

'You can't go down there, Mistress. Sorry.'

There was police tape and crash barriers blocking the sidewalk in front of the library. The officer who spoke to her wore a hi-viz jacket and protective headgear. She looked harassed and mildly frightened. Other officers, similarly attired, were ranged along the cordoned street as far as the clock tower. A small crowd of onlookers, students mainly, stood huddled against the office buildings on the pavement opposite.

'What's happening?' Amber asked the officer.

'I'm not at liberty to say, Mistress. We will be releasing information to the public as it becomes available. Until then, might I strongly suggest that you return to your place of residence?'

'Is anyone hurt?' Amber said, but the guardswoman was already gone, striding down to join her comrades at the makeshift barrier.

Amber hesitated, wondering if it might still be possible to gain access to the library quadrant from a different direction. You'll get yourself arrested, Amber told herself. What good is that going to do?

She stepped back from the barrier, moving towards the bystanders congregated beneath the tiled concrete portico of the College of Architects.

'Does anyone know what's going on?' she said. The eyes of the crowd turned upon her, fixing her with an expression caught midway between hostility and bemusement, as if she had spoken in the old language, or uttered an obscenity.

Finally one of them deigned to speak to her, a skinny girl with her hair in dreadlocks, a leather haversack resting on the ground between her feet.

'People are saying there's been a bomb. In the catacombs.'

'Runes, most likely,' another voice chimed in. 'There are prentices trapped inside apparently, at least twenty of them.'

The rune sept. Amber's mind reeled in confusion. There hadn't been a rune attack in years, not since she had come to the city, not against a public target anyway. The magisters' endless petitioning to shut down the library had become an accepted and tedious fact of city life. But killing philosophers? Even the more extreme factions would not countenance such an action. Jaen would most likely tell her later that the rumours were just that – scaremongering.

They had all those barriers up and it was just a broken drain, can you imagine? Typical guards' hysteria.

Amber craned her neck, shading her eyes against the fluorescent glare of the guards' helmet lights, trying to see through the darkness to the library itself. There were no lamps lit in any of the windows, which was odd, but—

Smoke rising from a hole in the Lower Tunsgate, a ragged space where a door had once been, streaks of white in the surrounding umber like old man's beard.

'Back, back!' The raised, terrified voice of one of the guards, then a juddering disturbance beneath her feet, as if something vast and subterranean were stretching its limbs. Then what sounded like a thunderclap, and the white noise of screams. Loose leaves of books and clumps of paper, raining down in ashen clods from a sky that stank, suddenly and unmistakably, of brimstone.

Great flames – dragons' breath – leaped like orange banners from the building's burst facade. The library's turrets seemed to be melting, crumbling away like icing sugar.

The guards scattered. A length of police tape, untethered, bumped and flickered against the paving slabs like a cast-off snakeskin.

'Jaen!'

Amber screamed their name aloud, its single, jagged syllable exiting through her gullet like a twist of barbed wire. As guards spilled from the entrance quadrant Amber ducked, unnoticed by any of them, beneath the broken barrier, flinging herself towards the blazing library across the paper-strewn grass.

West Edge House
Tarquin's End
Bodmin
Cornwall

Dear Andrew,

I'm allowed to make tea in my room. There's a fridge in the first-floor lounge where I can keep milk, and also butter and cheese if I want to make cheese on toast. I like to sit in the armchair facing the window, drinking my tea and looking out over the garden. In spring, Sylvia Passmore takes the deck-chairs out of the garage and arranges them on the back patio. There are six chairs altogether, but the only people who make use of them regularly are Jackie and Diz.

I've asked Jackie to come and have tea with me plenty of times, but she always says no. I think she's afraid of my dolls. We put the kettle on in the first-floor lounge instead. Sometimes we play a game of Snap! with the pack of animal cards from the games box in the tallboy. Jackie always wins at Snap! – she's incredibly fast. Each time she wins a point she slams down her hand on the table and laughs, as if that's part of the game.

It was August when I first arrived here. The fields were shimmering with heat haze.

I was told it would be for a month. Just until you get your strength back, they said. That was twenty years ago last month.

Of course I'm not a patient any more, not really – I have a job here. From nine until one I work in the office, typing up the patients' records on the computer and taking dictation from Dr Leslie. Dr Leslie doesn't like the computer, even though it was he who insisted we have one.

In the afternoons I carry on with my research into the life of Ewa Chaplin. I have been writing letters to the museums where her dolls are kept. I go over the replies and make notes. I write more letters. Sometimes I just like to reread Ewa's stories. There is so much I don't know yet, but I feel certain that one day all my questions will be answered.

You asked me how I first became interested in Ewa Chaplin and I told you it was because my friend Helen was in a play based on one of her stories, but that's not really true. I mean, it's true about Helen being in the play, but I didn't know the story was by Ewa Chaplin until a long time afterwards. I first saw a photograph of an Ewa Chaplin doll in Abraham Gold's book, *Costume Dolls of the Post-War Era*. If you have a copy you'll know the photograph I mean, the one called 'Serena, or Portrait of the Artist's Mother'. The doll is dressed all in black – even her petticoats are black, with grey stripes – and beside her is a rectangular wooden case, with a flute in it. The flute is just a toy but it looks like it could play, if you knew how to play it.

I knew that doll was special as soon as I saw her, that she wasn't just a doll and that Ewa Chaplin had made her because she was trying to tell me something. Well, not me personally, but whoever happened to be looking at the doll at any one time. The doll was like a picture, a painting of someone. I'm sure you know what I mean.

I read all the way through Abraham Gold's book, trying to find out more about 'Serena, or Portrait of the Artist's Mother' but apart from the small portion of text underneath the photograph saying that the doll was in a private collection in America she wasn't mentioned. I still remember how disappointed I felt. It would be romantic, wouldn't it, to tell you that I decided on the spot that I would have to write a biography of Ewa Chaplin myself, but that isn't true either. I don't know what I decided, or even if I did actually decide. I just started writing about her one day, or copying down some information out of another book, I can't remember exactly. That's often how these things happen, I suppose – by chance, like with the play Helen was in. It would be easy to pretend it was a big, decisive moment, an *epiphany*, but it wasn't. It was just a coincidence.

Ewa Chaplin sewed entirely by hand. She believed that only hand-stitching offered her the quality she wanted, that strangely lifelike look that all her dolls have, the feeling they give you when you look at them that they know you're there. Long after the war was over she carried on using the same basic materials she had grown used to: unbleached cotton and upholstery trimmings, fabric remnants and bits of old clothes. Her one extravagance was the very fine, very supple calf's leather she used to make the dolls' hands and feet.

She hated the very idea of mass-market models and numbered editions. All her dolls are unique. Towards the end of her life, Ewa Chaplin did start to become known as an artist, but she never moved from the small flat in Kensington she took out the lease on six months after she first arrived in England. She rarely travelled outside of London, and she never went back to Poland. She died in the winter of 1997, of pneumonia. A lot of people presumed she had died long before that, though she was only sixty-six. It's strange to think that when I went to London with the school, Ewa Chaplin was still alive, that for a couple of hours at least we were in the same place at the same time. I'd never been in a proper city before and I didn't know what to expect. Some of the children in my class had been to London with their parents, and they talked about it in loud voices all the way up the motorway.

Helen had been to Kew Gardens once, on her birthday, for an outdoor performance of *Cinderella*. The prince had worn a badger's mask, Helen said, and one of the children in the audience had screamed and tried to run away. She said it was something about the badger's head being bigger than the prince's real head, which I suppose could be very frightening if you thought about it too much.

Our school party was split into two groups. One group went to the Tower of London, the other went to Madame Tussaud's. We met up for lunch in Regent's Park and then we swapped over. I was in the group that went to the Tower first. I remember I'd been looking forward to seeing the crown jewels, but when we got there they were all behind glass and you couldn't get close enough to examine them in detail. A girl called Mallorie Spence had white silk gloves put on her and was allowed to pick up a tiara. A lot of the teachers liked Mallorie because she was clever and quiet, she never made a fuss about anything. What I remember most about her was her mouth, the way her lips were always slightly parted in the middle, as if they'd been painted on. It reminded me of a doll's mouth.

Madame Tussaud's turned out to be much more exciting than the crown jewels, in any case. There was a room with waxwork models of Henry VIII and his six wives. Anne Boleyn had her hair parted straight down the middle and a thin gold chain around her neck.

'I wonder if she had to take the chain off before she was executed,' Helen said. 'Or would the axe have sliced straight through?' She drew in her breath with a hissing sound, as if she were cold. I wanted to touch Anne Boleyn's hand to see what the wax felt like but I was scared I might set off an alarm.

The most valuable doll I ever owned was a Morgenkammer 'Janine'. I named her Rosamund. She was Helen's identical twin.

I don't have her now, of course. Every now and then I come across a 'Janine' in one of the online auction catalogues, but Morgenkammer dolls are very expensive these days and I couldn't afford to buy one even if I wanted to. I found Rosamund in a junk shop in Truro. She was sitting on a filing cabinet, holding down a stack of old fishing magazines. She still had her original clothes, only you couldn't see that at first because someone had put a pink baby's cardigan over the top of them. I had no idea how valuable she was. I was just amazed by how like Helen she looked.

Some people believe that stealing a person's image gives you the power of life and death over them. I didn't know how Helen would react when she saw Rosamund sitting on top of the bureau in my bedroom, whether she would be upset or even angry. What she actually did was laugh and put out her arms.

'Let me hold her,' she said. She pressed Rosamund's cheek to her own cheek and smiled, as if the two of them were posing for a photograph. 'I always wanted a sister.'

Helen only came to our house that one time. My mother followed her around as if she was afraid she might steal something. She barely spoke to her directly. She asked her questions through me instead in what I always thought of as her television voice: *Would Helen like another cup of tea*, or: *Would Helen like to wash her hands before we eat?*

After supper we went upstairs to my room. Helen sat on the floor with her back resting against the bed and told me about the play she was going to be in called *Amber Furness*. *Amber Furness* had been on in London, and had even been turned into a film, with a famous actress named Laura Plantagenet in the role of Amber. Helen told me how Laura Plantagenet had almost been killed in a car crash the year before, tugging her breath in over her teeth, the same as when she'd been talking about Anne Boleyn and the gold chain.

Helen's main ambition was to be an actor. She had a theatre programme from the Old Vic production of *Amber Furness* that had been signed by most of the cast. She called it her good luck charm. I told her she didn't need luck, she would be brilliant anyway. She looked at me in an odd way, then laughed.

The weather changed last night. I woke around four o'clock and felt it shift. I pulled the quilt up around my neck and listened to the rain coming down hard against the windows. By the time it grew light the rain had stopped, but the air felt damp and chilly with the memory of it. I was late down to breakfast. Sylvia

Passmore was in the kitchen, slicing bread for the eleven o'clock sandwiches.

'We're almost out,' she said. 'I meant to go to the shop yesterday but I didn't have time.' She rubbed her temple with the back of her hand, as if she had a headache. I offered to walk into Tarquin's End and buy the bread for her.

'Would you really, Bramber?' she said. 'That would be such a help, if you could. I've got so much on this morning.' She hesitated, as if she thought she should give me the chance to change my mind, then dashed away to Dr Leslie's office where the petty cash is kept.

'Two large white farmhouse,' she said. She gave me a five-pound note. 'Or get three, if they have them. I can always put one in the freezer. That should be plenty.'

Tarquin's End doesn't always show up on maps because it's so small, just a cluster of houses around the duck pond and the village shop. And the church, of course. The church is called St Ninian's. The last time I went there was after Jackie's father died. Jackie wanted to light a candle and say a prayer and she asked if Sylvia and I would go with her. Sylvia took us down in Dr Leslie's car, but when we arrived outside the church, she wouldn't let Sylvia go in with us. She wouldn't say why, but then that's typical of Jackie, she can change her mind in an instant and all over nothing.

'You come on your own,' she said to me. 'Or are you afraid of the ghosts?'

'There's no such thing as ghosts, Jackie,' I said. Jackie looked at me sideways, with a sly expression. I couldn't work out if she really was anxious about something or if she just wanted to get at Sylvia. Sylvia sat in the front seat looking furious. She knew better than to make a fuss, though – the last thing she wanted was to bring on one of Jackie's panic attacks.

The inside of the church was cool and grey. There are six stained-glass windows in St Ninian's, each showing a different scene from Noah's Flood. I glanced at the people and animals thrashing about in the water then looked away again. There was something horrible about the images, something you wouldn't expect to find inside a church. Jackie was standing a few paces away from me, bending over a marble sarcophagus. The blue light from the windows turned her red shoes purple.

'He looks just like my father,' Jackie said.

The tomb was carved with a marble figure, a man lying asleep with his hands crossed over his chest. A plaque on the side of the casket read: *Leonard Francis Tarquin 1798–1873*. He had a long, lean face, and wavy, shoulder-length hair, like a mediaeval knight. Jackie had once shown me a photograph of her father, a small, badger-like, balding man with round, owlish glasses. I didn't say anything. Perhaps Jackie's father really had been like a hero to her, in his way, her own Sir Galahad. The idea seemed sad to me but beautiful, too.

I miss my dad, so much.

Suddenly Jackie turned and walked away. Light tangled itself in her hair like strands of blue wool.

There were other Tarquin graves outside in the churchyard. Sylvia told me the last of the Tarquins was killed in the trenches, in the Battle of the Somme. An information leaflet in the church porch said the hamlet had originally been called Netherstone.

The duck pond had filled up overnight. In summer, the pond dries up and becomes much smaller but in autumn when the rains start, children come down with jam jars to fish for sticklebacks. There were no children by the pond this morning, which surprised me, until I remembered they would all be in Bodmin, at school.

The village shop sells bread, milk, eggs. Some vegetables and fresh meat too, if you get there early enough. If you need anything more than the basics you have to go into Bodmin. The woman who serves behind the counter is called Mavis Nash. When I asked for the bread she said I was lucky, they only had the one loaf left.

'Miserable morning,' she added.

'Yes,' I replied. 'The forecast says it's going to rain again tonight.' I picked up the loaf and left. I once overhead Mavis Nash saying they shouldn't have a mental home so close to where normal people live. Luckily, I don't see her that often because it's usually Sylvia who buys the bread and eggs. Sylvia doesn't live at West Edge House. She comes in every morning on the bus from Bodmin. When I arrived back at the house, Sylvia was outside, standing on the front steps. The door was wide open behind her.

She snatched the loaf from my hands and pushed me inside.

'Where on Earth have you been?' she said. 'I was relying on you.'

She slammed the front door and stalked off down the corridor without waiting for me to answer. When I looked at my watch I saw it was twenty to one, almost lunchtime.

I'd been gone for almost two hours. Time is odd like that

sometimes. You can't always tell where it's going, or what it might do.

It's strange, you know. I've never talked about West Edge House really, not to anyone. It's different with you. I feel as if I could tell you anything.

I hope you are well, Andrew,

Bramber

5 .

I FOUND THE SECOND EWA Chaplin story even more engrossing and enjoyable than the first. The idea of a fairy tale that didn't end happily ever after was fascinating to me. I liked the dwarf, too, Anders Tessmond. He didn't once apologise for who he was, and that was something I hadn't come across before – dwarfs in books are mostly villains, have you noticed? Either that or they're put there to be funny, or pathetic. Tessmond was just a person, with his own ideas about the world. I suppose you could argue that he was cruel, but I didn't see it that way. He was fighting for the woman he loved, that's all. If anything it was Amber who was in the wrong, for pretending to care for Tessmond more than she did. You could even say she betrayed him.

After finishing 'Amber Furness' I sat staring out of the window at the passing countryside. I could have started reading another story but I found I wasn't quite ready to leave the world of 'Amber Furness'. I watched the traffic instead, checking the road signs as we approached Salisbury, where I would be leaving the coach and catching the train for Exeter. Mostly though I thought about Ursula, because how could I not? I say I enjoyed Chaplin's story, but the truth was that it had shaken me badly. *How could she know these things?* I kept wondering. I understood that the most powerful stories of all are those that seem to speak to us directly, but in the case of 'Amber Furness', it was as if Ewa Chaplin had been able not just to see into my thoughts, but to unearth a secret passageway into my past.

I MET URSULA CASE at Woolfenden College, which is where I began my degree course after completing my 'A' Levels. Woolfenden specialised in business subjects, politics and economics, and was loosely affiliated with the University of London. Ursula was studying for a degree in commercial accounting. When I asked her about her choice of subject she told me the accounting degree had been her father's idea.

'He wanted me to learn a profession I could rely upon,' she said. 'He promised to help me as much as he could with whatever I wanted to do in life, on condition that I agreed to humour him over his back-up plan. An offer I couldn't refuse, right?'

I never met Ursula's parents and, aside from that one story about her father, she hardly ever talked about them. I knew that Ursula was from Whitby, on the North Yorkshire coast, and that her father owned a small chain of convenience stores in and around the Harrogate area. His name was Ranjit Case. He was more than twenty years older than Ursula's mother but Ursula never said how they met. Ursula's mother Herta was German, and came originally from a small market town in Schleswig Holstein.

Ursula returned to Whitby for the Christmas and Easter vacations of our first year at Woolfenden but over the summer break she moved out of college accommodation into a studio flat close to campus and went home only rarely. The week after our degree results came out, she bought the flat using money her father had given her for a graduation present as a deposit. I thought I might get to meet Ursula's parents at the graduation ceremony, but in the event, Ursula's one guest was a tiny, silver-haired lady in shalwar kameez that Ursula introduced to me as her Aunt Maryam.

I DECIDED TO STUDY statistics because I wasn't too bad with numbers and my father assured me the degree would stand me to good advantage when looking for work. I met Ursula in the college canteen. We were less than three weeks into term. It was a Wednesday, which was seminar day, and the place was pretty crowded. I saw Ursula standing close by with her tray, and as she was clearly looking for somewhere to sit I made room for her at my table. We ate our meals in silence. From time to time I found myself glancing at the brooch she wore, a large, oval onyx in an elaborate Victorian setting. I was struck also by the design of her jacket, a grey pinstripe with wider-than-normal sleeves, which seemed to me to be the height of elegance. As she got up to leave I asked her where she had bought it.

'I made it myself,' she said. 'It's my own design.'

I noticed she had the most extraordinary eyes: large, deep, with the colour and sheen of moss agates. She wore her hair pulled back from her face, accentuating her high arched brows and domed, slightly overhanging forehead. I learned that as a child she had suffered from rheumatoid arthritis, and that her finger joints were permanently swollen as a result.

I asked her if she would like to have coffee with me sometime. She knocked on my door later that same evening.

Her reaction to my dolls was one of delight. 'I love dolls,' she exclaimed. 'No one's ever too old for dolls.'

When I asked her if she wanted to be a fashion designer she shook her head at once. 'I hate the word fashion,' she said. 'I want to make clothes that will last, the kind you could fold away in a trunk and still be happy to wear twenty years later. Most clothes these days are designed to be worn for a season and then thrown away. A lot of material just goes into landfill. I think that's a terrible waste of the Earth's resources.'

She took up sewing when she was nine, as therapy for her hands. 'There were all these exercises I was supposed to do but they hurt so much and I hated them because they seemed pointless. At least with the sewing I had something to show for it. In any case, I was lucky. The disease went into remission when I was fifteen.'

Ursula owned an electric sewing machine of course, though she performed a lot of the more intricate work using an old manual Singer with a rotating handle. When I asked her to show me how it worked, she took a square of blue cloth and placed it under the needle, then showed me how to begin stitching by turning the wheel. The needle rose and fell like a hammer, pulling the thread along behind in a simple running stitch. I asked her if it was difficult to control.

'Of course not,' she said, and laughed. 'Not once you get used to it. It's easy.'

She kept a trunk beneath her bed, stuffed with fabric samples, which she collected from a variety of sources. When I expressed curiosity about it she pulled the trunk to the centre of the room and allowed me to empty its contents on to the floor. It was like being given permission to enter the store room of a small but very specialised museum. I recognised satin and velvet and damask, cotton and calico – Ursula seemed surprised that I knew their names. I loved the feel of the fabrics, their different textures and weaves, although I was by no means the expert Ursula seemed to take me for. There had been a small haberdasher's store in Welton, I told her, a cramped, musty-smelling premises called Percy's where my mother occasionally used to buy replacement buttons or zips. At the back of the store, long bolts of cloth stood upright against the walls, but my mother had no use for fabric by the yard. She bought her curtains and other soft furnishings ready-made, from Debenhams or Habitat.

'I remember when Debenhams had its own haberdashery department,' Ursula said. 'The one in Harrogate did, anyway. It's gone now. Hardly anyone makes their own clothes these days. I think it's a shame.'

It was Ursula who first suggested I try making a doll. 'You can start off using a pattern,' she said. 'But once you get the hang of the basics you can design your own.'

She found a book for me in the local library, *Let's Make Dolls*. The book was filled with diagrams that had to be copied on to tracing paper for use as templates. Ursula showed me how to enlarge the diagrams by working to scale, then helped me pin them on to calico. The next stage was cutting out, after which the pattern pieces had to be pinned together in pairs, ready for stitching. My first doll took me six weeks to complete, including her clothes. She was a classic Raggedy Anne, with the traditional stripy stockings and woollen braids. Her dress was sprigged blue cotton with a white petticoat under. The petticoat was trimmed with broderie anglaise.

As soon as she was finished I began making another, this time from a more complicated pattern. This new doll had long dark ringlets and Victorian silk pantaloons. As my experience increased, I began to enjoy even those parts of the process I had initially found tedious or overly time-consuming – the copying-out of the scale diagrams, for instance.

Ursula told me I was a natural, but I have come to believe the term is meaningless, that it is simply a matter of discovering the thing that engages your attention to such an extent that the world acquires a new clarity in the light of it. The thing you sense in your bones that you were born to do.

Ursula also showed me where to shop for materials. Some of the larger department stores still possessed haberdashery departments of some description, though these were not in the main half so interesting as those small, independent emporia that had been around for decades, surviving on local custom and pure stubbornness. Shops like these sold a more idiosyncratic selection of cloth, often at significantly reduced prices. I grew to love the interiors of these stores, dingy and chaotic but stocked from the owner's unique taste and therefore filled with the promise, each time, of finding something extraordinary.

There were also the vintage clothing boutiques and charity shops, and towards the end of each week Ursula and I would scour the local papers for announcements of jumble sales and church bazaars then head out by bus to school gymnasiums and village halls in obscure locations, returning in the evening with great armfuls of garments which we would cut up into usable squares of fabric, the variety of patterns and textures so thrilling to us it was like an addiction. And of course our haul of treasure cost us almost nothing.

Under Ursula's guidance I soon learned as much about fabric

as I already knew about dolls. I learned to recognise the difference between natural fibres and synthetics, to estimate the strength of a weave, to notice how the colours in a piece of old velvet were richer and stronger than those in its modern, mass-produced equivalent. Ursula taught me how to unpick a garment and then cut it down. Some items yielded yards of usable material, others no more than a scrap, but if the cloth was beautiful or unusual enough the effort was worth it. I remember one piece from that time in particular, a child's high-waisted dress with a large triangular burn-mark in the back of the skirt – clearly the result of an accident with an electric iron. The dress was made of silk, with glass buttons down the front of the bodice and on the cuffs. Ursula and I came across silk all the time, but this piece was special because of the colour: a mauve so delicate it gave the impression of transparency.

I kept the material for a long time before making use of it. In the end I turned it into a tunic for one of my troll dolls, a green-eyed girl named Livia with the face of a Karl Petersen shepherdess doll. She must have been dropped in her earlier life, because although her head was otherwise perfect, her right ear had been broken off, leaving a penny-sized, crater-shaped scar with the texture of compacted sand.

Ursula was right in what she said about nobody making things. The art of creating objects by hand has been almost entirely superseded by mass production. Goods arrive in industrial quantities from village-sized factories, staffed by underpaid vassals in these nuclear-age reconstructions of the feudal state. Raw materials are harvested indiscriminately, torn from the earth with scant regard for the devastation such demand might place on the environments that produce them. Nottingham lace, Sheffield steel, Staffordshire pottery – they may as well be the names of long-extinct life forms in the Natural History Museum.

This saddens and frustrates me, more than I can usefully express. When Karl Marx talked of workers becoming alienated from the fruits of their labours, I believe it was precisely this usurping of the necessary by the merely profitable that he had in mind.

I BECAME AWARE ONLY gradually that I wanted to sleep with Ursula. I imagined removing her outer garments, wondering if she made her own underwear too or bought it from Marks & Spencer like everyone else. Above all I wanted to know what she would look like with her hair down. I lay in bed at night, stroking myself under the covers and thinking about how it might feel to work my fingers beneath the narrow elastic of whatever Ursula might be wearing beneath her exquisite jackets and shirts.

These imaginings aroused me unbearably, but when I finally came, my climax was ground out in the guttering, distasteful light of memories of the acts I had performed, however unwillingly, with Wil. I found it difficult to reconcile the reticent, modest young woman who was my friend with the musk-scented, insatiable shadow who shared my bed. I could imagine the act in enough detail to drive me mad, but not what I might say to her afterwards, how our friendship might survive such a monstrous breach of privacy.

I never spoke a word to her of what I was going through. I think now that I should have done, that if I had, I might have discovered she was harbouring similar feelings for me. All the signs were there, I realise that now, although at the time I was terrified that if Ursula found out how I felt I would lose her forever. Whatever the theoretical outcome of such a confession is now irrelevant, though it could hardly have been more distressing than what eventually occurred.

Ursula disappeared from my life so suddenly and so completely it took me years to accept the fact that she was gone. After we graduated, she sold her accountancy books and began taking private commissions for bespoke clothing. I went to live in a rented flat above a laundrette in Hammersmith and started work as a data analyst with a private consultancy firm called Clark Cannings. I would meet Ursula for a meal every Wednesday evening at a wine bar just off Covent Garden, and every other Saturday we went shopping. On one of these Saturdays she simply failed to turn up, and when I telephoned to check if I had the date wrong there was no reply. I tried again, thinking I must have misdialled, but there was still no answer.

I phoned later that afternoon and evening, then twice every day for a week, letting the phone ring until the line cut out. The next time I tried there was no dial tone, just a click when I connected and a synthetic female voice telling me the number I was calling was unavailable. There was a light on in her flat sometimes, but no one ever came to the door. I sent her postcards and letters, some of them pleading with her to tell me what I had done wrong, others describing the minutiae of my life and my daily routine as if nothing had happened.

I scanned the newspapers daily, both local and national, dreading the sight of her photograph because of what it might mean – *woman murdered, woman abducted, woman urgently sought* – and yet hoping for it against all hope, because at least then I would know.

I even considered writing to her parents, then realised I didn't have their address.

Almost a year from the day of our last meeting, a new tenant moved into Ursula's flat, a tall, Scandinavian-looking woman with short blond hair and a red Honda moped. I didn't dare to approach her. For a while I continued to write, hoping that Ursula's post would be sent on to her new address but in the end I realised I had to stop. Sending the letters had been helpful at first. Now it was just painful.

A long time afterwards – five years or more – I saw a doll I had made for Ursula sitting in the window of one of the scores of antique shops along the Portobello Road. She was a copy of a Schindler original. Her dress was dove grey and very plain but her petticoat, a mass of soft pleats, had been created from more than a dozen different fabrics and had taken me most of a week to sew together. I marched into the shop, declaring I'd buy the doll before I'd even asked how much it was.

As soon as I got home I took off all her clothes and turned them inside out, examining the seams and pockets in the hope and almost certain expectation of finding something – a message, a code, anything – that would finally reveal Ursula's whereabouts and what had happened to her, but there was nothing.

I held the doll against my face and inhaled, hoping to catch a trace of Ursula's scent. Ursula never wore perfume as such, but I had always noticed and liked the aroma of the toiletries she used: a herby, yellowish smell, like sundried gorse.

The doll, whose name was Marnie, smelled faintly of chemicals, as if she and her clothes had recently been dry-cleaned. Every trace of Ursula's scent had been removed. If I had not made her myself, I would have found myself doubting she was the same doll.

I could not help feeling that this act of purging had been deliberate, a message that only Ursula and I would understand: our time together was over and somehow I must come to terms with living without her.

Dear Andrew,

I recognised my father's gift for mending things as a kind of
miracle, a means of giving life back to the dead. I also saw how
his work with machines gave him a fuller sense of who he was,
a place in the world where he felt comfortable. My mother never
seemed to feel comfortable anywhere, and if she came across
something broken she threw it away.

It was Mrs Hubbard who first taught me to use a computer.
Mrs Hubbard was Dr Leslie's secretary when I first arrived here.

'You're too bright to be shut away in here,' she used to say to
me. 'You know that already though, don't you? You'll leave when
you're ready, I suppose.'

Mrs Hubbard was enormously fat. She wore vast tent dresses
patterned with pagodas or windmills or oversized flowers,
and puffed like a broken engine as she moved. She had a soft,
moon-like face and tiny hands. Her nails were always perfectly
manicured, painted with satin sheen nail varnish in an endless
array of colours. Her first name was Meredith. She lived with
her husband in one of the fishermen's cottages on Salt Street, just
down from the village shop.

She died suddenly one day of a heart attack, on her way home from work. Dr Leslie was rushed to the scene immediately but Mrs Hubbard was dead by the time he got there.

The nearest hospital is eight miles away, in Bodmin.

'She was lying there blocking the pavement like a great beached whale,' said Sylvia Passmore, who happened to have stopped off at the village shop on her way home and so saw the whole thing. 'I know I shouldn't say this, but she was asking for it. She was well over twenty stone, you know. You can't expect to carry on like that and get off scot-free.'

She said that Meredith's husband had wept openly in the street. 'He was older than her by a mile, you know. Not that you'd know from looking at him. He's good-looking in a way, or at least he would have been when he was younger. How the two of them got together, goodness knows. He'll be married again before the year is out, you wait and see.'

A couple of days after Meredith died, Dr Leslie asked me if I would like to take over the computer. I thought Sylvia might be upset, but she said no, she didn't have time, not with all the other things that had to get done around here. 'Anyway, it'll keep your brain from going soggy,' she said. 'You can't be too careful in a place like this.'

It's my job to type up Dr Leslie's records, and keep them properly filed. I do the accounts now as well – it's not too difficult once you get the hang of it. Maths was never my best subject at school but Edwin once said to me that numbers are no more difficult to understand than words, once you learn their language. Edwin loved numbers, the same way my father loved machines.

Edwin was never my boyfriend, not really. I don't know what he was.

A new patient arrived here last night. Dr Leslie's phone kept ringing, which was unusual for that time in the evening. Every time it went off, Sylvia went charging down the corridor to answer it. Sylvia hardly ever stays at West Edge House overnight. I once overheard her telling the postman she thought the house was haunted.

The new patient finally arrived at around nine o'clock. I'd gone to my room by then, but when I heard the front doorbell go I came out on to the landing to see what was happening. There were a group of people clustered around the door – Dr Leslie and Sylvia Passmore, the two night nurses, someone else I didn't recognise but who must have arrived with the patient, a boy with long hair who kept hugging himself and laughing.

I watched them for a while then went back to my room. A short while later they brought him upstairs. The room next to mine was empty, so they put him in there. I heard him crying through the wall, a strangled, gargling sound, as if he were fighting for breath. I could hear one of the night nurses murmuring to him, a constant, even sound, like running water. Eventually the crying stopped and I went to sleep.

I didn't see the new patient again until tea time today. I went along to the first floor lounge to make some toast and found him sitting there on the sofa, next to Jackie. There was a cup of tea on the table in front of him but he hadn't touched it.

'This is Michael,' Jackie said. 'Michael Round. I made him some tea but he says he only drinks Earl Grey.'

'There might be some in the kitchen cupboard,' I said. 'I'll go and have a look.'

Michael Round was wearing grey flannel trousers that were too big for him and a green cardigan. His hair kept falling in his eyes and for a moment I thought how like Edwin he looked but then I realised he didn't at all, it was just the hair.

There was an old packet of Earl Grey teabags in the larder – I think they belonged to Meredith Hubbard – but by the time I got back to the first-floor lounge, Michael Round was gone.

'They've taken him away for questioning,' Jackie said gaily. She grinned. 'They won't get much out of him, though. He's trau-ma-tised.'

She spelled out the word deliberately, as if it were the answer to a quiz question, rolling the 'r'.

'Did he tell you why he's here, Jackie?'

'Of course he didn't. Saw his daddy knocked down in the street, probably. How should I know?'

I was telling you about Edwin. He was sixteen when I first met him. His family moved to Truro from Pangbourne, in Berkshire. I remember he started school three weeks into term, which doesn't sound like much but where school kids are concerned, three weeks can be the difference between a new person settling in normally and being treated like a freak. It didn't help that Edwin had also been kept down a year. People made up all kinds of strange reasons for this, mainly that he was retarded, or that he'd been brought up in a religious cult and hadn't learned to read until he was ten. None of it was true, but it was still a whole week before anyone said so much as a word to him.

He was six feet tall, and with his earnest expression and heavy spectacles he could easily have been mistaken for one of the teachers. He wore a navy-blue blazer over his school jumper and always had his tie done up to the top. Also, he never tried to hide the fact that he was clever. After only a couple of days the rumours about his being retarded became ridiculous – anyone could see how brainy he was – so they were replaced with new rumours about a mental institution.

But what set Edwin apart most of all was that he honestly didn't seem to care what anyone said about him. He responded politely when eventually he was spoken to but he didn't try to get in with people, or attach himself to any particular group. At break time he would wander slowly around the playing fields, reading a book. At lunchtime he sat on his own. There were teachers who made a fuss of him – who called him a prodigy and whispered about him going to Oxford – but he didn't appear to take much notice of them, either.

I used to stand and watch him from the other side of the football field and wonder what he was thinking about. I didn't approach him, though. I was afraid of looking an idiot or being told to get lost. If it hadn't been for Helen being in the play, Edwin and I might never have spoken at all.

I'm picking up where I left off but really this is two letters in one because I spent most of last week in bed with a cold and couldn't get down to the post box. Every time I tried to stand up I felt dizzy. Even when I did manage to dress myself I kept falling asleep in my armchair. At one point I dreamed about my mother, yelling at me for leaving the back door open when the gas fire was on. The next day I received a postcard from my father, telling me he was planning to spend Christmas with a cousin of his, in Spain. The postcard had a photograph of a donkey on it – not a Spanish donkey with a straw hat but an English one, in a donkey sanctuary somewhere in Dorset. The postcard had a musty smell, as if it had been shut away in a drawer for ages, and when I looked at the postmark I saw it was dated ten years ago.

It was strange to think of it circling round and round inside the postal system for all that time. I'm miles behind with Dr Leslie's files now, as well.

We had a concert here on Tuesday. Dr Leslie likes to organise outside entertainment for us sometimes, especially around Christmas or Easter. Last Christmas we had a conjuror. I wasn't well then, either. I remember lying in bed listening to the radio, when Jackie suddenly started screaming. The conjuror had asked if he could borrow her scarf ring, apparently – he wanted to make it disappear. Jackie went into a panic, so Diz said it was all right, the conjuror could have his Parker pen instead. That frightened Jackie almost as much as the idea of losing her scarf ring, although Diz soon got his pen back and that calmed her down.

My cold was getting better by Tuesday so I was able to go downstairs for the concert. It was held in the visitors' lounge. Diz helped Sylvia clear all the board games and old newspapers off the top of the piano, which they then wheeled to the centre of the room. There was a flute player and a pianist. The flute player wore skinny black jeans and a red velvet jacket. His hair was so blond it looked white under the lights, like some kind of precious metal. The pianist was Chinese. She had long dark hair in a plait and gold stilettos.

I've never really cared much for music. I prefer natural sounds, like the calling of birds or the chirping of crickets. The sound of the flute was so much louder than I imagined it would be, hard and bright, almost like a trumpet. The flute player seemed to dance a little as he played, swaying in time with the music in his black leather pumps. The pianist kept her body upright, and very still, her fingers scurrying swiftly about the keyboard like spiders, or mice.

About ten minutes into the music, Michael Round began to cry. His whole face was wet with tears, as if it were melting like one of the waxworks in Madam Tussaud's. Looking at him reminded me of my mother, though I never saw her cry, not ever.

Ewa Chaplin's mother Serena was a flute player, did you know that? Her teachers said she was a brilliant musician, and everyone believed she would go on to have a great career, but then one of her hands became injured in a fire. The fire started on the second floor of the Chaplins' apartment block, a few months after they were married. Serena's husband Jonas wasn't at home, and Serena was visiting friends in the flat above. She managed to climb out on to the fire escape, but the sash cord holding up the window burned through, bringing the heavy frame crashing down on top of her hands. She suffered five separate bone fractures, and the tendons in her right wrist were permanently damaged.

She recovered the use of her hands fairly quickly, considering, but her confidence was shattered. She said the feeling in her fingertips had been affected, that she would never play in public again, and she never did.

Ewa was born soon afterwards. People whispered that it was a miracle that Serena's pregnancy had survived, almost as if there had been a trade-off: her child for her music.

It snowed in the night, and Sylvia is in a foul mood because the bus was delayed. The only person who seems excited by the snow is Jackie.

Sylvia is in charge of putting up the Christmas decorations, but she always lets Jackie do the tree. My mother used to dress our Christmas tree beautifully. I remember how one year, Mrs Porter from down the road asked her if she'd ever been a professional window dresser.

'You have a marvellous eye, Elizabeth,' she said. 'You're very artistic.'

My mother smiled and thanked Mrs Porter for the compliment but I could see she was annoyed, that she didn't like the idea of Mrs Porter thinking she had once made her living by working in a shop, when she had studied at the Royal Academy of Music, in London.

A couple of days later my father accidentally let the back door slam shut when he was coming inside. Two of my mother's crystal sherry glasses fell over on the draining board and smashed.

'It's my fault,' my mother said at once. 'I didn't stack them properly. The old bat obviously didn't have a clue what she was talking about.' She pulled the dustpan and brush from under the sink and swept up the pieces. Her mouth was set in a hard line, as if she was trying to keep herself from screaming, or from bursting into tears.

The glasses had been a wedding present from the woman who gave me my first doll, Catherine Sharpe.

Dr Leslie wears a wedding ring, but he isn't married, at least not any more. That's what Sylvia told me, anyway. Goodness knows how she finds out these things.

'He wears the ring to stop women from pestering him,' she said. 'Women are always falling for doctors.'

When Sylvia is annoyed about something you can hear her Cornish accent but whenever she speaks to Dr Leslie she sounds like one of the programme announcers on Radio Four. Jennifer Rockleaze calls her the Countess. I once saw Sylvia push past Jennie on the stairs and nearly knock her over. She usually avoids Jennie completely if she can.

'She thinks I'm out to steal her boyfriend,' Jennie said, when I asked her about it. A grin spread across her face. She looked like a mischievous child.

'You don't mean Dr Leslie?' I said.

'Who else? The Countess has had the hots for him for years.'

Sylvia wears neatly tailored skirts and plain tops in pastel colours, a fresh one every day but they all look the same. Her shoes are amazing though. She must have a hundred pairs at least and she keeps them immaculate. Jackie can't keep her eyes off Sylvia's shoes – you can almost see her mouth watering – but I've never noticed Dr Leslie so much as glance at them. I occasionally catch Sylvia looking at Dr Leslie's wedding ring, and then I can't help wondering if it's true, what she says, that Dr Leslie wears it to keep women away.

'Do you think his real wife died?' I once asked Jennie.

'He might have murdered her, you never know,' Jennie answered. 'They say it's always the quiet ones.'

Trust Jennie to come out with something like that. I couldn't help laughing, though I found it difficult to imagine Dr Leslie becoming close enough to anyone to want to murder them. He's good with his patients but he finds it hard to deal with their relatives, you can tell. He doesn't know how to talk to them. He's become so wrapped up in his work he's forgotten how to live in the everyday world.

With love,

Bramber

THE ELEPHANT GIRL

by Ewa Chaplin

translated from the Polish by Erwin Blacher 2008

Zhanna Mauriac arrived in late May, on the morning Mila learned she was once again pregnant. Mila wondered later if that was what started it, if all her reactions that day were a little off-kilter. She had already been told about the new girl, who was brought along and introduced to the class by the headmistress. Mila smiled her best hello-I'm-your-new-teacher smile; Zhanna stared stolidly back at her with unfathomable mud-coloured eyes.

What an ugly child, Mila thought. *She's like the bad fairy at a christening.*

She tried to banish the thought but it wouldn't go. She'd never taken an irrational dislike to a child before but Zhanna Mauriac gave her the creeps and as the morning wore on she found the girl's presence in her classroom increasingly distracting. If her behaviour had been disruptive she would have known how to cope. As it was, Zhanna sat meekly in the place she had been allocated, her mouth hanging slightly ajar, her features so immobile there were moments when Mila caught herself wondering what would happen if she went up and slapped her.

She's like a horrible plastic doll, Mila thought. *The kind you get given for Christmas when you're ten and never play with.*

When Mila tried asking Zhanna a question, the child's eyes rolled blankly in her head like stone marbles.

Zhanna Mauriac had a pudgy moon face and mousy hair cropped in a straight line across her forehead. She was eight years old, a full year younger than most of the other children in Mila's class, but Mila had been forced to take her because apparently she was ahead in most of her subjects. She was a misfit in other ways too. It was true she'd had a tricky start – joining a class midway through term was something even the most confident child would find difficult – but that was far from being the sum of her problems. On the Friday of her first week in school, Mila found herself staring at Zhanna and thinking how *old* she looked, a peculiar shrunken old woman with nasty lumpen features and a secretive soul. A witch who would slap a curse on you the moment you crossed her.

That was ridiculous of course, she was just a child.

The other children called her the Elephant Girl. Zhanna Mauriac wasn't fat exactly but she moved as if she was, stiffly upright as a plump little penguin and with her arms projecting just a fraction to either side. She wore heavy black shoes with square buckles, the kind of shoes that might just as well have had 'cripple' stamped in capital letters on the lid of the box.

It was difficult to stop the other children from teasing her and, on those days when she was particularly tired, Mila found herself pretending not to notice what was going on. One lunch hour when she was on playground duty she came outside to find a dozen or so of the rowdier youngsters standing in a circle around Zhanna Mauriac and pelting her with gravel. The stones bounced off her stomach and thighs in a way that reminded Mila of the wooden Aunt Sally at the county goose fair you could pay to throw steel quoits at and win a prize. Zhanna made no attempt to escape or defend herself. Mila forced her way through the circle and grabbed her roughly by the hand.

'For goodness' sake, stop it,' she said. She marched the girl briskly inside. She felt taut with anger, not so much with the other children as with Zhanna. It was as if she set out to be bullied, as if she had deliberately brought the whole thing on herself.

Mila could not get rid of the feeling that Zhanna Mauriac was a bad omen, and as the term progressed the idea began to root itself more firmly inside her head. She supposed it was the result of the hormones flooding her system. Everyone said it was normal to feel off-balance during pregnancy, that many women fell prey to irrational thoughts. With the anxiety caused by her two previous miscarriages Mila guessed she would be particularly susceptible.

It was frightening though, nonetheless; it felt a little like madness.

The worst thing was her certainty that Zhanna was pretending idiocy to conceal her true nature. In the original Charles Perrault tale of *The Sleeping Beauty*, the bad fairy came to the christening disguised as a peasant. She blamed the queen for leaving her off the guest list, even though the queen claimed that not inviting her had been a simple oversight.

There must have been a reason though, Mila told herself. *You don't just forget people.*

In the version of the story her class loved best, all the fairies at the christening were named after saints, and the gifts they handed out to the newborn princess were qualities of attraction and magical powers. Sophia brought the gift of wisdom, Agatha granted the power of levitation and so on. Margaret kept a dragon trained to her side like a Rottweiler and promised the princess protection against demonic powers. Cecilia blessed her with the gift of music and divination.

The bad fairy had no name, and she had been excluded from the celebrations because she was ugly and senile and the only gift she had to offer was her preternatural talent for talking with ghosts. No one wanted to be reminded that the infant princess would eventually grow old and go crazy. It was said that the royal family was rife with craziness, that the queen herself was already beginning to show the signs.

The bad fairy was not really bad, Mila saw. She was just an unwelcome reminder of what was true.

Zhanna Mauriac couldn't speak or at least she wouldn't. Varvara Pilnyak, who taught the infants' class and who happened to live in the same street as the Mauriacs, told Mila that Zhanna's communication problems had worsened considerably since starting school.

'She does tend to get picked on, rather,' Varvara said. 'I suppose it's inevitable.'

When Mila asked her what was actually wrong with Zhanna, Varvara shrugged and said it was probably a form of autism.

'She's supposed to be very clever, but then children like that often are. I've been told she plays the piano very well.'

Mila listened to what Varvara was saying but found it hard to believe. When she was six years old Mila had been taken to a concert featuring the great Austrian pianist Vladimir de Pachmann, who had terrified her with his black cloak and peculiar manner of addressing the audience in mid-performance, and who yet at the same time had enchanted her so completely with the music he made that she had pestered her parents non-stop for piano lessons until they finally gave in and sent her for private tuition with a Madame Cluny. Mila began to nurture secret dreams of becoming a concert pianist. The first big disappointment of her life came with the realisation that she didn't have the talent to make her dream a reality. By her late teens she had given up music altogether.

The idea that Zhanna had what she lacked was somehow grotesque. When the school closed for the summer vacation, Mila clung to the irrational hope that when the children returned in September the Elephant Girl would not be among them. But on the first day of term there Zhanna was, stumbling across the playground in her hideous shoes. She gazed at Mila without seeming to recognise her, but Mila felt convinced she was pretending.

Her anxieties about the baby had eased off a little over the summer, but with her first sight of Zhanna Mauriac they returned in a rush. Less than a week into term, Mila asked the headmistress if she might request a meeting with Zhanna's parents. The headmistress seemed to think this was a good idea.

'The child still doesn't seem to be settling the way she should. Perhaps a chat with Mum and Dad might move things forward.'

Both the Mauriacs held down professional careers and the meeting took some arranging but finally the three of them were together in one room.

'We're worried about Zhanna's progress,' Mila said. 'Is she normally this quiet at home?'

'Zhanna doesn't talk much even with us, if that's what you're getting at,' replied Dunia Mauriac. 'She prefers to practise her piano.' Zhanna's mother was anaemically pale, with thin, almost colourless hair. Her voice seemed unnaturally loud, as if she was trying to make herself heard in a crowded room.

'I understand that Zhanna is musically gifted,' Mila said. 'Have you ever considered sending her to a specialist school? Somewhere better suited to her needs?'

'A special school?' boomed Etienne Mauriac. 'Are you trying to imply that Zhanna is retarded?' Etienne Mauriac was some sort of scientist, a large man with a florid complexion and heavy jowls. He looked to Mila as if he was heading straight for a heart attack. He hovered a few inches behind his scrawny wife as if he was trying to use her as a human shield.

'Of course not,' Mila said. 'In fact, she's ahead of her class.' She fought the urge to hiccup. She had come to recognise her hiccups as a sign of approaching nausea and another bout of the morning sickness that continued to plague her, even though common wisdom insisted it should be starting to ease off by now. When she made tentative enquiries about who looked after Zhanna when they were at work the wife barked out the name of a foreign au pair. The au pair had already been mentioned several times by both parents but Mila seemed incapable of remembering her name for more than five seconds. Her memory felt increasingly unreliable since the end of summer. She had heard pregnant women described as being 'away with the fairies'. She supposed this haziness with facts was one of the symptoms.

She was beginning to sweat. She dug her fingernails into her palms and tried not to think about the slice and a half of rye bread she had eaten for breakfast, the butter oozing yellowly, like pus.

'Would you excuse me for a moment?' she said, and hurried out of the room. She reached the ladies' lavatory just in time. She sank to her knees beside the toilet bowl; the close odour of spent urine brought her stomach contents rushing upwards in a hot pale stream. She stifled a sob. The Mauriacs were strange people, almost as strange as Zhanna herself, and she didn't like them. She had been stupid to expect their sympathy. The thought of them waiting for her just along the corridor made her heart flutter inside her chest like a panicked bird.

She stood at the basin and rinsed out her mouth, splashing water on her burning face. When she returned to the classroom she found the Mauriacs standing exactly as she had left them. It was as if they had gone into suspended animation as soon as her back was turned, snapping back into life only when she was actually present to see them. She realised that Zhanna resembled both of them and neither, combining their least attractive features in a puddingy amalgam of the monstrous. She wondered if her parents loved their daughter, if it was possible to love a child who seemed as unaware of herself as she was of others.

She wondered if they ever wished she didn't exist.

'I'm sorry about that,' she said. The two Mauriacs stared back at her expectantly. 'As I was saying, it's not that Zhanna can't do her lessons. It's more that she doesn't mix much with the other children.' She folded her arms across her belly and gripped her sides. She wondered what would happen if she fainted.

'Why would Zhanna want to mix with the other children?' said Dunia Mauriac. Her voice seemed loaded with a sour disdain. 'Zhanna isn't like other children, or hadn't you noticed? Other children bore her stupid. She prefers to discuss her music with Marielena.'

Marielena. Mila seized on the name triumphantly. *That's the au pair.*

'Well, that's fine then,' Mila said. The inside of her mouth felt painfully dry. 'Just so long as you think she's happy. That's the main thing.'

The encounter had drained her of all energy. She managed to escort the Mauriacs back along the corridor to the main entrance and then she went in search of Varvara Pilnyak. She was in the staff room, drinking coffee and catching up on her marking.

'I'm feeling like hell,' Mila said. 'Would you be able to take my afternoon classes if I go home?'

Varya, who had a free period, agreed at once. Varya was forty-five and lived alone. She'd had an abortion when she was eighteen, the unsavoury side-effect of a fortnight at the Black Sea resort of Sochi, a holiday Varya described as two straight weeks of accidental sex and intentional mayhem. When Mila asked if she regretted the abortion, Varya said no.

By the time her husband Niklas arrived home that evening Mila had a raging headache. She didn't feel hungry but she knew she must eat, for the baby's sake. She warmed some leftover chicken broth in a saucepan and added some vegetables. The smell of the soup against the metal pan made her feel queasy.

'I can't stand that Mauriac child,' Mila said once they were seated. 'She should be in special needs.' She pushed away her half-eaten soup and covered her face with her hands. She'd hoped that telling Niklas how she felt would help to disperse her anxiety but it had not.

'Is she interfering with the rest of the class?' Niklas asked. 'If she is then you must speak to the head. You shouldn't be made to take on extra work.' He carried on eating his supper, his spoon rising and falling in the bowl like a mechanized tool. Mila thought with irritation of Zhanna's immaculate exercise books, the dense, crabbed hand that made her assignments look as if they had been completed in a foreign language.

The girl couldn't seem to master joined-up writing but so far Mila had been unable to find so much as a single spelling mistake.

'She's not behind, so I can't say anything. I don't want people thinking I can't do my job.' She rested her cheek against the polished surface of the table. Its smoothness seemed to block the pain in her head, at least for the moment. 'I'm going to bed,' she said. 'I'm exhausted.'

'I don't want you getting upset,' Niklas said. 'Remember what the doctor said?'

'I'm not upset, I'm just tired.'

The doctor had told her repeatedly that she needed to relax, that her anxiety was becoming part of the problem. She had not exactly accused Mila of sabotaging her own pregnancy, but Mila thought she had come pretty close.

Stop fretting about the baby. The baby will look after itself if you leave it alone.

The doctor kept leafing through Mila's records, her striped green smock stretched tight over breasts the size of cow udders. Dr Beck had four children, two of them grown already and attending medical school. Mila thought she could afford to relax. She tried to imagine a future in which her visits to Rosa Beck's surgery were part of her past.

'I'll bring you a cup of tea,' Niklas said. He reached for her hand. Mila tensed.

'I don't want tea,' she said. 'I think I'll just read for a bit.'

'Well, let me know if you need anything.' He brushed her cheek with the back of his hand. His skin was rough, corroded by the repeated actions of turpentine and masonry dust. Niklas was doing overtime on the con- struction sites, ostensibly so there would be money for when the baby came. He hadn't been out on the town in more than six months. He insisted he didn't miss it, but sometimes Mila wished he would just go. Not just out with his comrades and cohorts, but completely away.

Perhaps if she were left in peace her child would survive. An image rose in her mind of Zhanna Mauriac, coming down the school steps one at a time, seemingly oblivious to the sniggers and catcalls that followed her progress. *She's a tough little beast*, Mila thought. *I wonder what keeps her going.* A child no one wanted, yet so obstinately insisting on being there. She read three pages of *The Kreutzer Sonata* before falling into a fitful sleep. She kept dreaming that the curtains were open and that people were staring in at her from outside. When she woke the next morning she felt more tired than she had been when she went to bed.

At assembly the headmistress told the children she had a surprise for them: a former pupil of St Saviour's would be coming to pay them a visit and give a special concert.

'She's the pianist Naomie Walmer. Some of you may have seen her name recently in the newspapers. We're very proud she was once a member of our school.'

The children, prompted by Varvara Pilnyak, started to clap. Mila saw to her amazement that Zhanna Mauriac was clapping too. It was the first sign of animation she had ever shown, although Mila could not believe she had even the faintest notion of what she was clapping for. She closed her eyes, overcome by a sudden vertigo, the sense that her insides had become the world and that if she didn't climb out of them soon she would be lost forever.

She had more or less stopped listening to music after her first miscarriage, but she remembered hearing Naomie Walmer on the radio once, playing the barcarolle from *The Seasons* by Tchaikovsky. The announcer had referred to her as a child prodigy.

Cecilia, Mila thought restlessly. *The patron saint of music and divination.*

The edge of the wooden seat was digging into her back. She didn't know she had fallen asleep until one of the other teachers nudged her awake.

The following morning she and Niklas went to the clinic for her five-month check-up. When the scan technician asked if they wanted to know the child's sex Niklas looked uncertain but Mila answered yes almost at once.

'It's a girl,' said the technician. She used a pencil to point at the murky little screen, indicating the baby's heart and lungs, the bunched-together knees, the heartbreaking curve of her spine. Mila was not surprised by any of it. She had felt her child's presence for weeks now. The baby's sex she had known all along.

Elisabeth, Mila said silently. *Elisabeth Cecilia Sayer.*

She had not discussed the baby's name with Niklas yet. It didn't feel safe. The technician was still talking but Mila found it difficult to focus on what she was saying. She kept her eyes fixed on the monitor, on the flickering point of light that said Elisabeth was really there and really alive.

'Are you OK, Mimi?' Niklas said. He was standing very still, and Mila had the sense that he was holding his breath, even though normally Niklas never seemed to worry about anything. He had always insisted that once her body was ready things would work out. *Perhaps he's right,* Mila thought. Niklas stroked her hair and asked the scan technician if everything happening inside Mila was happening normally. The technician nodded her head emphatically and then said yes.

'There's really nothing to feel anxious about, Mr Sayer. At this stage you should both start thinking of this as just an ordinary pregnancy.'

She asked Mila about her morning sickness and Mila said it was very much better. There were questions she wanted to ask but she held them back. When the only question that mattered could not be answered with absolute certainty, what was the point of asking anything else?

The first miscarriage had happened just ten days after Dr Beck confirmed that Mila was pregnant. She still grieved for the child, but secretly, as if admitting that it had ever existed was a source of shame. Her second failure had happened at eighteen weeks. Niklas had come home from work to find her curled up on the bathroom floor covered in blood. She had lain there for what seemed hours, terrified that she was bleeding to death and that her half-formed baby was dragging itself towards her across the tiles.

That child still haunted her like a revenant. She couldn't help believing she had let it down.

This third child had hung on inside her for twenty weeks. Everyone insisted it was third time lucky.

She had lunch with Niklas in a café near the clinic and was back at school in time for the junior book club. They were reading Friedebert Tuglas's *The Little Witch*. The children sat in a circle on the floor while Mila read aloud and asked the children questions. Zhanna Mauriac sat slumped forward with her legs apart and her head lolling in a manner Mila found faintly obscene. She could not rid herself of the thought that Zhanna was staring at her swollen belly.

She wants to take my baby, Mila thought. *I know I must be crazy to think that but I know it's true.*

Varya had told her that the Mauriacs were moving abroad, that Dunia Mauriac had landed a post at some foreign university. Mila hoped the move would happen soon. She felt certain that if they were gone before Elisabeth was born then everything would be all right.

That night she dreamed she was sitting up in bed in what she thought was her bedroom but turned out to be a hospital. The ward was filled with the sounds of people sleeping. Their snuffles and groans were frightening in the darkness. There was someone close by, perhaps a nurse. The nurse pressed a button in the side of her head and a light came on.

'We can't have you nodding off,' she said. 'Not when it's time for her feed.'

Mila recognised the voice of Dr Beck.

That's not the real doctor, she thought. *It's a copy*. Her bulky body loomed beside the bed. A wicker basket stood nearby on a metal trolley.

'Are you ready?' said Dr Beck. She tugged at Mila's nightgown, exposing a breast. Mila tried to ignore what was being done to her because she knew she needed to concentrate on the basket. Dr Beck kept forcing her back against the stack of pillows.

'There's nothing to be afraid of,' she said. 'Just try and relax.'

She turned aside. The pale rounds of her fat cheeks gleamed in the half-light as she leaned over the basket and reached inside. She lifted out a squirming bundle and held it towards her. Mila felt her terror rising. She knew her baby had been taken away and replaced with a monster.

The thing in the doctor's arms was white and naked like a grub. It opened its mouth in a blank wide scream and Mila saw it meant to close upon her breast. She tugged at the blankets in an attempt to cover herself but the blankets were gone and so was her nightgown. The creature thrusted towards her, swivelling its bulging head on its fat white neck.

'Maggoty,' said Dr Beck brightly. 'This is one hungry little elephant.'

Mila's eyes filled with tears. She found that she could no longer move, that she was attached to the bed somehow. In the instant before she woke she realised the thing in the doctor's arms was Zhanna Mauriac.

She lay there in the darkness, heart pounding. Her face was wet with tears, but she couldn't get away from the thought that they were not real tears, they had strayed over from the dream, which meant that at least part of the dream must really have happened.

She shuddered. She drew her arms across her belly and breasts and found she was naked. She could not remember taking off her clothes. An image came to her of the fat white doctor, tugging at her nightgown, hot hands groping.

It was three o'clock in the morning, always the worst time. Niklas lay unconscious and faintly snoring at her side. It came to her that Zhanna was out there somewhere, that she was responsible for her nightmare, that she had made it happen.

Why, though? Mila thought. *Why would she do that?* The answer came back at once: *Because she's jealous. She wants the whole world to be as ugly and awful as she is.*

She switched on the radio on the bedside cabinet, using headphones so as not to wake Niklas. The Home Service came on, a concert featuring the pianist Maria Yudina. Yudina had made radio broadcasts from Moscow throughout the war. Mila didn't believe in God, not really, but she thought she could believe in St Cecilia. She listened to Yudina playing

Bach's Chromatic Fantasia and tried to imagine what it had been like, recording Bach's music in a tiny basement studio while German soldiers poured over the border in a dull grey flood. *It's what St Cecilia would have done*, Mila thought. She could almost believe it had been St Cecilia herself who had given Yudina the strength to stand up to whatever the world and its tyrants happened to throw at her.

The thought calmed her and she was soon asleep again. When she woke the next morning the headphones lay beside her on the pillow, chattering out the news in tinny voices. She supposed they must have come adrift in the night, but when she asked Niklas if he had heard anything he said no.

Naomie Walmer's visit was the lead item on all the local news programmes. A news team came to the school and made a short film that showed Naomie Walmer arriving at the school gates in a black Trabant. After that the photographers had to go away because the headmistress hadn't wanted them filming inside the school. The seniors had decorated the lobby as part of their term project. There were pictures of Naomie Walmer on stage at concert halls all over Europe, images from her album covers, short essays on the life of Chopin or Medtner or Naomie herself. There was a photo of her as a junior at St Saviour's, sitting on the floor of the sports hall at morning assembly, a wafer-thin, nervous-looking child with an appealing smile.

The headmistress made a little speech, welcoming Naomie back to the school and to the new assembly hall, which hadn't yet been built when she was there. Afterwards, Naomie came onstage and played Chopin's Opus 34 Waltz in A Minor. She was wearing a shift dress in plain blue cotton and Mila couldn't help noticing the way it showed off her arms, graceful and white, smooth and polished-looking as the arms of a porcelain ballerina. Her hair was fine and curly and amazingly fair. It stood out around her head like a corona. Mila had expected her to play something light and cheerful but the waltz was almost painfully slow. The children sat and listened in what felt to Mila like an uneasy silence. One of the senior boys, a shy child called Stefan Reisz, who was president of the school chess club, started to cry. The tears on his cheeks looked sticky, like melting sugar.

Faintly and for the first time, Mila felt Elisabeth kick.

This can't be real, Mila thought. She wrapped her arms around her belly, wanting to seal the moment in with her forever. She could still hear the music, the long meandering coda that had always seemed to her like the sounds of someone talking in their sleep.

She had been able to play the piece by heart once. Hearing Naomie Walmer made her realise all over again how fruitless her efforts had been but the difference was that this time she didn't care. She shut her eyes. She could feel a presence in the room, a compassionate, all-knowing soul that was as old as time. *Cecilia*, she thought. *Cecilia, in the body of Naomie. She came to me after all. But it was never me she wanted to speak to, it was Elisabeth*. She thought she might faint with happiness and terror.

After what seemed a long time, the music stopped. Some of the other teachers started to clap.

'I'm sure you'll all agree that was very wonderful,' said the headmistress. 'It's not often we have such magic in our midst.'

Magic, Mila thought. *That's what this is*.

The children filed out of the hall, and the headmistress whisked Naomie Walmer off to the staff room. It had been arranged that she would spend some time with each class in turn. The children were restless, high on the break in routine. Mila handed out drawing paper and a variety of crayons and told them to make thank you cards for Naomie. There was a lot of swapping of seats and excited noise.

Only Zhanna Mauriac remained quiet. She sat hunched over her desk, scribbling intently with a plain lead pencil. When Mila passed by her on the way to the stationery cupboard she saw her paper was covered in musical notation.

It was the first thirty bars of Chopin's Opus 34 number 2.

'What are you doing, Zhanna?' Mila said. 'We're supposed to be making cards.' She snatched at the paper, wanting to get a closer look at it. Zhanna Mauriac pulled it away with a little grunt. The corner of the paper tore off in her hand. The girl at the next desk looked across and stifled a giggle.

The little freak, Mila thought. *How did she do that?* Zhanna Mauriac gazed up at her, open-mouthed. Her eyes wet and brown, like mud puddles. Mila suddenly realised she was crying.

'Don't get yourself in a state,' she said. 'I'll fetch you a fresh piece.' She turned away, for some reason terrified that Zhanna Mauriac was about to start screaming.

At that moment there was a knock at the door.

'Hello everyone,' said the headmistress. 'I've brought someone to see you. I hope Mrs Sayer doesn't mind us interrupting her lesson.'

The children whispered and fidgeted as Naomie Walmer came to sit in a chair at the head of the class. The girls in the front row sighed, as if in the presence of majesty.

'You won't remember Naomie from when she was at school here,' said the headmistress. 'She started playing the piano before you were born.'

Naomie Walmer stayed and answered questions for the rest of the lesson. At first it was only the more talkative children that would speak to her, but by the end they were all doing it, shooting their hands up and talking over each other in the hurry to take their turn. Mila had to tell them twice to simmer down.

Zhanna Mauriac stared blankly into space, the torn piece of drawing paper discarded on the desk in front of her. From time to time her lips twitched. When the bell went she got straight to her feet, stumbling after the others in her shapeless dress.

'The Elephant Girl's coming to get us,' said Simona Sandowska, a pouting beauty with wavy auburn hair and the beginnings of breasts. 'Let's run.'

They poured out of the room and down the corridor in a noisy stampede. Mila was left alone with Naomie Walmer.

'I'm sorry about that,' Mila said. 'They're a little on the boisterous side today.'

'You mustn't apologise,' said Naomie Walmer. 'I thought they were fantastic.' She stepped forward and took Mila's hand. 'Thank you so much for having me here. It's brought back so many memories.'

'Good ones I hope.'

'Oh yes. I loved being at school.' Close to, she still looked very young, hardly more than a child herself. And yet her hands, Mila could feel, were strong as a farm worker's, and there was a quality of separateness about her that Mila found almost frightening. It was as if she could sense the music curled inside Naomie Walmer, the way Elisabeth was curled inside herself.

'When's it due?' she said. She glanced down at Mila's belly and smiled.

'Not so long now,' Mila said. 'Just over nine weeks.'

'You must be very excited.'

'Yes,' Mila said. 'I am.'

She realised it was the first time anyone had spoken about her pregnancy so openly. People were afraid of upsetting her, of saying the wrong thing. Even Niklas had stopped trying to communicate with her on anything more than a practical day-to-day level. She knew this was her fault, just as she knew Niklas still loved her. But Naomie Walmer's innocent remarks seemed to open up the world to her.

Her words were like a blessing, like a gift. They made it possible for her to believe that Elisabeth was really here and really coming.

She showed Naomie Walmer the way back to the staff room then went out of the side door and on to the playground. It was a marvellously bright October day. The sky was stretched tightly above the rooftops like a swathe of blue cloth. Children chased each other across the tarmac or sat together in groups beneath the trees. There was no sign of the Elephant Girl and for the first time ever when she thought about Zhanna Mauriac, Mila felt a twinge of remorse.

If only Elisabeth can be all right I'll find the courage to start from the beginning again with Zhanna.

Courage? The word puzzled her until she realised it was true. She had never hated Zhanna, she had been afraid of her. Afraid she could harm Elisabeth by her very existence. She made her way back inside, meaning to go in search of Zhanna and bring her outside into the sunshine.

Suddenly she became aware that she could hear music. Somebody was playing the piano. Mila followed the sound along the corridor and right up to the closed double doors of the school assembly hall.

She pushed the doors open, suddenly nervous. The tall windows along the side mirrored themselves in pools of light across the parquet floor. Zhanna Mauriac was seated at the piano.

She was playing a waltz by Chopin, not the slow A Minor but its partner, the much faster Opus 34 in A Flat. Her stubby fingers flew across the keys, the knuckles bunched and raised, hands crouched above the keyboard like fat spiders. She played effortlessly, as if the very notion of the piano was something that had been invented for her own amusement. Her mastery of the instrument seemed complete.

Her clay face wore the same blank expression as always.

Mila marched towards her, her shoes skidding on the polished wood. As she approached the stage, Zhanna finished playing and stood up from the bench.

'Fryderyck Chopin was born near Warsaw on March 1st, 1810,' she said. 'His compositions make extensive use of Polish dance rhythms such as the polonaise and the mazurka. People say he invented the nocturne, but the nocturne was actually invented by John Field.'

Her voice had a gravelly quality, like that of a very old woman. She slowly put out a hand to touch Mila's belly.

'Your baby likes music already, I can tell,' she said. 'Your baby will be just like me.'

Mila slapped Zhanna hard across the face. The slap made a cracking report, like a gunshot, and for a second Mila saw the imprint of her fingers outlined in red across the girl's plump cheek.

'How dare you,' she said in a whisper. 'That's a lie.'

Then she felt herself begin to bleed.

6.

I ARRIVED IN SALISBURY JUST in time to miss the Exeter train.
I read Ewa Chaplin's 'The Elephant Girl' while I waited for the
next one, a mean, dark little story that nonetheless contained stark
elements of truth – more truth, perhaps, than some readers would be
prepared to countenance, especially since it was difficult to determine
where the author's sympathies precisely lay.

The introduction to Chaplin's collection – by a Polish academic
and specialist in post-war Eastern European literature named Krystina
Lodz – explained that Ewa Chaplin had been a gifted student, that
she had always cherished ambitions to be a writer and that she was
supported in her aspirations by the symbolist poet and essayist Delilah
Gopnik, whose classes the young Ewa had attended at Krakow
University.

The war, and her exile in London, had put an end to her studies:
*In common with many Jewish and dissident intellectuals who fled
to Great Britain and the United States following Hitler's accession to
power, Ewa Chaplin found herself in a country and a situation in which
her former dreams for her life – her intellect, her talent – were met with
incomprehension and indifference. Public opinion tacitly stated that in
the case of refugees like Chaplin, it was enough that they had escaped
the Nazi atrocities. Further than that, they were simply foreigners, and*

there on licence. The idea that a young female Polish Jew might have expectations for her life in her new country that extended beyond survival — that she might even criticise and make demands upon the society that had opened to embrace her — would not have been met kindly by her would-be saviours, to say the least.

Lodz described Ewa Chaplin's first months and years in London as being hard and isolated, stating further that she never gave up on the dream of being a writer, even after she found a measure of success and recognition as what Lodz dubbed a textile artist. Lodz made no mention of dolls. She seemed to shy away from the idea that dolls could be called art even, though she was happy to admit that the works Ewa created bore much in common with the prickly, often uncomfortable tone of the stories she continued to write until the end of her life.

Ewa Chaplin's view of the fairy tale is in no way escapist, Lodz wrote. *And yet neither do her stories adhere to the strict moralities imposed by earlier practitioners, most notably the Grimm brothers. Chaplin's tales speak of cruel reversals and secret triumphs in an unpredictable world. These tales thrill even as they terrify, because we sense instinctively that they could happen to anyone. Even to us.*

Elegantly put, I conceded, except that Ewa Chaplin's tales really did seem to be happening to me, making their presence felt in ways I found if not terrifying — a story was only a story, after all — then at least unnerving. The little girl in 'The Elephant Girl', for example — she was Jane Clarence to the life, only of course she couldn't be. Ewa Chaplin had died before Jane was born.

I dismissed the thought, chiding myself for reading too much reality into what was self-evidently a work of fiction. I got up from my bench and walked the length of the platform, hoping I might find somewhere to buy a sandwich or even a packet of crisps, but the ticket hall and the refreshment kiosk were both closed. My train was still not due for half an hour, and apart from myself the station seemed to be deserted. I became aware of an uncommon silence, the preternatural quiet of a hot midday. I returned to my bench, took the half-finished letter to Bramber from my holdall and added a detailed description of my surroundings: the weeds sprouting between the flagstones, the old stationmaster's house with its red window boxes, the parched scrap of yellow lawn to the side.

Once again I made no mention of where I was. In her last letter, Bramber had mentioned a recent illness, the resulting exhaustion, the impossibility of travel. As if she were in a fairy tale herself, I mused, a sleeping beauty. But if there were dragons to be slain, their identity was not so easy to determine.

Could lack of confidence be described as a dragon? Could low self-esteem? I smiled to myself. This was the stuff of self-help books. I had no right to presume. Through the course of her letters, Bramber had told me a great deal about her day-to-day life. I had come to know the occupants of West Edge House as if they were my own friends and neighbours. About her arrival in this institution though – her reason for being there – I knew remarkably little.

I heard Clarence's voice inside my head – *why don't you ask her then, seeing as you're so close?* – but shrugged it aside. Such an invasion of Bramber's privacy would be monstrous. And yet, for all that I now chose to think of West Edge House as a kind of sanctuary, a sanatorium along the lines of those that had once flourished throughout the spa towns of Europe, I could not deny that the woman I thought of as my soul mate was in a mental hospital.

What traitors words are, sometimes. What did it matter how the place might be designated, when my Bramber was sad, suffering, lost, as Ewa Chaplin had been lost, cut off from one existence and thrust wantonly into another, the reality of her life laid waste, even as a harsher, less trustworthy reality arose to replace it?

A great breach, a severing of past from present with no hope of return. Was it any wonder that Bramber found solace in studying her spiritual twin, in assimilating the details of her troubled life, in retracing her hesitant steps across a war-torn landscape?

Did Bramber look at Ewa Chaplin, and see herself? The idea made sense, and even if it did not explain everything, it explained much. The details – the *explanation* – could surely wait. We had a lifetime to get to know one another, after all.

As if in response to my lightening of mood, the station platform began to fill up with other passengers. When the train finally arrived, it was one of the old kind, with a through corridor and pull-down windows. I had not realised such trains still existed. I found a compartment that was not too full and managed to bag a window seat.

The train stopped at every station along the route: Wimborne, Yeovil, Axminster, Honiton, Clay. The countryside around Wade had been flat and expansive, but west of Yeovil the landscape became increasingly hilly. I glimpsed farmsteads and crossroads, clusters of whitewashed cottages, their gardens running down to the railway tracks. In the gardens, washing flapped brightly from rotary dryers, dismembered motorbikes glowed sullenly in the heat. As the train pulled away from Clay Station, I caught sight of the tower of St

Benedict's Church, the place, or so *Coastage's English Almanac* reliably informed me, where the noted archaeologist and curator Hermione Thorncoatts was buried. *Coastage's* described St Benedict's as 'a fine example of Norman architecture' and well worth a visit. I had originally planned to stop off in Clay and spend a night there, but although I searched the guide books and online listings exhaustively I had been unable to find any suitable accommodation.

Now that I saw the village, straggling out of sight between the trees, I felt glad to be passing through without stopping. From the train at least, Clay seemed to be a dingy, secretive place, its huddle of low-lying houses most likely chilly and plagued with condensation in winter. I did not want a repetition of my experiences in Wade.

I arrived in Exeter half an hour later. I made straight for the taxi rank, and asked the driver to take me to the White Hart Hotel, on South Street. *Coastage's* highlighted the White Hart as one of the oldest inns in the city, which also had the benefit of being close to the centre.

My room was on the second floor, under the eaves. There were stripped oak beams and a marble wash stand, a low door giving access to an en suite toilet and shower. The air was redolent with the scents of wax furniture polish and clean bed linen, and when I looked out of the window I saw that the room overlooked an inner courtyard, paved with cobblestones and planted with roses. A young couple were down there, sitting at a wrought-iron table sipping glasses of wine. I decided I would take a shower immediately, and emerged feeling re-energised and in a good frame of mind.

Wade had been a mistake but that was behind me now. This was a different day and Exeter – larger, more sophisticated, closer to my goal – was a different proposition. The doubts that had begun to assail me on the platform at Salisbury – that it was not just Wade that had been a mistake, but the entire venture – receded completely. I was back in the saddle.

EXETER IS TWINNED WITH Bad Homburg, a medium-sized German spa town to the south of Frankfurt. Its town hall is of Gothic proportions, its elegant, tree-lined boulevards overlooked by the former houses of the manufacturers and merchants to whom the town owed its fortune. When I visited the town – the same year I first took up my post at Clark Cannings, this was – I found it more bustling than I had expected, more commercial, yet aside from this fleeting impression of busyness, my memories of Bad Homburg itself remain vague. It was not the architecture I had come to admire, but the museum.

Since travelling to Bad Homburg those many years ago, I have made visits to all the major European toy museums, and for my thirty-fifth birthday I treated myself to a week's holiday in Montreal, so I could attend the World Symposium on Dolls and Automata, which that year boasted several notable guest speakers I was eager to hear. I kept journals of all my trips abroad, documenting my discoveries and collating information. I made many valuable acquaintances and more than a handful of friends. All seemed to agree that the Museum of Childhood in Bad Homburg was in a class of its own.

It is not just the size and extent of Doris Schaefer's collection that makes it remarkable, but her eye for quality. 'I am drawn to certain dolls not by the price they might command, but by their personality,'

Schaefer writes in *A Short History of Wonderland*. 'When I first began collecting, I had no notion of dolls as objects of monetary value. I saw them as beautiful little people with minds and stories and a history that was entirely their own. I felt an intense and painful longing to understand their world.'

In many cases, the dolls Schaefer acquired turned out to be both rare and valuable. A number of the dolls on display in the Museum of Childhood are thought to be the sole surviving examples of their lines.

While I was in Bad Homburg I bought a set of slides with accompanying hand projector that illustrated a selection of the museum's highlights. I had been back to Germany several times since – once to the Kramergalerie in Berlin, and twice to the famous Museum of Toymaking in Nuremberg – but I had never returned to Bad Homburg, or to the Museum of Childhood. I think perhaps I was afraid to – afraid that in repeating the experience I ran the risk of diluting my memories. But when I learned from an article in *Doll Collector* magazine that a cross-section of Doris Schaefer's collection was to go on loan to the Royal Albert Memorial Museum in Bad Homburg's twin town of Exeter I felt no such reservations.

A fortnight prior to my journey west, I had telephoned the Royal Albert Museum to make sure that the dolls would be on display throughout the period of my visit, and to check the museum's opening times. They confirmed that the show would still be running, and also sent me a leaflet with photographs and details of some of the exhibits – a Leinsdorff 'Helene', a Didier Montaigne 'Marie Celeste' and a rare Bertram & Tovey 'Alison' doll that had featured in one of my slides. It would be good to see these dolls again – the 'Alison' especially – but what I was counting on most of all was that the exhibition might include one of the Museum of Childhood's three Ewa Chaplins.

I was hoping I might be able to photograph the doll, or purchase a postcard of it, if such postcards were available, as a token I might offer to Bramber at our first meeting.

By the time I left the hotel it was four o'clock. The museum would be closing at five, but it was only a short walk from South Street to Queen Street and I wanted to go and see the Schaefer dolls right away. There would be time for a longer visit the following day, I told myself. Besides, I could use the fresh air.

Exeter was badly bombed during the war, the damage consolidated by the brutally short-sighted town planning of the 1950s. Of the buildings on South Street, only the White Hart itself and the cluster of houses and commercial premises in its immediate environs had escaped further injury. The rest of the street was a messy amalgam of fifties infill and seventies red brick. The soulless, concrete canyon that constituted the high street had fared no better. It was as if a great fist had descended from the sky, smashing the heart of the city into dusty oblivion.

The museum at least had emerged unscathed, an impressive Victorian edifice which, as the leaflet informed me, had recently been internally refurbished and extended. The entrance foyer was pleasantly cool. Laminated arrows signposted me towards something called the Arundel Collection, together with an exhibition of work by the South West England Society of Goldsmiths. There were also signs for a gift shop and café. I ignored these various temptations and proceeded upstairs.

A broad, carpeted staircase led to a first-floor landing hung with eighteenth-century portraits and still-life paintings in glowing oils. There was nobody about, presumably because it was so close to closing time.

The Schaefer dolls were being shown in the Albert Galleries, a series of interlinked spaces that occupied most of the first floor exhibition area. At the entrance to the galleries was a display of information, including a photograph of Doris Schaefer on the steps of the Museum of Childhood in Bad Homburg, the same image that formed the back cover illustration of *A Short History of Wonderland*. I studied it for a moment before passing through into the exhibition space. A small distance in front of me, a woman in jeans and a hooded sweatshirt was standing motionless in front of one of the cabinets. I hung back close to the entrance, scanning the contents of the cabinet closest to me: seven Tremmler dolls in Bavarian costume, each named for a day of the week. When I looked up again the woman was gone. I moved across to where she'd been standing, curious to see which of the exhibits had so absorbed her attention.

It sounds fanciful to say it, I know, but I wasn't in the least surprised to find it was a Chaplin.

The doll before me had not been on display when I visited Bad Homburg, I felt almost certain – she may have been on loan elsewhere – but I recognised her at once, not just from the photographs in Artur Zukerman's portfolio but also – inescapably – from my reading of 'Amber Furness' just a few hours before. She had long red hair and leaf-green eyes. Her black lace gloves were exquisitely fashioned, her plaid woollen cloak cunningly fastened with a golden pin-brooch in the shape of a beetle. A label at her feet identified her simply as 'Artist', and included the additional information that the companion-doll to 'Artist', 'Philosopher', was part of a private collection in Milan. The whereabouts of a third doll belonging to the set and known as 'Magister' were currently unknown.

The artist, and the magician. The maiden, and the dwarf. Bramber had never suggested that we trade photographs, nor any written information pertaining to personal appearance. I could only surmise that her dislike of the telephone extended to a similar distrust of the camera, and all other recording devices, be they visual or auditory. I had not pressed her on this – to demand that she reveal herself would be to invite her to demand the same of me. What would she think of me then: her manikin, her magister, her *dwarf*?

I had embarked upon my journey westwards in the belief that the mutual trust and affection and – yes – love that had arisen between us would be enough to overcome all obstacles. But what if I were deluding myself? What if Bramber recoiled from me in disgust or, worse still, indifference? This was a fear I had never dared voice, not even to myself.

Chaplin's 'Artist' doll, in her haughty innocence, seemed now to chide me for my own foolishness and hubris, in ascribing to my mission even the slimmest chance of success.

And yet I did still have faith, in spite of everything. If 'Artist' was a chastening reminder of my limitations, so was she also a talisman – a symbol of all Bramber and I had in common, and of my desire not only to be with her but to set her free.

The heavy yellow light of late afternoon suffused the room, coating it and its precious accoutrements in a layer of gold varnish. I reached forward, resting the outstretched tips of my fingers against the glass of 'Artist's' cabinet. 'Artist' stared back at me in defiance, or was it collusion? It seemed that she was not scorning me so much as daring me: *make it happen*.

Our reverie was interrupted by the sound of footsteps: a bulky security guard, peering in through the open doorway. The thought police, 'Artist' murmured, right on cue. I started back from the cabinet in guilty surprise.

'Good evening, sir,' said the guard. 'Apologies if I startled you. Just a reminder that we'll be closing in a couple of minutes.'

I glanced at my watch: almost five.

'I'm sorry,' I said. 'I lost track of the time. I'm just leaving.'

'Right you are, sir.'

He turned away from me and walked off along the first floor landing. By the time I crossed to where he'd been standing, he was out of sight.

Dear Andrew,

I once asked Helen how old she was when she first realised she
wanted to be an actor and she said she wasn't sure.

'I remember back when we were living in Wimbledon I was
in the school play of *Alice in Wonderland*. There were these three
other girls all squabbling about who was going to play Alice but I
always knew I wanted to be the Red Queen, so I could shout "off
with their heads".' She laughed. 'You can do anything you like on
stage and no one can stop you.'

A dreamy look came into her eyes, as if she were imagining what
it would be like, to see her name up in lights on a theatre hoarding
or spread across a cinema screen. For a moment I felt so jealous. Not
of her, but of how well she knew herself. I think a part of me was
shocked, that she could own up to wanting something that much.

If people know you want something it makes it easier for them
to take it away from you.

It made me think of my mother, sweeping up the broken
glass, with her mouth in a line and saying Bramber, go to your
room, don't you have homework to do? Even though it was the
Christmas holiday and there was no homework.

My mother wanted to be famous, like Helen did, and Ewa Chaplin's mother. Serena had a brilliant career in front of her, everyone said so, but then she was caught in the fire and her plans turned to dust. In just a couple of minutes, her whole life was changed.

Serena was always disappointed that Ewa didn't care about music the way she did. She left the family when Ewa was eight and went home to Berlin. It was Ewa's father Jonas who insisted that Ewa leave Poland. He said it wasn't safe for her, she was half-Jewish, she should go to London. He knew someone there – an old friend from his army days. Ewa stepped off a train at Victoria Station sometime in the autumn of 1938. Her only luggage was a small black suitcase, which contained some items of clothing and her story manuscripts, together with Jonas's life savings in old gold zlotys. Jonas had coated the coins in oil to hide their shine.

The reason I'm in West Edge House is because I killed someone. Dr Leslie says that's not true, that I should stop thinking that, but he's just being kind. Somebody is dead because of me, and that's the same thing, really, isn't it?

I know I should have told you sooner but I didn't know how. If you don't want to write to me any more I'll understand completely.

Your friend,

Bramber

7 ·

I LEARNED A LOT FROM Ursula, but she could not teach me everything. She knew about clothes, not dolls.

In the beginning, I attempted only the simplest kinds of patterns, rag dolls made entirely from cloth. As time passed I became more competent and more adventurous. I began examining the dolls I owned to find out how they were made. I was content at first to copy the masters. But in the end, like every artist, I aspired to the creation of work that was truly original.

Most dolls today are made exclusively from vinyl, but before the age of plastic and mass-production, doll-making was an art. Dolls' bodies were hand-made, usually from calico or leather, although there are numerous examples – mainly in museums – of dolls made from wood or wax. Dolls' heads, hands and feet were made from bisque porcelain. Such creatures had weight and substance. Even the least fanciful of children might hold one in their arms and dream it was real.

In time I came to know the premier suppliers – artisan workshops in Germany and Japan, where dolls' heads and eyes and feet were manufactured to order. By the time I graduated from Woolfenden College I had completed a copy of a Gilbert Sweeney 'Rose Marie' that was, with the exception of the age of the materials, all but indistinguishable from the original. Two years on from that, I was beginning to experiment with designs of my own.

Dolls were my life, but I never dreamed they would one day become my living. Clark Cannings specialised in running feasibility studies for fledgling businesses. I tabulated batteries of theoretical sales figures and calculated the potential for growth on a year-on-year basis. The work made use of techniques I had outlined as part of my final-year dissertation, with the significant advantage that I was now being paid. I turned out to be good at my job, and my usefulness to the firm was never in question. Any problems I encountered belonged, as usual, to the social sphere. From the beginning of my final year at Woolfenden onwards I had experienced a secret mounting anxiety at the prospect of returning to the outside world. If school had been bad, what would it be like working in an office?

For the first week or so, things were pretty much as I had expected. My father had worked for an old-fashioned firm of solicitors where, apart from the secretaries, all of the employees were men. Clark Cannings was very different. Most of the twenty staff were under forty and more than half of them were women. The office was open-plan. People chatted to each other throughout the day and drank coffee and ate packed lunches at their desks. Several of the women were in great demand, the men competing constantly for their attention. The banter was for the most part good-natured but there was no escaping the scrutiny of others. It was a situation I was completely unused to coping with.

No open hostility was directed towards me, but I often heard the sound of smothered laughter when I entered the room. Stationery went missing from my desk. One afternoon I returned from my lunch break to find a cartoon cut-out of one of Disney's Seven Dwarfs Sellotaped to my computer screen. I did my best to ignore these insults, focusing instead on the job in hand, which I enjoyed in the same way that some people enjoy solving crossword puzzles or playing chess. As for my work colleagues, I hoped that some new form of entertainment would eventually present itself, or that they would simply become bored with teasing me.

At least no one could accuse me of shirking. I finished assignments quickly, which rewarded my colleagues with considerable savings in both time and effort.

'You're a right little eager beaver, aren't you?' said my line manager, Jeremy Gordon, about a month into my time there. Jeremy was a cherub-faced, rather portly computer programmer in his early thirties who had recently become engaged to one of the other statisticians. He liked to style himself the office clown. I had asked him what might be the easiest way of altering one of my page setups. When he looked at my graph of results he seemed surprised.

'That moron Dominic would have taken twice as long to come up with this lot,' he said. 'Which is why we had to have him fired.'

There was a general outburst of laughter, before one of the others explained that Dominic Siddons had been the operator who had occupied my desk immediately before me, and that he had not in fact been fired, but had left to open a wine bar in Spain.

The atmosphere around me had altered, nonetheless. From that day onward I was known as the Beaver.

I was never one of them, exactly, but I did rise to become a sort of office mascot. They still made fun of me from time to time, but with the difference that this was now done openly rather than behind my back. And for anyone outside the office, jokes about my stature were strictly verboten. Once, when our central heating system broke down, the contracted repair technician made the mistake of calling me a shortarse. There was no real malice in his comment, but coming from an outsider it sounded wrong. He had been with us for most of the day, flirting with the women and ribbing the men. He had an easygoing charm and a clever way with words but after the comment about my height he suddenly found himself working in near-silence.

'Idiot,' said Jeremy Gordon, once the man had left. 'We won't be using him again.'

I felt comfortable at Clark Cannings, because within a relatively short span of time I was allowed to become part of the furniture. No one ever questioned me about my life outside the office – I think most of them assumed I didn't have one. It was Derek Coombs, one of the media reps, who stumbled upon my secret. He was rummaging in my desk looking for Sellotape, and happened to find a copy of *Dolls and Dollmaking* in one of the drawers. I was out of the room at the time, in the lavatory. I was gone for less than five minutes but by the time I returned to the office a small crowd had gathered.

'I've heard of picking on someone your own size, but this wins the race,' quipped Jeremy Gordon. 'Trust the Beaver to like them young.'

Everyone laughed. Derek Coombs replaced the magazine on my desk with a guilty thump. I could see he was blushing.

'I make dolls, that's all,' I said. 'It's sort of a hobby.'

My colleagues seemed to accept my explanation immediately, and with an air of relief. The cap fitted, as they say. Here at last was an explanation for what I was.

'He's like Pinocchio,' said Tanya Blackstaff.

'Geppetto, you mean,' said Jeremy Gordon. 'He would say that though, wouldn't he?'

'These are really beautiful,' said Jacqueline Stephens, who worked as a PA to one of the bosses, Charlie Clark. She had picked up the magazine again, and was holding it open at a photograph of two dolls in the 'Vagabond' series by Margo Cleverley. They wore soft velvet caps and embroidered smocks, their features – the Cleverley series were all one-off creations – were painted delicately in enamel and fired to a vitreous shine. Margo Cleverley had won awards for her enamelling alone, which was artistry of a very high order. It interested me that Jacqueline, who had no specialist knowledge of dolls so far as I knew, had picked them out.

'I don't do enamel work myself. Margo Cleverley has been in the field for twenty-five years. I could make their clothes though, or something like them.'

'My gran had a doll like that,' Jackie said. 'Her name was Queenie.'

'It's those dwarfish little fingers that do it,' said Jeremy. 'Nimble with the needle as well as the brain.'

People had started to drift back to their desks. The incident seemed to be closed. Then Martin Finlay, a junior programmer, asked if I accepted commissions.

'It's for my niece's christening,' he added hastily. 'I wanted to get her something different, you know, something really special.'

His enquiry threw me, I have to admit. I had never thought of selling my dolls, a fact that probably sounds unlikely now, given how things turned out, but that was true, nonetheless. I had made dolls for Ursula, and once, somewhat incongruously, I had given one to my father. To give a gift to someone I cared for and wanted to please was one thing. To hand over one of my beloved creations to strangers, for money, was quite another. Nevertheless, I liked Martin Finlay, who was working at Clark Cannings part-time while he studied for his doctorate. If we hadn't both been so shy we might have been friends.

'What's her name?' I asked him. 'Your niece, I mean?'

'Genevieve,' Martin replied. 'Genevieve Margaret Coxton. But everyone calls her Jennie.'

Jennie's christening was only a month away, which didn't leave me much time. I told Martin Finlay I'd think about it, then spent the remainder of the day and all that evening thinking of nothing else. By the time I went to bed that night, I'd made up my mind to accept his commission.

I was still making replicas really, rather than designing from scratch, and yet the doll I created for Jennie Coxton was more than just a copy. She was based on a Weathercoatts 'Lucinda' but the finishing details and accompanying trousseau were entirely my own. Her feet, hands and face were a set I had recently ordered from a craft studio in Stuttgart – white bisque with just the merest hint of rose. Her gown was of an Empire design: high-waisted, with the underskirt falling an inch below the hem. I made it from a piece of heavy ivory silk that had once formed part of the skirt of an Edwardian wedding dress.

I named the doll Imogen, and became so addicted to working on her that I ended up completing her with a week to spare. I used the time that remained to create a second, identical gown in primrose yellow, with a lace-trimmed silk tote bag to store it in.

I handed the doll over to Martin on the Friday before the christening. Everyone gathered round to inspect my handiwork.

'I can't believe you made this,' Martin said. He flushed bright red. 'I mean, this is incredible.'

Jacqueline Stephens put out her arms for Imogen as if she were a baby.

'She reminds me of Queenie,' she said. 'How can you bear to let her go?'

She lifted the doll high in the air. Imogen's glass eyes flew open: cerulean crystal with a single swirl of indigo trapped at the centre.

'Is she heavy?' said Tanya Blackstaff. 'Can I feel?'

The women passed her between them, stroking her cheek, smoothing her gown. The men looked on in silence, but how they stared.

'I've heard of living out one's fantasies,' mumbled Jeremy. 'But this is ridiculous.'

'How much do I owe you?' asked Martin. Until that moment I had barely considered the matter. We settled on one hundred pounds, which covered the cost of the materials and with a little to spare. The price was ridiculously low, of course, but then I happen to think I owe Martin Finlay a great debt of gratitude. Clarence insists this is a misconception, that true talent will always find its expression in the end, that it is a question of when rather than if. But whatever the whys and wherefores, when I turned up at work the following Monday it was to find Martin Finlay waiting for me on the stairs.

'My aunt would like to order a doll,' he said. 'And a friend of the vicar's wife would like one, too.'

I netted four further orders over the next six months, all from people who happened to encounter Imogen, either at Jennie Coxton's christening or afterwards, at the family home. I knew that something momentous had occurred when I received an order through the post from a Mrs Phillippa Dale, of Dartford, Kent. I had no idea who she was or how she had learned of my existence, and when I asked Martin about her he didn't know, either.

'Some friend of my sister's, probably. Or a friend of a friend.' He glanced again at her letter, written on smooth headed notepaper that bore a trace of expensive scent. 'Your stock seems to be going up, though – she's offering three hundred pounds.'

Mrs Dale explained that she needed the doll to be delivered in less than a month, and hoped the amount named would provide adequate recompense. Spurred on by her enthusiasm, I created for her a dark-haired baby doll named Annelise. To add to the sense of theatre, I arranged to have her delivered by courier in a covered Moses basket.

I received my payment in full, plus a generous tip, by return of post.

By then I had enough orders on my books to keep me busy for months to come.

THE BROUHAHA SURROUNDING THE troll dolls was pure accident. A private collector showed one to a friend, who happened to work as a desk editor at *Crafts* magazine, and things snowballed from there. One minute I was an anonymous amateur, creating dolls in his own time and mainly for his own pleasure. The next I was a 'contemporary maker' being interviewed for *Art Now*.

The article, when they finally sent me the proofs, was entitled 'Little Monsters'.

I wanted to call them and insist they change it but Clarence advised me strongly to leave things as they stood.

'They're journalists, remember,' she said. 'They have to have an angle. The title is provocative but there's no harm in that. People see the word monster and they want to know more.'

Clarence and I first met when *Art Now* hired her to photograph the troll dolls for the article. Clarence was working for the Crafts Council at the time, but she still did bits of freelance photography here and there. She introduced herself as Nadia Clarence, though I soon learned that everyone including her husband called her just Clarence. She was tall and well muscled, with a dark complexion and long and very wavy, black-brown hair.

'I was born in Bristol,' she told me. 'My mother came from Malaga originally. My dad was from Jamaica but I never knew him.'

She spent an hour or so photographing the troll dolls, then asked if I would be willing to take part in an exhibition she was organising for the Crafts Council of work by new craft toymakers and textile artists.

'I think your work is fantastic,' she added. 'Original and striking.'

I was already thinking about going part-time at Clark Cannings, and a year after the 'Little Monsters' article was published I found myself in a position to hand in my notice. I had never dreamed that such a life-change might be possible, but it appeared that at least a proportion of those gallery patrons who prided themselves on their instinct for quality were also willing to put their money where their mouths were. At some point I began to feel embarrassed at my own prices, which was when Clarence took over the business side and became my agent.

'Your dolls will always sell, because they're so personal to you,' she said. 'They communicate a unique vision of the world.'

Clarence has always maintained that it was signing me as her first client that gave her the confidence to go ahead and open her own gallery.

Of course I didn't coin the term 'troll dolls' – I don't even remember where it came from, just that it started being bandied about and then seemed to stick. I don't make that many of them. Indeed you could argue that I don't actually make them at all, that they are accidents of nature.

The first was called Nonie. I spotted her at a house clearance auction in Forest Hill: an exquisite Eduard Marshal, her loveliness concealed beneath a purple nylon peignoir with a faded 'Made in Taiwan' label poking out beneath the hem. I was staring at her in what I hoped was a covert manner, wondering if any of the other bidders might have their eye on her and what she might go for, when Brian Alperin came up behind me and blew my cover.

'She's worthless, mate.' He clapped me hard on the shoulder. 'Just look at that face.'

Brian Alperin owned a thriving antiques business in Wimbledon village but it was the auctions he loved best, the riskier the better. Our paths often crossed and I enjoyed his company, in spite of the fact that he treated my interest in dolls as a mental aberration.

'Nothing you can do with that,' he added. 'Not without making it look like something out of a field hospital in Vietnam.'

Half the doll's hair was off, but that was of lesser consequence. The damage Alperin was referring to was far more serious: a wide, crescent-shaped gouge in her right cheek, running from the corner of one eye to just below the base of the ear. It was impossible to guess at how it had happened, but judging by the depth of the cut it was a miracle the head was still intact.

The facial damage notwithstanding, she had luminescent grey paperweight eyes and refined, hand-moulded features of the utmost delicacy. I knew I had to have her. What I proposed to do with her afterwards I had no idea.

I acquired her for less than a quarter of the price you would normally expect to pay for a Marshal, but as Brian Alperin had suggested she was practically worthless. If anything I had paid too much. Once I got her home I discovered that in addition to the wound on her face she was leaking stuffing from a three-inch gash in her back, a tear that was impossible to close because the material had worn so thin it was almost transparent. Her leather joints were fraying and cracked. She wasn't even good enough for parts. I realised with horror that if I hadn't bought her, some other dealer would have paid a courtesy amount to the seller before smashing open her head to get at her eyes.

I was able to save her arms and legs without too much trouble, though the body I sewed them on to was essentially brand new. I threw away the revolting nylon peignoir and created a new gown for her, a simple yet elegant design based upon a 1920s flapper dress by Fortuny. As Alperin had said, there was nothing I could do about her face. I could have tried repairing the gouge with one of the composite fillers used by ceramics restorers, or I could have sent the head to one of my suppliers in Germany and asked them to attempt a re-firing. Neither procedure seemed worth the risk to me, especially since the chance of it being successful stood at less than fifty-fifty.

In the end I decided to leave her face the way it was. I replaced her hair in its entirety, cutting it high and straight across her forehead in a classic Charleston bob. The glazed patina of her skin was simply stunning: milky and lustrous in the way you only see in the genuine article, and by the time I finished working on her I had grown so accustomed to the scar on her cheek that she would have appeared odd to me without it.

THE WOMAN WHO CAME to interview me for *Art Now* was called Sylvia Chambers. She positioned herself opposite me in the faded green wing chair I had owned since my days at Woolfenden, staring at me relentlessly over the rim of her teacup.

'Most people think of dolls as idealised representations of humanity,' she said. 'Doll-face, living doll, that kind of thing. Your current work seems actively to be in conflict with that ideal. There are those who would argue it contradicts it entirely.' She bent forward to take a biscuit. 'Would you say you do what you do in order to help counteract stereotypical presentations of physical deformity?'

'I don't know about that,' I replied. 'Mostly I would say that I love old dolls. Antique porcelain has a unique quality. It seems a tragedy to waste it.'

Sylvia Chambers scribbled her notes. She wasn't satisfied with my answer, I could tell. 'I don't like to compare dolls with human beings,' I added. 'The two are very different.'

'Would you say dolls were alien?' She had brightened up considerably.

'Not alien exactly, just . . . their own thing.'

She wrote down what I said, humming faintly to herself in what I could only interpret as glee. I had officially fulfilled my remit as a weirdo. *Andrew Garvie sees his creations almost as representatives of an alien race*, was how Sylvia Chambers interpreted my remarks for her article. *His little monsters are an allegory for persecution and alienation in our pressurised and sometimes repressive urban environment.*

As with the title, I did not protest. I felt annoyed by the way my words had been twisted, altered selectively to suit the writer's own agenda. And yet I found I did not entirely disagree with what Chambers had written, either. My dolls were little dissidents, in their way. As human beings they would have faced lives of oppression, everything from run-of-the-mill name-calling to full social exclusion. *And yet they persist*, I told myself. Their very existence was a kind of protest, if not against anything so grand as 'the political consensus' then at least against those bullies and tyrants who saw it as their business to dictate to others – at whatever level – how they should be living their lives.

Yes, I was proud of them. I was proud of the *Art Now* interview, too, though I didn't fully realise it until much later.

THE TROLL DOLLS ALWAYS sell, and it is the children who like them best. I once happened to be at the gallery when a Mr and Mrs Halloran came in with their daughter to select a doll. Mrs Halloran was explaining to Clarence that their daughter had just won a scholarship to attend a prestigious summer school in the United States and they wanted to mark the occasion with a special gift. The Hallorans were both company lawyers, and highly paid. Their daughter Millie was ten years old, her tiny oval face so perfect she could have modelled in advertisements for soap flakes or yoghurt. It was unusual to see a child in the gallery – a contradiction that pained me constantly. Millie Halloran wandered among the displays for at least half an hour, hands clasped behind her back and with an expression in her eyes that was close to rapture.

Finally, she pointed to a doll I had only recently completed, a baby doll with unusual hazel eyes and the face and feet of a Gertrud Klasen 'Poppea'. Klasen had died young, and not many of her designs had surviving examples. Her most famous creation was a poupée modèle named 'Sara', a gamine with cropped hair and a beaded black shift dress that was daringly short, at least for the time. The 'Sara' doll had been a limited edition – only five hundred were ever made. 'Poppea' was one of Klasen's later designs. I had seen two perfect examples, both of them in museums. The doll I purchased – off a market stall in Coventry, of all places – had jagged, brittle stumps in place of hands. In addition to that, the glaze on the upper part of the face had pulled away during firing, leaving a surface with the appearance and texture of orange peel.

I found her new hands, of course, but they were ever so slightly too big for her. I dressed her in a two-piece romper suit of dusky pink velveteen, appliquéd with dozens of sequined butterflies. She was a most unusual and appealing doll, and extremely lifelike. I could understand perfectly why Millie had chosen her.

'I want this one. Please,' she added quickly. Up until that moment the girl's parents had been sitting at the reception desk, drinking their complimentary coffees and making small talk with Clarence's PA. When they saw the doll their daughter had selected, they glanced at one another anxiously, not saying a word. Mrs Halloran put out a hand to stroke 'Poppea's' hair then swiftly withdrew it.

'I think there's something wrong with that one, darling,' she said. 'Why not choose another?'

Millie shook her head. 'I like her,' she said. 'She looks like a little baby but really she's old.'

Clarence reappeared at that point, as I knew she would. She began explaining the troll dolls to the Hallorans, using phrases like 'found artefacts' and 'unique properties' and 'reclaimed antiquities'. The Hallorans seemed reassured. As the father drew out his credit card to complete the purchase, he even made a comment about the superior quality of European porcelain.

'Is it German?' he asked. When Clarence confirmed that it was, he nodded vigorously, as if the 'Poppea' doll had been his preference, all along.

Whenever I create a troll doll, it is like reclaiming a fragment of the past. Old porcelain harbours the light. When complemented by the right glaze, it has a glow that is soft and liquid, tender as flesh. Clarence never questioned the troll dolls, she saw the point of them at once. But then Clarence has Jane.

JANE'S BIRTH WAS BESET by complications. Clarence's labour lasted forty-eight hours. Jane spent the first two weeks of her life in an incubator, and even when she was strong enough to go home, the doctors warned Clarence there might be difficulties later.

What they meant was that Jane might be brain damaged. When Clarence came to my flat for that first photo-shoot, she arrived with

Jane strapped to her back in a canvas sling. Jane seemed large for an infant, flat-faced with pale blue eyes.

'She looks heavy,' I said.

'Getting that way,' Clarence said. 'But she cries her head off if I put her down.'

Clarence talked to me about the shoot, then set up her tripod and backgrounds, all with the baby girl tucked into the space between her shoulder blades. The child seemed to stare at everything and yet register nothing, her eyes the vacant, insipid blue of burnt-out delphiniums. After about twenty minutes she laid her cheek against her mother's back and fell asleep. Clarence simply carried on working. Some years later she told me it had been impossible to leave Jane by herself – or with anyone else – for even a couple of minutes.

'She would scream as if she thought I had died,' Clarence said. 'Even if I just went to the bathroom. It was so frightening. I kept thinking about what they'd said at the hospital, about Jane being brain damaged. I didn't tell the doctors though. I didn't want her being messed around with. I knew they'd only make things worse.'

On the evening we spent together in the pub, Lucan told me that Jane still sometimes slept in their room.

'You must think I'm some sort of monster,' he said. 'Resenting my own child.'

'Have you ever told her how you feel? Clarence, I mean?' I stared into my beer glass and tried not to look at him: the heavy, beautiful hands, the dark blotches of sweat staining his shirt under the arms.

'How can I? It's not her fault. It's not anyone's fault. It would be easier if I wanted to leave, but I don't. I love them.'

What Lucan meant was that he loved Clarence. I love Clarence too, but I have never wanted to sleep with her. The largeness of her makes the thought indecent, somehow. Clarence often wears heavy, bulky clothing that makes her look even larger: fishermen's jerseys and army greatcoats and high-top Doc Martens. I have sometimes wondered what her body might actually be like under all those layers: the musky skin and heavy breasts, the pubic hair as crinkly as the hair on her head. I feel no desire for her, yet the thought of Lucan inside her makes me get hard immediately.

Lucan's hand brushed mine across the table, and for a second I dared to wonder if he was sending me a signal that the evening might end up being about more than two acquaintances having a drink together. The idea was preposterous, of course. Lucan left the pub soon afterwards on some vague pretext, and our brief moment of intimacy was never repeated. The next time I saw him at his and Clarence's flat he seemed embarrassed, as if he had been caught out in an indiscretion. I realised then that he had only confided in me because I was not connected in any way with his and Clarence's social circle. Most likely he barely even counted me as an actual person.

Jane will be tall and broad, like Clarence, but whereas Clarence's movements are dynamic and confident, Jane's limbs seem slack and slow. Aside from her hands, that is. It is as if the musical life of her mind has sapped her body of all energy.

When Jane was four, Clarence tried taking her to a small private nursery school in Highgate village. By then it had become possible to be apart from her, for shorter periods anyway, because Jane had learned to tell the time. Before leaving her at the nursery, Clarence would point to the clock on the wall and tell Jane what time she would return. Jane would then sit silently by herself until Clarence came back, making drawings with wax crayons or simply reading. She didn't seem unhappy, but she refused to have anything to do with the other children.

After six months of this behaviour, the headmistress asked Clarence if she would step into her office.

'We're worried about Jane,' she explained. 'I'm not entirely sure how we should play it.'

She told Clarence that although her daughter already possessed the reading ability of a seven-year-old, she was non-communicative and passively obstructive. She continued in this vein for around five minutes, then told Clarence about another nursery that might be better suited, a nursery that catered for special needs.

'They're doing some outstanding work there,' she said. 'They might help to bring her out of her shell.'

Clarence told me she felt numb all over. She thought of the doctors again and of their warnings. But she thought also of the slow, careful way Jane always kissed her goodnight, the way she put her head on one side when she was reading, as if she were listening to music.

In the end it proved to be music that was the key.

'We were in the village one day,' Clarence said. 'I'd had a doctor's appointment, and then we were going to feed the ducks in Waterlow Park. As we were crossing the road, Jane suddenly asked me straight out why we didn't have a piano. I told her I wasn't sure, but would she like one? She just nodded, like a little old lady, as if I were the stupid one for not knowing that already. It was remarkable.'

Soon after her fifth birthday, Jane started to attend the Monica Brundle School, a school for children who showed exceptional musical talent. For the first time she had friends: a Chinese boy named Yundi who played the violin and a twin brother and sister who lived with their aunts in a dilapidated Georgian villa on Highgate Hill. Jane sometimes went there after school to play trios and have tea.

I'd seen the Ibsen twins once or twice. It was impossible to tell them apart, or at least it was for me. On the surface they seemed more taciturn even than Jane.

'I'm sure they've got rats in that house,' Clarence said, with a shudder. 'I suppose it's all right, though. I don't want to stop her going.'

I am sure Clarence thought the odd rat running around under the floorboards was a small risk to take for the sake of Jane finally having some children her own age to spend time with. It must have been good for Clarence too, to have the place to herself for a while. Even when Jane was out of sight you could never forget she was there. The emotional current she generated was so intense it seemed almost audible, a low-level background hum.

'Do you think Jane is mad?' Lucan asked me as he left the pub. 'No one uses that word these days, do they? No one's allowed to.'

'Jane's not mad,' I said. 'She's different, that's all. Special.'

Just Jane, is what I should have said. I supposed Lucan would have heard the word special about a thousand times already. Enough times to make him sick and tired of it, anyway.

West Edge House
Tarquin's End
Bodmin
Cornwall

Dear Andrew,

Thank you, so much, for everything you said to me in your last letter. I'm so glad we've become friends. I don't think I've ever told you this, but when I put that advertisement in the magazine I never imagined that anyone would actually reply. It was like a dare I put on with myself, just to do something, something that would prove I didn't always have to do what people expected. No one would expect me to do this, I thought. I told myself that if anyone ever found out – anyone from here, I mean – I could say it was for research. That's why I said I wanted help with my work on Ewa Chaplin. But really I wanted to see if anything would happen.

I think of my mother driving me out to those unknown houses and villages in the car, the way I would sometimes imagine what it might be like to wander off into the background of whatever place we ended up in and start a new life there. A different life, with different people and different thoughts. Writing to you does that to me. It makes me feel as if the world could turn into something else at any moment. I hope you don't mind me saying that.

Since getting to know you I have started to think again of how I might leave this life behind – of packing a bag and catching the bus and coming to London. I would arrive at your door and you would let me in and we would talk and talk until it got dark. We would set the world to rights, as my dad used to say.

Maybe Dr Leslie is right, though. I'm not well enough to travel. Even the thought of buying a ticket sends me into a panic.

I used to believe that Helen and I would never be parted. I can see now that this was untrue, that someone like Helen would never really be friends with someone like me. It was as if I'd walked into someone else's life by mistake and no one had remembered to throw me out yet. Helen didn't care what I thought about things, she just liked talking to me, the same way Anne Frank liked talking to her friend Kitty when she wrote her diary. Because she knew that Kitty would always be interested in what she had to say.

Kitty didn't really exist though and neither did I.

My mother was against my friendship with Helen right from the start. 'These unequal friendships never last,' she said. 'I know what I'm talking about, believe me. You'll end up getting hurt.'

I wasn't sure what my mother meant by unequal, whether it was just that the Masons had more money than us or some other reason. The Masons lived in one of the large detached houses on Wimbush Hill. Helen's father was an orthodontist. He sometimes dealt with emergency cases at the big new NHS hospital in Plymouth but most of his work was with his private patients at his clinic in Truro. He had an angular, elegant profile, a large fair head and a nose that reminded me of Robert Redford's. The main time I used to see him was after school, when he would drive up outside in his Daimler to take Helen home.

Mrs Mason had beautifully shaped long legs and wide hazel eyes. She worked three days a week at a farm shop near Devoran but mostly she liked doing the garden. The first time I saw her she was down on her knees, weeding the flower beds in the Masons' front garden. She had grass stains on her jeans, and yellow trainers.

I found it difficult to imagine what kind of conversations the Mason family might have when they were alone together. It was true that Helen didn't really talk to me when we were at school, but then she didn't speak to anyone else much, either. She wasn't particularly popular, with the rest of our classmates or with the teachers. She usually scraped by in exams but she never seemed to care much either way. Sometimes when a teacher asked her a question in class she would stare at them blankly and then shake her head, as if she'd just woken up. The only time she seemed fully present was in English class, when Mrs Beasley made us take turns reading Shakespeare. Most people hated those classes, especially the boys – they reckoned reading aloud made them look like idiots.

Helen was always the first to volunteer. I remember once when we were doing *Othello*, she recited the whole of Iago's first act soliloquy from memory. Her voice sounded different, as if everything she had said up till that moment had been play-acting, and only this self – her Iago-self – was real.

When she finished, there was silence. Then one of the boys in the back of the class threw a wolf whistle and everyone laughed.

I looked across at Helen and she was gone. I don't mean

physically gone – she was sitting right there. But there seemed to
be a space around her, separating her from the rest of the class
and from Mrs Beasley and from everything that was happening
around her. She hadn't even heard the wolf whistle, I could tell.
Suddenly she looked straight at me, and smiled. As if only she and
I in the world understood what had just happened.

Except I didn't understand, not properly. I hated *Othello*. I
couldn't understand why Desdemona didn't just tell Othello
she'd lost the handkerchief and have done with it. I even found
myself wondering if she wanted to die, if deep down she regretted
walking into a life with Othello when she barely knew him. He
was a soldier, after all, he was used to going out into the world
and fixing things. Desdemona was used to another kind of life
entirely.

They reminded me of my mum and dad, in a way, how
different they were. By the time I was in the fifth form Mum and
Dad were barely speaking to each other. Not in an angry way,
they just had nothing to say. I began to hate going home after
school. My mother would usually be out on one of her drives.
When Dad came home from work he would take his boots off in
the kitchen then fall asleep in front of the television until supper
time. It frightened me to see him so exhausted. More and more
often, rather than go straight home, I would go to Truro public
library instead. Edwin would sometimes be there, holed up in
one of the study booths with a pile of science books. Some of the
books were ancient. Others had tight shiny covers and looked as if
they'd never been opened.

Once, when Edwin left his desk to go to the toilet, I leaned across and had a look at what he'd been reading, a fat red volume called *The Metaphysics of Physics*, filled with complicated three-dimensional diagrams that seemed to rise up off the page. If you stared at them long enough you could almost convince yourself they were solid objects. I turned the pages, trying to make sense of them and failing. I didn't realise Edwin had come back until he was standing right behind me.

'They're optical illusions,' he said. His voice made me jump. I thought he might be angry, that I'd been interfering with his things, but he didn't seem bothered, not at all. 'A lot of them are used as the basis for modern computer graphics. Like this one.'

He pointed to one of the diagrams, a series of cubes that appeared to expand and contract even as I looked at them. The sensation of movement made my head hurt. In the end I couldn't help but look away.

'Two dimensions can be bent into three,' Edwin said. 'Think of a Möbius strip.'

I asked him what a Möbius strip was and he showed me how to make one by tearing a strip of paper from the back of his exercise book. He twisted the paper around itself then stuck the two ends of the strip together with a piece of Sellotape.

When he cut the strip in half along its length, the two parts remained joined together, like links in a paper chain.

'It's a common conjuring trick,' Edwin said. 'Anyone can do it. It looks like magic, but it's just a simple rearrangement of space.'

Helen was very keen for me to go and see the play she was in. She kept asking me what day I was coming, and when I said

I wasn't sure yet, because I needed to get the money from my father, she gave me a free ticket for the Saturday matinée.

It wasn't a school play. Helen belonged to a small theatre company that put on productions in the Old Chapel. They weren't as popular as the Truro Players but Helen said she much preferred them because they did modern plays. 'Not the same old Noël Coward stuff,' she said. I'd never seen a play by Noël Coward so I wasn't sure what she meant by that, but I did know that Helen was the youngest member of the company. I had an idea there had been some bad feeling over her joining, that some of the older members had tried to keep her out, especially after she auditioned for the part of Amber Furness. I think that might have been why she wanted to have me in the audience – so she'd know she had a friend close by.

I would have gone every night if she'd asked me, and helped her to learn her lines, but she never did.

The play was set in Glasgow, although the programme notes said the original story the play was based on took place in an unnamed country in Eastern Europe. The main character apart from Amber is Gareth Maitland – the cast list describes him as 'an alchemist'. He rents a room above a noisy pub on Renfrew Street. Gareth Maitland is a dwarf, although it took some time to work this out, because the actor who played him was actually quite tall. The only way you could tell was by watching the way the other characters reacted to him.

Amber Furness is the landlord's daughter. Her father wants her to marry the son of a friend of his, a local businessman, but Amber, who is a gifted scholar, wants to travel to Germany and study mathematics. Amber and Gareth become close friends because of their shared interest in science and philosophy. At the end of the first act, Amber tells Gareth about her plan to run away.

Gareth Maitland falls deeper and deeper in love with Amber. He becomes convinced that together they will discover the secret of alchemy. He is on the point of asking Amber to marry him when he catches sight of her on the street outside, talking to a man he's never seen before. The man is Joachim Blum, a student from Göttingen. Gareth drops the tickets he has bought for the Eurostar into a drain in the pub's back yard. When Amber comes to his room later, to talk, he says nothing of what he has seen. He makes tea and listens, the same as always. Afterwards, when Amber has left the room, Gareth pours away the dregs of her tea and rinses out the cup.

Nothing seems to change at first. Amber looks the same, at least to the audience. It is only as the third act wears on that you notice the way the other characters are beginning to shy away from her. Right at the end, Joachim Blum arrives at the pub, looking for Amber. When Amber appears onstage, Joachim Blum draws back from her, as if she has the plague.

'I'm sorry,' he says. He throws a coin on the floor in front of her. 'Buy yourself some soup.'

Joachim doesn't recognise her. It's only then you understand she has been turned into a monster.

On my way out of the theatre I caught sight of Edwin. I had no idea he was there until that moment. He saw me at the same second I saw him. He came over and asked if I felt like going for a coffee somewhere and I said yes without even thinking about it. He was wearing the same blazer and trousers he wore for school. I wondered if he ever wore jeans, like everyone else.

I should have been nervous, but I wasn't. Being with Edwin felt normal, as if we'd known one another for ages, since before I'd known Helen, even. He asked me what I thought of the play.

'I'm not sure I understood it,' I said. 'If Gareth Maitland had really loved Amber, he wouldn't have given her the tea.'

'You're talking about the Platonic ideal of love,' Edwin said. 'Desire is different. Desire can drive you to anything, even murder.'

He told me about a painting by Velazquez called 'Las Meninas'. 'It shows the Spanish infanta, with her court dwarfs,' he said. 'There's a song by Schubert, too, called "The Dwarf". When the dwarf discovers the queen has betrayed him, he strangles her with her own scarf and throws her body into the sea.'

We talked some more about the play, and what an interesting idea it was, to have a play about an alchemist set in the twentieth century. Then Edwin started telling me about one of the teachers at his old school, an asylum seeker from Poland who had spent time in a Russian labour camp. The one thing neither of us mentioned was Helen – Helen in the role of Amber Furness. I remembered her big speech at the end of Act Two, standing on the corner of Renfrew Street with the light filtering through her hair, making it stand out around her head like a golden crown. The actor playing Joachim Blum wore torn jeans and a leather motorcycle jacket. He handed Helen a grey school exercise book, filled with what he described as equations of the infinite. Helen clasped the book to her chest as if she were afraid someone might steal it from her. *We think the same way, you and I*, she said. *We dream the same dreams.*

Helen lit up the stage like a firework. People say things like that all the time about famous actors, but it's the only way I can think of to describe her. It was as if the Helen I knew from school was only half of her, a pale ghost. The Helen lighting up the stage was someone else entirely, someone I never believed in until the moment of seeing her. She was beautiful, I realised, and also terrifying.

No wonder she never seemed to care what the teachers thought. Why would you, when you had this other person blazing inside you?

The following week I bought a card for her, a black-and-white photograph of marguerite daisies in a crystal vase. I wanted to tell Helen how remarkable she was, how much her performance had affected me, but I couldn't think how to say that, not properly. I suppose that was when I finally understood what my mother had meant about an unequal friendship. Helen would never really care about anything or anyone as much as she cared about being on the stage. In a way that was all right and in another way it wasn't.

What would happen to someone like that, if they couldn't get to do what they dreamed of doing, if they failed for some reason?

I never sent the card. I put it away in a drawer, still sealed in its Cellophane wrapping. It might still be there, for all I know. For a while I wondered if things might have been different if I had sent it, if Helen and I would have become close in the way

I wanted us to be but then I realised I was being stupid. Helen didn't want to be close to me – the idea would have horrified her. I don't know what she wanted.

Thinking of you, dear Andrew.

Your friend,

Bramber

8 .

*W*E WOULD TALK AND *talk until it got dark*, she wrote. *As if the world could turn into something new at any moment.*

Her words filled me with the kind of gladness I had only felt on very rare occasions – my last day of school, for example, or the time Ursula accidentally locked herself out of her flat and ended up spending the night on the sofa in my living room. Those doubts that occasionally gnawed at me – that the closeness between us was and always had been a figment of my imagination – vanished like beads of frost in an autumn sunrise. Clarence was wrong, I knew that now for certain, and I had been right all along: Bramber needed me and wanted me and her letter proved it.

I felt an all but insurmountable urge to respond in kind, to make my confession, as it were. To lay bare not only my feelings but my past as well. I wanted Bramber to know everything about me, my darkest memories as well as my brightest hopes, so that there would be no shadows between us at our first meeting, and we would come together not as curious strangers but as trusted intimates.

I restrained myself, not wishing to overburden her, though the thoughts pressed in on me. People and places I had not thought of in years continued to resurface. Natural enough, I supposed – the past tends to come back most strongly precisely in those moments when we are breaking away from it. Yet the memories were painful, all the same, if only because they served as a reminder of how lonely I had been throughout those years, the years before Bramber, before the ongoing, dreamlike present, before the future that seemed so nearly within my grasp.

ABOUT TWO YEARS AFTER Ursula went out of my life I started seeing Runymeade Saxe. Run lived in an immaculate mews cottage off Swanns Lane, at the lower end of Highgate village and less than fifteen minutes' walk from where the Ibsen twins lived, though the twins and their bramble-clad, peeling monument of a home were still years in my future.

I met him one Friday in a bar close to Covent Garden, an area I still sometimes frequented, if I am honest, solely in the hope of seeing Ursula. Run asked me if I was looking for someone. I gazed up at him for a moment – the delicately arched eyebrows, the starched white shirt front – and then said yes. He reminded me of Wil, which in a strange way made things easier. He flagged down a taxi on the Strand and gave the address of a hotel somewhere near Aldgate.

I went with him as if in a dream. I gazed at the traffic beyond the windows, the lit-up hoardings, the tide of Friday-night revellers pouring from the entrances and exits of a thousand bars. I understand now that I was afraid, although at the time I felt so distanced from my actions I seemed almost not to be there in person, but rather looking down on myself from a great distance: a tiny clockwork figure with his eyes on the road.

Run said something to me about the warmth of the evening,

then asked if I'd seen a comedy that happened to be playing in one of the theatres off Seven Dials, then simply took my hand. His skin felt smooth as calf's leather. I noticed he wore a gold signet ring on his left little finger.

By the time we got out of the taxi it was spitting with rain. From somewhere in the middle distance came the glittering fandango of thrown glass breaking, swiftly followed by the sounds of laughter and running feet. From somewhere closer to hand I caught the unmistakable odour of blocked drains. A fizzing neon sign said 'Hotel Atlantis'. Run steered me through the shabby foyer and then upstairs.

It was my first full act of intercourse since leaving Wil. I took off my jacket and dropped it on the dressing table. I remember how careful Run was with the rest of my clothes, folding them carefully over the back of the bedside chair, a squat and ugly thing, button-backed, upholstered in pink velour. At some point he must have asked me my name because he kept calling me Drew – Drew, Drew, Drew, right through it all. I don't know how, but he seemed to know I could never bear to be called Andy. Afterwards, just once, he called me boy.

I wiped myself on the flimsy sheet then fumbled my clothes back on, half-tripping over my trousers in the process. I heard the sound of running water, splashing against the pink porcelain of the ancient washstand. By the time I turned to face him, Run was fully dressed.

'Would you like to go downstairs and have a drink?' he asked. 'The bar isn't bad here, surprisingly.'

'Not now,' I said. I tried to think of a passable reason why I could not stay, but it seemed none was necessary. Run passed me my jacket, then a shade more deliberately my wallet, which had fallen out of my pocket on to the floor. I opened it, counting money into his hand until he closed his fingers around the notes and put them away.

'Will you be all right getting home?' he said. I reassured him that I would be and then left. There were taxis outside the Atlantic but I ignored them and carried on walking until I came to the underground. When I arrived back at Hammersmith I bought a newspaper from the all-night supermarket just outside the station entrance and then continued up the road to the Orion. I was just in time for last orders. I usually avoided the Orion, especially at the weekend – it was the kind of pub where people went to get drunk – but on that particular evening the ribald anarchy of the packed saloon bar was a blessed relief. I sipped at my brandy, letting the thoughts and images that coursed through my brain gradually wear themselves away into dust.

Raucous laughter erupted as someone vomited outside the gents' lavatories, then everyone was turned out into the street. The rain had stopped. Backlit by the moon, the muggy West London sky was mottled with cloud.

It wasn't until a couple of days later that I found Run's business card in my jacket pocket – he must have put it there while I was getting dressed. I was relieved to find it, though I didn't call his number for almost a month. When I finally rang him, he gave me the address of his house in Highgate, where he showed me into a small, spotlessly clean bedroom at the back and performed his services upon me. Afterwards we sat in the kitchen. Run made tea and we talked. Sometimes, if he didn't have to go out later, we would eat a meal together. Run collected theatre programmes and other stage memorabilia that I enjoyed looking at. He in turn was fascinated by my dolls.

On the second Christmas of our acquaintance I presented him with Adrien, a narrow-waisted, long-limbed doll in the traditional black-and-white silks of a pierrot. Under the harlequin's hat, her beautifully domed china skull was shaded along the hairline but was otherwise bare. Her feet were glorious: high-arched, with each toe distinct and just a little longer than would usually be considered normal.

'Is she a girl or a boy?' Run asked, after he'd unwrapped her.

'I hadn't really thought about it,' I said. 'Does it matter?' In fact, Adrien looked a little like one of the Ibsen twins, although of course I couldn't have known that at the time.

I stopped seeing Run six months after I began writing to Bramber. I knew by then that I loved her, you see, and my relations with Run seemed wrong, suddenly. I would have liked to continue with the second part of our visits – the meals, the theatre programmes, the conversation – but Run had never given any indication that he wished for our relationship to be anything other than it was, and I did not want to take advantage of his good nature.

Clarence knew all about Ursula but I never breathed a word to her about Run. When I told her what Bramber had written to me in her letter – about wanting to come to London, to change her life for me – her reaction was strange.

'It'll never work out,' she said. 'It's a crush, that's all. People say all sorts of things in letters, but they don't really mean them. They can pretend anything they like.'

'Bramber's not like that,' I said. Bramber always used the same paper for her letters, pale blue and semi-transparent, like airmail paper. She wrote in ink with a very fine nib and her small, back-ward-sloping script was difficult to read on occasion. I had never shown any of her letters to Clarence. I felt no need to prove anything. Bramber had told me things about herself that would be impossible to fabricate. It is not so easy to invent a life as people make out.

'I think you'd like her,' I added. 'I've told her all about you.'

Actually this was not true. I had named Clarence as the owner-manager of the gallery that represented me, but that was all. I didn't want to mention Clarence too often in case Bramber got the wrong idea. Clarence never asked me a single question about what Bramber and I said to each other in our letters, and as time wore on I began to feel as if there were whole layers of my existence that remained hidden from her.

As Bramber became more real to me, Clarence became less so. What was strange was how little I minded.

I LEFT THE MUSEUM and returned to my room at the White Hart. I lay down on the bed and closed my eyes, listening to the noises that seeped through the walls: the opening and closing of doors, the muted chatter of televisions and radios, the creaking of the floorboards at the top of the stairs as other guests passed to and fro along the landing. I found these sounds restful, and I fell into a light doze. By the time I went back downstairs it was seven o'clock.

My mobile battery was almost on empty, so I telephoned Clarence from the payphone in reception. It rang and rang, and I found myself hoping that Clarence had gone out somewhere, that I wouldn't have to talk to her. When she finally answered she sounded distracted and out of breath.

'Is everything all right?' I said.

'Oh Andrew, we've lost Anneke. Jane won't stop crying. You know how she loves that doll.' I felt a stab of dismay, not so much for Clarence but for Anneke, a curly-headed toddler doll based upon a little-known Denis Chaud model named 'Clarice'. I had presented her to Jane on her ninth birthday. According to Clarence, the two were rarely parted.

'How did it happen?'

'I'm not sure. It must be at the Ibsen twins'. Jane's been round there all day.'

An image came to me of the mansion in Highgate, the vast garden with its rotting outbuildings and overgrown pathways. You could hide a double decker bus there, if you felt so inclined.

'When did Jane tell you?'

'Not until we were home – she was obviously too upset to say anything earlier. And the Ibsens' phone line is down again, so I've not been able to call. If Jane goes on like this I'll have to drive over there.' She paused. 'That place gives me the willies in the dark.'

'Is Lucan not home from work yet?'

'He had to fly back to Rome, first thing. It's a long story.' She sighed. 'I'm tearing my hair out here.'

What she meant was, she wanted me with her. Clarence believes I have a special way with Jane.

'Have you tried putting on one of her records? The Scarlatti? Tell her you'll go and look for Anneke tomorrow, as soon as you've had breakfast. So long as they stayed in the garden she can't be far.'

Limp platitudes, but they were the best I could muster. I didn't want to be talking to Clarence, much less cooped up in the flat with her and Jane. I wondered if that feeling might change, once Bramber and I were together in London, or whether it would be better if I started seeing less of Clarence altogether.

Suddenly the pips went.

'Shall I call you back?' Clarence asked.

'It says no incoming calls,' I lied. 'I'll call again once I've charged my mobile.'

There was a long pause. I asked Clarence if she was still there, then realised we'd already been cut off. There was a click and the line went dead. I replaced the receiver. I wondered if Lucan really was having an affair, whether Clarence knew and didn't want to talk about it. The thoughts irked me but didn't intrude. Clarence might as well have been speaking from another world.

I had been planning to eat in the hotel restaurant, but on the spur of the moment I decided to find somewhere in town instead. The phone call had made me feel restless again, and there was always the chance that Clarence would look up the number of the White Hart and try and call me back anyway.

I crossed the road and followed a sign for the cathedral, leaving South Street via a narrow cobbled passageway between a fast food outlet and a florist's. After walking for a hundred yards or so I found myself in Cathedral Yard.

The heat of the day had diminished. I caught the scents of honeysuckle and wisteria, as well as the greener, more astringent aroma of nettles and yarrow, the kind of wild plants that will flourish anywhere, even in the heart of the city. Ivied stone walls concealed the Dean's residence and the chapter house, the famous Exeter Cathedral School. The cathedral itself was magnificent and pleasingly robust. I stood for some minutes looking up at the tower, watching the sunlight as it lit up the great west window. There was an atmosphere of unblemished serenity, a sense of timelessness that existed in marked contrast with the rest of the city. I felt almost as I had done in Wade: that I had discovered another town, a truer town, hiding behind the facade the place presented to the outside world.

I chose a restaurant overlooking Cathedral Green, a pleasant seeming Italian with whitewashed walls and a flagstone floor. I ordered the ham risotto and a bottle of Chianti. I had eaten nothing substantial since breakfast and so I was hungry but my appetite for the wine was even stronger. The smell of it made my head spin. By the time the waiter brought my risotto I had consumed a third of the Chianti and the edges of things were beginning to blur. I knew it was unwise to drink on an empty stomach, but all the same I felt gratified and semi-blissful. Thoughts of Clarence, the idea of her almost, seemed far away.

The food brought me back a little and I became more aware of my immediate surroundings. To my left sat a middle-aged couple, the man running to fat but the woman still handsome, with strong, patrician features. Each time she turned her head, the diamond ear-rings she wore snatched greedily at the light. The table to my right was occupied by a younger man, eating alone. He wore a canary-coloured short-sleeved shirt. His forearms were tanned and muscular, the arms of someone who is used to working out of doors. When the waiter came to refill his glass, the man thanked him in Italian. After the waiter had gone, he caught my eye.

'Lovely evening,' he said. He had a Scottish accent. I have never felt comfortable exchanging small talk with strangers and normally I would simply have agreed with him and left it at that. As things were, the man's proximity, coupled with the effects of the Chianti, made me feel more loquacious.

'It is indeed,' I said. 'A fine night for drinking fine wine.' I raised my glass to him. Quite suddenly I felt glad of his company. His grey eyes displayed the usual curiosity about my appearance but on this occasion I found I didn't care. I leaned back in my seat, letting him have a good look.

'And what are we celebrating?' he asked finally, nodding towards the half-empty bottle of Chianti at my elbow.

'Running away from London,' I said impulsively. 'Going west to rescue the woman that I love.'

The Scotsman laughed. 'Congratulations,' he said. 'It's not every day one crosses ways with Sir Galahad.'

I smiled back at him, then drained my glass. I remembered Bramber's own reference to Sir Galahad in one of her letters, the one where she was telling me about Jackie and her father. It occurred to me that until that moment I had spoken of Bramber to no one apart from Clarence. Doing so now made me feel giddy, as if I'd fought myself free of a fear I barely knew I had.

'Well, "rescue" is putting things a bit strongly, perhaps,' I conceded. 'But maybe I can be forgiven, since I actually will be venturing close to the birthplace of King Arthur.'

'Your girlfriend's from Cornwall, then?'

'She was born there. She's been staying in a village near Bodmin, called Tarquin's End.'

'I've not heard of it.'

'It's very small. Not much more than a hamlet, really.' I spoke as if I knew the place well, as if I'd visited frequently. Soon after receiving Bramber's first letter I had been into WH Smith's and purchased the Landranger ordnance survey map for Bodmin and the surrounding area. It took me some time to locate Tarquin's End, which was represented by three black dots midway between the villages of Ravensbridge and Polbrock. Less detailed maps, as Bramber had said, most likely wouldn't show it at all.

'Back of beyond, eh?' The man chuckled. 'There be dragons.'

He signalled to the waiter, and asked him to bring us another bottle of wine. 'This one's on me,' he said. When it arrived he downed a glass straight off, as if it were water. I told him Bramber had been ill for a while, but she was better now.

'The past year has been really hard on both of us,' I said. 'But she needed a break from London and I couldn't afford to be away from work.'

In an earlier letter, Bramber had told me she'd been to London once with the school. She lost her packed lunch on the tube somewhere between Tower Hill and Baker Street. The Scotsman had left his own table and come to sit at mine, his brawny forearms sprawling, relaxed, across the tablecloth. The material of his shirt, I noticed, was strikingly attractive, a kind of crushed linen.

'Is she beautiful then, your girl?' he asked.

'She is to me,' I said. 'I've known her all my life. I've never met another woman like her.'

'You should hold on to her then, my man, or she'll disappear on you, that's all I'm saying.' He stared at me hard, as if daring me to contradict him. His manner seemed to have changed suddenly, becoming simultaneously more aggressive and more vulnerable. I wondered how much he had had to drink before I arrived. 'People can change. Leave her alone for too long and you might find it's you who needs rescuing.'

'She hasn't been alone,' I said. 'She's with friends. And she has my letters.'

The Scotsman sighed and struck the rim of his glass. 'Don't mind me. The truth is I envy you. Reckon it's my own wife I've been talking about but that was a long time ago.'

He excused himself and went to the gents. His walk was slow and heavy. He was clearly very tired or very drunk. I signalled the waiter and paid my bill. I stayed seated at the table for a couple more minutes out of politeness, but when my drinking companion did not return I put on my jacket and left.

It was past ten o'clock. Cathedral Green was empty of people, and when I touched my fingers to the grass they came away damp. The sky was infinite: violet, pinpricked with stars. I wondered if it looked the same from Tarquin's End.

The bar of the White Hart smelled of beer and overcooked meat. I went upstairs to my room and switched on the television, flicking from channel to channel before settling on a hospital sitcom in which the chief administrator had obviously been modelled on Margaret Thatcher. I found the frenzied actions of the doctors and nurses curiously calming. The programme finished and the news came on. I watched the headlines and then had a shower. I thought about the Scotsman, wondered where he was travelling to, or from.

He missed his wife, that would be clear to anyone.

Was she dead, or had she left him? I had found it exhilarating, to play at having a wife, a dress rehearsal, perhaps, for the life to come. The Scotsman had seemed to find it natural and acceptable that I would have a partner, someone I loved and who loved me. He had urged me to hold on to her.

Clarence was wrong when she said we barely knew each other. As I had insisted to the Scotsman, we had our letters. What difference did it make, if all our talking had been on paper instead of out loud?

We had a lifetime of words still to share. But these, our early years, would always be special, and we would always have our letters to remember them.

Dear Andrew,

I keep thinking I really ought to tell you more about Edwin and what happened between us. I don't want to hide anything. I think it's important that we're truthful, don't you? It all happened a long time ago, after all. I feel like I was someone else then, a completely different person. Does that sound ridiculous?

Edwin and I became closer as the summer deepened. We went for long walks, out across the allotments, or along the old Newham railway line, to the fields beyond. You'll ask me how I felt about Edwin and I'll find it hard to answer. When people talk of being in love, they speak of yearning or terror or agony, of revelation. I never felt any of those things when I was with Edwin, I just felt normal. As if I'd found the missing piece of a jigsaw puzzle that had been there in the box all the time.

I thought we'd always be together because how could we not be? I was scared sometimes when I thought about the summer ending. The weather would turn colder, which would mean fewer walks, and then there'd be school. Even then I didn't worry all that much. We would still have the weekends, the public library after classes, the same as before. The idea of a future beyond that was too huge to think about, yet at the same time it didn't seem to matter at all. Edwin liked to say there was no such thing as the future anyway, just a continuous present, only with some of it too far away to make out the details.

'Time doesn't really exist,' he said. 'It's a human construct.'

He said he could prove it to me, that all we had to do was stay up all night and I'd see how the future was really the present all along. We laughed and swore we'd do it, that we'd take blankets and food up to the allotments and wait for daylight, that we'd feel the planet revolving beneath our feet like a great spinning top.

We didn't go through with our plan, though. It was just too complicated. I kept imagining my dad going into my room and finding me gone, the trouble it would cause. I guess Edwin imagined the same, or something like it. We were still children, really. Children tend to think of danger in terms of what they see on television: wars, or getting lost on a mountain, or a forest fire. The kind of random disaster you can fight or run from.

Danger can be ordinary, though. Something that doesn't seem threatening at all, until it sinks its teeth in.

The old Newham line used to run from Truro to Sweetshouse before joining the Hayle branch line at Par. Originally it was part of the old china clay railway. Later it was amalgamated into the West Cornwall line, which lost more than half of its branch lines and stations in the Beeching cuts. My father didn't get angry at people as a rule, not even customers who were late paying, or who didn't pay at all – he always said that losing your temper over money was to pay to devil's wages – but he hated Dr Beeching, who he referred to as a robber baron. Dad said Beeching didn't care what losing a station could do to a town, that his appointment had been a travesty and a sin.

Many of the branch lines were torn up and built over. Some, like the Newham line, eventually came to life again as cycle paths. The Newham path ran in a loop around the western outskirts of Truro then climbed uphill over the old viaduct. People tended to stop walking before they got that far, and the upper stretch of the pathway could get quite overgrown. On the day I'm telling you about, I remember the scent of greenery was overpowering, that there were butterflies sunning themselves all along the top of the viaduct.

When we reached the other side, I flung myself down in the grass and looked up at the sky. Edwin sat down beside me and took off his glasses. I remember he looked different without them, younger. He leant back on his hands and gazed up at the trees.

'There's a saying around here, that if you fall asleep under the viaduct you'll dream about the ghost train,' he said. 'A local folk singer wrote a ballad about it – I looked it up in the library. He's in an old folks' home now but there are still people who believe the old quarry trains never stopped running. They say that on a still night you can hear the whistle blow, if you listen hard enough.'

'You don't believe that though, do you?' I said. 'You don't believe in ghosts?'

I knew about the old quarry pit – we'd learned about it at school, how the china clay deposits dried up and there wasn't enough work left to keep the trains running. The clay diggers moved east to St Austell and the quarry was shut down. There was talk of flooding the quarry pit, of turning it into a reservoir, but that never happened.

You can still go there, if you want. The pit has been fenced off now because it's dangerous but you can see it through the bushes still.

Dr Leslie told me a local charity has started campaigning to turn it into a nature reserve.

Edwin said he didn't believe in ghosts the way they were in films, the spirits of the dead come back to haunt us. He believed most ghost sightings were more likely to be people who happened to be living in parallel universes.

'Parallel universes?'

'Like if there was another version of reality right next to ours, a version of the world in which the quarry never closed down, and so the trains kept on running. And maybe sometimes people in our world can hear them, the way you can sometimes hear people talking through the walls in the house next door. There are plenty of scientists who believe in the possibility of parallel worlds. More than who believe in ghosts, anyway.'

'Because they're less frightening?'

'Because they're more likely.'

I asked him if he believed in God and he just laughed. 'I'm not much of a one for beliefs,' he said. 'I prefer observations. Things that can be proved by science.'

He touched the side of my neck, removing a blade of grass. Then he ran a hand down over my shoulder and around the curve of my right breast, as if he were outlining me in chalk, like the police do with dead bodies in the TV detective shows, or maybe just proving my existence. He laid his arm on the grass next to mine as if comparing their lengths.

'Let's get back off the path,' he said. 'Someone might see us.'

We fought our way through the undergrowth to a sun-striped, grassy clearing between the trees, young green oaks, their foliage bright and sharply outlined against the blue sky. The air was very still. Edwin took off his trousers and knelt above me, his penis hard and tight against his belly. I reached out to touch it. The feel of it was curious, like soft leather stretched over stone. The blue veins stood out starkly, like aquifers in granite. He stroked the hair back off my face then reached down and touched me between my legs. I could feel his fingers, pushing gently and then more vigorously, going deep inside. I closed my eyes, flinching slightly as if I'd been stung.

'Does it hurt?' Edwin said. 'Should we stop?'

'It's all right,' I said. I touched his wrist where it moved between my legs, felt the reedy, fragile bones working his hand. He withdrew his fingers then lay down on top of me and put in his penis. It hurt less than I thought it would, though being joined with him in that way felt strange to me, almost as if in becoming one we had been made to give up a part of who we were. I knew that sex was supposed to bring us closer, but in those moments when it was happening I felt more distant from Edwin than I'd ever been.

Perhaps it was too soon for us. I really don't know. All I can say is that when I think of that afternoon I still feel sad. I wish we had talked more afterwards – that might have made things all right – but we were both so young.

A short time later Edwin gasped, then rolled away from me. I touched his hair, his forehead. He felt hot, sticky with sweat. Broken leaves and pieces of grass clung to my bottom and thighs. I heard the scatter and rush of birds in the depths of the trees, then from somewhere further away a train blew its whistle.

'It's the ghost train,' Edwin said. 'It'll come for us now, you'll see.'

I laughed. 'I thought you didn't believe in ghosts,' I said. My voice sounded unreal to me, like a tape recording, although Edwin didn't seem to notice and as time wore on and the sun bore down I began to come back to normal. This is the way things are supposed to be, I reminded myself. You'll soon get used to it. The thought that I *could* get used to it made me feel stronger and older and, in a curious way, protective of Edwin – Edwin who knew so much, but who still did not know these thoughts of mine and never would.

We must have fallen asleep then, but not for long. We walked back into town along the cutting, then went our separate ways. I hoped I might find the house empty but both my parents were at home. My father was in the lounge, sitting in his armchair watching the football scores. Bars of sunlight filtered in through the closed curtains, criss-crossing the carpet with fuzzy yellow lines.

'You look like you've caught the sun,' he said. He smiled. 'It's good to see you getting some fresh air.'

He looked tired, even though it was a Saturday and he'd most likely been asleep all afternoon.

The radio was on in the kitchen. My mother was singing

along to the music, a pure, high keening that was utterly unlike her normal speaking voice. The music made me shiver. The idea that a person who produced such sounds could also be my mother seemed ridiculous. I couldn't make out any of the words, and after a moment I realised she was singing in a foreign language.

'It's German,' said my father, as if reading my mind. 'Lizzie learned German at college, as part of her training. She had to know French and Italian as well. All part of her training,' he repeated. He closed his eyes.

'Why did Mum give up? Her singing, I mean,' I asked him, much later. After I came to West Edge House, Dad sold the house on Harlequin Road and went to live in Swanage to be closer to his sister. For a while – before he had to go into hospital, I mean – he still drove down most weekends to see me. If the weather was warm enough we would sit on the patio, in Sylvia's deck chairs, looking out over the garden and exchanging news. We never spoke about my mother, except for that once. It was as if the curtains parted, just for a moment, and then slid closed again.

'She fell over on stage,' Dad said. 'It put her off her stride and she forgot all her words. She asked if she could start again, but then she dried up completely. Everyone said it was nothing, just a college recital, she should forget all about it. Her confidence was destroyed though. I used to think it was how a tightrope walker might feel. You perform this miracle every night of the week for years and years, and then one night you look down at the ground and the only thing you can think about is how far you have to fall. Lizzie never sang in public again after that and it broke her heart.'

I still think about what Edwin said, about parallel worlds.

What if there were a world where my mother had never tripped up on stage, where I had never pushed Helen in front of the ghost train and where my father had found my mother dying that night instead of me?

Can you imagine a parallel universe? I think you can. Sometimes when I go to sleep I think about what it might be like, to wake up in that world instead of this one, how quickly everything that happened here would seem like a dream.

Dear Andrew. I do hope you don't mind me telling you these things.

Your friend, always,

Bramber

My dear Andrew,

Jackie told me she still remembered the night she won a pierrot at the Tavistock goose fair.

'It was on that game where you have to catch a rubber duck with a fishing line,' she said. 'I was nine years old. I called the pierrot Ponchinello, like the leprechaun in the song we learned at school. My brother was so jealous. He spent all his pennies on the rifle range but he didn't win a thing.'

It was the first and only time she ever mentioned a brother. I asked her what had happened to Ponchinello but she didn't reply.

'I always loved the fair,' she said instead. 'Even if you didn't win anything, there was always the feeling something marvellous was about to happen.'

Something marvellous. Her words made me think of Jennie, and what she had said about her and Paul running away with the circus. Ewa Chaplin wrote a story about a travelling carnival. Freak shows and carnivals were very popular in Eastern Europe. It was only the war that did away with them. I always assumed freak shows were a bad thing, that they exploited people who had no other way of making a living. But the carnival in Ewa

Chaplin's story acted as a kind of refuge, a sanctuary for people who would have been rounded up and killed by the Nazis otherwise.

When I was little, my father used to take me to the goose fair in Truro. I liked the candyfloss machine, and the treacle toffee stand, but I was afraid of the fair people, of the way the lights from the stalls and rides threw strange shadows across their faces. The fair is a different world, I think, the kind you have to be born into to understand properly. I remember the huge carousel with its painted horses, the contest to guess the weight of a large black pig. Dad always had a go at the hammer. I kept hoping he might win a goldfish but he never did.

By the time we were doing our 'A' Levels, the goose fair was a thing of the past. We had the bank holiday fête instead: stalls selling cakes and assorted jumble and a bran tub full of prizes that weren't worth winning.

It was Edwin who suggested we should go. 'There's going to be an elephant,' he said. 'They're bringing it in from Helston zoo and if you pay three pounds you can have a ride on it.'

He sounded excited, as if he'd never seen an elephant before, which perhaps he hadn't. All I could think about was how they were going to get the elephant from Helston to Truro and whether it would be frightened, having to be led up and down among all those people suddenly. It was the only time I ever felt older than Edwin and the feeling scared me. It was as if, for a tiny moment, I had glimpsed another Edwin, an Edwin who played football in the park with all the other kids and who would laugh in my face if I so much as mentioned parallel universes.

The fête took place on the last Monday in August, the bank holiday. I kept thinking about how a month from now we would be back at school. There was bunting strung from the fence posts and a bouncy castle under the trees. One end of the football field had been roped off, and people were standing in line outside a striped marquee. The thought of the elephant inside unnerved me, the prospect of something mythical and terrible all at once.

Suddenly I spotted Helen, standing at the edge of the crowd, craning her neck to see over the heads of the people in front of her. I started at the sight of her. I hadn't known she was going to be there and I felt guilty, I suppose. I hadn't spoken to her since the start of the holidays and I'd been spending so much time with Edwin I'd hardly thought about her.

She turned around then and caught sight of us, her hair flashed bright in the sun. I raised my arm and waved.

'Who are you waving to?' Edwin asked.

'Helen,' I said. 'She's over there, by the tent.'

Edwin shrugged, as if the name meant nothing to him, and I wondered if he remembered her, even. 'Would you like an elephant ride?' he said. 'I'll pay.'

I shook my head. I found I hated the idea of it, the poor elephant being walked in circles at the end of a rope, the people looking on, as if the elephant were part of a freak show, something monstrous and wonderful to be gaped at and then discarded. All those cameras pointing, all those instamatic cameras chirping like crickets. 'Helen might, though.'

I offered her name as a consolation, a way of saying no to Edwin without making him feel that his suggestion had been

unwelcome. And of course Helen would want an elephant ride –
for someone like Helen, an elephant's back was just another kind
of stage. She had worked her way to the front of the queue by
then, anyway.

I watched as the elephant was made to kneel, as Helen
mounted the short flight of wooden steps that had been placed
beside it. There was a cloth on the elephant's back, a patchwork
of satin and velvet in scarlet and gold. Helen's light summer dress
rode up around her knees, revealing her freckled shins and lower
thighs. As the keeper led the elephant around the top corner of
the football field, Helen let go of the red silk rope that formed
the elephant's harness and raised both arms above her head. Her
cheeks were flushed, and her hair stood out in fuzzy corkscrews
about her ears. A couple of people in the crowd began to clap.

As the elephant came to a standstill outside the marquee, Helen
fixed her eyes on me. For a moment her expression appeared
utterly blank. Then she smiled.

'It's like feeling the world turn,' she said, as she came towards
us. 'You should try it. You might never get a chance like this
again.'

'I'm scared of heights,' Edwin said. The way he spoke to
her made it sound as if he knew her, as if they'd talked together
before, many times. Once again I glimpsed that other Edwin,
the Edwin who would say something just to be funny. His words
sounded made up to me, like small talk, the kind of thing people
say to each other in films.

Were they in a film now, Edwin and Helen? I found I could
picture it, quite easily, Helen in one of those cartwheel hats with

roses around the brim, Edwin as the young country doctor, thin and rather earnest but still good looking.

'You were in the theatre, weren't you? I remember seeing you,' Helen said.

Edwin blushed. 'Do you feel like getting something to eat?' he said. 'We were just thinking about going for hot dogs, weren't we, Bramber?' He turned to look at me as he said it, but didn't quite meet my eye. I realised I had become insubstantial to him, a piece of stage scenery. He never used my name like that when he spoke to me, not normally.

'I can't, I'm sorry,' Helen said. 'I have to go home now. My dad's taking me to an audition.'

'See you later, then,' said Edwin, as if he really might.

We headed away from the elephant tent and back towards the food stands, where Edwin bought us both hot dogs, though I no longer felt hungry. Then I asked Edwin if he'd like to come back to my house. I felt startled by my own suggestion, almost panicked, but in the end there was no need to worry because my father was asleep in front of the television and my mother was out. I led Edwin quickly upstairs, the taste of grease and fried onions still thick on my tongue.

Sunlight flowed in through my bedroom window, unspooling itself on the bed, the luminous, depleted warmth of a day that is almost spent.

Edwin examined the books in my bookcase, picked up a framed photograph of my father standing beside a 1950s racing car. Dad looked young in the photo, so young I could almost not recognise him. Edwin put down the photograph and picked up the snow globe, the one with Hampton Court Palace inside that I'd been given for my birthday when I was a little girl.

'I can't stop thinking about her,' Edwin said. 'Ever since we saw the play, it's as if she's become trapped inside my head. You're her friend. Do you think if I asked her to go out with me she'd say yes?'

He held the snow globe up to the light, flooding the palace rooms with afternoon sunshine. Then he shook it, hesitantly at first and then with more vigour. The little world under the dome turned instantly white.

'I don't know,' I said. There was a kind of harsh ringing in my ears, the sound of an electrical device that won't switch off. 'She's not really my friend. I know her to say hello to, that's all.'

We hung around my room for a little while longer then Edwin said he should go, that he was supposed to be home in time for supper. Then he went. That was the last time we were together, just the two of us. I felt empty inside, an empty vessel. People use that phrase to describe someone who turns out to be less than they seem, but I can still remember how I felt at that moment and in the hours and days that followed, as if I really had become a china doll, a painted surface with nothing inside, so fragile I had to move carefully in case I smashed apart. I became afraid of loud noises, of traffic, of the casual collisions and glancing contacts that are experienced daily with people in the street. The world felt too noisy, cartoonish, and I wondered how I'd managed it before, how I had moved through it without thinking.

I remember how I felt, but not the feeling. Perhaps I don't want to. I do sometimes wonder where Edwin is now, how he ended up, even though I don't want to speak to him and never could. He is in his world and I am in mine – parallel universes. Does that make sense?

In Ewa Chaplin's story – not the one about the carnival, the one about the duchess – the street where the actress lives with her husband has the same name – Golovinsky Street – as the street where Ewa's parents were living when she was born.

With love always,

Bramber

Happenstance

by Ewa Chaplin

translated from the Polish by Erwin Blacher 2008

I was scared of Aunt Lola at first, because she only had one eye. I was about five when she first came to stay. I'm sure she must have stayed with us before that, when I was a baby, but I'm talking about the first time I remember. Aunt Lola was my father's sister. No one had warned me about the eye beforehand – perhaps everyone assumed I would remember – and that was why I was scared.

When I say she only had one eye, I don't mean she lost one in an accident or anything, I mean she was born like that. Her left eye was perfectly normal. On the right side of her face, where the other eye should have been, there was just a pinkish, wrinkled hollow, like a thumb print in Plasticine.

Other than that, I thought she was pretty. She had delicate, birdlike hands and a sweet, soft smile. Her chestnut-coloured hair was like a per-fumed cloud. I stared at the monstrous concavity on the right side of her face and wondered what it might feel like to touch it: whether it would be soft, like her cheek, or whether I would be able to feel a phantom eye moving about beneath the skin, slimy and gelatinous and cold.

The eye she did have was long-lashed and golden, just like my father's. She wore a strand of beads that matched the colour exactly and when Aunt Lola bent down to kiss me I grabbed them. They felt warm and glistening in my hand, like pieces of toffee. When Aunt Lola tried to straighten up, the string broke. Beads flew in all directions. Everyone was suddenly on their knees.

'You could try to help, Sonia,' said my mother. 'Seeing as this is all your fault.'

'Don't worry, Dorrie, it was an accident,' said Aunt Lola. 'I think we've got them all now anyway, haven't we, Chimp?'

My father's name was Charles, but Aunt Lola called him Chimp, a private nickname from their childhood that made my father sigh in a resigned way and that annoyed my mother. Aunt Lola smiled at me, her cupped hands brimming with golden beads. An elf queen, I remember thinking, hoarding her treasure.

Once the adults had had coffee, Aunt Lola came to my room and gave me one of the beads as a souvenir. It was large and oval and shiny, like a boiled sweet. When I held it up to the light I could see there was something trapped inside it, some type of insect. It seemed to be missing one of its legs. Aunt Lola told me the bead was made from the blood of trees, which was called amber.

'That little fly must have got its feet stuck in the amber and then died there,' she said. 'It's millions of years old. As old as the dinosaurs.'

I held the bead tight in my fist. 'Did it hurt when they took out your eye?' I said.

She laughed. I knew my mother would have told me off severely for mentioning the eye, but Aunt Lola didn't seem to mind at all. 'Sometimes things go wrong with a baby when she's in the womb,' she said. 'The building instructions get mixed up. That's what happened to me, and so I have a missing eye.'

'Could that happen to any baby?' I said. 'Could it have happened to Daddy?'

'It could have done. But it didn't.'

I rested my head on her shoulder and stroked her hair. I felt safe with her, for some reason, as if she really were an elf queen and I her trusted subject. I felt different about the missing eye from that time on. I held a secret belief, that it was my mission to protect Aunt Lola from the pointing fingers of other people – stupid people, who did not understand about missing instructions for making babies, and dinosaur-flies caught trespassing, like naughty schoolboys, in the blood of trees.

My mother disliked Aunt Lola, but it had nothing to do with the eye.

My mother disapproved of her husband's sister because she wrote detective stories.

'There's something very unhealthy about a woman going on about murder all the time,' she said. 'It's as if she's obsessed with death. I know Lola has been disadvantaged, but really, I can't see what good it does her to be so morbid.'

Disadvantaged meant the missing eye. Although my mother never spoke about the eye directly, she always managed to bring it into the conversation by other means. My mother sold cosmetics, and she was good at her job. She organised makeup parties at other women's homes, for which there was always a long waiting list. I was forbidden to touch her samples, but every now and then she would give me some she had left over, sachets and tubes that had already been opened and partially used. I would steal my father's shaving mirror out of the bathroom, lay out the cosmetics on top of my chest of drawers and pretend I was in a beauty parlour.

I liked strong contrasts: deep vermilion lips, sooty lashes, heavy-lidded lavender eyes. Aunt Lola wore no makeup at all, or if she did it looked so natural you didn't notice it. My mother wouldn't have her books in the house but when I was fourteen I took some of my Christmas money and went into town, where I found a whole shelf of Aunt Lola's novels on display in the Crime section of our local bookshop.

The book I chose was called *Happenstance*, and was about a film director who discovers that her actor husband has committed a murder.

It wasn't long before my mother found out what I'd been reading. 'Fancy wasting your money on that rubbish,' she said. She was furious, I could tell, though she didn't try to confiscate the book – I had reached an age where such a sanction would have seemed unreasonable. I read the book through to the end, but I didn't enjoy it much. From the way my mother harped on, I had imagined the story would be exciting, bursting with bloody weapons and murdered corpses. As it was, I found the plot difficult to follow and you didn't even get to witness the actual murder, which had already been committed before the book started.

I didn't bother buying any more.

When I told my parents I was going to art college, their reaction was not positive, to say the least. My father did his best to stay out of it, but my mother wouldn't let the subject rest. She had her heart set on me going to university to study law, of all things. That sounded like hell to me and I said so. Neither of us realised it at the time, but what I really wanted to do was follow in her footsteps. By the end of my first year in college, I knew I had no interest in painting pictures or, as the tutors insisted on calling it, 'making art'. I wanted to work in the theatre as a makeup artist.

I had always been amazed at what makeup could do. From an early age, I had watched, fascinated, as my mother turned dull women into beauties, shy women into vamps. There was something of the miraculous in such alterations, a craft that skirted close to alchemy. I longed to discover its secrets for myself.

In the end I dropped out of college and started looking for work. So far as my mother was concerned, I made that situation even worse by moving in with Aunt Lola. Her place was more than big enough for the both of us, Lola insisted, and the rent she was asking was so low for the city, no more than a token, so I thought why not?

I had never visited Aunt Lola in her flat, and it wasn't until I turned up there with all my junk in tow that I understood how successful she was as a writer. Her apartment was on the Merkelgasse, and very spacious. The room she had picked out for me was twice the size of my old study bedroom in college, and it had its own bathroom. The ceilings of the apartment were high and the windows were large, though all the rooms seemed dark. I thought at first this was because Lola's apartment building faced north-east, but the longer I lived there the more I became convinced that the dim, almost turgid atmosphere of the place was down to the sheer accumulation of dark things Lola kept there: the varnished mahogany furniture, the brown velvet curtains, the heavy, block-printed papers that covered the walls.

'You look tired,' Lola said, when I arrived. She put out a tiny hand for one of my bags. 'You should have let me book you a taxi.'

It sounds silly, I know, but seeing Lola there in her own private kingdom made me feel shy of her, almost afraid. Throughout my child-hood she had been a beloved figure, someone I always looked forward to seeing and missed when she went abroad or just wasn't around. Once I started college she figured less – perhaps inevitably – and we fell out of touch. As she welcomed me into the hallway of her very serious, almost impossibly large apartment I found myself staring at her face – at the pinkish, wrinkled dent where her eye should have been – and wondering if I'd made a terrible mistake.

I needn't have worried. Lola turned out to be easygoing – she never interrogated me about where I was or who I was with the way my mother would have done – and for a while at least we seemed closer than ever. She didn't go out much herself but that seemed to be mainly because of her work. And she was always taking phone calls – some of them went on literally for hours. She laughed a lot during the calls, a low, sweet chuckle, her one eye smiling and flashing like a bead of polished amber. On the other side of her face you could see the two little dents her teeth made where they met her lower lip. When you caught sight of her suddenly and from a certain angle, it was difficult to understand what you were looking at.

When I finally plucked up the courage to ask her why she wrote about murder, she laughed at that, too.

'You wouldn't believe how many times I've heard that question,' she said. 'All crime writers get asked it, I think, but women crime writers especially. People tend to think we share an unhealthy interest in violence, but it's not that at all. Not for me, anyway.'

She said it wasn't the act of murder itself that fascinated her, but the circumstances that led up to it and what happened next.

'Murderers are a minority group. I'm interested in what drives them. If you ask a roomful of people if they think they might be capable of murder they'll mostly answer no. Some will cross that line, though. Even the most unassuming person can turn out to be a killer, given the right circumstances. What pushes them over the edge – that's what I want to know.'

I was interested by what she said – interested enough to give her fiction another try. I began reading her most recent novel, which was set in a Hong Kong law firm and concerned a kidnapping. The blurb on the flyleaf said that Lola Danilow had travelled extensively in South-east Asia and had twice been the recipient of the Beata Stasinska Award for Detective Fiction. Both snippets of information were new to me.

There was nothing about her eye, no photograph, either, which didn't surprise me. I wondered how many of her readers even knew.

My first real job was with an independent film company and paid so badly that if it hadn't been for Aunt Lola and her peppercorn rent I would have barely got by. I loved it, though, because I knew I was finally doing what I was born to do. I imagined this was how Aunt Lola must feel about her detective stories, and when I received my first miserable pay cheque I decided to blow the lot on taking her out for a meal, a thank you and celebration all in one.

I agonised for a long time over where we should go. I didn't fancy heading to any of the bars and restaurants I knew near the centre and although I told myself that this was because I thought Lola would prefer somewhere quieter, away from the tourist crowds and noise, if I'm honest it was because I didn't want to risk running into any of my colleagues from the studio. I didn't like to think of how they might look at Lola, at how they might look at me for being with her. I always answered questions

248

about where I was living with some non-committal statement about lodging with family. I didn't want to have to explain things in any more detail.

In the end we went to a small Italian place, just around the corner from the flat. As we arrived, a woman and a young boy were coming out. The boy stared up at Aunt Lola, tipping his head back and clinging fast to the door handle. His upper lip was crusted with sugar. His mother glanced at us briefly then tugged on the boy's arm, forcing him to let go of the door.

Aunt Lola turned to me and made a remark about never having been to this restaurant before and how pleasant the place seemed. She seemed unconcerned by the boy's behaviour and I felt relieved. There is something almost superstitious in most people's attitude towards disfigurement – it is as if they believe deformity might be contagious, or spread bad luck. I found such ignorance appalling, but at the same time I had begun to resent Aunt Lola also, for provoking such a reaction.

She cramped my style, in other words. I had my own life now, my own friends. Aunt Lola was a problem I had not signed up for and had no idea how to solve. It didn't help that those friends of hers who did come to the flat bored me rigid. Other writers and literary critics mostly, drunk on success or failure and forever banging on about subjects so terminally dull they could send you to sleep just by being in the same room.

I kept thinking I should move out, but I couldn't afford to, not if I wanted to keep living close to the city centre. I gave myself a deadline: another twelve months at the most and I would be out of there.

The first two productions I worked on – a romantic comedy and a prison-break drama written by an ex-convict who had become something of a national celebrity – were not technically challenging, but I put in a lot of overtime, nonetheless. I wanted to show I was serious. Also, I enjoyed the buzz of being around a film set. I used my time off to increase my repertoire, practising on myself as I had always done until I perfected the particular effect I wanted to achieve. I gave myself bullet wounds and acid burns. I aged myself forty years. Once I gave myself a black eye, then popped out to the local mini-mart to pick up some groceries. Judging by the weird looks and concerned glances, the results were convincing.

It was on the evening I recounted this anecdote – I was with a group of tech support in the Maraschino bar – that I first happened to exchange words with Wilson Krajewski. Wil was a screenwriter and editor, though I didn't know that then. He was often around on set and I had an idea he was one of the lighting crew.

I was intrigued by him, I suppose. He wore black jeans and a plain T-shirt like everyone else but it was difficult to tell how old he was. If you had asked me if I thought he was good looking, I would probably have said yes, but I would have found it difficult to say exactly why.

Instead of laughing at my fake black eye anecdote like everyone else, he responded with a disapproving stare, and that intrigued me, too.

Stuck-up smart-arse, I thought. I didn't even know what his name was. When Karl from sound told me it was Wilson I thought I'd misheard.

'My mother is American,' Wil explained, once we were better acquainted. 'It's a family name.'

I'd had a couple of flings since I'd come to the city – guys I'd known from college – but nothing serious. On paper, Wil was the last person I'd have imagined ending up with. The first time he took me out on a date, he spent the entire evening talking about his work. I listened carefully, trying not to say anything that would have him mark me down as an idiot, feeling vaguely bored but, as I say, intrigued. After dinner we went back to his place – a loft apartment in a converted factory five metro stops away – and fucked. I hadn't intended for us to end the evening in that manner but something about the way he rolled his cigarettes really turned me on and anyway, it was more interesting than listening to him going on about Verfremdungseffekt.

We started seeing each other regularly after that. It turned out Wil was in his forties, with two highly rated commercial successes under his belt and another half-dozen independent projects in the works that wouldn't make him any money but would win him a serious number of brownie points with the critics.

He was intense and self-obsessed but he didn't flirt with other women when he was with me and he was good in bed. He could also, when he was in relaxed mode, be great fun to be with.

A friend of mine from wardrobe told me she'd always fancied him rotten, which was the icing on the cake, really. There were no hard feelings.

I was drunk the evening I took him back to Lola's. I don't think I'd have done that otherwise, and then how very different all our lives might have been. It was the night we wrapped the prison-break drama and we were all high on relief, not least Wil. He had spent six months working alongside the celebrity criminal, who still got to take most of the scripting credit in spite of – and these are Wil's words, not mine – not being able to string a sentence together that did not include the word cunt. It was close to midnight when we left the Maraschino, and I suddenly got it into my head that Wil might get a kick out of seeing where I lived, the Merkelgasse and all that. I'd told him I lived with my aunt, but not who she was. I didn't want to spend my time with Wil talking about Lola, and I had no intention of introducing them. Not yet, anyway.

Lola normally retired to bed at around eleven and I thought the chances of us disturbing her were slim. Like I say, I was drunk.

Wil's reaction as we went up in the lift was suitably gratifying. The lift was pre-war and rattled like a lorryload of loose ironmongery, but that was all part of what you might call the period charm.

'I can't believe you never told me you lived in this building,' Wil said. 'You do know it's famous? Tobias Angell lived here. And Marek Adorno used the facade in *The Wolf of Warsaw*. This is incredible.'

'My aunt's lived here for years,' I said, breezily. 'Since before I was born, I think. I suppose I take it for granted.'

I hadn't heard of Tobias Angell or *The Wolf of Warsaw*. Wil was always dropping the names of films and books – he was the kind of person who feels more alive in invented worlds than in the real one. I flicked on the hall lights, four low-wattage bulbs in wrought-iron sconces. The light they cast was very dim, a kind of ochre glow that was supposed to look like candlelight. The hallway ran the whole length of the flat and the poor lighting made it look even more cavernous. Our shadows hunched and leaped like dwarfs in a funhouse mirror maze.

'Here we are,' I said. 'Home, sweet home.'

'I can't get over this. It's spectacular.'

I felt a surge of self-satisfaction at my achievement – finally we were talking about me and not him. Wil moved slowly along the hallway, examining the pictures. There were three of them, all murky oils of the kind Aunt Lola seemed to go in for. Two were landscapes, forested ravines with ruined castles that looked like something out of *Dracula*. The third was a portrait, an adolescent girl sitting on a bed in what appeared to be a dingy hotel or more likely a lodging house. She looked terrified to me. The painting gave me the creeps.

'What a superb painting,' Wil said. 'Do you know who it's by?'

'I'm not sure,' I said. I'd grown so used to the clutter in Lola's apartment I'd stopped noticing it ages ago. I wished now that I'd paid more attention. 'My aunt will know. I'll ask her.'

Wil nodded. He was still gazing at the painting and seemed almost to have forgotten I was there. After a moment he moved away from the picture and into the living room. One of the table lamps had been left on, but there was no sign of Lola and that at least was something.

'I'm going to change my shirt,' I said. I'd spilled wine on it earlier, in the bar. I was beginning to sober up and the soiled shirt was just one more way in which the situation was beginning to feel out of control. 'I won't be a moment. Then I'll fix us both a drink and we can relax.'

Wil made a noise of assent. 'Hurry back,' he said, though it was clear he was more interested in what other unexpected treasures might be available for his delectation on the mantel and sideboard. I returned to find him standing in front of Lola's huge carved bookcase, hands thrust deep in his pockets. There were books all over the flat, not just on shelves but lined up along the skirting boards, perched precariously on top of cupboards, everywhere. The ones in the bookcase were all hardbacks, all first editions, all crime novels of some description and many of them Aunt Lola's own works. Lola had been with the same publisher throughout her career, and all her books had a similar cover design: the title in black against a grey background, and always with a hornet somewhere about, the stripes on its abdomen highlighted in gold foil. Clever.

Wil ran his finger along the smooth grey spines before taking down one of the books, *Belladonna*, which was about a woman who has her own sister committed to a mental asylum so she can steal her child.

'I thought this was terrific,' Wil said. 'Very well written. I read it when it first came out.'

'It's my aunt's,' I said automatically, then instantly regretted it. Whatever the initial rush it had given me, I could see now that bringing Wil here had been a mistake. Never mix business with pleasure, or aunts with lovers.

'You mean your aunt collects first editions?'

'No,' I said. My heart sank. What if he demanded to meet her? 'I mean my aunt is the author. She's a crime writer.'

'Your aunt is Lola Danilow?'

I nodded. Wil turned eagerly to the back flap, searching for a photograph, presumably. I could have told him he wouldn't find one. He seemed genuinely awestruck, more so even than when he'd been looking at the paintings in the hallway, but I took no pleasure in it.

'I'll go and get those glasses,' I said. I turned to leave the room, and almost ran slap bang into Aunt Lola, who was standing in the doorway, dressed in her grey silk kimono and matching slippers. It seemed almost uncanny, the way she had crept up on us so silently. Her face was half in shadow and for a moment it appeared normal, the hollow where her right eye should have been merely the shaded concavity of an ordinary eye socket. Then she tilted her head slightly and the light from the standard lamp fell fully upon her. I found myself recoiling, just a little. I tend to forget how shocking her appearance must be to strangers.

'I thought I heard voices,' she said, smiling. 'Would anyone like coffee?'

Her voice, so refined, so melodious, and always with that chuckle bubbling away beneath the surface. She didn't turn her head or try to hide herself from Wil, even though she'd never met him before. She was getting on for fifty by then, but she didn't look it. Her body was still trim and graceful but that wasn't the whole source of her appeal, or even the half of it. There was something elfin about her, something entrancingly childlike. It was as if the world and everything in it were perpetually new to her. I wondered if in some strange way this quality of freshness, of transparency, was something that had arisen directly out of her disfigurement. Lola had never lived a normal life, and so had never grown bored or tired the way ordinary people often do.

I glanced quickly at Wil, trying to gauge his reaction. Would I see in his eyes what I had seen in the eyes of so many others: that fleeting expression of horror, swiftly concealed behind a mask of smiling acceptance? Once the mask was safely in place, people would take their time observing her, hiding behind pleasantries and chatter, noting and cataloguing every detail of what they perceived as her tragedy.

I saw none of this with Wil.

'You're Lola Danilow,' he said. He stepped forward to greet her, steadily meeting her gaze. He was still holding her book, *Belladonna*. He held it out towards her like a tribute. 'I admire this novel tremendously,' he said. 'I've always thought it would make a marvellous screenplay.'

'It was actually under option for a while,' Lola said. 'Nothing came of it, though. The film business is so fickle.'

She smiled at him, that sweet, soft smile, half beautiful, half monstrous. 'If you'll excuse me for just a moment, I'll go and fetch that coffee.' She turned and left the room. She hadn't asked Wil his name and I thought how strange that was, almost as if she knew him already. They were both writers, after all, both relatively well known within their own small circles. It was possible, at the very least, that they had friends in common.

Wil replaced *Belladonna* on the shelf and took down the book next to it, *The White Castle*. When I looked at it the following day I saw that the plot concerned a murder at an international chess tournament. I couldn't imagine anything less enticing.

Wil replaced this second book also, then began wandering around the room with his hands behind his back, examining the sepia-tinted photographs of film stars, the two bronzes Lola kept on the table beside her phone. The bronzes were weird: intricately detailed, slightly larger-than-life sculptures of a scarab beetle and a common toad. They were by an American sculptor who had been a friend of Aunt Lola's for years. The photographs were a mystery. I found it hard to imagine Lola choosing them herself – it would seem almost perverse, for her to surround herself with images of such beautiful people and I assumed they must have come with the flat. They certainly looked old enough.

There was silence between Wil and I, the awkward, stagy kind that exists between two people who know that every word they speak will be overheard by a third. Eventually, Aunt Lola returned, bearing a mahogany tray laden with three espresso cups, her silver coffee pot and the ornate, claw-footed sugar bowl that went with it. Wil hurried forward to help her but she waved him aside.

'You two make yourselves comfortable,' she said. She began pouring the coffee. Wil sat down in one of the twin leather armchairs opposite the sofa. I settled myself on the floor at his feet, resting the back of my head against his knees, the kind of gesture a screenwriter might have used to indicate that the younger woman wished to assert her dominance over the older one: hands off, bitch, he's mine. Which I guess sounds dodgy now, given everything that followed, but I'm pretty sure the only thing I was thinking at the time was that I was bored.

I drank my coffee slowly and kept my mouth shut. Wil toyed with my hair, jabbering away with Aunt Lola about goodness knows what. The more they went on, the more it became clear that they did have friends in common, acquaintances at least, and that Aunt Lola was familiar with both of Wil's films. I wished they'd stop. In spite of the coffee, the alcohol was catching up with me and it was a struggle to keep my eyes open.

I came awake with a jerk. Wil's hand was on my shoulder.

'Away with the fairies, you were. Your aunt's gone to bed. I had no idea how late it was.'

In fact it was after one thirty. The bed in my room was a queen-size, another of Lola's heavy brown antiques. The heating had gone off and the air was chilly. We undressed quickly and got under the covers. Wil's lovemaking was urgent, almost brutal. I got off on it, but it freaked me out a little, at the same time. Normally, he was slow, cautious even, and I couldn't help wondering if the thought of Aunt Lola, just a few doors away, was acting as some kind of weird turn-on for him. He fell asleep soon afterwards but I found myself fully awake suddenly. The apartment creaked and groaned around me as it did most nights, only that night I felt certain that Lola was wide awake also, lying flat on her back and staring up at the ceiling through her single golden eye.

I covered my right eye with the palm of my hand. The view didn't change much, though the darkness of the room seemed more intense, somehow.

Around two months later, the studio started work on a brand new project, a World War Two drama this time. We were all doing a lot of overtime and I was exhausted. Throughout the final fortnight, before the wrap, I barely saw Wil at all and when I did see him I felt on edge. Some of the thrill seemed to have gone out of our relationship, but I put that down to stress.

I was so preoccupied with work it never occurred to me that Wil might be cheating on me, though in hindsight it was obvious. In all the weeks since our peculiar evening in Lola's apartment, Wil hadn't asked me a single question about her, or the famous building, which anyone would think was odd, given how taken he'd been with both. Not that I was going to broach the subject myself. I'd made sure Wil was out of the flat before Lola was up, and I had no intention of bringing him back there any time soon. I knew Lola wouldn't say anything – she never asked me questions about my private life. I allowed myself to believe that was the end of it.

Except that it wasn't. I found out on a Wednesday. I'd stayed over at Wil's the night before and forgot to set the alarm. I was fighting the day in an uphill battle from the moment I got up, which was probably why I managed to spill a whole cup of coffee over myself, scalding my arm and soaking my T-shirt into the bargain. I normally ate lunch in the hospital canteen, which did an all-you-can-eat buffet and was just across the road from the studio, but I decided to nip back to Lola's instead, so I could have a quick shower and change my clothes. I stank of coffee and my bra felt sticky. I've always had an aversion to feeling unclean.

I thought the flat was empty when I arrived. If I wondered about that at all, I suppose I presumed Lola must be out on an errand – the mini-mart probably, or else the library. I remember feeling relieved – I'd be able to get in and out without having to explain why I was home or hang around chatting. My room was the second on the right along the hall, next to the big cupboard where we hung up our coats and stored the vacuum cleaner. The door was open a crack but I thought nothing of it. With it being just me and Lola, I never made a point of keeping it closed.

She was lying on her back, her head towards the foot of the bed and facing the wall, her hair spiralling across the covers like an inverted crown. She was completely naked. As I entered the room she turned to look at me. Her single eye flashed gold. Her cheeks and neck and collarbone gleamed with fresh sweat. You would have thought she would react with horror, me seeing her like that, but I swear to you she was smiling.

Of course Wil never saw that. He was lying between her legs, embedded in her up to the hilt like a knife in butter.

'Oh Christ,' he said, when he finally realised what was happening. He flung out an arm, tugging at the bedclothes in an attempt to cover himself. They wouldn't come loose, though – Aunt Lola was lying on top of them, pinning them down.

'Sonia,' he said. Just that.

'If I'd known you were into freaks I wouldn't have bothered,' I said. The room stank of their sex, I realised, and once I'd started smelling it, it was all I could smell. My words seemed to spread slowly through the tainted air, vibrating outwards like oily ripples on a stagnant pond. I ran from the room, remembering only belatedly that it was my own room I was running from. All my clothes were in there, including the dark grey jersey top I'd been intending to change into.

I went back to work. There seemed no other choice. I got through the day somehow and then later at the Maraschino I asked my friend Dina from wardrobe if I could stay at her place for a couple of days.

'My aunt's thrown me out,' I added. As explanations went it sounded suitably dramatic, and might even have been called truthful, if only partially. Dina always relished scandal, so she was happy to help, even going so far as to pay a visit to Aunt Lola's the following day to collect some of my belongings.

I'd counted on Lola not saying a word to her beyond the necessary and I counted right.

I should have left things there. I'd more or less decided I had to move out of Aunt Lola's anyway, and if I were honest with myself I knew already that Wil and I weren't going to last. We were just too different, and wanted different things. If he'd had an affair with someone else – someone I didn't know, or even someone I did know who wasn't my aunt – I think I could have moved on. After a bit, anyway.

As it was, rather than fading away, the horror of it – both what I had seen and what I had said – dug its claws deep into my mind and would not let go.

Most of all, Lola's smile. A smile that said: *You know nothing, silly girl, now run along.*

I tried to tell myself I had imagined it, that the expression I had caught on her face had been one of shock, her lips stretched wide in distress and heartbreak, but I knew that wasn't so.

I faced a terrible choice: either believe my own, falsified version of what I had seen, or accept that everything I thought I knew about Aunt Lola – her grace under fire, her affection for me, her fundamental goodness – had all been a lie.

I think it was this, in the end, that helped me decide. Once the pain of personal betrayal had begun to wear off, I found the business of Wil was just a distraction from the question of Lola.

Who was she really and what was her game? If she could behave that way to me, her beloved niece, what might she have done to others, down the years?

I know how melodramatic that sounds, believe me. You'll ask me why I couldn't settle for the simpler explanation: that Lola and Wil really had fallen for each other, and didn't know how to tell me. They had more in common than Wil and I did, that's for sure, and they'd both have felt awful about deceiving me.

And still I couldn't forget her smile. That gloating, knowing smile that told me none of this had happened by accident, that she had planned it. I'd better get out of her way now, while I still could, or . . .

Or what? I didn't know, and I would have felt ridiculous, trying to explain my fears to any of my friends. In the end I phoned Dad. I was still in regular contact with my parents and since I'd landed the job at the studio even my mother seemed resigned about my career choice. I think a part of her was even pleased, though she would never have said so, and it was no good talking to her about Aunt Lola, either. My mother had always held fast to the idea that Lola was a tragic, helpless woman who wrote about murder because she couldn't get a man. If she ever found out about what happened with Wil – information I was determined would never see the light of day – she would come over all smug and I-told-you-so. She'd be convinced that Lola's actions arose out of simple jealousy, and I'd be no further forward.

I called after supper. I knew Mum would be out, hosting one of her parties, and I wanted to speak to Dad without her knowing. Once we'd got through the pleasantries, I told him I'd moved out of Aunt Lola's and into my own place, a box-sized studio apartment that was four flights up over the central market but that had the notable advantages of closeness to work and being seriously trendy into the bargain.

'Were you not getting on with Lola?' Dad asked me at once. I was surprised, that we had come to the point so soon. I had expected more prevarication, more dancing around the point like nervous teenagers on a first date.

He'd made the first move. I owed it to him – to both of us – not to play dumb.

'We've not spoken since I moved out,' I said. I could hear him at the other end, breathing slowly in and out and waiting to hear what I would say next. 'Dad, how do you feel about Lola? I mean really?'

By that point I was expecting an outpouring, a series of anecdotes about how Lola had bullied him senseless when they were kids, how she'd always managed to get her own way, how she would exert a terrible punishment if he tried to cross her.

Once again, I was wrong.

'Keep out of her way, Sonia. Whatever happened, it's best to leave it. Just get on with your life.'

'I thought you were close, though.' And now I was prevaricating, but the baldness of his response had caught me off balance. That feeling you get when you're afraid to tell someone something in case they think you're crazy, or lying, only to have them turn round and tell you no, you were right all along.

I should have been pumping my fist in triumph, but what I actually felt right then was frightened.

'I was close to my sister,' he said slowly. What I noticed most of all was the way he stressed the word 'sister', instead of 'was'. An odd way of putting it, I thought, and one I picked up on immediately because of the way our line coaches were always banging on about the importance of emphasis, the way a sentence's meaning could be changed entirely simply by laying the stress on one word instead of another. 'Lola was . . .

my inspiration. I adored her. The night she went missing was one of the worst times of my life. Of all our lives.'

'What do you mean, went missing?'

'She was on her way to visit a friend, just down the road, but she never arrived. I was six at the time, Lola was nine. Our parents never worried about us running around by ourselves. It was a small town, everyone knew everyone, it was perfectly safe. But Lola just vanished. My father went door to door, looking for her, but no one had seen her. He and some of our neighbours were just getting a search party together to scour the patch of woodland us kids called the Spook when Lola reappeared. Her skirt was all torn and there were scratch marks on her arms from brambles but she kept saying she was all right and she didn't seem upset at all, so the fuss soon died down. Everyone assumed she'd wandered off and lost track of time. The Lola who came back wasn't my sister, though, that's all I can say. It's something I've never talked about, not to anyone, but I know it's true.'

'What do you mean, Dad, not your sister?'

'I don't want you digging into this, Sonia, I don't like it. Just promise me you'll keep away from her. Promise?'

I promised, though I mentally reserved the right to go back on my word, should it become necessary. I needed time to think.

'Did she ever say where she'd been?' I asked.

'Only that she'd gone looking for fairy gold and got lost in the woods.'

'But you didn't believe her?'

'Yes, I believed her.'

I let him go after that. I could tell how much it cost him, to tell me even that much, and I felt concerned about my mother coming home suddenly and interrogating him over what we'd been talking about.

I understood what Dad was saying, in any case: he believed Aunt Lola was a changeling. You read of such things in the tabloids sometimes, though I'd never known anyone it happened to personally.

I remembered all those times when I was a kid, me saying to Aunt Lola that she was my elf queen and I her loyal subject.

She always smiled so sweetly when I said that. How foolish she must have thought me, even then.

How do you go about killing a fairy queen? There are no books on the subject – I know, I searched – and ironically I found myself falling back on Lola's own. After largely ignoring Lola's oeuvre for most of my life, I now devoured it eagerly, reading all of her books in sequence right through from her debut – *Cousins* – to her most recent novel *The City Gates*, which had been published to ecstatic reviews just six months before.

I found her plots as opaque and dull as ever, but one potentially useful discovery I made, and made quickly, was that Lola was obsessed by detail. Not just the forensic details that were central to solving crimes, but the practical and other mundane details of how they were committed. Toxicology was a favourite subject of hers, as was ballistics. In one novel – *End of Service* – she even had an excruciating five pages describing the commonest materials for making an effective garrotte, and where best to source them.

I wondered how she knew all this stuff, how much of it was true. I couldn't see myself wielding a gun, much less a garrotte, because I knew I was almost certain to make a hash of things. If I didn't get killed myself, I'd almost certainly be caught, and then I'd be sent to prison for life, with the entire courtroom believing I killed my poor disabled aunt because she stole my boyfriend.

It would have to be poison. Aunt Lola's books furnished me with enough information to begin hatching a plan, but that still left me with the problem that had been bothering me from the start: did what worked for humans also work for the small folk? Would arsenic kill an elf queen, or would she wolf it down like sherbet, and lick her lips afterwards?

I had no idea.

Aunt Lola made the procurement of deadly chemicals sound like the least of a would-be murderer's difficulties, and she turned out to be right. There are more things in heaven and earth, Horatio, and a city this size boasts more establishments selling under-the-counter merchandise than you might imagine. Poky little shops in the factory district, hole-in-the-wall outlets down every proverbial back alley, all seeking to do business and all without attracting the kind of attention that might prove harmful to trade.

You would be surprised, how many substances are listed under the general designation of rat poison. Anyone would think it was the fifteenth century, the amount of rat poison that gets sold nowadays. There was a place I found, a grubby emporium advertising itself as Warbinski's Iron-mongery and General Stores, where the proprietor would weigh out bismuth and antimony by the ounce, using the old-fashioned kind of brass-levered weighing scales you find in every grandmother's kitchen.

'And you don't mind working with this stuff?' I asked him, a red-nosed, runny-eyed gnome of a man I presumed must be Mr Warbinski. I wasn't buying anything that day. I had decided to use Warbinski's as a testing ground, to see what kind of reaction I might get when I started asking the kind of questions I needed to ask.

I posed as a radio journalist, of all things. I told him I was researching a programme on old family businesses.

Warbinski shook his head. 'Used to it,' he said. 'None of these materials are dangerous, so long as they're treated with appropriate respect. Don't want strychnine ending up in the sugar bowl now, do we?'

He laughed uproariously, his nostrils flaring wide. I managed a smirk because I knew it was expected but it was difficult for me not to imagine that his supposed joke had been at my expense. When he offered me a cup of tea I quickly refused.

'Just one more thing,' I said, as I was leaving. 'Do you sell anything for fairy infestations?'

'Good Lord,' Warbinski said. He was doing his best to look outraged but I could tell it was a put-up job by the way his gaze was momentarily diverted towards the back of his shop, as if he were suddenly afraid I might be a decoy, and that even now a team of detectives were trashing his storeroom in search of blacklisted substances. 'We don't go in for that kind of thing here, indeed no. The materials you are referring to are only available under special licence. Costs an absolute bomb and definitely not worth the blowback if some idiot gets their sums wrong, indeed no.'

I decided I would have to take a chance. I took out my wallet and placed a note of a painfully large denomination on the counter. I made a real meal of it, too, licking my fingertips and staring into his eyes as if we were both actors in some low-rent spy movie. 'I'm sure you know where such *materials* might be available, though,' I said, deliberately. 'What with your family ties to this part of the city being so extensive?'

He hesitated for less than a second before grabbing the note. 'Zivor-ski'll set you right,' he said. 'Under the bridge and then right into Gagarin Street. Only I would strongly advise you against. Not to be messed with, those fae buggers. Don't say I didn't warn you.'

'This is just research,' I reminded him. 'My enquiry was strictly theo-retical.'

'Right you are, then,' said Warbinski, brightening up again. I knew he didn't believe me for a second, but by his reckoning he'd done his moral duty and that would have to be enough.

Zivorski's turned out to be a jeweller's, and judging by the stones on dis-play in the window, quite an expensive one – not what I had expected at all. I peered in through the bowed, nicotine-stained glass, trying to work out if Warbinski had been taking me for a ride after all.

In the end I decided to chance it and went inside, pushing at the peeling door in its warped frame until a bell sounded, summoning the eponymous Zivorski. I was surprised by her youth, I suppose because the shop itself was so decrepit.

What surprised me even more was that she was a dwarf. A human dwarf, I assumed, rather than fae, although the shock of seeing her, given the reason I was there in the first place, almost made me turn around and leave before I got in any deeper.

I remembered Warbinski's words: I advise you strongly against.

What did I think I was doing in this part of town, anyway? My mother would have a fit.

'Good afternoon,' said Zivorski. 'How can I help?'

She spoke quietly but firmly, without that edge of deference adopted by most service personnel. Her dress – a grey silk shift – was obviously expensive but without looking flashy.

She knew how to play down her disadvantages, that was for sure.

'Warbinski sent me,' I said. That at least was the unvarnished truth.

'Leon? What's he been up to?' Her guard seemed to drop at the mention of Warbinski's name. The two were genuinely acquainted then, which at least was something.

'I only met him today,' I said. I was about to launch into my radio journalist spiel but something in this woman's expression gave me to understand that we were beyond that. 'I went to his shop because . . . I have a problem. Warbinski said you might be able to help.'

'Don't tell me you're intending to kill someone? There are easier ways of solving problems, believe me.'

'She's fae,' I said quickly, my trump card, although I had an idea this Zivorski would have worked that out already. Why come to her otherwise? For executions of the common or garden variety, Warbinski's stock of pathogens would be more than adequate.

'I'm sure Leon will already have told you this isn't a good idea,' she said at once. 'So let's skip that. It won't be cheap.' The figure she quoted was indeed the better part of two months' wages. Something of my dismay must have shown in my expression because she gave a wry smile. 'These family feuds are best forgotten, you know. What was it your father said? Get on with your life?'

I felt the blood drain from my face. 'Come on,' Zivorski said. 'That's just ground-level telepathy. It's perfectly harmless. The things your aunt could do to you are a hundred times worse. If she finds out, I mean. Have you thought about that?'

'That's why I need her gone.' My voice sounded dry as a rusty hinge.

'I can't go on like this. Always wondering what she might do, what she might be thinking. It's driving me mad.'

'Well, it's your funeral.' Zivorski sighed in a way that suggested she dealt with fools like me every day of the week and was getting tired of it. She came out from behind the counter and I had the chance to observe how oddly shaped she was, the trim elegance of her upper body contrasting dramatically with the squat pelvis, the plump bowed legs, the unnaturally tiny feet. There was something powerful about her though, a decisiveness in her movements that said she didn't care how she might be perceived, her body was splendid to her and she wouldn't change it even if she could.

I couldn't help noticing how beautifully she did her makeup: flawless lips in deep magenta, navy eyeliner, an almost-nude luminescent powder that made her spotless complexion gleam like pearls.

Expensive, like her dress. She bent slightly to unlock the back panel of the window display then reached inside, drawing forth a tray of gemstone rings. She placed the tray on the counter before selecting one, an incredible square-cut topaz set in gold. The stone seemed to wink at me as if it knew something. I shivered. The topaz looked unnervingly like my aunt's single, all-seeing eye.

'There's a tiny catch just under the stone, here.' Zivorski pressed lightly against the metal with the ball of her thumb. The topaz sprung open like a miniature door, revealing a tiny golden cavity beneath. Inside the cavity lay a spherical tablet, or capsule. It had the sheen of nacre.

'This will dissolve in any liquid, alcoholic or otherwise. It runs through your victim's system much like human tetanus, but at a hundred miles an hour. She will curl and shrivel before your eyes. It can be distressing to watch, I warn you, especially as she'll probably be conscious until the very end.' She paused. 'I might be able to give you something back on the ring afterwards, if that's any help.'

I left Zivorski's with the ring in a leather casket and my bank account more or less empty. I walked back towards the centre of town, navigating the refuse-smelling backstreets and questionable retail outlets as if I'd lived in the slums of the factory district all my life.

And it may well come to that, I thought, if any single part of this goes wrong. I wondered if it would really be so bad. No one knew me here and rents were bound to be dirt cheap. I could set up a beauty parlour. I'd have clients coming out of my ears in no time at all. I was surprised and a little appalled by how appealing it seemed, the idea of sliding out of one life and into another. I couldn't help thinking about what Aunt Lola had said when I first went to live with her, about anyone being capable of murder, given the right circumstances.

Did I truly mean to go through with this? I clasped my satchel to my chest, the trick ring inside. Zivorski had told me the poison in the capsule would only work on fair folk.

'Which gives the product an inbuilt advantage, you know, if you happen to have made a *mistake*,' she added, leaning heavily upon the last word as if she were offering me one last chance to resolve my predicament in a less radical way, and save myself some money into the bargain.

The problem was that I didn't want to save the money, not any more. I had even lost some of my hunger to see Lola dead. At some point during the planning process, my anger and hatred had reshaped themselves into something less visceral and more chilling: curiosity. I had become like one of Lola's protagonists: secretive and introverted, obsessed with minutiae.

It sounds incredible I know, but what I wanted most was to discover if I could get away with it.

Like Ernst Meier in *The White Castle*, I had come to think of myself and Lola as natural adversaries: two evenly matched opponents in a struggle carried out in silence but that was nonetheless a fight to the death.

I waited three days, just to steady myself, then gave Aunt Lola a call. She sounded delighted to hear from me, her voice trembling with emotion. Or was that simply the result of a bad telephone connection?

'Sonia, dearest. I've been longing to talk to you. It's been so difficult to know what to say.'

'I should have called sooner,' I said. My heart was pounding. I couldn't remember ever having been in a situation where what I was saying felt so violently at odds with the thoughts in my head. The feeling was exhilarating, a sense of being ahead of the game, of knowing something my enemy – for was she not my enemy? – could never have guessed at. It was easy to see how this kind of power might become addictive. 'I hate us not speaking. Can we meet?'

'That would make me very happy. Oh my dear, I can't tell you how wonderful it is to hear your voice.'

She asked if I would prefer to meet up in town – neutral ground was what she meant – but I said no, I would come to the flat, the flat would be fine.

I hadn't been near the apartment since the day I found Lola in bed with Wil and the thought of going there now made me sick to my stomach. Nonetheless, we agreed that I would call round at three o'clock the following day. I would be on set all morning, but one of our key actors was filming a TV commercial in the afternoon, and we'd be clocking off early.

I rode up in the lift as normal, the rusty chugging sound so comforting in its familiarity that I could almost imagine another version of myself – the Sonia-before – calling off the murder plan and agreeing to move back in here, to let bygones be bygones.

Then I remembered the crucial element that had been missing from our phone conversation: Lola hadn't mentioned Wil, not once, which must surely mean the two of them were still together. If they'd split up she would surely have told me, or at least dropped a hint.

It suddenly occurred to me that Wil might even be living with her now. I'd glimpsed Wil around the studio from time to time but I'd deliberately avoided him as much as possible and those friends of mine who were also friends of Wil's kept a diplomatic silence. I had no idea how he was or what he was doing, which suited me fine. But this did also mean I'd left myself open to nasty surprises.

I rang the bell. The familiar, harsh buzzing, then silence. I tried to compose myself, to be the person I was pretending to be – the person who had turned up on this same doorstep eighteen months ago with two bulging holdalls and a broken suitcase, in fact. It was only then that I realised that person no longer existed, that whatever happened in the next forty-five minutes she was gone for good.

Then the door burst open and there she was, my aunt, wearing a beautiful hand-finished trouser suit and smiling like a movie star.

Her hair looked as if it had been recently styled, the wispy auburn curls both softer and brighter. She looked radiant. If I'd had any doubts about how things stood between her and Wil, those doubts were gone now.

I wondered if Wil knew what she was, if he even cared.

'Sonia,' she cried. She threw her arms around me, kissed my cheek. 'You look lovely, dear. Come inside.'

She didn't even sound like her old self: mildly sardonic, wryly amused, cautious and consistent. It was as if she believed the whole world must now share her happiness, a joy so pure that its origins in deception no longer mattered.

The truth is difficult, isn't it? I want to tell you how this story ends, but I'm not sure how to do that. I could tell you about how we sat down together in Aunt Lola's living room with the photographs and the books and that ugly bronze beetle of hers, how Lola talked and talked, insisting that when she first went for a drink with Wil it was just that – a drink – because they'd enjoyed each other's company so much the previous evening.

'You have to believe me, Sonia, I didn't plan any of this.' She even blushed. 'I think I might have been a little crazy for a while.'

Just for a while? I thought, but didn't say. I kept my smile on and said it was all right, I understood, that's what love does to people. She leaned forward in her chair then – the same chair Wil had been sitting in the night he met Lola – placed her hand on my arm and said yes, that was it exactly, and I did understand, didn't I, that she loved Wil, that it was the real thing, that she wouldn't have dreamed of coming between us otherwise.

'I still feel ashamed,' she said. 'Not of Wil and me, but of the way it all happened. You finding out like that. I can't tell you how dreadful I feel. I wish I'd found the courage to tell you properly.'

She was shaking all over by then, trembling like a harvest mouse, steaming with the ecstasy of self-disclosure. That's not my phrase, it's Lola's – from the scene in *Cousins* where Petya is confessing to Hanna that he killed her father.

I patted her shoulder and said she should stop blaming herself, that Wil and I had been on the rocks and that the past didn't matter now anyway because I was with someone else, a jazz drummer named Marco I'd met when his band played the Maraschino three months ago.

'Really?' gasped Lola. 'Oh Sonia, that's wonderful. When do I get to meet him?'

She sounded genuinely pleased for me, too, suggested we should come round for dinner as soon as possible, me and the non-existent Marco, who I think I might actually have fancied if he'd been real. If Lola thought she had a monopoly on creative invention, she was wrong. I smiled and smiled, all the time thinking that if she said one more word about her and Wil and how *maaahvellous* they were together then I might just have to kill her.

Which was funny really, because I was going to kill her anyway.

'Let's have tea,' she said at last. 'And you can tell me all about Marco.'

She hurried off into the kitchen. I heard the sounds of running water and the rattle of crockery and at one point I even heard Lola singing although I might have imagined that. I got up from my seat and moved slowly around the room, running my fingers over the spines of the books in the bookcase, gazing at the framed photographs of film stars just as Wil had done and wondering if any of these things would pass down to me when my aunt was dead.

She came back at long last, placed the tray on the low coffee table between us. As well as the tea things there was a plate of the elegant sweet confections – Viennese wafers and iced petit fours – that I knew she must have bought specially from Süssmayr's Pâtisserie, which was quite a hike from the Merkelgasse and way past the mini-mart. I should be so honoured.

We waited while the tea brewed, talking of nothing. Lola finally plied the pot, the liquid falling in a perfect amber arc, making that inimitable sound tea makes as it flows into a cup. It was only once she'd finished pouring that Lola realised she had forgotten the milk. Lola always took her tea black, in the Russian fashion, with a lump of sugar. Normally she would have remembered that I prefer mine white. Either she was just nervous or, what with me being out of her life for so long, she had genuinely forgotten.

'How silly of me,' she said. 'I won't be a moment.' She hurried back to the kitchen. It was now or never. I hadn't practised the manoeuvre at home because I was afraid it might jinx me. Perhaps I was just lucky, but I needn't have worried. The whole thing went perfectly, as if I was used to poisoning people's beverages for a living. A quick movement forward, press with the thumb, a tiny sound – plink! – like a solitary drop of water falling from the tap into the bath. The tablet dissolved so quickly I barely saw it happen. Which made it easier to tell myself afterwards that the horror of what occurred next was not my fault.

Zivorski had warned me that it might be upsetting to see Lola die, to watch her agony, though in fact it was not. Rather I *beheld* it, as I might have observed something that was happening on a television screen, or the final day's rushes from whatever film project I was currently working on. Assessing them for bungled lighting or muffed lines.

I think I would be right in saying that this was a perfect performance. Lola raised her cup to her lips, blew gently on the liquid to cool it as was her habit, took one quick sip and then another, grimaced slightly then replaced the cup in its saucer. I had just enough time – a second or so – to curse myself for not asking Zivorski how much of the liquid had to be consumed before the poison was effective, before Lola began to die.

A look of terrified surprise came into her eye, an expression I can best describe as acute awareness. Then her muscles went taut, all of them, at once. She jerked bolt upright in her seat, as if she'd been turned into a line drawing of herself, all points and angles. Her fingers gripped her knees like the talons of birds. I could see how she was trying to unclamp one of her hands, to reach for me, for the table, for anything, but her joints were locked tight. She couldn't speak either, or scream.

Instead, a terrible gurgling, the only sound her constricted throat could now produce.

I sat and watched, gazing at her as the knife-bright awareness in her eye changed to the dull fog of delirium, as her spine bent itself backwards in a paroxysm of desperation – I heard it crack – and her bent knees beat against her chest like demented drumsticks.

Blood coursed from her mouth, together with some other substance – bile, probably – streaming down her chin and flooding the gold-flecked front of her expensive pant-suit as the room filled with the mingled aromas of her shit and piss.

Someone's going to have one hell of a cleaning up job on their hands. The thought floated through my brain, light as air and blue as a robin's egg, as a stray piece of confetti.

The whole process took less than two minutes. A brief interlude, I suppose you might call it, unless you were Lola. When it was over her whole skeleton seemed to fold in on itself, a bunch of twigs wrapped in soiled rags, that's what she looked like, her head lolling crazily off to one side like a broken doll.

Suddenly I needed the bathroom. I reached the toilet just in time, my bowels voiding themselves in a mess of stench and heat, as if in some bizarre tribute to what had just happened in the room next door. I remained crouched there for several minutes, breathing hard, and gradually the churning in my stomach seemed to subside. I knew I still had the teacups to deal with and I couldn't afford to relax or even think much until that was done.

When I felt able to move I returned to the living room, where I lifted the two cups carefully from the table and carried them through to the kitchen. I emptied their contents down the sink, chased them down with hot water. Then I washed the teacups and carefully dried them, returning my own to the correct cupboard and replacing Aunt Lola's in its previous position on the tray. I poured her another cup of tea, then dusted the handles of all receptacles with a clean cotton handkerchief I had brought specifically for the purpose.

There would be other prints of mine, everywhere throughout the flat, but then why shouldn't there be? I had lived there for more than a year, after all. I had visited my aunt this very afternoon, and found her quite well.

You wanted that to happen, didn't you? That was the ending you were hoping for, don't try and deny it. You can't have a decent murder story without a gruesome death scene, whatever Lola might say. Have a think about your own secret wishes before you go pointing the finger at women who happen to write crime novels.

Now have another think, about how you'd feel if I were to tell you that this *wasn't* the ending after all, that it was all in my head. Would you feel disappointed, or relieved? You could have your cake and eat it then, couldn't you? A horrific murder, followed by a happy ending. You decide.

I did buy the ring, but after a couple of sleepless nights I trudged all the way back to Zivorski's and asked if I could have a refund. Zivorski said she didn't do refunds, that she'd be leaving herself open to all sorts of abuses if word got around. Which it would, she said – word always does. But she offered to buy the ring back from me at sixty per cent. I agreed on the spot, and after she'd shut up shop we went for a drink together in the Spider Monkey, a joint near the Old Market that looked dubious from the outside but that was actually a hangout for students and chess players.

'I'm buying, and no arguments,' said Zivorski. Her first name was Catherine. Clearly everyone in the Spider Monkey knew her – her appearance at the bar didn't turn even a single head. I liked her a lot, I realised. She had a way of being herself that I sorely envied. When she came back with the drinks I asked her how she'd ended up in the jewellery business.

'I took over from my dad,' she said. 'I grew up over the store and I guess you could say the gem trade is in my blood. Us dwarfs are good with loot, or hadn't you heard?'

The shock must have shown on my face because she burst out laughing. 'Oh come on,' she said. 'I don't give a shit what folk call me, so why should you?'

I think that was the moment I realised I could love this woman. Love her, and be in love with her. She seemed everything I wasn't. 'What about the other side of the business?' I asked. 'Did you learn that from your dad, as well?'

'We don't talk about that,' she said. She folded her arms across her chest. 'My granddad on my dad's side was a changeling and he taught me stuff, introduced me to people. My dad always warned me to keep away from that side of the family, but business is business, that's what I say. And it would be a shame to let the old knowledge die out.'

'Aren't you afraid?'

She shook her head decisively then changed the subject. 'What made you change your mind?' she asked. 'About your aunt, I mean?'

I considered her question for several long moments before replying. Why had I changed my mind? There were so many reasons I could have given her but what it came down to was that I didn't have the stomach for it. I wasn't a murderer. Not this time, anyway. And I really did want to move on.

'Too messy,' I said to Zivorski. 'I never could stand getting muck on me.'

Zivorski laughed until there were tears in her eyes and then asked me if I fancied supper. 'They do a mean dumpling stew here,' she said. 'Or we could go somewhere else?'

'Here's fine,' I said. 'I like it.' And it was true, I did. I wondered what Lola was doing and then stopped wondering. I had better things to think about and, after all, in a funny sort of way she had done me a favour.

9 ·

I FOUND IT DIFFICULT TO sleep after reading 'Happenstance'. Once again, the peculiar coincidences between the story and real life – the way Wil in 'Happenstance' had betrayed Sonia, for instance: was that not a darker, stranger version of Edwin's betrayal of Bramber? And that was before I even considered the starker, still more disturbing coincidence of Wil's name. Wilson Krajewski the playwright, Wilson Crosse the collector of automata, the pederast? I felt ripe with coincidence, shaky with it, as if I were being manipulated somehow without my knowledge. As if – and I know how this sounds – I were myself a character in one of Chaplin's stories.

Yes, you can laugh, as I know I would be laughing myself if this hadn't really happened, if these coincidences hadn't unfolded before me on the page in black and white. As it was, I lay awake for a long time, listening to the hotel winding down for the night and trying to make sense of it all, and when I finally did drift off to sleep it was only fitfully, a rest repeatedly punctuated by some fresh vision, imaginary noise, or my own thudding heart.

When I opened my eyes to find the hotel's bedside clock – a flickering digital anomaly amidst the analogue splendour of the White Hart's more skilfully chosen accoutrements – displaying 6:55, a reasonable hour at last, I felt a disproportionate relief, the relief of a prisoner becoming alive to the rattle of the keys that would precipitate his release from torment into the outside world. It was all just fiction, after all. What's in a name?

I went down to breakfast at half past eight and then checked out. I had originally planned to spend the whole day in Exeter as well as an additional night at the White Hart, but such a delay to my journey now seemed pointless, a waste of time. The Scotsman's insistence that I not leave Bramber alone, coupled with the destabilising effects of a seriously disturbed night, had put me into a state of nervous tension. For my own peace of mind I knew I needed to keep moving westwards, to reach Bodmin before nightfall.

But I did still want to pay another visit to the museum. I would have my luggage with me this time – an inconvenience – but seeing as the museum was directly en route to the station I did not want the greater inconvenience of backtracking to the White Hart to collect it before I left.

I want to stress that what happened next was not part of my plan. I intended to take one last look at the Ewa Chaplin doll, buy some postcards for Bramber and then head for the train. Which goes to show how our lives, much more than we know, are governed by chance.

I arrived at the museum just after it opened. An elderly woman was hauling herself up the steps to the entrance, a carrot-headed child on either hand. The children resembled each other in looks as much as the Ibsen twins, but were twice as lively. They hurried the old woman forward, as if presenting her as a prize.

'I want to see the dollies,' said the little girl. She tugged at the old woman's arm, yearning towards the poster tacked to the railings.

'We're going to see the crocodile,' the boy insisted. He began hopping up and down on the steps, thrusting his face in close to his sister's and snapping his teeth. 'Crocodiles eat dolls up.'

The sun shone on his hair and on the turquoise T-shirt he wore, rendering their vivid colours strident as poster paint. By contrast the old woman shared the pallor of a ghost. I assumed she was the twins' grandmother, although she bore them no likeness whatsoever.

The foyer was full of Americans, clearly a coach party. They milled around, exclaiming in loud voices over the architecture, before streaming into the café. A large man stood aside to let them through, and I recognised him as the security guard from the evening before. I hurried past him up the stairs, hoping vaguely that he wouldn't notice me, though what I had to fear from him I could not have said. Not then, anyway. The upper floor seemed deserted. Then, just as I reached the entrance to the Albert Galleries, the fire alarm went off. A member of the museum staff – a woman – hurried out of the exhibition space, looking harassed.

'It's done that twice already this morning, would you believe?' she said. She smiled, raising her eyebrows, then headed quickly downstairs.

The gallery was empty. I was alone with the dolls. I moved at once towards the central aisle, towards Chaplin's 'Artist'. When I arrived in front of her cabinet I discovered something extraordinary, not to say impossible: the glass door was standing open. I looked about myself, bemused – surely someone would come running? – but there was no one in sight. I realised then that the museum worker, in her hurry to deal with the fire alarm, must have left the cabinet open by accident.

What are you waiting for? said 'Artist'. Some accidents are meant to happen.

An odd feeling swept over me then, a kind of quiet frenzy. It came to me that here was my chance to do something, to prove myself to Bramber, to show her that even if I could not give her the world, I could give her the thing in the world that she most desired.

'Artist' was right, I realised – the open cabinet was an omen, a sign. I remembered the last time I had been in the room: the golden afternoon light, the way 'Artist' had seemed to urge me to set her free. Then the security guard had intervened, but now the security guard was downstairs and it was just the two of us. Laughter bubbled up inside my chest and throat. I choked it down only with difficulty. I was in a state of near-hysteria. The only thing keeping me from throwing myself around the gallery in a paroxysm of joyful derangement was the knowledge that for my crazy scheme to stand even a hope of succeeding I would need to stay quiet.

Call it delusions of grandeur, temporary insanity, whatever, but I was not myself. The sight of the open cabinet door had unlocked something inside me, a mental anarchy I had not experienced before, except perhaps in the dreadful days immediately following Ursula's vanishment. It did not occur to me to think about surveillance cameras, or alarm systems – not that I would necessarily have recognised such gadgets for what they were anyway. The point remains – I did not think of them. I could hear 'Artist' laughing delightedly. My course was set.

I inched forward cautiously, inserting first my hand and then most of my right arm into the cabinet. My fingers brushed 'Artist's' skirt, then her shoulder. Beneath her dress her stocky, pliant body felt soft yet firm. I set both hands about her waist and lifted her free. She came easily, almost falling into my arms. A dozen images flew through my mind: trains departing from stations, lovers meeting. I saw these scenes as through a clouded window, barely registering my actions save through the fluttering of my breath against her hair, the rapid thudding of my heart, which would not be quelled.

I unzipped the holdall at my feet and thrust 'Artist' inside. How fortunate, I thought dimly, that I had chosen to bring it with me after all, rather than deciding to leave it behind in the hotel's storage room, to pick up later. With the bag finally closed, a curious calm descended. There was no trace now of the theft – the crime – I had just committed. All that remained for me to do was to leave the museum like any other visitor.

Suddenly I heard the sound of voices on the upper landing. They should not have been familiar, yet somehow they were.

'Dolls are boring. Indian canoes are much better than dolls.'

It was the boy I had glimpsed outside the museum, the noisy carrot-top with the twin sister and the wraithlike grandmother.

'Dolls aren't boring for Angel though, are they, Squirrel? We can go back and see the canoes again afterwards, if you like.' The grandmother, her voice firmer and more confident than I would have expected from her frail appearance, the voice of a respected headmistress in a prosperous market town.

'Don't call me Squirrel. I don't like it.'

'I'm going to choose my favourite,' the girl said, unperturbed. 'Both of you have to guess which one it is.'

They had appeared in the doorway now, the boy sulky with his hands in his pockets, the girl leading her grandmother eagerly by the hand. The boy slouched over to inspect a lively display of Bildnis girl-soldiers. I moved towards the exit, struggling with my holdall. The grandmother edged aside to let me pass. As she turned her head to look at me her eyes froze.

'Stay where I can see you, Squirrel,' she said. She raised her voice, as if to address a crowd.

'I'm sorry, I'm in your way,' I said. 'It's just this bag.' I stepped swiftly towards the doorway, raising the holdall as if to emphasise the annoyance it was causing us both. The grandmother pursed her lips, her red-headed granddaughter clinging tightly to her arm.

'Look at the little pixie!' squealed the boy. Lads of his type fear nothing. I hurried out of the gallery and along the landing. I kept expecting someone to stop me, but no one did.

I arrived at Exeter St David's with less than five minutes to spare. The train to Bodmin was a stopping service, calling at every station along the coast. It was packed with day-trippers bound for Dawlish and Teignmouth, and for the first part of the journey I was forced to stand. In many respects I was grateful – the cramped conditions made me much less conspicuous – though the temperature within the carriage became increasingly uncomfortable. After Newton Abbot the train emptied out and I was able to sit down. I lodged my holdall under my seat, praying that its precious cargo would not be damaged, terrified to check its contents for fear of attracting attention. My encounter with the grandmother and the two children had unsettled me – I felt certain that the boy especially would remember me, if it ever came to that.

My main preoccupation for the immediate future was to put as many miles between myself and Exeter as I reasonably could.

You have to understand that on some level I still did not properly believe in what I had done. Not only because it was out of character – until that day I had never so much as raided the stationery cupboard at Clark Cannings without asking permission – but because there was still no evidence of my misdemeanour in the outside world. No one was running or pointing, there was no sound of police sirens. Everyone around me was behaving as if nothing had happened, which allowed me to believe in my pretence that nothing had.

As the train rolled over the Royal Albert Bridge, Brunel's greatest gift to the West Country and the point of magnificent transition from Devon to Cornwall, I even allowed myself to imagine that if I were to unzip my holdall then and there I would find nothing more remarkable inside than the clothes I had packed for my journey, *Coastage's English Almanac*, and the battered 'Laura Louise' doll I had purchased in Wade.

You wish, 'Artist' murmured.

I did not wish her gone, though, for how could I? Here at last was the adventure I had longed for, the sense of a shuttered life becoming real. The Scotsman would be proud of me, I thought. He would chuckle, and call me Sir Galahad. Then he would raise his glass and wish me well.

My dear Andrew,

There are times when this place frightens me. Not because of anything that has happened here – hardly anything happens here – but because of the memories it holds. What else is a house but a box full of memories? No one who ends up here ever intended to, not since West Edge House became a hospital, anyway. People come here to forget who they were and where they came from and what they have done. But the house remembers.

I expect you think it's strange, an idea like that. I don't know what's put me in this mood. Sylvia Passmore, probably. She finally asked Dr Leslie to go out with her and he turned her down. Not that it's any of my business, but I happened to be in the office at the time and so I heard the whole thing.

Sylvia was waiting for Dr Leslie in the corridor. She told him someone had given her two tickets for a concert in Truro and she'd been wondering if he might like to go with her.

'It's a recital of piano music, by Chopin,' she said. She mumbled something about the pianist, a child prodigy who had just won an important music competition in Poland. I didn't catch exactly what Dr Leslie said in reply but a few seconds later Sylvia came barging into the office and slammed the door. I don't think she realised I was in there because when she caught sight of me she blushed bright red, like someone who has been caught out in a lie.

'What are you doing in here?' she said. She sounded furious. Before I could think of anything to say in reply she turned away and pretended to look for something in one of the filing cabinets. A moment later she left the room without a word. The air seemed to rock from side to side, like water in a jam jar that's been picked up and shaken. I could still smell her perfume, a sweet, flowery fragrance that always reminds me of the clothes she wears, the pastel cardigans and tailored skirts, the immaculate shoes.

I hadn't intended to mention the incident to anyone, but later in the afternoon I found myself telling the whole story to Jennifer Rockleaze. I thought it might make her laugh but instead she seemed angry.

'Sylvia's a fool,' she said. 'Even if she got what she wanted, he would make her life hell.'

'Why do you say that?'

'She likes the idea of marrying a doctor because she thinks it sounds better than a plumber or a tractor driver but all she really wants is someone she can get dolled up for.' Jennie laced her fingers together and steepled them. Her nails were painted with a pale pink varnish that looked like mother of pearl. 'Maurice doesn't care about things like that. Sylvia could come into work dressed in a bin bag and he wouldn't notice. What on Earth would they find to talk about?'

Sylvia phoned in on Friday to say she was ill in bed with a

cold, and after that it was the weekend. When I saw her again on Monday she seemed back to normal. She was wearing a pair of dark brown court shoes, the leather so smooth and so shiny you could see your face in it. She barely said a word to me all morning, but that was nothing unusual. She brought Dr Leslie his coffee at eleven thirty, the same as always, with a buttered scone.

Dr Leslie is like two different people, depending on whether you're speaking to him as a doctor or just as himself. As a psychiatrist, he pays attention to everything you say, even down to the tiniest details of what you had for lunch or where you went on holiday when you were ten. I don't know if his doctor's memory is really photographic but it must be close to that. And yet if you happen to talk to him just in passing, in the office for example, you often have to say something twice to get his attention. It's like what Jennie said about Sylvia's shoes – Dr Leslie simply wouldn't notice a thing like that. He walks around in his own world, his own private bubble. I've known Dr Leslie for almost twenty years but I don't know what he's like – him, I mean, the real Maurice. The food he likes to eat and the books he likes to read, that whole thing about whether he really was married or not. I just don't know.

I've never thought about this before – it's part of the way things are here – but coming to know you, the way we are with each other in our letters, has made me realise how little of themselves people give away. It's like when you see a terrible crime reported on TV. The murderer's neighbours and work colleagues all look stunned, and keep saying how normal the murderer seemed, how quiet he was, how he was always helping old ladies across the road. This is the moment when they realise they didn't have a clue what he was really like, that the person they thought they knew was a total stranger.

When I first came to West Edge House I was supposed to have consultations with Dr Leslie twice a week, although it usually ended up being more than that. Dr Leslie insisted that I should keep going over the events of that summer until I came to accept what he always referred to as the facts of the case, as if it really was a crime that we were talking about.

I kept expecting him to ask me about my mother: did I love her and did she love me? Did we have a row that day? How did I feel when I came home and saw the ambulance by the front door?

Did I still believe that my mother's death – her *suicide* – was my fault?

I hate the word suicide. Not because of what it says but because of what it doesn't say. Suicide is a Latin word, formed from the preposition sui, meaning oneself, and the verb caedere, meaning to cut, to strike or to kill. It is a snaky, sinuous word – that double 's' sound – a word that seems to squirm around the truth of what it means. For me it does, anyway. Don't say suicide, I think whenever I hear it. Say what you mean. She killed herself. She decided she would rather be dead than keep on living in the world, in the house on Harlequin Road with my father and me.

How could she have been that unhappy? Did you know your mother was unhappy? I kept expecting Dr Leslie to ask me, and I would imagine myself laughing, laughing into his face because of course I knew, how could I not know when being unhappy was not just something my mother did from time to time like anyone else, it was what defined her. Her unhappiness was so familiar it was part of the scenery, like the ugly green wallpaper in the downstairs toilet that my father kept meaning to paint over but never got round to. No one liked it but we were used to it. In some ways the house wouldn't have felt right if it were no longer there.

Would you say your mother was depressed? I honestly couldn't say, Doctor. I didn't really know her all that well.

Dr Leslie never asked me these questions though, or if he did I don't remember. He seemed more interested in the other things that had been going on at the time: Edwin, and Helen, and my father's illness. When he talked about the night my mother died, it was Rosamund he asked me about, the doll that looked like Helen and that I smashed to smithereens after Edwin confessed to me that it wasn't me he loved, but Helen, even though he didn't know Helen, he didn't have a clue about her.

'Do you still believe you were doing harm to your friend by destroying the doll?' Dr Leslie asked.

I shook my head and said no. 'How could I?' I said. 'It was only a doll.'

'A doll that looked like Helen.'

'Yes,' I replied, although the way he said it made it sound more like a piece of prosecuting evidence than an actual question.

'Do you know what a graven image is, Bramber?'

'A graven image is an idol,' I said. 'A picture, or a statue that is supposed to represent the power of God.'

Dr Leslie began talking then, about the power of the human image across all world religions.

'There are those who fervently believe that harm can be brought to a person, simply by destroying a model of that person, or by burning their photograph.'

I found him interesting to listen to, because I liked him, I suppose. Dr Leslie is a gentle man, who works hard and gets tired. I knew he wanted to reassure me that what I did to Rosamund didn't have anything to do with my mother's suicide, but I didn't believe him. I couldn't expect him to understand, because he wasn't there.

It was almost dark when I went out, past nine o'clock. My mother was upstairs in the bedroom, my father was in the living room with the TV on. I can't explain what made me take Rosamund, what made me destroy her, only that I still loved her and that her presence had begun to distress me beyond endurance. I had no definite plan in mind when I left the house – only that I had to be outside, away from that place, and that Rosamund had to come with me.

'You must have been angry about Edwin's interest in Helen,' Dr Leslie said.

I told him no, not really, not at all. 'I told him he was being stupid, that Helen didn't care about him, or about anyone. All she wanted was to get away to London, to be an actor.'

'Did your mother ever hug you, Bramber?'

I laughed. 'Why would she? We weren't that kind of family.'

I carried Rosamund carefully downstairs, cradling her against my shoulder like a child. Her fair hair tickled my cheek and for a moment I felt an aching sadness at the thought of being parted from her. There was no one about, and when I reached the path that led to the viaduct I almost turned back. It was so dark, you see. I hadn't thought about how dark it would be, not really. I remembered the times Edwin and I had talked about sleeping out on the allotments and thought what a ridiculous idea it was, once you really thought about it. The bushes crowded around me like—and I know it sounds silly to say this, but I kept imagining they were alive, the secret people of the woods, come down to take a look at what I was doing. I had never felt afraid of the dark before, but the lumpy, massed shadows of the trees and bushes made me feel I'd never properly understood how different night was from day, until that moment.

Every sound I made seemed vast. I held on tightly to Rosamund and spoke a few words to her. Her hair took on the glow of the moonlit sky.

I hadn't been back to the viaduct since the afternoon I'd been there with Edwin. The place seemed different, too: stranger, and in the brittle, glassy light of the moon it was easy to imagine the stone viaduct as the dividing line between this universe and another one, as Edwin had said, a universe where trains still ran down to the quarry and where people believed in ghosts and where Edwin and I would spend next summer Interrailing in Europe, just as we'd planned.

Except now that would never happen, because I had been living in the wrong universe all along.

I lifted Rosamund high above my head to show her the moon. She is lovely, I thought, and once again I felt a terrible loneliness at the idea of her leaving me. When I dropped her from the bridge, she disappeared from my sight almost immediately, slipping into the darkness like a stone slipping into deep water. After what seemed a long time later I heard a faint tinkling sound, like a summer breeze passing through wind chimes. For a moment I stood perfectly still, leaning over the parapet and staring down. There was nothing to see. The night yawned beneath me like a black pit, lukewarm and smelling of nettles. I buried my face in it, like an old blanket. I was alone.

I walked home after that. By the time I reached the house it was after midnight. When I think about that night now, I like to imagine it like this: I come in through the back door. My father is still in his armchair in front of the television. The late news is on. Dad has the gas fire turned on full, even though it isn't cold, not at all.

'Where have you been?' Dad says. 'I didn't hear you go out. I was worried.'

'I went for a walk, that's all,' I reply. 'Are you OK, Dad? It's boiling in here.'

'It's my fingers, I can't seem to get them warm, these days.'

I kneel beside him and take hold of his hands. His palms are damp with sweat.

'How long have you been feeling like this?' I stroke the clammy skin, desperate to switch off the fire.

'A couple of months,' he says. 'About a year, maybe.'

'You should go and see the doctor. Tomorrow.'

'Oh Ba,' he says. 'I worry about you sometimes. You are so like your mother.'

He releases one of his hands from my grasp and touches my hair and for a moment he seems almost all right again and so do I.

I had always believed it was Dad I took after, but perhaps I only thought that because I loved him. It was true, what I told Dr Leslie: I barely knew my mother at all.

I never thought I'd say these things to anyone, except Dr Leslie, but he doesn't count. Dr Leslie doesn't care what I say, except for how it fits into some picture he has. Writing to you feels different. It feels like you're really listening. I never believed that talking would help, but with you it really does.

Your friend always,

Bramber

I O.

AFTER CROSSING THE ALBERT Bridge, the train seemed to enter not just another county but another world. Rolling green hills were replaced with scabrous, parched-looking moorland, whitewashed cottages with angular, bare-faced homesteads constructed from granite and surrounded by loose agglomerations of rickety-looking outbuildings, roofed with asbestos shingles or corrugated iron. Here and there, the broken towers of abandoned tin mines reared up from the sparse vegetation like ruined castles.

The landscape seemed derelict, barren. The train called at numerous one-horse stations along the route, disgorging clumps of dishevelled passengers on to mostly empty platforms. Eventually, even the straggling villages petered out, and there was nothing beyond the windows but the dung-coloured, featureless expanses of Bodmin Moor.

It took most of another hour to reach Bodmin itself. I was alone in the carriage by then, although I had once again become preoccupied by the conviction that I was being watched, that there were CCTV cameras somewhere, or a two-way mirror. I stared fixedly at a poster over the door, an advertisement for an amusement park somewhere near Land's End, wondering if it might conceal a hidden microphone. I knew these ideas were ridiculous even as they occurred to me, but ever since boarding the train I had felt like a fugitive.

It was the doll, of course – 'Artist', my secret cargo. I was a thief, a common thief. In my head the words sounded outrageous, even comical, yet they remained true, nonetheless, and my increasing awareness of that fact and of the doll's presence only made them seem more so.

Don't sweat the small stuff, 'Artist' murmured. You set me free. Don't I deserve to be free? Museums are no place for the wicked. I'd rather be in a prison than in a museum.

I understood what she meant, though I doubted a court of law would be so easily swayed.

As the train ground to a halt, I disembarked in front of a small cluster of granite buildings: a stationmaster's house, a boarded-up waiting room, and the ticket hall itself, which appeared to be unattended. There was no one about and, after a minute or two of waiting, the train released its brakes and sidled away. I glanced briefly at my watch: ten to five. I realised it was pointless to think of going on to Tarquin's End that evening, that I would have to look for somewhere to stay in Bodmin itself.

I passed through the station building to the access road beyond, then set off in what I took to be the direction of the town centre. My holdall was heavy and I felt very tired. I cursed myself for not having foreseen the necessity of booking ahead – I had planned my earlier overnight stops so carefully, so why not this one? I could only suppose it was because I had found it difficult to imagine anything beyond my meeting with Bramber. I hoped it would not be too difficult to find a reasonable hotel, though the desolate air of the town's approach road was not exactly encouraging.

BODMIN TOWN CENTRE, WHEN I finally reached it, was larger than I expected and not so down-at-heel as I had feared. Neatly kept granite houses lined the high street, which led on to a central square, planted with trees. Facing on to the square I noted a variety of local businesses, now mostly closed for the day. Cars stood parked at the kerb, their erstwhile occupants gathered on wooden benches outside a pub. The pub was called The Tarquin. As well as the chalkboard menu and a banner advertising a Sunday carvery I was relieved to see a signboard for bed and breakfast.

I made my way briskly through the crowd of evening drinkers and into the saloon. The man behind the bar had shaggy, shoulder-length black hair and wore a T-shirt printed with a design of a fist clutching a rose. When I asked him if there were any vacancies, he said there were two rooms left, one with an en suite bathroom and one without. I asked to see the room with the bathroom. I had made up my mind to take it, whatever, at least for tonight.

The Tarquin must have been twice the size of the Bluebell Inn at Wade. It was also much older. The downstairs consisted of two large bar areas and a billiard room. A staircase near the public lavatories gave access to a long upper landing leading to five or six bedrooms. The uncarpeted floorboards were creaky and uneven, blackened with age.

'This is the en suite,' said the barman, opening a door. 'Overlooks the back yard, so it's quiet enough.'

He had not offered to carry my holdall. I couldn't decide whether this oversight had arisen out of rudeness or out of respect.

I had not expected much from the room, and my first impressions were of dowdiness and mild discomfort. The space was dominated by an enormous brass bedstead, the mattress covered by an ancient-looking eiderdown patterned with roses. A worn rug lay on the floor to one side of the bed, but otherwise the boards were bare. There was a half-height gentleman's wardrobe in one corner and a straight-backed wooden rocking chair in another. There was no television. An inner doorway led to the en suite facilities, which consisted of an old-fashioned, high-cistern toilet and a chipped enamel bath.

'Breakfast's from half-past eight,' said the barman. 'If you want it, that is.'

I wasn't sure which he was referring to, the breakfast or the room.

'It's a beautiful room,' I said, deciding for both of us. 'I'll take it.'

The barman nodded, then handed me an iron Chubb key attached by a piece of string to a wooden number three. It wasn't until after he'd gone that I saw that the room truly was beautiful, after all, the simple arrangement of necessary objects creating an ambience of quiet authenticity that made my room at the White Hart seem false and ostentatious by comparison. The well used furniture had a comforting solidity, the waxed floorboards shone pale gold in the evening light. On a low table at the foot of the bed stood a china tea service, together with a radio with a leather hand strap and a Bakelite case.

I crossed to the window. Immediately below lay a concrete yard. A row of wheelie bins stood lined up against the retaining wall. On the other side of the wall was West Moor, a vast tract of lichen and heather, on fire with gorse. Birds darted amidst the twilight, gathering insects. A woman passed along the horizon, walking her dog. I stood quietly for ten minutes or so, relishing the stillness and taking in the scene in front of me as if it were a sequence from some minor but visually arresting art-house film. Nothing was happening, and yet everything was. It was as if my life, for those brief moments, were being held in stasis. There was no past, no future, just that room and its contents and the view beyond.

It occurred to me that my journey could end here, that I could spend this one night in The Tarquin, then instead of going on to Tarquin's End I could return to Bodmin Station and from there, home.

What if Clarence was right, and my relationship with Bramber Winters was all in my head? A fantasy that, were it revealed to her, could only provoke embarrassment and revulsion.

At least if I backed out now there would still be our letters. Letters contained worlds after all, you could read anything into them.

You don't mean that, surely? 'Artist' hissed at me from the holdall. I know people call you names, but 'coward' has never been one of them.

Her. She didn't even have a name, only 'Artist', which surely said everything about the kind of madness she had inspired in me. I turned away from the window and seized the holdall, dragging it from where I had deposited it just inside the doorway into the space between the bed and the entrance to the en suite. I felt suddenly appalled at the prospect of opening it, at being confronted with the evidence of the crime I had committed.

I would have to admit then that the doll was there, that I really had stolen her. The action seemed already distant, impossible, and yet it had happened.

She was lying on her back, apparently sleeping. As I raised her slowly towards me her eyes flew open. The green transparency of her gaze – bright as phosphor – was almost shocking. I had thought her expression imperious. Closer to, it seemed defiant, the expression of an elf queen on the warpath. *You think you command me, sir? Then think again.*

I was also disconcerted to discover that her hair was real. Such a detail should not have surprised me – synthetic dolls' hair remained uncommon until the 1950s and, even then, many of the smaller manufacturers stuck with mohair because it was cheaper and more readily obtainable. Yet something about 'Artist's' auburn tresses unsettled me deeply. I remembered Ewa Chaplin's flight from Poland, from Hitler's armies, and from there I found it was impossible not to think of the Nazi death camps, the vast mounds of human hair that had been left behind in the wake of genocide. Such images were disturbing, inappropriate, and yet they persisted.

You should understand that I felt no love for her. I realised that in taking 'Artist' I had transgressed, not merely against the law but against the boundary between the kingdom of reason and the world of desire. In ways I could but dimly understand, I was now her prisoner. I began to wonder if she had engineered this even, drawing me to her in the knowledge that she was my fate, and I hers.

My act of theft, when I thought about it now, seemed ludicrously easy: the preoccupied attendant, the open door, the silent alarm bell. Even a practised felon could not have bargained for such a cavalcade of lucky coincidences, might have considered the challenge unworkable and therefore dangerous.

And yet, I had done it. There was no hue and cry, no uproar. I laughed to myself then, a little, anyway. If this happened in a film, you would not believe it.

Just go with the flow, young master, said 'Artist'. This is what you wanted, is it not? It is you who talked of dragons, of rescue. A quest without hidden dangers is no quest at all.

I could not now remember whether it had been me who had mentioned dragons, or the Scotsman in the yellow shirt. Not that it mattered much. My stomach grumbled, reminding me of how hungry I was. Enslavement to an elf queen did not preclude the usual human frailties, it seemed. I could have ordered a meal at the bar but decided against it. The saloon bar had seemed unpleasantly crowded, and the outside tables were mostly full. I wrapped 'Artist' loosely in one of my used shirts and replaced her inside the holdall – not exactly royal apartments but she would have to make do.

I pocketed the key to my room and went downstairs. Some of the drinkers at the bar turned to look at me as I passed through, but their casual curiosity did not bother me. In comparison with the contents of their glasses, I was of scant interest.

I set off across the square, choosing one of the side streets almost at random. Cooking smells drifted from the open windows of the cottages, making my mouth water. The road led to an area of tarmacked hardstanding. There was a bicycle rack, recycling receptacles for glass and aluminium drinks cans, a footpath leading directly on to the moor. In a cul-de-sac just off the tarmacked area I spotted a fish and chip shop called the Jolly Roger. The shutters were open and a small queue had formed outside.

I felt for my wallet. There were perhaps five people in the queue ahead of me. The young woman serving seemed to know all of them by name. The lanky boy directly in front of me bounced a black-and-white football repeatedly against the concrete. He wore a grass-stained white T-shirt and shorts, and had a grazed right knee. He kept glancing at me sideways, his narrow face set in a frown. Suddenly a girl ran up to him. She was younger than he was, curly-headed and chubby with a face full of freckles. She wore a Manchester United T-shirt with matching red socks.

'You've forgotten the money,' she said to the boy. She waved a ten-pound note at him, as if to prove her point.

'Elephant,' said the boy. 'Heffalump.' He chucked the ball straight at her, bouncing it off one of her thighs. The girl caught the ball expertly and held on to it, taking a swipe at the boy with her other hand. The boy made a noise like a machine gun and then darted away across the tarmac. The girl took his place in the queue, wedging the football under her arm. She stared at me openly, her sweet moon face broken in a half-smile.

'It's nice out here tonight, isn't it?' she said. She inclined her head as she spoke, enunciating each word carefully, like lines she had learned from a play.

'It is indeed,' I replied. 'I'm getting hungry though, aren't you?'

She grinned at me then, showing her teeth, her bright button eyes narrowed to slits. I waited to see if she would continue our conversation, but she did not. When her turn came in the queue she ordered four portions of haddock and chips. The young woman behind the counter, dressed in a sailor's cap, packed the food into a cardboard carton and handed it down.

'There you go, Binnie,' she said. 'Say hi to your mum and dad for me.'

The child grabbed hold of the carton and sped away. Before disappearing around the corner she looked back at me once and waved.

I ordered battered cod and a double portion of chips, then walked the twenty yards to the edge of the moor. The grass had grown damp with dew but I sat down anyway. The sky above me was the soft, transparent, twilight mauve of amethyst. I rested the packet of fish in my lap and began to eat. I was aware of cars starting up, of the background chatter of the people still waiting for their food, but these things did not intrude upon me. I felt miles from anywhere and for the first time that day entirely at peace. I sat still and gazed upon the moor, at the neat grey cottages with their well tended gardens. I was struck by the cleanliness of the place, by the fact that there were no crushed drinks cans or discarded food cartons on the forecourt of the Jolly Roger. It would not have been like that in the city. I looked around for a waste bin so I could dispose of my own litter and quickly spotted one close to the recycling station, alongside a post box and a telephone kiosk.

If the pay phone hadn't been there I would never have made the call. I had left my mobile charging in my room at The Tarquin and in any case, I had not intended to telephone West Edge House in advance of my visit because I had no idea of the protocol. What if, by alerting those in authority there, I inadvertently put the whole purpose of my journey in jeopardy? I had briefly considered asking Clarence to call, pretending to be a relative, just to see how the land

304

lay, but given Clarence's antipathy to Bramber, that idea was clearly out of the question.

The telephone box was one of the old red ones, with an old-fashioned rotary-dial telephone inside. It could even have been that which finally prompted me to call. I couldn't remember the last time I'd seen one of those old phones and I was curious to find out if it still worked.

I dialled Directory Enquiries, then asked for the number of West Edge House, Tarquin's End.

'Business or Residential?' asked the operator.

'Business,' I said, hoping this was correct. Bramber had always skirted around the exact designation of West Edge House, but I presumed it was run as some sort of convalescent home. The operator was silent for a moment, then asked me if I had a street address.

'There isn't one,' I said. 'It's just the name of the house, then Tarquin's End.'

'Do you mean the hospital?'

I hesitated for a moment and then said yes. There was a sharp click, then an automated voice read out a number. I felt in my pocket for a pen and noted it down. The number had only five digits, which meant a non-digital exchange. I thought all such numbers had become obsolete years ago. I looked at my watch. It was now getting on for eight o'clock. I half-convinced myself it was too late to call, that it would be better to stick to my original plan and wait until the morning.

In the end I dialled the number only because I felt certain no one would answer. Either that, or the line would be dead. In fact, my call was picked up almost immediately. There was a short silence, then a tremulous female voice recited the number I had just dialled, the intonation rising towards the end as if to indicate a question. For a moment I forgot it was I who had placed the call.

'Is that West Edge House?' I said. Silence. I spoke again quickly, stumbling over my words in my haste to get my message across before the woman at the other end decided to put down the phone. 'I'm sorry to call so late, but I was wondering if it might be possible to speak to Bramber Winters?'

It felt good to say her name. It struck me that the woman I was speaking to would almost certainly know Bramber, might be friendly with her even. In spite of my nervousness I felt a rush of excitement.

'We're not supposed to speak to the papers.' The woman's voice was suddenly much louder, forcing me to hold the receiver away from my ear slightly. 'Dr Leslie said that if the papers called we should always put the phone down immediately.'

'I'm not from the papers,' I said. 'You've made a mistake.' Before I could say any more, the line went dead. I dialled the number again. The same woman answered.

'Go away,' she said.

'If you could just let Bramber know that Andrew called? There's really no need to worry. I'm a friend of hers.'

I listened carefully for her reply, pressing the receiver tightly to my ear again, but the only thing I could hear was a low hissing. I wondered if the telephone had developed a fault suddenly. Then I realised it was the sound of people whispering.

'Bramber?' I said. My heart was thudding loudly in my ears.

'How are we supposed to know you're not one of those *paparazzi*?'

A man's voice this time, much firmer than the woman's and with an educated accent.

'Are you a doctor?' I said. It was only after I had spoken that I realised how ridiculous my words sounded, a line straight from a film.

'You can't prove I'm not,' the man said. 'I passed all the examinations, you know. I took a First.' There was a strange, bumping sound, which I took to mean that the man had covered the receiver with his hand. I strained my ears to listen. I could just catch the muffled, panicky chatter of the woman.

'I told him to go away,' she said. 'I promise I did.'

'It's not your fault, Jacks. I mean, it's not as if you called him.'

I heard a third voice somewhere in the background, muttering something unintelligible that sounded like 'boots, boots', and then the man again.

'This is Dr Leslie. How do you know where we are?' Before I could answer, the third voice said 'boots' right into my ear and then the line went dead again. This time when I redialled I got the engaged tone.

I replaced the receiver in its cradle and stepped out of the booth. A deep twilight had settled upon the moor, making it appear as boundless as the sea. The neon sign fronting the Jolly Roger gave the faces of the people in the queue an orange cast, as if they were warming themselves before a bonfire. I made my way slowly back up the lane towards The Tarquin. I thought about calling Clarence but I was afraid to. I knew she would tell me to come home, and I was feeling so unsettled by what had just happened that I knew I might be tempted to obey her.

I was afraid of other things too, but found it difficult to name them. My mind kept replaying the way the woman at Directory Enquiries had said the word 'hospital': deliberately, as if spelling it with a capital 'H'.

I couldn't help wondering what it might do to someone, being shut away in a place like West Edge House for twenty years. I was bound to admit there was at least a chance that Bramber would reject me entirely, not out of repulsion but through fear of the outside world.

BOTH BARS OF THE Tarquin were full to bursting. I went straight upstairs to my room, which was alive with the hazy, amber glow of the outside security lights. I quickly drew the curtains then ran a bath. I could hear the laughter of drinkers downstairs in the bar but the sound was not oppressive and in fact I found it soothing, a comforting confirmation that I was not alone. By the time I got out of the bath I felt more relaxed. I made tea in the large china pot and decided I would write to Clarence. It was only once I dug out my writing pad that I realised I didn't have a clue what I wanted to say to her. I settled on a postcard instead, a view of Exeter Cathedral at dusk. I looked at the card for some moments, studying the lighted facade with its saints and angels. I wrote 'wish you were here' on the back and then put it away.

The pub had gone quiet and I saw it was long past eleven and approaching midnight. Time had scurried away from me again. There was no noise from the landing and I wondered if, after all, I was the only guest. It occurred to me, ridiculously, that the word 'guest' sounded unnervingly similar to the word 'ghost'. For some reason I kept remembering the voice I had heard on the phone, the man with the Oxford accent who had pretended to be a doctor, if he had been pretending. I switched on the radio to blank him out. Piano music tumbled out and after a second or two I realised it was a piece I recognised, although I was unable to remember the title or the composer. I assumed it was something of Jane's. I thought of the way Jane sometimes closed her eyes when she was playing, her plump, pale hands scuttling like blind mice over the keyboard.

I had always found Jane's talent unnerving, supernatural almost, though of course I never said as much to Clarence.

I reached out and twisted the dial, drowning the music in a burst of static. Eventually I hit on a local station that was broadcasting a phone-in discussion on the foxhunting ban.

'The change in the law has been disastrous,' a caller was saying. 'It's destroyed our way of life. How can politicians understand anything about the countryside when they barely set foot outside Westminster from one year to the next?' The caller pronounced the word 'year' as 'yar'. Her voice reminded me instantly of the man on the telephone.

'A century ago and you'd have been using the same argument to justify hanging,' another caller objected. He had a thin, reedy voice and he sounded upset. 'Just because it's tradition doesn't mean it isn't barbaric.'

The third caller was also a man. He spoke with a local accent so thick I had a struggle to understand him. 'That's all very well,' he said. 'But what are we going to do with all the hounds?'

'I'll take a hound,' said the other man quietly.

'It's ridiculous to compare hunting with hanging,' said the woman. 'Foxes are vermin. Ask any farmer.'

'You might be interested to know that the police around here still use dogs to catch criminals,' the local man added. 'It's all bloodhounds nowadays, but foxhounds are just as good if it comes to a chase.'

'Dogs are the best friends we have, if you ask me,' said the woman. 'I'd trust a dog over a police officer any day of the week.'

'If anyone out there has anything to add to that we'd love to hear from you,' the presenter said smoothly. She gave out the number of the radio station and then a pop record came on the air. I got into bed and switched out the light. The mattress was old and deeply sprung and very comfortable. The pop song seemed to go on forever, and it was only when I came awake that I realised I'd been asleep. I woke up suddenly, convinced I was not alone in the room. The radio station had closed for the night, replaced by quiet static. I threw back the covers and made a grab for the radio, hugging it against my chest as I fumbled for the off button. The static subsided. I fell back against the pillows, heart racing.

Why didn't you just put the light on? said 'Artist'.

Her voice seemed to come from close by, from beside me in the bed even. I thought of her eyes, green as razors, her stiff little limbs.

In spite of myself I felt aroused. I masturbated furiously, bringing myself to a swift climax. The aftermath was dizzying. I listened to my own breathing as if from a great distance. It was as if I were two separate people, one in my bed at The Tarquin, the other far away, prisoner of a realm as dark and forbidden as my cruellest desire.

What nonsense you talk, said 'Artist' drowsily. We fucked, so what? I hope it was as good for you as it was for me.

The old house creaked and groaned as if it too were breathing. From somewhere amidst the darkness I heard a cough. A door banged shut downstairs. I closed my eyes, then opened them again. On the bedside table, the luminous dial of my watch read half-past three.

West Edge House
Tarquin's End
Bodmin
Cornwall

Dearest Andrew,

Three days ago I had a visitor. I hadn't slept well the night before
and when I finally got up it was after nine. The first thing I heard
was Michael Round, crying through the wall. A couple of minutes
later Jackie and Diz came along the corridor and stopped outside
his room. They whispered together for a moment or two then one
of them knocked on the door. I heard Michael Round's bare feet
shuffling across the lino as he went to open it.

'We're setting up a whist drive,' Diz said. 'Would you care to
join us?'

I didn't catch what Michael said in reply but by the time I came
downstairs the three of them and Livia Curran, who looks just
like Ingrid Pitt from *Countess Dracula*, were outside on the patio,
a pack of cards between them on the table. Jackie was dealing. I
noticed that Michael Round was still in his pyjamas.

I went into the kitchen and made myself some toast. Sylvia
doesn't like people helping themselves to food between meals
but everyone does it. I ate the toast at the kitchen table and
then washed up my plate. I ran into Dr Leslie in the kitchen
corridor.

'You're not usually late for breakfast,' he said. 'You're not feeling unwell, are you?'

I told him I was fine, just running behind with things, then he told me there was someone here to see me, if I felt up to it. I wasn't sure what to say at first. I hadn't had any visitors since my father died. When I asked who the visitor was, Dr Leslie just smiled and said it was a surprise.

'They must have got the name wrong,' I said. 'Are you sure it's really me they've come to see?'

I know how impossible this is going to sound and please don't go thinking I really am crazy but my first thought was that my visitor must be my mother. I sometimes wonder what would have happened if my father had died first, instead of my mother. I think of her selling the house on Harlequin Road and moving to a large, bright apartment in Bath, or Salisbury. I imagine us writing letters, exchanging news, talking to each other in a way we never did when she was alive.

I wouldn't be writing from here, of course. I can't imagine where I would be writing from, who I would be. But I like to imagine her smiling. Do you think that's silly?

'There's no mistake,' Dr Leslie said. 'Your visitor has travelled a long way to see you.'

He said we could use his office. At that time in the morning, Sylvia Passmore would normally have been in there, sorting through the post. I wonder what reason he had given her, to keep her away.

She would find out about the visit soon enough, in any case. It's impossible to keep anything secret here for more than five minutes.

When I first heard her footsteps I thought it was Sylvia after all, but that was just from the way her shoes click-clacked on the parquet. She hesitated in front of the doorway, as if she was worried she might have come to the wrong place. Then she tapped on the door. I felt so nervous I couldn't say anything, not even 'come in', but that turned out not to matter because she came in anyway. Her shoes were made from cream-coloured leather, so pale it was almost white. The heels were high and polished, the same colour as the shoe.

Blond hair often darkens with age, but if anything, Helen's had grown even lighter. It stood out around her head in flyaway curls, just as before.

'You haven't changed,' was the first thing she said. 'You haven't changed at all.'

She came fully into the room and closed the door. I gazed at her, this apparition. Was she beautiful? Did I know her? Was she older?

I remembered how she had looked on the day of the elephant, arms raised above her head, the light from her hair leaping up into the sky like reverse lightning.

Like a doll, a living doll, an image you might see in an old book of fairy tales: *Plate 3 – The Birthday of the Infanta*. Or else captured inside a snow globe, maybe.

Yes, she was older. This woman was still beautiful, but she seemed leached of colour and substance, like a woman in a photograph. Probably it was the clothes she was wearing, all that pale linen, though there were lines around her eyes as well. Tiny ones, but they were there.

'I've changed a lot,' I said, not knowing if it was true or not. Twenty years seemed like seven days suddenly. I kept thinking I was going to be sick.

'What a weird place this is,' Helen continued, as if I hadn't spoken. 'It's taken me weeks to persuade them to let me see you. Months. I don't know how you stand it. Don't you ever feel like breaking some of the rules?'

She plumped herself down in the swivel chair behind Dr Leslie's desk and smiled, a tight, breakable gesture, like the rim of a wine glass.

'There aren't any rules,' I said. 'I can get out of here any time I like.'

'Well, there are rules if you want to get in.' She leaned forward in the chair, propping both her elbows on Dr Leslie's ink blotter. 'They asked me so many questions anyone would think it was Checkpoint Charlie. Your doctor is worried my presence here might be triggering, apparently.'

She snorted with laughter, then inhaled, drawing her breath down over her teeth. Her Anne Boleyn gasp. I noticed the scar across the palm of her hand, a hard pink contusion, convex and sharply contoured, almost like piped icing. It looked as if someone had once attacked her with a food mixer.

'Dr Leslie didn't tell me you were coming,' I said. 'I only found out five minutes ago.' I found I was still staring at her hand. I knew I shouldn't, but I couldn't take my eyes off that scar. Helen's face was expertly made up in shades of pink and mauve and grey, but she wore no rings, and her fingernails were unvarnished and cut short. She didn't want to draw attention to her hands, I suppose. If Jennie had been there she would have wanted to know all about it: how the accident happened, whether it had been painful, everything. Jennie isn't afraid of asking questions. Not like most people.

Helen blushed and then smiled. 'It happened when I was filming,' she said. 'On an oil rig, would you believe? Some stupid thriller. It could have been much worse. The doctors say I could get a skin graft but it doesn't seem worth it. Not to me, anyway. I hate hospitals.'

'West Edge House isn't a hospital,' I said.

'If you say so.' She was silent for a moment. She pitied me, I could tell, but her pity seemed a long way off, like mist over a lake, like weather over the border in another country. I knew she was lying about her hand. What I didn't understand was why she was here.

'You have to get out of this place,' she said at last. She spoke especially slowly and clearly, enunciating each word as if she thought I might have difficulty understanding. 'What happened with your mum was years ago, Bramber, a lifetime. We were both just kids. You must know I didn't mean what I said. It wasn't your fault. Haven't the doctors told you the past is the past? I thought that was what these places were for.'

'My father died,' I said.

'I'm sorry,' said Helen. 'I liked your dad.' She fished a handkerchief out of her bag and twisted it between her hands. There were tears in her eyes but she didn't try to wipe them away, I suppose because she didn't want to spoil her makeup.

'I want to apologise,' she said. 'I should have come ages ago, I realise that. I was scared. I'm such an idiot. Can you forgive me?'

I wasn't sure how to answer. 'I didn't think I'd ever see you again,' I said. I didn't realise until I said the words how true they were. Since coming to West Edge House, I had thought of Helen in the past tense. I had wished her dead, I remembered that now. But wishing something is not the same as it being true. 'What were you scared of?'

'I don't know. That you would hate me, I suppose. That you would be angry. I would be angry, if I were you.'

'You thought I was stupid.'

'Not stupid. Just – naive, I guess. You were such a pushover. I was so messed up though, back then. I bloody hated Truro, especially school. I had this fantasy of blowing the place up, like Christian Slater does in *Heathers*. I liked imagining the expression on Dad's face when he found out what I'd done.'

'Did you get your place in London?' I asked.

'Yes,' she said. 'A garden flat in Peckham. The parents hate Peckham, they think it's a rough area. I remember when I got my first bedsit I told them I had rats, just to see what they'd do.'

'And what did they do?'

'Nothing much. But it started another row.'

We had coffee after that, I think. I can't remember how long she stayed exactly, maybe an hour or two? The strangest thing was that when I finally mentioned Edwin she didn't seem to remember him. Not at first, anyway.

'You don't mean the nerdy guy? I have no idea what happened to him. I don't keep in touch with anyone from school.' Then she repeated the line about me needing to get away from West Edge House. 'You're killing yourself in here,' she said. She blushed. 'You know what I mean.'

You blame yourself for what happened to Elisabeth, Helen said, but you were not to blame. *Elisabeth*, she said, as if she knew her, as if the two of them had been friends. But I could have stopped it, I want to say, I could have saved her. The words lodge themselves in my throat, hard and square, like a piece of apple.

People can choke on pieces of apple, like Snow White in *Snow White and the Seven Dwarfs*.

When the time comes for Helen to leave I accompany her to the door. I watch her step on to the path and walk towards the road. The sun drifts out from behind a cloud and makes a nest in her hair. Helen turns to look at me, shading her eyes from the light with her injured hand.

'I'll come again,' she says. 'Soon. And I'll write letters. Lots of them.'

I take a single step forward, wondering what will happen if I try to follow her. I am afraid that by the time I reach her side she will be gone.

There is always a day when summer fades into autumn, sometimes in the space of a single hour. The light changes colour and the leaves soften, become fragile. Everything goes to seed. I always try to ignore that moment, to pretend it isn't happening, but I am always aware of it. Every time it makes me wonder how many summers there are left.

Helen had seemed surprised, at the end of that summer, when I called round to see her. She even looked embarrassed. I had never come to her house before without being invited.

'Hey,' she said. It was a Saturday morning. She shoved both hands into her jeans pockets, a gesture that was new to her, a role she was learning. 'How are you feeling?'

The way she spoke to me made me think of Kimberley Grove, a girl in our class who went down with pneumonia the year before. She was off school for a month, which to us seemed a lifetime. When she came back after the Easter holidays, people spoke to her differently, as if they thought she might shatter or go into hysterics at any moment. One morning in assembly I overheard two girls in the row behind me whispering that Kimberley Grove had almost died.

'I'm all right,' I said. 'I thought we could go for a walk.'

Helen said OK but she didn't sound keen. Our friendship was over, I suppose, though neither of us seemed prepared to admit this outright. We talked of other things, the horrors of returning to school, the approaching exams. When we reached the section of the path that led directly to the viaduct, Helen came to a standstill.

'Let's go back,' she said. 'I don't like it up here. It's creepy.'

'That's just the trees,' I said. 'If you listen you can still hear the road.'

What I meant was that civilisation was not far away. We walked on, side by side, both of us straining our ears for the sound of a car. It was true that from the top of Wimbush Hill you could normally hear the traffic dashing to and fro on the bypass but for some reason at that moment it was perfectly quiet. I shuffled my feet in the dirt, making the leaves rustle. The sun poured down through the trees, cross-hatching the path with streaks of yellow. Like rancid butter, I thought. Its brightness amongst the gloom dazzled my eyes.

'I liked the play,' I said to Helen. I realised this was the first time I had mentioned it, even though it had been months ago. We were on the bridge by then. The sun was hot, one of the last hot days of that year. We leaned our arms against the parapet, soaking up the warmth. Mica sparkled in the granite, and I thought about how diamond is the hardest substance on Earth, and yet it is made of the same stuff as coal, or the fragile lead in pencils.

A simple rearrangement of space.

'Thanks,' Helen said. I thought she might want to say something more about the play but she changed the subject almost immediately. 'I love this warm weather. It always makes me feel I could live without food.'

I bent over the parapet and looked down through the trees. The leaves were beginning to turn, but only just. I gazed and gazed, wishing I could transport myself into that other universe Edwin had talked about. You'll want to ask if I missed my mother, but I can't answer, not honestly, because I can't remember. It was my father I missed, even though he was still living and breathing and making sure I ate a proper meal at least once a day. I know that probably doesn't make sense to you but that's how I felt.

The ground beneath the parapet was scattered with leaves, the first leaves of autumn, and yet I imagined I could see something else, down there in the cutting, something small and white. Its brightness against the leaf litter made it distinct, made it stand out a mile. It was Rosamund, of course, her broken remains, though mercifully she was too far away for me to see her properly.

'What's that?' Helen said, catching sight of her too. 'Let me see.'

'It's just a piece of paper,' I said. 'It's nothing.'

'It looks like a dead baby,' Helen said. 'I'm going down to have a look.' Her cheeks were flushed, with excitement maybe, or with the prospect of having something to talk about besides ourselves.

'It's not worth it. It's probably just an old Sainsbury's bag.'

'What's the matter? Or is ignoring dead bodies getting to be a habit with you?'

There was a light in her eyes, the light of goblins dancing. I understood even at the time that what she said had nothing to do with me, that it was something deep within her, an anger at the world, but the fury in her voice – the laughing contempt – was so potent and so keenly directed it was like an earthquake. I could feel my limbs shaking yet the space inside my head seemed utterly still.

I thought of the nurses, the paramedics, trying to comfort me, my father saying nothing, the weeks of skating around the facts like a hole in the ice. Helen might be a selfish bitch but at least she had it within her to speak the truth.

'I wish you were dead,' I said, quite calmly. 'Then I could ignore you, too.'

'People are saying that you left her to die. That you came

in and saw her lying there and then went out again. That you deliberately didn't call an ambulance.'

'Why would I do that?'

'I don't know. Because you're crazy? Everybody thinks so – crazy and pathetic. The way you keep hanging around me makes me sick.'

A rushing within me, like a wind gathering. A blissful sensation, because in those moments I allowed myself to hate her. I'm not good at hating, Andrew, because I've never been brave enough. Another moment and it would be too late. I would love her again, or at least understand her.

Helen was right. I really was pathetic. But then I heard the ghost train coming – its strident whistle, like a signal, *do it* – and that was enough.

I caught her by the hair, so soft in my hands, like thistledown, like Traveller's Joy. I think I really did mean to push her over the parapet, but she pulled away from me and went sideways, into the barbed wire fence that separated the cycle path from the drop into the culvert. She raised one hand to her head, to where I'd torn at her hair, and used the other to steady herself, grabbing at the barbed wire as if it were a lifeline.

She screamed, the sound of a rabbit caught in a trap, and I saw the blood pulsing up between her fingers from where the claws of the barbed wire were lodged, deep in her palm.

'Get it off me,' she cried. 'Get it off.' She was weeping now instead of screaming, her face, when she turned to look at me, blotted out by pain.

Her heart is broken, I thought. Isn't that how all fairy tales end, really?

'Get it off yourself,' I said. I turned then and walked away from her, back along the shaded pathway and into the town.

With all my love,

Bramber

THE UPSTAIRS WINDOW

by Ewa Chaplin

translated from the Polish by Erwin Blacher 2008

I remember a conversation I had with him once, at the private view for his first major London show.

'What's the difference between a spy and a secret agent?' he asked me. It sounded like the set-up for a joke.

'Are you serious? There's no difference, surely?'

'Perhaps not, if you're going by the dictionary. But did you ever hear of anyone being shot as a secret agent?'

Niko insisted that although in theory the words shared a meaning, in practice the term 'secret agent' made you think glamour and heroics, whereas 'spy' was a dirty word, synonymous with treachery. It was a put-up job, Niko reckoned. What side of the line you ended up on came down to who got to write up the report.

'Think about it,' he said. 'The Rosenbergs were convicted as spies, and died in the electric chair, whereas James Bond gets to blow heads off for a living because some spook in some back office has given him a licence to kill.'

It didn't seem to occur to him that James Bond didn't actually exist, that he was a literary invention owned by a film franchise. I asked him what the big deal was, but he'd gone all deadpan on me. Niko could be a pain like that. He had a habit of holding forth on heavy subjects, and once he got into his stride there was no stopping him. Tell him to lighten up and he'd look at you as if you'd suggested that dropping the atomic bomb had been a good idea.

'You wouldn't be asking that question if it were you facing the firing squad,' he said.

We were standing in front of a painting of his called 'The Tower', which was typical of the work he was doing back then. From a distance it looked like a dense mass of abstract colours. It was only when you saw it up close that you could see how complicated it was. 'The Tower' was made up of hundreds of tiny squares, painted one above the other like a giant stack of matchboxes. Inside each box was a different object: a pink transistor radio, a commemorative mug, a plastic doll with only one arm, the kind of mindless jumble of trash you find stuffed into the backs of cupboards or jumbled together in cardboard boxes in your local junk shop. When I asked Niko if the objects were supposed to mean anything he refused to say.

Some of the critics reckoned 'The Tower' was the Tower of Babel, that the random collection of objects was supposed to represent the lack of understanding between people or between nations or whatever. As far as I was concerned, this theory didn't hold water: even though they had different titles, Niko's paintings all looked pretty much alike.

'Time Machine', 'Fortress', 'Meridian' – whatever the paintings were symbolic of, the show sold out. No one called Niko's work weird or quirky either, they called it playful or ironic. I saw one review that described the Camden paintings as having 'all the freshness and vitality of a well drawn comic strip'. Each time Niko was interviewed, he was asked to spill the beans on what the paintings were about but he always kept stumm. He said the meaning of a work of art depended on who was looking at it. Art talk bores me, to be honest, so I didn't pay much attention. What I do know is that Niko seemed to be doing all right back then. I admired him, and I liked his work. What I disliked was everything that went with it, all that art school bullshit. I've always believed that good journalism is about saying what you mean in as few words as possible. When it comes to the art world you often end up getting the exact opposite.

Niko and I never really discussed Laura Plantagenet. My friendship with Niko was a coincidence in any case – Laura and I split up more than a year before I first ran into Niko, and it wasn't Laura who introduced us. Niko and Laura had been in and out of each other's lives since they were at college, but I think he understood her even less than I did. I can't remember if it was me or Laura who first suggested we get married. Whoever it was, we were a disaster waiting to happen. But because of the Angola brief and the film that came out of it I thought I was God in the making and I had the money to go with it. Laura had just finished shooting *Gethsemane*, the film that made her famous, propelling her out of the art house and into the glossies. Ivan Stedman and Laura Plantagenet, the proverbial golden couple. Except that we weren't.

After Laura I stayed single. I don't mean I stayed celibate – far from it. But I made up my mind to steer clear of anything too serious and not just for my own sake. Work and relationships don't mix, or at least not for me. When I come back off a job I'm exhausted, not fit for human company. I like to unpack my kit, junk the worst of it, steam-clean the rest, then lie in the bath for hours listening to the pipes grumble. I like to enjoy the sensation of feeling safe. There have been times when I've asked myself if I do what I do simply because I know that feeling will always be waiting for me at the end of it, but I decided that was bollocks, just the tiredness talking.

If all I wanted from life was some uninterrupted downtime I would have chosen a profession less likely to get me killed.

It was during one of these furloughs that Niko turned up at my flat. I hadn't expected to see him again, to tell the truth. He'd made a mistake, and a bad one. Such actions have inevitable results. I distrust idealism. I've seen enough of it in practice to know it's rarely about the other man. You might even call it the ultimate expression of arrogance, but whatever you call it, it's not worth dying for. Niko looked terrible. He stank like he hadn't washed for days and there was an ugly-looking cut beneath his right eye that had only partially scabbed over. I assumed it was police work, though it turned out to be a souvenir of a fight Niko had got into in some pub on Newport Street. Looking at it made me feel tired. It was one stupid thing after another with him.

I'd followed the trial on TV of course, and as if that weren't enough, Niko's girlfriend Mica mailed me all the press cuttings. But I was in Kuwait while it was going on and for once that seemed like a bonus. I wanted no part of it, least of all as a witness. Mud sticks and I didn't want to draw attention to myself. Do that in my line of work and your sources are liable to dry up overnight. For all his talk of secret agents and spies, Niko never seemed to grasp that.

Seeing him standing there in the hallway, my first thought was what excuse could I come up with, to tell him he couldn't stay?

'You'd better come in,' I said. 'Let me fix you a drink.' I decided I'd let him rest up for a couple of hours, then tell him I had a plane to catch. Asking for more would be unreasonable, even for Niko.

'Thanks,' he said. 'I could definitely do with one.' His hands hung limp at his sides, and there was grime under his fingernails. It looked like motor oil. I wondered what had been the final straw for him – the threat of execution, the crap in the papers, the wholesale public destruction of his work. I poured him a Scotch. He held the tumbler up to the light then took a quick swallow. When he rested the glass on the sideboard I could see his greasy fingerprints on the crystal.

'I'm going to make a run for it,' he said. 'I know someone who can get me out.'

'For God's sake, Niko,' I said. 'It's not worth the risk. If you jump bail and they catch you, you've had it. Sit tight and you get five years, maybe less. It's hardly the end of the world.'

'If I stay here I'm finished as an artist. They may as well kill me now.'

'Don't be so melodramatic. It'll all blow over. Get some commercial work, just for a while. You might even find this business works out in your favour eventually. People like notoriety, they lap it up. You'll end up with more commissions than you can fulfil.'

'I'm not like you, Ivan. I'm not prepared to play their games.'

'I resent that.'

'You've never been afraid to compromise. That's how you get by.'

'I make sure no one interferes with my freedom, if that's what you mean. If I have to adjust a paragraph here and there, then I'll make that sacrifice. It's a matter of priorities.'

'I won't have anyone telling me what I can and can't paint.' He snatched at his glass. His hands were trembling, though whether from anger or fear I could not tell.

'So long as they leave you alone, who cares?'

'And if they keep demanding more compromise, which they will?' Niko said. 'What then?'

I thought of all the examples I could give him, colleagues of mine who had been forced into far worse corners just to keep their passports: Estrella Finzi, Duncan Patel, Martin McEwan. I bit my tongue, though. I was tired enough as it was, and I couldn't face the fallout if Niko thought I was comparing myself with Martin McEwan.

'Let's talk about this tomorrow,' I said. 'You look like the walking dead.'

Laura managed to extricate herself, of course. She'd stopped seeing Niko on any kind of a regular basis at least six months before the case was brought, for a start, and she was required to appear in court only once, via a video link. Her lawyers maintained she had no idea that Niko intended to utilise her image in the creation of blasphemous material, which is probably true, to be fair. Laura is blind to anything that bores her, which would have included Niko's endless tirades against the Rouse government and what he called their draconian persecution of the creative impulse.

I ran into her on the street, not long after Niko pulled his disappearing act. I was just coming out of Green Park tube. She was crossing Piccadilly, in front of the Ritz. I'm lucky I suppose. If Laura was bored with Niko then God I was bored with her. The fact that I can recall that feeling precisely, a tedium so intense that I occasionally toyed with the idea of killing her just so I wouldn't have to hear her voice again, is what made it possible for me to stop in the street and have a civilised conversation with her. To enjoy her company, even. Niko never reached that stage of enlightenment. I guess he never will now.

'Laura,' I said. 'How are you?'

'Fine, thanks,' she said. 'I'm gasping for a drink, though. Do you fancy some lunch?'

She swept off her shades, a pair of vintage Versace's that would have set me back a month's earnings in the old days. It is no accident that so many of the film journalists and critics who have eulogised Laura over the years have found themselves unable to resist mentioning her eyes, which are a soft, powdery blue, shading to mauve around the margins of the iris. It was those eyes I first fell in love with, like everyone else. It wouldn't be an exaggeration to say I believed in them, the way some people still believe in God. Even now I wonder how it is possible for eyes like that to conceal such deep reserves of pettiness and self-absorption. I don't mean that Laura is stupid, quite the opposite – she was always smart as a whip and twice as sharp, able to grasp a situation in less than a beat. Her intelligence is what makes her such a great actor, I suppose, that ability to sum people up. It's what comes with it that drives me insane: her habit of dismissing at a glance anybody or anything that does not directly concern her person or her interests.

Being looked at turns her on like a spotlight, yet it was in those moments when she believed herself alone that I was most in love with her. Moments in which she might scrape distractedly at the edge of a fingernail with a worn-down emery board, or lie sprawled on her back on the sofa staring up at the ceiling. I used to wonder what went through her head at such moments, whether I might see her differently if I were able to read her mind. Probably not, and in any case these moments of reflection never lasted. The second she realised I was watching her she began to perform. She became someone else then, the person I found unknowable and in the end couldn't stand.

We went to a Greek place at the far end of Curzon Street. Quiet. Once I'd got the drinks in, she cut straight to the chase.

'Did you know Niko was planning to jump bail?'

'I was still in Kuwait,' I lied. 'I had no idea.'

'Simon says he's a fool. We could have found him a decent lawyer, if he'd only asked.'

You'll have heard of Simon Caultham, of course, the maverick auteur who kicked off his career with that incomprehensible alternative zombie movie, *Feet of Clay*, and who first directed Laura in *Amber Furness*. Caultham had been married twice already and no one believed for a moment that he and Laura would last five minutes but they seem to suit each other. Perhaps it's the inherent one-upmanship that turns them on: two equally monstrous egos, locked in a perpetual stalemate.

'Niko doesn't have that kind of money,' I said. 'Not any more. You know that.'

'Isn't that what friends are for? That's the trouble with Niko – always so insistent on his pathetic principles.'

'Have you heard from him, Laura?'

She glanced down at her plate, and I thought how that was the one thing about her I still found touching: her inability to lie without being detected.

'Not a thing,' she said. 'I haven't laid eyes on him since the trial.'

I didn't pursue it. There was nothing to gain, and in any case I was sick of the subject. Later on that day I admitted to myself it wasn't just Niko I was sick of, but everything. I was even sick of my apartment in New Cross, with its damp-smelling airing cupboard and perpetually dripping bathroom tap, minor annoyances I kept meaning to get fixed but never found time for. I fingered the travel documents I'd picked up that morning, the stamped visa and boarding pass for the Dubai shuttle, and felt a wave of relief sweep through me. I knew that so long as I could get on that plane I would be able to sleep, that my current bout of exhaustion would be at an end.

For the first time ever I began to give serious consideration to Sallie Stowells's invitation for me to join her bureau in Melbourne. I'd known Sallie for years. We shared a room in the press corps hotel during the third Iraq war. She'd been urging me to join her for a while, complaining that her best reporters kept getting themselves killed.

'Either that, or they leave after six months to work in TV,' she said last time we spoke. 'I need a safe pair of hands.'

I'd always turned her down before, but even with the wildfires and the mass shootings I was beginning to see the attraction. It would be a new start.

That first London show was so successful that Niko could have painted full-time if he'd chosen to. He decision to stay on at St Martin's was just one more example of his naivety if you ask me. He approached his teaching commitments as he approached everything else: with missionary zeal.

'It does me good to be around the students,' he insisted. 'There's a raw energy about them, a passion. If you met them you'd know.'

'There's already too much bad art in the world, Niko,' I said. We were in the Pillars of Hercules, on Greek Street. He had specks of yellow paint all over his hands, and the back of his sweatshirt was white with plaster of Paris. He reminded me of Van Gogh in that made-for-TV biopic, the one starring that German actor who went on to be an expert on UFOs.

Madness on both counts. I found it amusing that if Niko hadn't been my friend, I would probably have despised him as a matter of form.

Laura was right about the legal side of things. There's a Cromwellian fury at the heart of this nation, a cesspool of bigotry that wields the law as a weapon of revenge rather than the tool of justice it was created to be. You might even say that this propensity for score-settling is part of our character, that England's damp and chilly climate has corroded our souls. The Bishops call it a theocracy and insist there's no fairer form of government, but so far as I can see, Rouse's so-called divine revolution was founded on envy, political in-fighting and the old-fashioned lust for power. But Niko's work had its effect, even on me.

I always knew he painted portraits as well as abstracts. No gallery would take them of course, not after the Bermondsey Statutes, but he had whole sketchbooks and portfolios full of them, everything from pencil studies to finished oils. In spite of the strict prohibition laws on depicting the human form in painting, sculpture, art photography – they even had a clause against costume dolls – Niko was still able to find students who were willing to sit for him. It felt risky to them, I suppose – art as the new punk rock. Not that anyone seemed to give a damn what Niko was up to. Until the Laura paintings.

The first of Niko's models was a stringy, dark-haired twenty-year-old named Joanna Newbis. He painted her naked, elongating her arms and fingers and coarsening the texture of her skin. Niko showed me some reproductions of drawings by Egon Schiele and I could see what he was getting at, but even so, I didn't like them much, there was something of the butcher's shop about them. When he'd finished with the figure studies he painted her face in close-up. Then he painted her cunt, over and over again. At first it looked so raw you could almost smell it. In the end you grew so used to seeing it, you forgot what it was. It became a thing in its own right, a ragged, reddish-brown ellipsis, slightly puckered along its edges, like a split fruit, or like one of those bizarre single-celled pond organisms you can only see with the aid of a microscope.

I saw him do the same trick with a scorpion tattoo on the shoulder of one of his other models – a kid named Dwain Khan – and also with the lace edging of a silk camisole. He highlighted colour and texture, emphasising the abstract qualities that lay dormant in the most concrete, the most specific of subject matters. His paintings were enthralling and disturbing at the same time. To dismiss what he did as pornography is the cheapest brand of ignorance.

If you get the wrong judge though, even having the right lawyer might not save you. There's more than a whisper of corruption about our courts these days, but for me the most terrifying judges are those who actually believe in the sentences they're handing down. In a way they're just like Niko. There's no reasoning with absolute faith.

I left him to make up the bed and then sent out for food. When it came he scoffed the lot. It was as if he hadn't eaten for days. He looked better after that but there was still an air of futility about him, that panicky look rebel insurgents get when they realise that every safe-house has fallen and there's nowhere left to run. He lay back in his seat and closed his eyes. I could see them flickering back and forth beneath the lids, like nervous mice. He was clearly exhausted.

'Where will you go?' I asked. I refused to imagine a scenario in which the morning came and he refused to leave, postponing his departure from one day to the next until the police arrived. I dismissed the idea at once, not because it seemed far-fetched but because I couldn't deal with its implications. As it turned out, I didn't have to. Niko had his plan already worked out.

'I'm going to Leipzig,' he said. 'There's a guy who has a ticket waiting for me in Brussels. He says I won't have a problem crossing over, provided I can get on the Eurostar in the first place. But I have that sorted, too. Stefan Rogers up at the college knows someone who's supposed to be in Maastricht this weekend, for a conference on pharmaceuticals. He reckons I can buy his ticket. It's all arranged.'

'But this is crazy, Niko. What will you do in Leipzig, even if you get there?'

'Teach and paint. As I do here.'

'You know that's not going to happen. You've not been east of Frankfurt in years. I have, and I can tell you the infrastructure's just not there any more. The universities are a joke – just glorified military academies. And unless you feel like teaching maths or Chinese to twelve-year-olds there aren't any teaching gigs.'

At best he'd get some sweeping-up job in a canteen or factory. At worst he'd end up as manual labour on one of the reconstruction sites. That's about the only positive thing you can say about Eastern Europe these days: there's always plenty of building work going.

Niko knew these things as well as I did. I think that was at least partly why he looked so tired.

'I'll manage,' he said. 'At least I'll be able to work.'

'In one of those blasted high-rises with the concrete cancer? Or in a basement that fills up with sewage whenever it rains?'

'If I have to.'

'Have you been to see Mica?' That was probably the wrong thing to say right then but I'd run out of arguments. Niko shuddered.

'I can't face it,' he said. 'I'll write to her.'

'Does she know you're here?'

'God, no.'

Mica Okonkwo lived on a decrepit house boat on the Regent's Canal. Not the park end of course, but the eastern stretch, over towards the King's Cross basin. Her studio was a sub-let, part of a converted warehouse complex in Camden. She taught English part-time at a local primary school but even so I think she found it difficult to make ends meet. Once during the summer I'd seen her stacking shelves in Tesco's. In certain lights she looked haggard and crazy like one of the bag-ladies who camp out on the sidings at Waterloo Station, but then she'd turn her head and smile and you'd see someone else: a woman who knew her own mind and intended to use it. I don't know how she met Niko. As far as I knew, she lived alone.

Mica worked in ceramics, building tiny sculptures using rolls of clay that she left to harden then scraped smooth with a flexible steel kidney. The finished objects resembled beach flotsam, or artefacts from an ancient burial site. I have no idea how she coped with Niko's women. That was something none of us talked about, least of all Mica.

The strangest thing about her was her sympathy with our esteemed leader, Bishop Damian Rouse. Not that Mica was in favour of the Bermondsey Statutes – she had been as enraged by the reintroduction of the death penalty as Niko – just that so far as her own work was concerned, she said she found it easy to comply with them.

'It is still possible to say big things in a small way,' she insisted. She and Niko were always arguing over this. Mica had conducted a considerable amount of research into isolated societies where photography was still seen as a major religious transgression, so she knew all about the sanctity of the human image. When Niko's work was going well, he appeared to thrive on these discussions. When he was having difficulties he would get drunk and accuse Mica of collaborating with the enemy. He could actually become quite aggressive, which was unlike him. Mica had her own ways of dealing with him, no doubt, but she never backed down in an argument.

I knew Niko had asked Laura to model for him, but I didn't know the half of it. If I had, I'd have told him not to be an idiot. It was as if he had a death wish or something. But then again that isn't exactly uncommon among artists.

He worked up the portraits of Rouse from the photographs in the Mackinnon biography. That book was hard to come by, even then, although it wasn't until after the trial that it was officially banned. Niko's masterpiece showed Rouse as he appeared during his Cambridge days: the velvet blazer and horn-rimmed spectacles, the blond hair flopping forward into his eyes. It was at Cambridge that Rouse developed his signature style – the studied nonchalance of the outcast intellectual – and although he's lost his hair and gained some weight since then, the frilled shirts and heavy specs remain the same.

Laura he painted from life. I have to say it was a shock, seeing her like that, even though I knew the scene Niko had painted was entirely the figment of his imagination. In a way it was that image – Laura on her knees with Rouse's dick in her mouth – that finally made me realise that she and I were over, that we had run our course, that there was no way back. Naturally, she looked glorious – you could say it was her best role yet. And then that side panel: Noah Pinkowski, seated behind a lectern taking notes, an onyx fountain pen between his fingers, his denim-clad, foreshortened legs drawn up on his stool. The scale and technical accomplishment of the painting suggested that Niko had started work on it long before Pinkowski's execution, yet the timing of its unveiling – less than a month afterwards – seemed to suggest that it had been painted as a direct response.

Pinkowski's was not the first state execution to be carried out in the wake of the Bermondsey Statutes, but it was the most notorious. Pinkowski's alleged crime was his authorship of *The Rotterdam Club*, a scandalous and suspiciously well documented account of Damian Rouse's alleged association with the Golden Gryphon, the neo-Nazi organisation that was said to be behind the metro bombings in Paris and Budapest. That was the official version anyway, though there were certain insider factions who insinuated that Rouse wanted Pinkowski removed from circulation because he had scored higher yearly averages than Rouse when they were both at Cambridge.

Score-settling, in other words. Pinkowski being a dwarf may have added some colour to the news coverage, but it certainly didn't help him on the stand.

The title of Niko's painting was 'The Magdalene'. He may as well have called it 'The Suicide Note'.

He went out like a light. I managed to get to sleep OK but woke again in the small hours, filled with that sense of foreboding you get when you know something is wrong but cannot immediately remember what it is. Outside, it was raining hard. I listened to the water sluicing down the faulty guttering, hoping the window seal in Niko's room hadn't begun leaking again.

I traded the Fulham place for the New Cross flat more or less the minute Laura moved out. Laura loathed south-east London, which was probably the main reason I decided to move there – I knew she would never be tempted to try and come back. She referred to my place in New Cross as the roach motel, which was actually a misnomer as I never had cockroaches, the flat was too damp for them, too close to the river. The money I had left over I salted away. I lay in the dark with my eyes open, wondering if Niko would take any of the money if I offered it to him. It seemed like a waste to me. I imagined him getting off the train in Leipzig and knew he would stand out a mile. He'd most likely get mugged in the first five minutes if his comrades didn't send him a minder.

I didn't have much more than spare change in the flat. I fretted about how things might look later, if the police came knocking, if they discovered I'd withdrawn a huge wad of cash on the very day my old friend and criminal associate Nikolaus Schilling jumped bail and fled to Europe under an assumed identity.

I got out of bed at around six o'clock. I didn't want to wake Niko before I had to, so I washed and shaved at the hand basin in my bedroom. The basin was square and heavy, supported by a cast-iron bracket secured to the wall with giant masonry screws. There was a blue-grey tidemark halfway up the bowl that I couldn't get rid of, no matter how hard I scrubbed at it. Like everything else in the flat, the sink had a pre-war feel, a robust ugliness that had disgusted Laura on sight but for which I felt a grudging respect.

The basin seemed to insist on its rights. Perhaps that's why I'd never had it removed, even though for three hundred and sixty-four days of the year I found no use for it.

When I went through to the kitchen to make coffee I found Niko already there. He was fully dressed and seemed more in control of himself than he had done the previous evening but the sight of him unnerved me, all the same. If I tell you he looked like his own ghost, you'll think you know what I mean, but you'll only understand a part of it. Yes, he looked gaunt and pale and nakedly preoccupied. But looking at him, leaning against the kitchen counter in his tatty old Levi's, I became suddenly and painfully aware of how irretrievably he had lost his place in the scheme of things. He could not walk into a travel agency and book a seat on an aeroplane, nor could he apply for a teaching post outside of his current postcode. He could not send mail without knowing it would probably be opened by the Home Office censors. He could not broadcast, he could not publish, he could not vote.

I experienced a sudden twinge of vertigo, as if these strictures applied to myself instead of to him.

'I'm going to call Stefan Rogers,' I said. 'It's safer if I do it. Then I'll need to go out for an hour or so. Will you be all right here by yourself while I'm gone?'

He nodded. In the time that remained to us, we barely spoke two words to each other that weren't essential for basic communication. I downed half a cup of coffee then took the tube up to Shoreditch, where I telephoned Stefan Rogers from a public call box and arranged to meet him in a burger bar opposite Charing Cross Station. I called in at the bank, then went to a grubby little shopping mall I knew just off Cheshire Street and bought a waterproof rucksack, a pair of black Doc Martens and a selection of own-brand T-shirts, sweatshirts and jeans. Niko was an inch or so taller than me and I was a couple of pounds heavier than him, but we were more or less the same size and I knew the clothes would fit.

I walked into the burger bar just after ten thirty. Stefan Rogers was already there, sitting at a corner table flicking through *Time Out*. I ordered myself a cup of coffee and he asked me about the Kuwait job. As I got up to leave, Stefan handed me a paperback book, an ancient and dog-eared copy of *Dr No*.

'Thanks for lending me this,' he said. 'I'd forgotten how good it is.'

The Eurostar ticket was tucked inside, still wrapped in its Cellophane seal. Stefan and I had agreed upon the book ruse instinctively, caught halfway between mutual terror at exposing ourselves to risk on another's behalf, and excitement at starring in our very own spy movie.

At six forty-five that evening I said goodbye to Niko on the concourse of St Pancras Station. It was still the rush hour. Streams of commuters pushed past us on every side. I looked at Niko and shrugged. We embraced briefly and then he disappeared into the crowd.

I never saw him again.

I went to the Odeon cinema on Shaftesbury Avenue. They were showing Wendell Schwarz's *Passover*, a new director's cut, and I went in just as the film was about to start. I fell asleep more or less as soon as the lights went down and woke up a couple of minutes before the final credits. I'd seen the film with Laura when it first came out. We were in Istanbul, on one of our rare trips abroad together, and we'd gone into the cinema because it was the only place the air conditioning appeared to be working. I remember Laura took her shoes off under the seat, then spent the entire film reading the *Paris Review*. Most of all, I remember how happy we were. Things always seemed easier between us when we weren't in London.

When I came back out on to the street it was raining again. I walked down Charing Cross Road with my head down, bought a copy of the *Evening Standard* at the station entrance. There was nothing in the paper about Niko and my heart lifted at that, even though I knew it was still far too soon to start imagining that he – or I – was out of the woods. When I arrived back at the flat I made myself busy fixing supper. It wasn't until after I'd eaten that I went into the spare room. The bed was made, the corners of the undersheet tightly folded as if Niko had been to the kind of school that set a value on such things. Perhaps he had. Belatedly I realised I had no idea.

There was an envelope on the bedside cabinet, one of the standard white office variety I recognised as my own stationery. It was addressed to Mica Okonkwo. The flap was stuck down, and when I tried it with the edge of my fingernail the seal held firm. I took it through to the kitchen and used the kettle to steam it open. The letter inside was written in blue biro on two pages torn from a ring-bound exercise book. Niko's writing was cramped and spidery, a predictable mess. He had crossed out liberally, leaving heavy indentations in the cheap paper.

I put the letter back in the envelope without reading it. It was harmless curiosity I had felt, nothing more, a child's longing to know the end of a story. I understood it was wrong, all the same, a kind of theft. Even if Niko never found out, it was a base impulse and I refused to succumb to it. I re-sealed the envelope with Prittstick and once the glue was dry I ran over the flap lightly with a steam iron. Good as new.

A month went by before I was able to deliver it. When Mica finally picked up her phone, we arranged to meet in a pub we both knew, not far from Warren Street tube. I arrived there before her. I bought myself a drink then sat down to wait at a table near the entrance. Mica turned up about five minutes later. She was carrying a zip-up nylon holdall, her bushy hair held back from her face in a striped bandana. She came to sit beside me, shoving the holdall under her seat and resting her feet on it. She looked worn out, even more so than usual.

'Where have you been?' I said. 'I've been trying to get hold of you for ages.'

She shrugged. 'I had to go away for a bit. My brother's been home on leave.'

I remembered she had family somewhere in the Midlands: a sick mother who had once been an opera singer, a brother in the army. I knew nothing about them. Nor did I wish to.

'He's gone, hasn't he?' Mica said. There was a fierce light in her eyes but no tears, at least not yet. I thanked God for small mercies.

I nodded. 'To friends in Leipzig. That's what he told me, anyway. He left this for you.'

I handed her the envelope. She tore it open straight away. I was surprised by that. I had assumed she would secrete it away somewhere, save it for later, when she was alone. The flap of the envelope came up all of a piece, without tearing. I wondered if Mica would notice such a telling detail, which of course made me think of Niko, all his crazy talk about spies.

She scanned the letter while I sat there, moving her lips from time to time as if trying to memorise the words. After a couple of minutes she put it back in the envelope, which she tucked into the inside pocket of her anorak.

'Did you persuade him to take some money?' she asked.

'Of course.'

Her question startled me with its practicality. I noted the dark bags under her eyes, the closed expression, the accumulation of years of worry and vague disappointment, pain she was so used to bearing it had become the norm.

'What will you do?' I asked.

'Wait,' she said. 'It's what he wants.'

Once again, I felt surprised. I had expected Mica to flood me with questions, to demand to know the final details of Niko's escape so she could make plans to follow him. When such demands were not forthcoming I began to understand something of Niko's decision to leave without attempting to see her. He needed something to believe in, some last shred of hope. Times changed after all, and so did regimes. What did the artist in exile dream of nightly but a return to the land and to the people that inspired their art?

A light left burning in an upstairs window, as the sun went down.

Mica Okonkwo would know this. She would take care to ensure that the light did not go out.

Mica went into the tube at Warren Street. I carried on down Tottenham Court Road, wishing I had a plane to catch. It was Saturday, and as I drew closer to Centre Point the crowds increased until I found myself having to step off the pavement to avoid getting jostled. The latest techno-gadgetry sparkled from the windows of the electronics franchises, and I thought about a shop front I had walked past in Budapest once, where knocked-off cameras and fake Walkmans fought for space alongside hunting rifles and World War Two gas masks. The gas masks had been fitted with modern chemical filters, although they still looked like death traps to me.

By Percy Street a bank of widescreen TVs in the window of the

344

Sony Centre lingered over the same image: a child dressed in prison yellow being forced down a board ramp into what looked like an empty swimming pool. I lingered for a moment, trying to work out what was happening, and realised with a jolt that the figure in overalls was not a child but Noah Pinkowski, that the screens were displaying a rerun of his execution. Pinkowski's eyes were sunken and haunted, dark with fatigue. The guards to either side of him carried electronic stun guns of the kind more usually found in slaughterhouses. They had taken away Pinkowski's glasses, which was probably the reason I hadn't recognised him. He was wearing leg irons.

Shots of the crowd showed people with their mouths open and fists raised, visibly heckling. Either the sound had been muted or the reinforced glass prevented me from hearing what they were shouting. Either way I was glad.

As I turned away from the screens I saw two women come out of the store. They were clearly mother and daughter, the one a fast-wind-forward of the other. They each held a plastic carrier emblazoned with the crown-shaped logo of one of the newer satellite companies.

'Let's go to that new place, on Charlotte Street,' the older woman was saying. 'I'm dying to take the weight off my feet.'

The younger woman laughed and shook her head. 'I told you those shoes would kill you,' she said.

It's strange, isn't it, the way our lives all turn on moments rather than epochs? If those women hadn't come out of the shop precisely then, I would probably still be in New Cross, living out of suitcases and agreeing to tolerate whichever fresh act of madness the Rouse regime chose to perpetrate in any given week. As it was, their words – so innocently spoken, cruel to the point of blasphemy when considered against the atrocity playing out silently on the screen behind them – acted upon me more potently than all my reasoning and counter-reasoning had so far been able. I went straight home, and as soon as I'd taken off my coat I made two phone calls, one to Foxton's estate agents on New Cross Road, the other to Sallie Stowells's office in Melbourne.

'How soon can you start?' said Sallie. She really did seem delighted.

'How soon do you want me?' I said.

There was no reason to tell Laura I was leaving but I called her anyway. When she insisted on coming over to say goodbye properly I did not try to dissuade her.

'This place,' she said as she entered the flat. 'I never thought you'd sell it.'

'You hate it, Laura, you know you do. You've hated it from day one.'

'I said it's a mess. That's not the same thing at all.'

Her hair had been recently styled, clinging close to her skull like a piece of expensive silk headgear. As I helped her off with her coat her familiar scent came wafting out, vanilla and roses, the aroma of delight accomplished, with a vague undertow of corruption.

She crossed to the window, staring out over the office blocks, renovated tenements and boarded-up garages of New Cross Gate. I went and stood behind her, pulling her against me, letting her feel how hard I was.

'You're a bastard, Ivan,' she said. I began to unbutton the top she was wearing, a cropped-off cream-coloured cardigan in silk cashmere. We made it slow. At the end I sat on the edge of the bed and let her come sitting astride me in the way she liked. Once she had finished I rolled her on her back and dug into her, hard, climaxing in a single thrust. When I opened my eyes I found her staring right into them, her blue-mauve irises darkened to the colour of lupins.

'You're a bastard, Ivan,' she said again. She laughed softly. I kissed her on the mouth for the last time.

We put our clothes back on and I made tea. While going through my stuff for the house clearance I discovered I still had the Meissen à deux tea service one of her girl friends had given us as a wedding present. If Laura remembered it she passed no comment. Her feet were still bare, legs crossed at the ankles. The skin over the bone was taut, delicate, bluish-white like the porcelain.

'How will you stand it?' she said. She took a sip from her cup. 'They say Australia is going down the tubes.'

'I need a change,' I said. 'If it's too ghastly I can always come back.'

I knew I wouldn't, though. I think Laura did, too.

In summer you can lie on a hammock strung beneath the eaves and watch the lightning setting off bush fires. For some reason and in spite of all the times I've come under bombardment, the lightning terrifies me. One night in an effort to forget about it, I wrote the first six pages of a novel about a firefighter who had been disfigured in a bomb blast. The following morning I was on a plane to Hong Kong to report on the aftermath of the stock exchange shootings. I had a lot on my mind, but at the same time I found I couldn't forget about that imaginary woman and the life I had begun to invent for her. I'd never written fiction before. I had never really seen the point of it, until now.

Once I'd checked into my hotel I hooked up the laptop and had another look at what I'd written so far. The words seemed both mine and not mine. The sensation was strange to me and curiously exhilarating. I couldn't help wanting to know how the story might end.

I I .

I WAS LATER DOWN TO breakfast than I had intended. A place had been laid for me in the bar. I saw used cutlery and plates at several of the other tables, which suggested there were other guests staying at The Tarquin after all. There was no sign of them now, whoever they were. I sat down to wait, and after a minute or so the barman from the evening before came through to take my order. His hair was tied back with a bootlace, and there was a red smear across the back of his hand that appeared to be ketchup.

'Full English or continental?' he asked. I opted for the cooked breakfast. Bramber had always been at pains in her letters to stress that West Edge House didn't cater for guests, and I thought it would be unwise to count on getting lunch there. When the barman reappeared with the food I asked him about buses to Tarquin's End.

'There's the ten twenty to Padstow,' he said. 'That stops at Tarquin's Cross. You'll have to walk from there but it's only a mile.'

I thought he might ask why I wanted to go there but he didn't. As he came back to clear the table I got up to leave.

'Do you know why this pub is called The Tarquin?' I asked, as an afterthought. 'Does it have any connection with Tarquin's End?'

He shrugged. 'The Tarquins owned most of the land around here at one time, so I suppose it must have.'

'Were they farmers?'

'They were rich, that's all I know. The churchyard at Tarquin's End is full of them.'

'Are there Tarquins still up at the house?'

'You mean the loony bin?' For the first time since I arrived, the man seemed curious about me. 'Is that where you're going?'

'I have an interest in historic houses,' I said. 'That's why I'm here.'

'That place never had anything to do with the Tarquins, so far as I know,' he said. 'Huge, it is. Bit of a rabbit warren. A mate of mine went up there once, on a carpentry job. He said the corridors inside went on forever. Miles, he said. They paid him on time though. You can't say fairer than that.'

'Is it still in use as a hospital, then? I thought it had been closed down.'

'They don't lock them up these days, any road. They're allowed to come and go as they like, apparently. Bit of a peculiar set-up, if you ask me.' He stacked my dirty plates in the crook of his elbow. 'Ask the driver. He'll tell you where to get off.'

'Do they still take new patients?'

'I couldn't say. A real white elephant, anyway. I dread to think what they spend on electricity.'

He shrugged again then left the room. I waited, hoping he might return – my mind was full of questions suddenly – but he seemed to have disappeared. I went back upstairs to my room to collect my holdall. I hadn't wanted to bring it down to breakfast with me in case anyone asked me what was in it, a precaution that now seemed somewhat foolish, to say the least. I came down to find the door to the street standing open, bright sunlight splashing the tiles. From somewhere upstairs I could hear the muted hum of a vacuum cleaner. It was already ten past ten.

The bus stop was on the square. A small crowd had already gathered, mostly women and children. The women carried bulging tote bags and rolled up towels, presumably bound for the beach and seaside amusements at Padstow. As I joined the queue I caught sight of the two children I had seen outside the Jolly Roger the evening before. When the girl saw me she looked down at the pavement and tried to hide herself behind a tall, brown-armed woman in a yellow sundress. When the bus arrived she jumped quickly on board and ran straight to the back. The bus itself looked ancient, its sides streaked with rust.

I asked the driver for a return to Tarquin's Cross.

'Three fifty,' he grunted. For a wonder, he barely glanced at me. I handed him the money then sat down near the front. The vehicle's interior smelled of warm plastic and dry earth.

'Frog prince, frog prince,' crooned the plump girl's brother.

'Get off, you're hurting,' said the girl. I turned briefly in my seat to look at them. He was tugging at her hair. When he noticed me watching he covered his mouth with his hands and began to laugh.

The woman in the yellow sundress told him to stop, her darkened lashes dipping low over her eyes. She looked just like him. The girl sidled away and pressed her face to the window. The last of the town's granite houses fell away.

The bus turned on to the potholed B-road that skirted the moor. The landscape was stark and barren, the heathery scrubland frequently pierced by outcrops of rough granite. Here and there I spied the ruins of cottages or barns. There was little traffic. The road ran due north for a couple of miles then dipped south-west, following the line of an ancient and mostly eroded river valley. I could see a crossroads up ahead, one route branching northwards in the direction of Pentland and Padstow, the other cutting east-west across the moor. The bus began to slow down. I got hastily to my feet.

'Which way to Tarquin's End?' I asked the driver. He pointed west, then jammed his finger on the button that opened the doors. I stepped down on to the tarmac. The bus remained stationary for a moment then did an abrupt right-hand turn and lurched away towards Padstow.

The road as it continued was dusty and narrow, scarcely more than a track. The moor stretched away to the horizon on either side. After half an hour of walking I came to a dry stone wall and soon afterwards a humpbacked bridge. The river that ran beneath it was all but dry. The duck pond, I thought – that must feed into the duck pond. The bridge I recognised from the large-scale ordnance survey map I had bought back in London. On the other side of the river was Tarquin's End.

I counted eleven low-slung cottages including the post office stores. They were built from red brick, a marked contrast with the granite facades I had seen in Bodmin. The duck pond was fringed with dead bulrushes and almost empty of water. In the reeds close to the bank, a child's wooden sailing boat dangled helplessly by its rigging, its red hull criss-crossed with scratches. One of its triangular sails had been torn away.

I passed a pillar box, a red telephone kiosk. Unlike the phone box in Bodmin, this one had no telephone inside, just a faded directory and a sheet of paper with 'out of order' scrawled across it in loose, handwritten capitals. The adhesive tape attaching it to the glass had begun to peel away.

Brick access paths twisted their way between the cottages. Weeds grew up through the cracks, tufts of thistle and ragwort, their stems coarse as horsehair. I started towards the post office stores, meaning to ask for directions, then saw it was closed. In the long back gardens of the other cottages I could see washing hung out to dry on nylon clotheslines, children's toys scattered haphazardly on the patchy grass. Music drifted from an open window, a chart hit from the 1970s that had been a secret favourite of my father's. I tried to think of the name of the band but couldn't remember.

The road sloped upwards past the cottages, following the curve of the valley. To my left stood the Church of St Ninian's, a modest but well proportioned building with a square tower and Norman arches. Whereas the mean red cottages could only ever emphasise the bleakness of the landscape they stood in, the church seemed to exert the opposite effect, wresting from its surroundings an impression of uplifting purity that was unexpectedly exhilarating.

Beyond the church lay the open moor. I hesitated, wondering if I had taken a wrong turning somehow, then carried on up the track. After a further twenty minutes of walking the road ended. There, in the shallow cleft of land between one tract of moorland and another, lay West Edge House.

Had I been expecting a vision of mullioned windows and ivy-clad walls I would have been disappointed. In reality, West Edge House was a three-storey 1920s villa that had obviously seen better days. The exterior paintwork was peeling badly, the pebbledash render – clearly once white – had turned a dingy grey. The large and ugly bay windows on the ground floor lent the building an air of graceless angularity, whilst the entrance porch – a pillared portico in a mock-Classical style – seemed like a later addition and entirely out-of-keeping with the whole.

A wide, unkempt front lawn swept down to the road. A broken water sprinkler gushed fruitlessly, flooding one strip of grass to a greenish mulch while the turf to either side went bald in the harsh yellow sun. Where the lawn met the moor, dandelion and thistle sprouted in droves. A line of faded pink paving slabs made a rudimentary path to the front door.

Not exactly Brünnhilde's mountain top, is it? said 'Artist'. I did my best to ignore her, though I could hardly disagree with her analysis. Although in my darker moments I occasionally imagined something in the manner of a Victorian lunatic asylum, complete with bars on the windows and spiked iron railings, if I nursed any preconceptions at all, they had mostly featured the hushed green ambience of one of the more modest and less frequently visited stately homes, a haven where damaged souls and fragile bodies might retreat from the world for a while to recuperate in peace. Gazing at the drab and oddly ramshackle exterior of what lay before me, I found myself reminded of the formerly grand hotels in ageing seaside resorts – Eastbourne, Bexhill – that had been sold off in their hundreds after the war and converted into bedsits or retirement homes.

Close to the house, a lone woman paced to and fro across the lawn. She was pushing a baby carriage, an old-fashioned perambulator with enormous silver-spoked wheels and a fringed canopy. She traipsed back and forth between the broken water sprinkler and a concrete bird bath, covering exactly the same distance each time, as if she were counting out the steps, which maybe she was. As I came slowly up the path towards her, I saw that the pram was empty. I hesitated, wondering how the woman might react to my presence, but she didn't appear to notice me at all.

The front door was standing ajar, revealing a doormat, a tiled square of hallway and beyond that another door. On the other side of the glass I could make out a stretch of corridor surfaced in what looked like brown linoleum. Go on then, said 'Artist'. This is the proverbial it.

I reached up and pressed the doorbell. There was a harsh, clattery ring. The inner door was opened almost immediately, as if someone had been lying in wait just behind the glass. Standing before me was a woman in what looked to be her mid-fifties, dressed in a chequered woollen pinafore dress and red open-toed sandals. Her grey hair hung straight to her shoulders, the front portion held in place with a pink plastic hair slide.

'You must be Mr Allman,' she said. 'Do come in.' She smiled a bright, artificial smile, like an actor in a toothpaste commercial. Her voice sounded familiar suddenly and I realised this was the woman I had spoken to on the phone the evening before.

'My name is Andrew Garvie,' I said. 'I'm Bramber's friend. Bramber Winters? I think I spoke to you yesterday.' I paused. 'Are you one of the nurses?'

She had seemed to be on the point of letting me pass, but at the mention of the word 'nurse', she moved swiftly to block my way.

'Of course I'm one of the nurses,' she said. 'And you can't come in.'

'I don't mean any harm,' I said. I could hear 'Artist' sniggering

355

from inside the holdall. 'I only want to talk to her. I did try to phone.'

The woman's mouth fell open slightly. I could see the tip of her tongue protruding between her teeth.

'You're not on the list,' she said. 'Mr Allman is on the list.'

'Perhaps you could just tell Bramber I'm here?'

'No one's allowed to see her. Not without permission from Dr Leslie.'

'Well, perhaps I could talk to Dr Leslie then? I don't mind waiting.'

The woman hung her head and refused to look at me. At that moment a door opened at the far end of the corridor and a small group of people emerged. At their head was an extremely tall man in a white coat, his bony wrists protruding from the sleeves. Around his neck hung an instrument I initially took to be a stethoscope but on closer inspection revealed itself as a bizarre arrangement of rubber tubing and metal clamps, the kind of instrument one might imagine in the possession of a Dr Frankenstein. As for what it might actually be used for, I dreaded to think.

'You must be Dr Leslie,' I said. I stepped forward and extended my hand. 'I'm here to see Miss Winters.' I had hoped my use of Bramber's surname would inspire confidence in him: here was someone who was clearly a professional, who was used to speaking with doctors on equal terms. As it was, my words came out in a rush, almost a gabble. I realised I probably sounded as confused as the woman in the red sandals.

'Who told you she was here?' barked the doctor. He turned away to address the woman in a way that seemed deliberately designed to exclude me. 'Jackie, you know what I told you about talking to strangers.'

The woman put her hands behind her back, carried on staring at the ground. She looked as if she might be about to burst into tears. One of the men who had arrived with the doctor stepped to her side.

'It's not your fault, Jacks. They'll try anything, these people.' He placed an arm around the woman's shoulders. He wore a moth-eaten long-line cardigan the colour of pea soup and a pair of grey flannel trousers held up with braces. In contrast with the doctor, all his clothes seemed too big for him. He appeared to stoop beneath their weight, and seemed much older than the woman, although his voice remained surprisingly firm.

'We're not used to this kind of intrusion,' said the doctor. 'We're very private here. When you're working with vulnerable patients, you have to be.' He folded his arms across his chest. 'Pretending to be one of us, too,' he added. 'Some people have no morals at all.'

At first I had no idea what he was talking about. Then I saw that two of those accompanying him were also dwarfs. One of them, unlike me, was a true achondroplasic, with the characteristically prominent jawline and foreshortened limbs. He looked to be in his early twenties, a robust youth in button-fly jeans and a grey sports vest. Beneath his high-domed forehead his deep-set eyes were shadowy and huge. He was more or less exactly my own height. Beside him stood a young woman with silver toenails and matching sandals, her long, silky-textured hair the colour of wheat.

'Keep your eyes to yourself, mate,' said the youth. 'She's with me.' He slung an arm around her waist and pulled her closer. Their bodies made audible contact at the hip. The girl sniggered. She reminded me of 'Artist', I realised. Two mad queens.

'If you go now we'll say no more about it,' the doctor was saying. 'I don't want to bother the police, not if I can help it. They have enough to be getting along with as it is.'

He came straight at me, his thin arms outstretched. I was so surprised by the turn of events I had no time to step aside. I went down hard on the floor of the porch, landing on my backside with a painful thump.

The front door banged swiftly closed. I was alone, outside the house, almost as if the past ten minutes had never happened. I stared up at the facade, feeling furious as well as confused. I reached for my mobile, thinking I would keep phoning until they at least agreed to let Bramber know I was there, then realised I had forgotten to load the number into my contacts.

I heaved myself to my feet and made my way back down the pathway past the broken water sprinkler, the base of my spine still throbbing from the fall, the woman with the pram still continuing with her guard duty on the ill-nourished grass.

I think I was in shock at that point. I had never had a physical altercation with anyone, not since school, and although the doctor's assault on me could hardly have been described as violent, it had nonetheless left me feeling confused, shaken, and utterly deflated. If he even was a doctor – I had only his word for it, and the man hadn't come across as exactly reliable. Was Bramber being held here against her will, after all? I realised I couldn't even be sure she was on the premises.

Looks like you'll have to break in, then, said 'Artist'. I could hear her quite distinctly, even from inside the holdall. Desperate times call for desperate measures, Sir Lancelot.

'Galahad,' I muttered. 'The Scotsman said Galahad, not Lancelot.'

Whatever, said 'Artist'. You're not going to let one mad doctor stop you, surely? If you let these people win you're no knight at all.

She was right, of course. I couldn't just leave. In every sense of the word, I had come too far. I reasoned I would probably not have to actually break in either, not to the extent of smashing a window or forcing a lock. As 'Artist's' kidnapper, the last thing I wanted was to attract the attention of the police. But it would do no harm to see if this perplexing, ramshackle building had another entrance.

I turned left at the end of the path, following a line of gorse bushes that appeared to mark the official dividing line between the garden and the surrounding moorland. The flatness of the landscape meant that I would easily be visible to anyone who happened to be watching me from inside, but so far as I could tell, no one was. West Edge House stood silent and closed. Even the woman with the pram had gone indoors.

The gorse bushes petered out alongside a gravelled pathway which appeared to offer access to the rear of the property. I followed it with rising excitement, only to find myself thwarted again by a stout wooden fence which effectively cordoned off the entire back garden. My heart sank at the sight of it. Without the use of a ladder, my way was barred. Brünnhilde's mountain top, indeed.

Then I realised that one of the fencing panels was actually a gate. Unsurprisingly it was bolted shut, though this time my luck was in: the bolt was on the outside, effectively making the garden into a prison yard.

Fortunately it was easy to open.

I slid back the bolt, peered cautiously through the gap. I saw a lawn, cracked and dishevelled as the grass that fronted the building, a sort of circumscribed wasteland. Closer to the house was a concreted patio area. Canvas chairs stood in a shabby group around a plastic table. Large French doors overlooked the patio. For a second I glimpsed the dwarf boy, staring at me, aghast, from behind the glass. I reeled backwards, heart racing, and so did he. I realised I'd been fooled by my own reflection.

I moved quickly out of sight of the windows and towards a long rear extension that jutted out from the main house, forming an 'L' shape. The kitchens maybe, or consulting rooms for the doctors. The windows in that part of the building were high up and narrow, almost like windows in a castle. I felt hideously exposed, consumed by the same paranoia I had experienced in Wade, my body shrinking before the glare of invisible telescopes. I dodged around the back of the extension and into a concrete passageway that ran down between the house and fence and that led back, or so I assumed, to the road at the front. Here at last I felt safer, less spied upon, which was probably why when I saw the door in the wall I felt less surprised than I might have done otherwise. The balance of West Edge House had tipped in my favour, it seemed. I had stumbled upon another way inside.

The door was of the modern UPVC variety, with frosted glass panels. I pulled down on the handle. The catch clicked and I felt the door open. I hesitated for just a moment, and then went inside.

I found myself in some sort of vestibule, the floor surfaced with the same brown linoleum I had glimpsed in the main hallway. Opposite the door, two metal filing cabinets stood either side of an ancient corduroy sofa. Running directly off this apparent waiting area, a flight of stairs led upwards to the first floor. I hurried up the steps, my feet making rapid tapping sounds on the bare linoleum. At the top was another door, furnished with reinforced glass and leading to a spacious landing. From here, a wide corridor ran what seemed to be the entire length of the house. A number of doors led off. Tall windows bathed the landing in late morning light. The walls were covered with a faded paper, patterned with roses, the kind you might expect to find inside the home of an elderly aunt. From somewhere I could hear the mellow, curiously restful sound of a ticking clock. The ambience here was reassuring, comforting even, a thousand miles from the chaotic lunacy I had encountered downstairs.

I made my way carefully along the corridor, the carpeted floor-boards creaking softly beneath my feet. All the doors looked identical. I felt like the bumbling soldier in Andersen's fairy tale, 'The Tinder Box', afraid that if I picked the wrong door the doctor would come, or the dwarf boy, that this miraculous chance would be wasted and I would lose Bramber forever.

It was the postcard that saved me – the postcard of Bramber castle I had sent to Bramber soon after we began our correspondence. I had not expected to see it again, but suddenly there it was. Someone – and I could only presume it had been Bramber herself – had placed it in a frame and hung it on the back of one of the doors. Finally I had arrived at my goal. X marks the spot.

The white-painted door stood ajar. I tapped softly and waited, hoping I might hear her voice, telling me to come in, that she was glad I was here.

Impossible thoughts, silly daydreams. How could Bramber know

I had arrived when I had never even told her I was on my way? When there was no answer I knocked again more loudly and then pushed open the door. You'll say I shouldn't have done that, that the room was Bramber's private domain and I had no right to be there.

What choice did I have, though? I had travelled so far, so many miles heading westwards with her in my thoughts. She held my future in her hands without even realising. I had to tell her I was here at least. After that it would be up to her.

I don't know what I expected to see. An invalid's room, perhaps, the curtains drawn against the sunlight, a figure propped up in bed, shrouded in white? In reality it was just a bedroom, larger than average and bright with sunshine, overlooking the garden. There was a high wooden bed with a green quilted cover, a low-backed chintz armchair, a battered 1930s bureau in walnut or teak. On top of the bureau was a polished wooden jewellery casket and beside that a glass snow dome containing a miniature model of Hampton Court Palace. There was also a photograph, a framed snapshot of a girl in a pleated tartan skirt and navy jumper. The girl was seated on a wall in front of a house, one hand half raised, as if she'd been about to wave and then inexplicably decided not to. Her fair hair stood out from around her head in a wispy cloud.

I recognised her at once as Helen Mason.

Bramber's dolls were seated on a wooden chest at the end of the bed. They were nothing special, the kind of attractive yet common-place examples that offer a gateway to doll collecting but are never its ultimate goal. Most dated from the 1890s, and only one had any real value, a dreamy-faced LaQuelle 'Marie-Therese'.

I crossed to the window and looked down into the garden. It

looked different from up there – neater and more inviting. A green lawn strewn with daisies, a sun-warmed patio where people could sit and talk and drink lemonade and play cards.

I had been crazy to believe I could make a difference here, that my intrusion could represent anything but an embarrassment. What could I know of Bramber's life, of what she really needed, let alone wanted?

No fool like a little fool, said 'Artist'. Unkindly, I thought.

'You can talk,' I said. I felt ready to laugh suddenly, even though my eyes were full of tears.

Touché.

I took 'Artist' from the holdall, lifting her carefully into the light of the room like the brittle, surly thing she surely was. 'What now?' I said. 'Seeing as you're so clever.'

I held her up to the window, green eyes blazing. And that was how Bramber found us when she entered the room.

I did not hear her approach, because I did not expect to. I think I had given up at that point, stopped hoping for any kind of resolution, and so she was the last person I expected to see. The first I knew of her presence was when I heard her cry out.

'Anders?' she said. More of a whisper, really. I wheeled around, still clutching 'Artist'. Steady on, 'Artist' grumbled. You're hurting. But I scarcely heard her.

There she was in the doorway, Bramber Winters. My Bramber, if you like, though I would not have dared call her that. The first thing I noticed was that her feet were bare – another reason I had not heard her coming. She was wearing jeans and a T-shirt with a sequined butterfly across the front, ordinary clothes, the kind you might find in any high street chain store. Her face was round and faintly freckled, a nice face. She reminded me a little of the girl I had spoken to outside the fish and chip shop in Bodmin.

Her hair was cut short: mid-brown, beginning to go grey. I think it was this last detail that moved me, most of all.

'I'm sorry,' she said. 'Were you looking for Paul? I only thought because . . .' Her words petered out, and I realised she had mistaken me for a friend of the dwarf boy, the handsome lad in the sports vest with the dark brown eyes – freak calls to freak.

I felt disappointed, not because of what she had said but because it was she who had said it. I had hoped she might be different, that she would see me – truly see me – and not just my height.

Unfair of me, of course – we had only just met – but even dwarfs dare to dream.

'You thought I was him,' I said. I laughed nervously. 'Anders Tessmond, from the story by Ewa Chaplin.'

She blushed rose pink, and if I had not already been in love with her I think I would have fallen for her in that moment, then and there.

'How would you know?' she stammered. 'I mean, I don't under-stand.'

'I have Ewa's book – *Nine Modern Fairy Tales*. I've been reading the stories on the way.'

'On the way?'

'Here. To see you. I know I should have written and told you but I was afraid you'd say no.'

I saw confusion and anxiety on her face, the question of who I might be still unresolved. Then she caught sight of the doll in my arms and her eyes widened.

'That's the stolen Chaplin,' she said. 'They were talking about her yesterday, on the local news.'

I held 'Artist' out to her, because what else could I do? Sunlight clawed at her russet hair, turning it the ragged, last-ditch auburn of autumn leaves. 'I brought her for you,' I said, stupidly. 'I know you've always wanted a Chaplin doll.'

If you think you're leaving me behind in this dump you've got another think coming, 'Artist' said. I ignored her.

'Andrew?' said Bramber. Her voice was filled with wonderment. 'My goodness, are you all right? You look . . .'

Again, words failed her, and it was only then that I became aware of the state I was in: the grass stains on my shoes and the elbows of my jacket, the sweat on my forehead, the dust coating the seat of my trousers where I had fallen down. In addition to that, I had been walking in hot sunlight for what seemed like most of the morning. I was filthy and overheated and confused.

'I'm sorry,' I said. 'I lost my bearings once or twice. This place is hard to find.'

'I did try to warn you,' she said. She smiled, with the kind of faraway longing that made me imagine she must be thinking of someone she loved. 'Would you like a cup of tea?'

West Edge House
Tarquin's End
Bodmin
Cornwall

Dearest Andrew,

Jennie and Paul are leaving. I knew something was wrong, because of Paul. He was much quieter than usual, and his face had filled up with a darkness that looked like rage. He's so cheerful normally. On Sunday afternoon I went up to the first-floor lounge as usual to collect the used teacups and found Jennie and Paul in there, sitting opposite one another on the sofa with their knees touching. Paul looked like he'd been crying. I left immediately without saying a word, but half an hour later Jennie came to see me in my room.

'I didn't want you worrying about us,' she said. 'Everything's going to be all right.' She used both hands to push back her hair, then told me she and Paul were going to live with Paul's parents, in London.

'It's not ideal,' she said. 'Paul's mum can drive you mad. But it'll do until we find a place of our own.'

'Where will you get the money?' I said. I felt stunned.

Jennie shrugged. 'Paul's good with numbers. He hates to admit it, but he's actually a qualified accountant. Again it's not ideal but it means we can manage until we get the business up and running.'

'Farewell to the circus,' I said, to make her laugh, but suddenly her eyes were bright with tears.

'It'll be all right,' she repeated. She wiped her eyes with the back of her hand. 'It'll have to be.' Then she took an envelope out of her jeans pocket and handed it to me. 'I don't really want to talk about it,' she said. 'But if you read this you'll understand.'

The letter in the envelope was from Maurice Leslie. I knew that even before I saw the signature because I recognised his handwriting. He wrote about how he was in love with Jennie, and then went on to describe the things he wanted to do to her. He dwelled on her body, articulating his perverse fascination with her in precise, almost scientific detail. He even wrote that Paul could be involved in their arrangement, if that was what Jennie wanted. *I really don't mind*, was how he put it. *He's a beautiful boy*.

I read the letter through twice then put it back in its envelope. I felt numb.

'Has he – tried to touch you?' I said at last. Even speaking the words aloud felt wrong.

Jennie laughed bitterly. 'He's examined me so many times I've given up thinking about it. I never noticed anything but that's pure Maurice, isn't it? It's always the quiet ones.' She rubbed at her forehead. 'We can't stay here though, not now I've read that letter. Paul's been beside himself. He can't get over thinking he should be doing something – about Maurice, I mean. But I just want to get away.'

'Don't you think – I mean, what if Maurice, if it's not just you?'

'I might be able to think about that some more once we've

put this place behind us. Think what to do, I mean. But not right now.'

I reached out and took her hand. It was tiny, porcelain-white, almost a doll's hand. Maurice Leslie's hands were large, nimble-fingered, with prominent blue veins and a light ticking of hair across the knuckles.

Paul was strong for his size, but he was a full eighteen inches shorter than Dr Leslie.

'It's time we were going, anyway,' Jennie said. 'You know what people say – hang around in a madhouse long enough and even the doctors can't tell if you're crazy or sane. I'm looking at this as a wake-up call.' She sighed, and squeezed my hand. 'Maybe you should do the same.'

A fortnight after my mother died, my father bought me a doll. She was a 'Pamela Anna', from the Chisholm factory, in Stoke-on-Trent. We were in Truro for my doctor's appointment. I noticed the doll afterwards, when we were on our way back to the car, in the window of a tiny and expensive antiques shop on Cuthbertson Road.

She had straight brown hair and a green velvet dress. She looked nothing like Rosamund and I felt glad.

'Do you like her?' said my father, when he saw me looking. 'I know you love those old dolls.'

I don't remember what I said in reply, but Dad went into the shop and bought her anyway. I stood outside in the street, watching through the glass as the woman behind the counter took the doll out of the window and wrapped her in tissue paper. I don't think my father had ever bought anything that expensive before, not even as a gift for my mother.

He came out of the shop and placed the package into my arms.

'You know you can always talk to me, don't you?' he said. 'About anything.' I nodded, because I knew that was what he wanted, though in fact we hadn't talked at all, not even after the ambulance crew had loaded Mum on to a stretcher and driven away.

What was the point? She was gone. There was nothing to say.

The doctor's consulting room was in a large Victorian house not far from the library. The sun was shining on the day I first went there, I remember that, although I also remember my father was wearing gloves. There was a fish tank in the waiting room, angel fish gliding about amidst underwater ferns. I don't remember the doctor's name, only that he spoke with a Scottish accent.

'Death is difficult to make sense of, however it happens,' he said. 'Would you like to tell me something about your mother?'

I stared down at my hands, folded in my lap. I wanted to return to the waiting room and watch the fish swimming back and forth in their glassy prison.

'Do you remember how you were feeling the evening she died? Would you like to tell me about that, instead?'

I smiled at him and clung fast to the pain. So long as I still felt the pain, I could convince myself my mother was still in the world. I thought she was sleeping, I imagined myself saying. She was lying on the bed with her back to me, that's what I remember. The curtains were shut, but that was all right, because it was getting dark outside anyway. I noticed how heavily she was breathing, like a dog snoring, or a pig grunting. I thought that was funny and awful at the same time. *Gross*, Helen would have said. Gross was one of her words.

Mum was lying very still. So still she seemed inanimate, which is another word for dead. It was scary, seeing her like that, I remember that too. What if she is dead, I remember thinking, and my heart lifted just for a second, because my mother was always unhappy and I was tired of it. I thought about going over and touching her shoulder, just to check she was OK, just so I could prove there was nothing wrong.

What could be wrong, though? She was asleep, that was all. If I woke her up she would have a go at me, she'd ask me where I thought I was off to at this time of night.

Did I understand that she had taken an overdose?

Did I smell the vomit on the pillow, by her face?

Did I see the empty pill bottle on the bedside cabinet?

All my life I've told myself yes, you did see those things. You could have saved her if you'd told someone, called an ambulance. You left your mother to die because you were jealous and selfish and because – even if it was just for a moment – you wished she was dead.

The truth is, I have been over that night in my mind so many times I can no longer properly remember what really happened, if those details are details I can remember, or bits and pieces I picked up from what I found out afterwards. When I arrived back at the house after dropping Rosamund off the viaduct, I found Dad waiting for me, outside on the pavement, still in his slippers. He told me my mother was seriously poorly and that an ambulance was on the way.

'Dad?' I said.

'You couldn't have known, Ba, you couldn't have known.'
He was, in his way, beside himself, a silent shriek. There wasn't
enough room for him in the ambulance, so he said he'd follow in
the car. When I offered to go with him he said it would probably
be best if I stayed at home.

He didn't ask me where I'd been. I don't think he properly
realised I'd been out.

The moon was very bright, I remember that. How stupid, I
remember thinking. Mum won't see the moon again now, not ever.
I felt faint but I bit down on my knuckle and that brought me
back.

I sat in silence for the appointed hour in the doctor's office then
Dad drove me home. The living room was bright with sunshine
so I went upstairs to my room and drew the curtains. Later on
that afternoon I dreamed that Helen came to the door and asked if
she could see me. My mother told her I was sleeping, and sent her
away.

Dear Andrew, you have become my lifeline. I don't know what
I'd do without you.

Always your

Bramber

12.

'YOU KNOW THERE WERE times,' Bramber said to me, 'when I had to ask myself if you really existed. It's not forbidden to have friends from outside but I forgot what that was like. It felt a bit frightening. At first it did, anyway. I started wondering if I'd invented you, the way Ewa Chaplin invented characters to put in her stories.'

'You knew my letters were real, though?' I said. 'Weren't they proof of something?'

'It's hard to explain. I knew there was a real person named Andrew Garvie writing to me, a man who made dolls and collected art books and travelled the world. I was afraid I was reading too much into you though – into our friendship. You sounded too good to be true, I suppose.' She laughed. 'I felt as if we'd known one another forever. I expect that sounds silly to you but that's how it was.'

'It doesn't sound silly at all. I felt like that too.'

We had been talking for what seemed a long time, though in reality it was not quite an hour. I had been anxious at first that someone – the doctor, the youth – would burst in on us, demanding that I leave West Edge House immediately before the police were summoned. The more time passed the more I sensed that this would not happen. Bramber's room seemed a place apart, an oasis in time.

Bramber told me she hadn't been well, that she hadn't been properly herself since her mother died.

'Helen said I've let life get away from me and she was right,' she said. 'Being in here has made things worse, I can see that now. I should have left years ago but I was afraid I wouldn't be able to manage.' She paused. 'I'm so glad you're here, Andrew. Are you upset, that I mistook you for Anders Tessmond? Do you think I'm crazy?'

'I think Anders Tessmond is a great character,' I said. 'I wouldn't call him a role model, exactly, but he's more interesting than most of the dwarfs you find in other people's stories. And he has better dress sense.' I glanced down at my crumpled shirt and we both burst out laughing. Then she leaned forward in her seat and took my hands. Her touch, not just the delectable warmth of her skin on mine but the very fact that we were touching, that after all my plans and dreaming we were finally here together in the same place, made my heart hammer and my head spin. I could see that Bramber was just an ordinary person, edging towards middle age as I was, yet to me she was enchanting. I gazed upon her as I had once gazed upon the glowing reproductions of Pre-Raphaelite paintings in the books in the art section of Welton public library, taking in the magical arrangement of colours, the aura of mystery, above all the promise of stories yet to be written and still to be read.

She was ravishingly, uniquely alive, her eyes enlightened not so much by experience as by rapt hope. I once read somewhere that the true definition of love lies in acknowledging that the person standing in front of you is as alive and filled with purpose as you are, as deserving of scrutiny. If this is so then I knew in that moment that I loved Bramber Winters, as I love her still.

I did not speak of my feelings. I knew it would be wrong of me, the kind of emotional greed that is liable to destroy everything it touches, especially if that thing is fragile, and very nearly brand new. Could Bramber ever care for me as I cared for her? I did not know, and had no wish to ask her. Unlike the dwarf in Schubert's song, I felt no desire to kill my queen or, like Anders Tessmond, to destroy her integrity.

Simply to know that I was with her in this room, on this plane of reality, in this universe – that was enough.

'What will you do?' I asked her instead. 'Have you decided?'

'I'm going to leave,' she said at once. 'I've already told Dr Leslie. I want to finish my research – maybe I really could write a book about Ewa. Then I thought I might try and track down my mother's friends – those who are still alive, anyway – and find out about what she was like before she gave up music. There might be a story there too, don't you think?'

'I'm sure there would be.' I hesitated. 'You could come and live with me. There's a spare room. You would be – completely private.'

I was blushing like a fool. She squeezed my hands. 'It's lovely of you to think of that,' she said, 'but Helen has offered me a room in her flat. She says I can stay as long as I like, until I get settled. She says she'd like the company.'

'And you've said yes?' I swallowed the lump in my throat.

She nodded. 'But you and I – we'll be able to meet now, won't we? Meet more often. If you'd like to?'

'Of course I would.'

'I'll write to you with Helen's address as soon as I get there. You will stay for lunch? Here, I mean. I'm sorry about what happened earlier. Diz and Jackie can be nervous around strangers but I know they'd love to get to know you properly.'

And of course I wanted to say yes, to grab every loose thread of time and bind her close, bind her close for always, but I knew in my heart this would be a mistake. If we were to have a future, this place – this enchanted mountain top – should not be a part of it. Orpheus-like, I knew I would be better to turn my back and trust that she, my Euridice, would fit her footprints into mine and follow me back into the light.

It came to me that once I left here I would have no way of contacting her. She would soon be gone from Tarquin's End, and I had no idea where Helen Mason lived, other than that it was in Peckham. Peckham is bigger than most small towns, and swallows people whole. Again, I had no choice but to trust her.

How do you bid adieu to the person you love? Not in the company of strangers, that is for sure.

'I would love to, but I can't,' I said. I invented something – an auction in Truro – that I was supposed to be attending, that I didn't want to miss. Did she look disappointed? For a second maybe, as if she had briefly glimpsed a new and shining world, only to see it go tumbling down the sky, lost forever from view. Then something else – relief? – won the upper hand.

'Well, if you're sure,' she said. And then: 'What about her?' She nodded at 'Artist', who had been sitting on Bramber's bed all this time, lounging against the pillows like an imperial courtesan. I had forgotten all about her.

I thought about saying that 'Artist' was a copy, an identical replica, but anyone who knows anything about dolls would know immediately that this was a lie. There are no Chaplin replicas. None like 'Artist', anyway.

'I just borrowed her for a bit,' I said finally. 'I'll see she gets home safe.'

'Be careful, won't you?' There was a glint in her eye, a quiet amusement that seemed to hint at an unspoken pleasure in the mischief I had caused. I hoped this was so.

'You can be sure of it.'

I stumbled to my feet, wondering if it would be permissible to embrace her. Then Bramber stepped forward and put out her arms. I stepped into them, incredulous, rested my head against her chest, against the butterfly T-shirt. I could hear her heart fluttering. Worlds made and unmade themselves, parallel realities slipped in and out of synch. This is where you *strike*! cried Anders Tessmond. The world is a dangerous place, said Ivan Stedman. Mind how you go.

Outside the window, the summer sky was painted the false, saturated blue of plastic picnic cups. Ridiculously, I thought of Lohengrin, the knight of the grail, forced to leave his bride before their wedding night.

He had bound Elsa with a pointless promise. I would not do the same.

'I'm so glad things are working out for you,' I said. 'I'm so happy we met.'

I stroked my hand across the back of her T-shirt. I felt her lips touch the top of my head, and then we drew apart.

I RETRACED MY STEPS to Tarquin's Cross. The distance seemed much shorter than it had done on my way out, and in passing through the hamlet of Tarquin's End I noted the presence of three or four children, lobbing chunks of dried mud at each other and into the duck pond.

'Hey, Grumpy,' one of them called after me. 'What did you do with the other six?'

The children dissolved into spasms of laughter, elbowing each other and doubling over in their merriment. I walked past them without stopping and on up the road, the scene – not just them, but me alongside them – etching itself into my brain like a woodcut illustration from one of Grimms' fairy tales.

Heigh ho, I thought to myself, and laughed aloud. I arrived at the crossroads where the bus had dropped me. There was a bus stop sign, I noticed, but the timetable was either missing or stolen. I had no idea how long I would have to wait – it could even be that there were no more buses that day. I decided to give it an hour. If I was still waiting after that I would have to go back into Tarquin's End and ask at the post office – someone there would surely have the number of a taxi company.

In the event, a bus hove into view just twenty minutes later. I bought a ticket for Bodmin Station, hoping I would not have to wait too long there, either. Bodmin, like all the towns and villages I had passed through on my journey west, had suddenly become too painful for me even to think about, its streets and cottages and shop fronts symbolic of my unsatisfied yearning and of my grief. For it was grief I felt, alongside my happiness, a soup of pain so thick it threatened to choke me. You have not lost her, I kept reminding myself, your goodbye was temporary. But in the half-hour on that potholed B-road that did not feel true.

I realised with horror and frustration that I would have to call in at The Tarquin to collect the rest of my luggage. What I wanted was to be on a train and heading back eastwards as quickly as possible.

'Artist', to do her credit, spoke not one word. I felt glad of her presence, though I would not have admitted it, least of all to her. She understood what I was going through, I knew that, and was grateful. 'Artist' would know what it meant to play for high stakes. She would know about grief, too, even though she would consider it beneath her dignity to speak of it.

It was only once we were actually on the train that she made her suggestion: that we should stop for the night in Dawlish, before heading home. I was resistant to the idea at first – I wanted to be back in London – but 'Artist' insisted.

You're exhausted, she said. You'll feel like hell if you don't take a breather. She said she'd write, remember? Anyway, I want to see the sea.

At her mention of the sea I felt something inside me unclench a little. When was the last time I had looked upon it, stood beside it, scented its salty exhalations? I could not remember. I imagined a room, small and clean and high up, overlooking the water. Good coffee and fresh croissants in the morning, then the journey home.

'Yes, all right,' I conceded. 'I suppose we could do that.'

I know an OK place, 'Artist' said. You'll like it, I promise.

'Why are you being so decent all of a sudden?'

She was silent for a moment. Because you're a king amongst

men and don't know it, she said. Either that or I'm losing my edge. You decide.

WE ARRIVED IN DAWLISH at around five o'clock. The shops were just shutting, dusting the streets with that aura of faded glory that is the inimitable preserve of the Victorian seaside resort in decline. Liquid sunlight slipped like syrup from the striped awnings of seafront cafés. The town's famous black swans lumbered nonchalantly around the ornamental lake that formed the centrepiece of the municipal gardens, alternately grooming each other and pecking for food. The atmosphere of the place – retrograde and somehow defunct – served only to accentuate my mood.

In spite of the affectionate manner in which we had parted, the mere fact of Bramber's absence from my side – the increasing distance between us – had set up within me a cycle of self-doubt and apprehension I was finding it impossible to reason away.

Had she truly meant what she said about us meeting again?

Was I a fool for leaving so hurriedly?

What must she think of me for being so candid about my feelings?

This disconsolate town with its down-at-heel amusement arcades and tattered bunting served only to put me in mind of how many similarly desperate no-hopers must have washed up here through the decades, how many weekend break-ups, broken-down addicts, hotel-room suicides . . .

Enough already, 'Artist' grumbled. Who do you think you are, F. Scott Fitzgerald? Keep walking.

I followed where she led, along the seafront and then up through the town, the famous cliffs flamed to scarlet in the last of the sun-light, like a Martian landscape. The gradient exhausted me but I was glad. The climb gave me something definite to focus on, at least. At the head of a narrow side street, a flight of stone steps took me still higher, between two sandstone columns and into the courtyard of a hotel named, somewhat improbably, Castle View.

'This better be it,' I muttered. A sign in the window indicated that there were indeed vacancies, as well as a three-star restaurant actually on the premises. So far as I could recall, the hotel was not listed in *Coastage's English Almanac*, but then again I had not planned on spending the night in Dawlish, so my memory might well have been faulty in that regard.

'No wonder there are vacancies,' I said to 'Artist'. 'You could put yourself in hospital just climbing those steps.'

Never mind, 'Artist' said. We're here now.

The young man at reception welcomed me courteously and asked if I would prefer their queen-size room or the super-king. He was a beautiful youth – elegant, gold-rimmed spectacles and the face of a poet.

'Whichever one faces the sea,' I said at once.

'The super-king, then. Fourth floor.' He made a note in his ledger, then enquired if I would be dining with them this evening.

'Most definitely,' I assured him. When he asked if I needed help with my luggage I declined. The lad aroused intense emotions in me and I found his presence disturbing because of that. I wanted to get away from him, from everyone. 'Artist' was right. I was exhausted.

The room, when I finally reached it, was a kind of paradise. Its wide bow window offered a one-hundred-and-eighty-degree view of the ocean, its position beneath the eaves removing it entirely from the hackneyed tawdriness of the town below.

The sun was finally going down, immersing itself, like Phaeton's chariot, beneath the softly rippled surface of the glimmering sea. I gazed for long moments, bewitched, alive only in the present, a gift that is offered to us only seldom, and that we rarely accept.

Then I lay down on the bed, losing consciousness almost immediately. I slept for two hours. When I awoke it was getting dark, the backlit horizon glowed a pale orange. When I went to close the curtains, 'Artist' asked me not to.

I want to look at the lights, she said. Could you let me have some air, do you think?

I took her out of the holdall and sat her on the wide window seat that ran around the edge of the bow window. I couldn't see any harm in it – we were too high up for anyone to look in and besides, I had more or less given up worrying about the police. 'Artist' did not want to be found, and for this reason alone I pitied the detective who had been tasked with attempting to discover her current whereabouts.

I showered and changed and went downstairs to the dining room. This would be the last of my meals away and, in spite of my persisting anxieties over Bramber, I experienced a twinge of nostalgia for my brief period of life on the road. The menu at Castle View was traditional and some would say old-fashioned, but the coq au vin I ordered was substantial and delicious. Now I was rested and had food in my stomach I felt somewhat less melancholy, distanced from myself, as if the lone man sipping Merlot at the corner table were the subject of a fascinating yet somewhat depressing documentary on the British seaside.

I, the real Andrew Garvie, bestowed my supercilious gaze upon him from somewhere just outside the frame, pronouncing myself an idiot without having to be one.

I ordered the lemon tart for dessert and then a snifter of Armagnac. When eventually I returned to my room I had no other plan in mind than to watch *Newsnight* and then catch an early night, but 'Artist' started in on me right away.

When are we going to talk about this? she demanded.

'Talk about what?' I said. I could hear myself sounding testy, though I wasn't so much irritated as bone-tired.

About what happens tomorrow?

'What happens is that I go to the post office first thing and buy one of those Royal Mail packing cartons. Then I send you back to the museum, recorded delivery.' This was at least one definite decision I had reached over dinner. My words as they came out sounded positive and sane.

They're like prisons, those places, you do know that?

'They are not like prisons. You get to travel the world. You have thousands of people to wait on you instead of just one.'

From the inside of a glass case.

I sighed. 'I can't keep you, you know that. I was never meant to be a criminal. I'm hopeless at it.'

All artists are criminals, to a degree. Have you thought about that?

'I'm too tired for philosophy.' I gazed out over the water, the black waves lapping at an invisible shore. It seemed to me that I could just make out something on the horizon, a blacker blackness, pinpricked about its midpoint by tiny lights.

Our ship, 'Artist' said. I could show you such things.

'I don't want such things. I want to go home. I want to get back to work. I want to try and form a real relationship with Bramber, if she'll have me.'

Have you ever thought, my dear Sir Galahad, that the real purpose of your crusade was not to end up playing house with that foolish woman but to bring us together?

'Bramber's not foolish. She's a good person. I believe in her. I believe in us.'

I began to weep then, to weep like a child as I rarely if ever had done when I was a child. I wept for myself, and for Bramber's lost years. I wept for Wil, and the way he had used me, for my never-to-be consummated love affair with Ursula. I wept for Clarence, whom I adored, and whom I had treated so selfishly these past few weeks.

I wept, as the poets say, because I must.

You were never meant for this kind of soap opera, Prince Andrei, 'Artist' said coldly.

'Why? Because I'm small?' Such a response would have been monstrous and yet so predictable – so melodramatic – I would almost have welcomed it.

Because you are great. Imagination comes with burdens as well as privileges. Solitude is one of those burdens. But is that so bad?

She said other things too, but I had mostly stopped listening. I stood captivated by the dark thing, the hulk on the horizon, which as it drifted closer revealed itself as a ship. Not a yacht or a cruiser but a tall ship, with three masts and numerous sails, a spider's web of lights festooned in the rigging.

Your cabin is prepared, 'Artist' whispered. And your queen is already on board. Her name is Ambergris.

What a beautiful name, I thought. I started forward, unlatching the window. Night air poured in, blissfully cool and sweet. The ship's lights blazed in the offing and I marvelled. I thought of the miraculous lands we might travel together, 'Artist' and I, the silks and beads and lace I would purchase, the visions that would spring to life beneath my hands.

Had not my dolls always been my world, from the moment I first glimpsed Marina Blue in Prendergast's window?

A king among men, 'Artist' had called me. She had been pulling my leg, of course, trying to cheer me up. But even so, to sail forever in pursuit of one's dreams – to be king of that glittering kingdom, if only for a moment – was that not an enviable fate for a poet of kapok and calico such as myself?

Was not love imagined often more glorious than hope fulfilled?

I leaned forward towards the night. She brushed the tears from my face with her chilly hands.

Come home, you idiot. Clarence's voice, so clearly imagined I could almost believe she was there beside me in the room. *You went on holiday, that's all. Holidays always make you feel rotten, it's a fact of life.*

And then, another image: Bramber, in her room at West Edge House. She was sitting at her desk, writing a letter. Her cramped, meticulous script flowed freely across the pale-blue airmail paper I knew so well.

Today was like a miracle, she wrote. *I keep wondering if I dreamed it, but I know I didn't.*

How could I have thought of leaving her, even for a second? The world was a dangerous place, as Ivan Stedman had said. But it was still my world. I would be damned if I would relinquish my place in it, even for a king's ransom.

I drew back into the room and closed the window. In the bay the ship, with its starlit rigging, shimmered brightly into focus just for a moment and then blinked out of sight.

✧

The Garden Flat,
143 Asylum Road
Peckham
London SE15

Dearest Andrew,

You'll see I have a new address now – Asylum Road! People
would find that amusing I'm sure, given my history, though you
will probably know that an asylum in mediaeval England was a
place of refuge. Helen's flat is actually a maisonette, and it has
its own entrance. My room is on the first floor, overlooking the
garden, which meant I felt at home here as soon as I arrived.

I left behind most of the things from my old room at West
Edge House. The armchair and the bureau weren't mine to take
anyway. I have my sea chest, and my jewellery box, my Hampton
Court snow dome, and the brooch in the shape of a beetle that
belonged to my mother. And of course there are my dolls to keep
me company.

I think Sylvia Passmore was sorry to see me go. She even
hugged me, which was unlike her, though she's been a lot less
moody in general since Jennie and Paul left. On the evening
of my farewell supper she started telling me about a scheme
she'd dreamed up for redecorating the rooms on the first floor.
She seemed quite excited about it, although it was probably the

prospect of having Dr Leslie all to herself that was doing the talking.

I don't think Sylvia has a clue about the letter Dr Leslie sent to Jennie. She'll find out soon enough – Jennie told me before she left that she had decided to go to the police, once she and Paul are settled in London – but it wasn't my place to tell her and so I didn't. It will be good for Sylvia to have a change of scene, anyway. Nothing is the same as it was. In a way, the life of the house as we knew it is already over.

I almost forgot to tell you – Diz and Jackie got married. They've gone to live in Diz's old house, in Horsfall. Jackie showed me a photograph of it, a square, red-brick end terrace with ivy twisting around the porch. Jackie seemed excited about the move, especially as it means she'll be living closer to her daughter.

She wore white at her wedding, a high-necked, 1920s-style dress in lace brocade. Her daughter Teresa was wearing a blue silk trouser suit and a pair of sunglasses with silver frames that made her look like a movie star. She arrived at Tarquin's End the day before the wedding and arranged for someone to come over from Bodmin to do Jackie's makeup and hair.

Jackie looked beautiful, like brides do in old photographs, as if she had been returned to a time and a place that was more her own.

On her way out to the car, she smiled at me almost shyly. She raised a hand to the back of her hair.

'I was always worried about Teresa finding out how her father died,' she said. 'I think she might already know, though. Do you think she minds?' She looked down at her feet. She was wearing the most exquisite shoes, a pair of silver stilettos. Sylvia Passmore had given them to her as a wedding present.

'He killed his first wife, you know, Teresa's dad,' Jackie added in a whisper. 'I didn't know that when we first got together but after I fell pregnant with Teresa I was so afraid. Afraid for her, I mean. I couldn't settle, not with that criminal in the world, knowing what he'd done and with everybody believing he was such a gent. He kept hinting he'd do for me as well if I said anything and I believed him. People say that about murder, don't they? That it gets easier after the first time.'

'Jackie,' I said. 'It's your wedding day. We can talk about this later, if you still want to.'

I'd heard all sorts of rumours about Jackie and why she was in here but they no longer seemed important. Whatever she had done or hadn't done, it was a long time ago.

Jackie turned her face away. Her profile seemed delicate and very young-looking and for a moment I barely recognised her.

'Teresa loves you,' I said. 'She knows you've done nothing wrong.'

'You don't know that,' Jackie said. 'I could have done anything.'

St Ninian's was filled with white roses. While Jackie and Diz stood having their photograph taken at the church door, Teresa approached me and thanked me for coming.

'My mother talks about you a lot,' she said. 'Thanks for everything you've done for her.'

'Jackie's my friend,' I said. We stood together in silence for a couple of seconds. I would have liked to continue the conversation but I couldn't think what to say. In the end Teresa smiled again and walked away.

The churchyard was bursting with sunlight. There was confetti on the pathway, and in the grass.

West Edge House felt completely different with Diz and Jackie gone. The night before I left, I lay in bed listening to the house murmuring to itself and wondering what would happen to it – when everyone finds out about Dr Leslie, I mean. Will it be pulled down, or will it begin a new life, with new occupants, new stories?

Houses are like trees, they have long memories. I'm not sure if I want West Edge House to remember me, or not.

I booked a taxi to take me to Bodmin Station. I could have caught the bus from Tarquin's Cross, but I couldn't face it. I didn't want people from the village asking me questions – I've had enough of questions. The main road through Tarquin's End was strewn with autumn leaves, and just below the duck pond I caught sight of Janey Morris – that's Meredith Hubbard's granddaughter – playing hopscotch with a couple of other girls I didn't recognise.

I felt more emotional than I thought I would, I have to admit that. As the taxi drove past St Ninian's I had to look away.

I'd never been on an Intercity train before, can you imagine? I sat back in my seat, watching the fields and rivers and villages fly past the windows and wondering if I would ever in my life see these places again. I took out Helen's letter, just to look at it, the London postmark on the corner of the envelope, the blue writing on the white paper inside. I'd read it so many times the paper was beginning to fall apart along its folds.

Paddington Station was busy, much busier than I was used to. I felt myself picked up by the crowd, swept along towards the ticket barriers with my single suitcase like a visitor who had just arrived from the planet Mars. I fumbled my ticket into the slot and passed through to the other side. I didn't see Helen at first, and for a moment I wondered if I had made a mistake – arrived at the wrong station somehow, or simply imagined it all. Just as I was starting to panic she appeared from out of the crowd and grabbed my arm.

'There you are,' she said. 'I was waiting on the wrong side of the station. The Penzance train normally arrives on to Platform 3.'

She put both her arms around me then, rocking me from side to side as if in mild astonishment that I was there at all.

'This is great, isn't it? Two mad, bad ladies, out on the town?' She punched my shoulder gently, then smiled. 'I'm glad you made it out. Do you think you'll be OK to get on the tube?'

I said of course I would, and I was, though I felt very nervous. That was a month ago, and I'm getting used to it now, though I avoid it during the rush hour if I can.

I'm going to apply for a reader pass at the British Library, because I'm hoping I can gain access to information about Ewa Chaplin from when she first came to London. I also want to find out where her unpublished story manuscripts are being held – I know they exist. I'm even thinking I might try learning Polish, so I could read them in the original. The new library in Peckham is a good place to work in the meantime. It's modern, and full of light, and different from anything I might have imagined before I arrived. I have the money my father left me, so I'm all right for now, but I want to get a job soon, anyway. I'd like to work in a library, or maybe a bookshop. Anywhere but a hospital!

I have such plans, Andrew. Helen keeps telling me I shouldn't get ahead of myself, that there's plenty of time, but I feel I've wasted enough time already. Do you understand?

I am sorry it's been a while since my last letter but so much has been happening. I would love for us to meet again, and soon. Helen says I must get a mobile, but I'm putting that off for as long as I can because I really don't like them. Give me a call on the landline, and we can arrange a time.

Thinking of you, always,

Bramber

1 3 .

MY MOBILE WAS ABOUT to die on me. Luckily Clarence answered after only three rings.

'I can hardly hear you,' she said.

'It's this phone,' I said. 'The signal's awful.'

She groaned, and asked me when I was going to cave in and get a proper smartphone. I imagined her in her kitchen, sitting crosswise on one of the high stools, swinging her long legs back and forth under the breakfast bar. I thought of the way she always played with the telephone cord as she talked, twisting the coils around her fingers like a spring.

I have seen paintings in the Prado and in the Louvre that remind me of her: oils by Goya and Velazquez of Spanish queens.

I could hear the chatter of the radio, an arts show panel game, and somewhere in the background the sound of Jane, practising the piano.

'Do you want to come round?' Clarence was saying.

'I should get back to the flat first, dump my stuff.'

'Wait by the Praed Street entrance,' Clarence said. 'I'll come and pick you up in the van.'

I was home. The station concourse heaved and throbbed about me, a microcosm of the city I had come to call my own. The whole of London tugged at my sleeve, urging me onward: *So she said you were a king, so what? They say the streets of this town are paved with gold and you know what rot that is. Unless it's drunks' piss you're talking about.*

The vast glass arch of the station's roof thrummed headily with the sound of falling rain: thrash thrash, like kids chucking gravel. The summer was over.

I smelled the smell of London's streets, ancient and immutable, slick with grey water. And I had work to do: dolls to create and letters to write, a kingdom to rule. There would be changes, of course. Telling Clarence how I felt about Bramber, for a start, telling her properly. I had hidden my real self away for far too long. Hiding is a form of deception, and deception always hurts people, in the end.

I had the strangest feeling, as if the city I had left behind on my journey west was in one world, and the city I was now returning to was in another.

I smiled. Edwin again, all his talk of ghost trains and parallel universes. Whatever universe he had found to live in, I wished him well. I could afford to be magnanimous. I was a king, after all.

ACKNOWLEDGEMENTS

Huge thanks to my editor, Jon Riley, and the marvellous team at riverrun for bringing Andrew's journey to fruition, and to my amazing agent Anna Webber of United Agents for her sage advice and staunch support for me and for this book. Thanks to my friends and fellow jurors on the Clarke Award Shadow Jury project – Maureen Kincaid Speller, Paul Kincaid, Megan AM, Victoria Hoyle, Jonathan McCalmont, Nick Hubble, Vajra Chandrasekera and David Hebblethwaite – who inadvertently helped lay down the runway for *The Dollmaker*'s completion. Thanks are also due to the many friends and talented colleagues whose conversation, crisis management and comradeship provide constant inspiration, including and in no particular order Matt Hill, Helen Marshall, Vince Haig, Anne Charnock, Garry Charnock, Emma Swift, Carole Johnstone, Priya Sharma, John Clute, Judith Clute, Elizabeth Hand, Douglas Thompson, Cleaver Patterson, Cath Trechman, Ella Chappell, Mike Harrison, Cath Phillips, Phil Maloney, David Rix, Rob Shearman, Colin Murray, Lisa Tuttle, Sam Thompson, Neil Williamson and Maureen Weller. A special mention to Angela Luxford, who started the whole thing. Thanks and love to my mother, Monica Allan, for always being there, and to my partner, Christopher Priest, for being the best.

A different version of 'The Elephant Girl' originally appeared in *Shadows and Tall Trees 3*, edited by Michael Kelly for Undertow Press (2012) and a different version of 'The Upstairs Window' was originally published in Interzone 230, edited by Andy Cox and Andrew Hedgecock for TTA Press (2011).

A NOTE ON THE TYPE

In 1924, Monotype based this face on types cut by Pierre Simon Fournier c. 1742. These types were some of the most influential designs of the eighteenth century, being among the earliest of the transitional style of typeface, and were a stepping stone to the more severe modern style made popular by Bodoni later in the century. They had more vertical stress than the old style types, greater contrast between thick and thin strokes and little or no bracketing on the serifs.